**"I dare you to read a 'Kurland' story and not enjoy it!"** —***Heartland Critiques***

In "To Kiss in the Shadows" by **Lynn Kurland**, Jason of Artane has his heart set on a noble quest—but his plans change when he meets a mysterious young woman who hides behind her tapestry frame yet manages to capture his heart.

**"[Madeline Hunter is] an immensely gifted new author." —Jane Feather**

In **Madeline Hunter**'s novella, a noblewoman beset by her brother's creditors offers a cherished tapestry to a man with more on his mind than settling her debts.

**"Sherrilyn Kenyon's imagination is as bright as her future." —Teresa Medeiros**

A lovely scholar's dream of deciphering a mysterious tapestry comes true when she meets an enigmatic stranger in **Sherrilyn Kenyon**'s breathtaking adventure.

**"Karen Marie Moning is destined to make her mark on the genre."** —***Romantic Times***

**Karen Marie Moning** tells the tale of a young woman who, after mysteriously receiving an ancient tapestry, is transported to medieval Scotland to break an evil spell cast by a naughty sailor.

Lynn Kurland
Madeline Hunter
Sherrilyn Kenyon
Karen Marie Moning

JOVE BOOKS, NEW YORK

TAPESTRY

A Jove Book / published by arrangement with the authors

PRINTING HISTORY
Jove edition / September 2002



Visit our website at www.penguinputnam.com

ISBN: 0-515-13362-0

A JOVE BOOK®
Jove Books are published by The Berkley Publishing Group,
a division of Penguin Putnam Inc.,
375 Hudson Street, New York, New York 10014.
JOVE and the "J" design
are trademarks belonging to Penguin Putnam Inc.

PRINTED IN THE UNITED STATES OF AMERICA

10 9 8 7 6 5 4 3 2 1

# Contents

# To Kiss in the Shadows

Lynn Kurland

# *One*

*'Tis said that in a woman's solar the course of wars and* the fate of countries is decided.

'Tis also said that therein is determined the fate of men and the manner of their course to a woman's bed.

Lianna of Grasleigh suspected that a woman had said the former and a man the latter, for 'twas a certainty that no man she knew would have accorded a woman the cleverness to determine the destiny of his realm. But if any man had heard the plotting and scheming going on behind her, he would have perhaps thought differently. At the very least, he would have quivered in fear for the fate of his own poor soul.

"Bind him," suggested the first of the other women in the solar.

"Nay, lure him," said the second.

"Help him slip into his cups, lure him, and *then* bind him," said the third. Then she gulped in surprise, as if that thought were too bold a one to voice.

Lianna let the peat smoke, perfumed oils, and stratagem flow over her. She had no stomach for joining in the talk—not that the ladies behind her would have allowed it. A member of court though she might be by command of the king, she was not accepted by that court. It had troubled her at first, that shunning, but she had grown accustomed to it. Besides, 'twas better that she keep to the work under her hands. Let the tapestry of the court be woven without her single thread running through it. She had her own pattern to see to.

She tilted her frame to catch the final shaft of sunlight that bravely entered the chamber despite the daunting thickness of the walls. To have fully succeeded in seeing her work, she would have had to turn her face to the women behind her, but that she could not do. Instead, she sat with her back to the chamber and made do with less light than was needful.

Much as she did in her life.

"Lie in wait for him," said the first. "In the passageway, where he must speak as he passes."

"Lie in wait in his bed," corrected the second with a lusty laugh, "and then see if he can pass on such an invitation."

"I would lie anywhere," said the third breathlessly. "Mayhap he would tread upon me."

"He will not be trapped by such simple ploys," said a fourth voice in a tone that cut through the speculation like a sword through living flesh.

Silence descended, silence broken only by Lianna's needle as it pierced the cloth again and again. She was powerfully tempted to look over her shoulder and see the looks the other women—save the one who had spoken in the end, of course—were wearing fixed to their no-doubt quite pale visages. But drawing their attention would only draw the attention of their sharp tongues as well, so she forbore. Perhaps listening to what she was certain would be a severe rebuke would be amusement enough for the afternoon.

"Kendrick of Artane will not be trapped by foolish gels who have no head for strategies," Maud of Harrow said, and she said it so decidedly that only a fool would have dared argue with her. "He is cunning and shrewd. To catch him, one must be his equal in stealth."

"But," said the woman who had spoken first, sounding rather hesitant, "would he not find it unpleasing to have a woman as full of wit as he?"

Lianna stitched contentedly. Adela was certainly lacking in wit, so that would not be a problem for her.

"I still say it matters not what wits you have, if you have enough of them to find yourself betwixt his sheets," said Janet, Adela's sister, whose most heartfelt desire seemed to be to find herself betwixt sheets—anyone's sheets—as often as possible.

"I agree," said the third timidly. She was Linet of Byford, and of the women behind her, the least vicious, to Lianna's mind. At least Linet flinched when Maud's tongue began to cut. "Surely," Linet continued, "his preference is a woman warm and willing in his bed."

"Many women have tried," said Maud, "but he refuses them all. Nay, the way to have him must come from a more subtle attack."

*And how would Maud know?* Lianna wondered. Perhaps she had given the matter much thought in an effort to find a diversion from her own terrible straits. And why not, given the life she had? The woman was wed to a man with a tongue so cruel few could bear him. Lianna shuddered. Had she been wed to such a man, she soon would have been reduced to cowering in the corner, of that she was certain.

Maud never cowered, not even before her lord. Then again, her tongue was as sharp as his. Lianna knew this because she'd listened to Maud use that weapon on her vile husband more than once. And, of course, she'd felt the bite of it herself—which was part of the reason she placed herself with her back to the chamber. There was little to be gained by giving Maud or her companions a constant view of her ruined visage. Maud tormented her enough while facing naught but her back.

But none of that explained how Maud knew so much about Kendrick of Artane's habits. Had she tried to have him in the past and failed? Did she intend to try again now? She was at Henry's court whilst her husband was off on an errand for the king in France. Mayhap she considered this a perfect time to trot out a new strategy.

"We might have more success with his brother," Linet offered timidly. "The one still free. The youngest."

The numerous swift intakes of breath were startling. Then there was absolute silence for the space of several heartbeats.

"Jason of Artane?" Maud asked. Her voice could have been full of what another might have termed fear.

Lianna was so surprised, she ventured a look over her shoulder. To her astonishment, Maud looked as frightened as the rest of the women.

"He isn't of Artane," Linet said. "Well, he was. But now he is of Blackmour."

And the women, as one, crossed themselves.

Lianna wondered if she might have passed too much time during her youth with her face pressed against linen to judge its usefulness for her stitching purposes. Obviously, she had missed several delicious rumors.

"The Dragon of Blackmour's squire," Adela agreed.

"You're a fool, sister. Jason de Piaget is the Dragon's *former* squire," Janet corrected. "He's his own man now. And likely as full of evil habits as the old worm himself."

"I hear he's handsome," Linet ventured.

"He was trained by Blackmour, who we know is a warlock," Maud said crisply. "No doubt Lord Jason, as fair of face as he might be, mastered many dark arts at his master's hand. Would you sell your frivolous souls to such a man in return for his deadly kisses?"

There was a bit of low murmuring, as if the other women considered it. Lianna was spared further speculation by the abrupt bursting open of the door.

"He's here!" a body announced breathlessly.

"Jason?" Linet asked with a gasp, sounding so terrified that Lianna could only assume she had reflected a bit more on Maud's words.

"Nay, Kendrick," the voice from the door said. "He's here!"

"Have you seen him?" Maud demanded.

"Nay, but I heard tell—"

Apparently, that was enough for the women, even Maud, though Lianna wondered what Maud's husband would say when he returned from his journeys and found out his wife was pursuing one of the most sought-after knights in the realm. For herself, Lianna was unsurprised by Maud's actions. She had ceased to be appalled by wedded women hunting desirable, unwedded men, even though in her home such a thing would have been unthinkable. Her parents had been devoted to each other. The thought of her mother having looked at a man other than her father never would have occurred to Lianna.

Of course, that was before, before her family had been slain, before she had been fetched by the king's courtiers and brought to court, where she had seen many things she never would have believed possible. 'Twas little wonder she passed most of her waking hours in the queen's least-used solar, hiding from the intrigues and horrors of court, and trying desperately with needle and thread to recapture some of the beauty she'd lost.

The door banged shut, and the excited shrieks of the women faded. Silence descended swiftly, leaving Lianna with nothing to face but her own thoughts. She looked over at the window and marked with dismay the waning of the daylight. Dusk meant she would have to descend to the great hall and take her place at the king's table.

How she loathed evenings! A pity she couldn't hide herself in some darkened corner of the hall. Nay, her place was determined by the vastness of her father's holdings.

She often wondered why Henry hadn't kept those lands for his own, but perhaps he had enough to fret over without them. Far better to sell her and her soil to a man who could manage the both of them. The king had need enough of allies, and she, after six months at court, had few illusions about what her fate would be. Her only surprise was that she hadn't met that fate yet. Surely her freedom couldn't last much longer. Even she was old enough, and wise enough, at a score to understand that.

But even though her holdings and her station guaranteed her a place at supper, they didn't guarantee her freedom from stares and smirks.

Would that they could.

The door behind her opened softly. She sighed but didn't turn her head. That was something else she'd learned at Henry's court: to hide her face. Tongues were cruel and never more so than when gazing on her poor visage. Better a knife in her back than words to pierce her soul.

There was a substantial pause, then a soft footfall that came her way. Lianna ducked her head. A long form settled across from her on one of the stone benches set into the wall. Lianna glanced up long enough to see that it was a man, but not one dressed in the trappings of a lord. Given his clothing, he was nothing more than a squire, and a poor one at that. She had nothing to fear from such a man. She could dismiss him easily.

She bent her head to her stitchery. "You shouldn't be here," she said firmly.

"Aye, there's a goodly bit of truth," he said with feeling. "The saints preserve me from the intrigues of a woman's solar."

Given that such had been her thoughts as well, she risked a look at the man facing her. And the beauty of his visage, even cast as it was in the last rays of sunlight, was enough to make her catch her breath.

His breath caught as well, and a small sound of dismay escaped him. But that brief flash of pity was gone so quickly, she almost wondered if she'd imagined it. He smiled a smile that would have felled her instantly had she not been so firmly seated on her chair.

"The pox," he noted. "I had it, too. I'll show you my scars, if you like."

She blinked at him.

"They aren't on my sweet visage, as you can see."

She made a strangled noise of denial, hoping fervently that the man wouldn't feel the need to strip down to his altogether to ensure her comfort.

His smile turned into a mischievous grin that had her smiling in return—regardless of any desire she might have had to do otherwise.

"Your maidenly eyes are safe," he promised with a wink. He stretched out his long legs. "Who are you?" he asked. "And where are your fellows?"

"Lianna of Grasleigh," she answered promptly, then realized that perhaps giving an unknown man her name wasn't wise. "And the ladies are coming back immediately," she added hastily.

"Off hunting, are they?" he asked.

"Hunting?"

"Aye," he said easily. "I know their kind. Always after some poor fool or other."

"The poor fool for the afternoon is Kendrick of Artane," she said with a scowl. "The handsome, wealthy, apparently infinitely desirable Kendrick of Artane."

"You seem to know much of him."

"I've been forced to listen to a listing of his virtues for the past se'nnight."

"But surely you must believe the reports," he said.

"How could one man be so perfect?" she asked. "I daresay the tales are magnified far beyond the truth." She listened to herself and was surprised to find that her courage was magnified far beyond its usual bounds. Speaking so freely to anyone not of her family wasn't her habit. Perhaps her tongue had reached its limit in patience.

"And what are those tales?" he asked, looking quite interested. "I've always a ready ear for ladies' gossip."

Lianna jabbed her needle into the cloth with vigor. Why not? If he had nothing better to do than listen, she had little better to do than talk. Besides, he wasn't laughing at her, nor was he insulting her. For that alone he deserved to be indulged. Perhaps he, too, sought only a respite before the torture of supper.

She let her needle fall and watched as the thread untwisted. "They say," she said, picking the needle back up, "that he has a visage to rival any angel's and a smile to set an abbess swooning into his arms."

"Sounds unlikely."

"Aye," she agreed. "Of course, that is but the beginning. They say he has seduced so many women to his bed that he's lost count and skewered so many of their lords on his sword that the blade won't surrender the bloodstains."

"Poetic," he said with a sigh. "Truly."

"That he has bedded so many?" she asked sharply. "Or that he has slain so many?"

"The latter, surely, but the first is more interesting."

"How so?"

He shrugged. "A man does what he must in matters of love."

"Better that he had denied himself now and again."

The man lifted one eyebrow. "The pleasures of a woman's bed? Think you?"

"If he has no control over his passions before he weds, how will he have any after he weds? Should he manage to distract some daft wench long enough to drag her before a priest, that is."

The man laughed. "You've given his bride much thought, I see."

"Aye, poor girl." She pursed her lips. "Surely she would expect more from him than so many indiscretions."

The man looked at her thoughtfully for a moment or two, then shrugged. "For all you know, tales of his prowess are false."

"Are they?" she asked skeptically.

"Tell me the tales, then let me judge. There are more reports of his antics, aren't there?" he asked hopefully.

"Aye. Enough to nauseate you for days."

"Tell on, then. I can hardly wait to hear them."

Who was she to deny this poor fool his little pleasures? She picked out the last handful of stitches she'd put in awry, then carried on with the gossip she'd heard over the past handful of days.

" 'Tis said," she continued, "that he consorts with all manner of odd folk, from faeries to warlocks. He has unholy skill with his blade. He escapes from impossible perils and emerges from all battles unscathed."

The man laughed. "By the saints, what a fanciful bit of fluff. Now, if bogles and ghosties are your fancy, rather you should concentrate on his younger brother. 'Tis Jason who consorts with warlocks and other such horrors. I daresay Kendrick, poor lad, hasn't the stomach for such things. Rather, he no doubt finds himself more comfortable in the pleasant and undemanding company of women."

"Then he'd best not come here," Lianna muttered, "for this collection of shrews is anything but undemanding."

"Perhaps with luck he'll avoid them," he said. "And you, lady, are you able to avoid them?"

Lianna wove her needle into the cloth to hold it, then rubbed her eyes with a sigh. "If only I could—"

A sudden commotion at the door made the man spring to his feet and pull the hood of his cloak close around his face. Lianna looked over her shoulder to find Maud and her companions sweeping back into the chamber as if they'd been royalty. And royalty, Lianna knew, was what they most certainly were not. Indeed, they were lower in station than her mother had been—making them lower in station than she herself was.

Yet another reason for them to hate her.

Maud looked at Lianna's companion. "This is a woman's solar, you fool. Who gave you permission to enter?"

" 'Twas a mistake, my lady," the man said, bobbing his head respectfully.

"Or did you invite him?"

Lianna realized Maud was glaring at her only because she felt the heat of the other woman's gaze. Perhaps the gossips had it wrong. Jason of Artane might have consorted with witches and warlocks, but he was likely just a man and possessed no unearthly powers. Maud, however, seemed to be fair burning a hole in Lianna's head with her gaze alone, which led Lianna to wonder about whom the woman really consorted with in the dead of night.

And by the time she'd thought that through, she found Maud's clawlike grasp encircling her wrist. Maud hauled her to her feet.

"How one as ugly as you could entice a man, I don't know," Maud said harshly, "but you'll not sully my solar with your whorish ways. This will teach you your place."

Lianna watched as Maud's other hand came toward her face. She'd never been struck in her life, and she could scarce believe it was going to happen to her now. The other thought that occurred to her was that this wasn't Maud's solar. It was the queen's solar, but since the queen was not at the keep, the right of the place likely should have gone to the woman of highest rank.

Which, as it happened, was Lianna herself.

Maud's hand continued toward her face. Lianna winced in anticipation of the blow.

A blow which never came.

Lianna opened her eyes, realizing just then that she'd closed them, only to find Maud's hand caught in another larger and stronger grip.

"Do not," commanded the man.

"And who are you to stop me?" Maud spat.

The man flipped his hood back with his other hand and smiled pleasantly.

"Kendrick of Artane!" squeaked Linet. "By the saints, Maud, 'tis him!"

"Silence, you silly twit!" Maud hissed. "I *know* that."

Lianna's first act was to gape at him in astonishment. Then she latched onto the urge to slink back into a corner and hope that Kendrick would forget her and everything she'd said about him in the past quarter-hour. She pulled her other hand from Maud's slackened grip and backed away, feeling her cheeks grow suddenly quite hot. By the saints, she had thoroughly insulted the man—and to his face, no less!

She was spared the humiliation of having to look at him, however, because he stepped in front of her and spoke to the other women.

"Perhaps I might escort you ladies to supper. I understand His Majesty plans to lay an uncommonly fine table tonight, and no doubt you'll want to seek your places early."

"But," Maud protested, trying to step around him and finish what she'd started.

Indeed, Lianna saw her hand still twitching, as if it itched to slap her.

"There is nothing here that warrants your further attention, Lady Harrow. Aye, I recognized you from your sapphire-like eyes, didn't you know? Tales of your beauty precede you wherever you go."

Maud snorted in frustration, but Kendrick seemed not to notice.

"Let us be off," he said. "I can see nothing here that either you or I need mark any further, can you?"

Lianna wondered if she should be stung by his words or expect them. But as he with one hand dragged the women from the chamber, he was with the other giving her a friendly wave behind his back.

She watched them leave. The solar door shut firmly behind them. The relief that flooded through her was enough to weaken her knees. She sank into her chair, grateful and not a little bemused. She had just thoroughly insulted the most eligible knight of the realm, yet he had accorded her the gesture of a conspirator. And he had also rid her of her banes—at least for the moment. A pity she could not find such a man to wed her, that she might be forever without such scourges.

The thought of Kendrick of Artane wedding with such a one as she sent renewed color to her cheeks. He was too brilliant a star in the firmament. Even had she possessed her beauty still, she could not have borne him as a husband. She wanted to be far removed from court, from pitiless tongues wagging at her, from being forced to attend a king who had no use for her except that she was connected to her land.

Ah, that a man might come and rescue her, free her from the king's wardship, and take her home. A pity she could not find one who was even uglier than she, that he might be grateful to have her.

She looked at her stitchery, then ran her fingers over her work, over the dark threads that depicted the scene laced with shadows. At least in those shadows made of thread there was somewhere to hide. Perhaps that was all she dared hope for herself, a piece of shadow somewhere where she could hide and forget her ruined visage.

But if she hid in the shadows, how would any man find her?

She pushed her work aside, surprised at the foolishness of her thoughts. It mattered not whether she hid or stood in full sunlight; no man would ever want her. The poor fool who would eventually be forced to wed her would like think his nuptials the blackest day of his life.

She rose, turned toward the door, and put her shoulders back. Dinner called and 'twould go worse for her if she were late, for then she would be noticed the more.

She left the solar with her head down.

# Two

***Jason of Artane rode through the barbican, cursing his*** father, his next older brother, and the weather, the last of which had been foul for the past pair of fortnights and was fair now only after he'd suffered out in it for a month. The early morning sunlight streamed down fiercely, as if it sought to pound good cheer into him with its rays. He stifled a hearty sneeze in his sleeve and wondered why he'd ever agreed to humor his father by following his brother from one end of the island to the other.

It had been a miserable journey from Artane, he had been sent on a useless errand to distract him from his true purpose, and he was certain he'd caught a healthy case of the ague the night before from having to sleep in a drafty stable instead of the nice warm inn he'd selected. He supposed he had only himself to blame for the latter. If he'd kept his cloak pulled together and his lips clamped shut, he wouldn't have been recognized. Instead, he'd given his name when asked and let his cloak fall away from the blood-red ruby in the hilt of his sword. The usual reaction had occurred.

Men had crossed themselves.

Women had screamed and fainted.

Jason had sighed in disgust, downed the tankard of ale he'd managed to obtain, flipped a coin to a speechless patron in return for the rough bread and hunk of cheese he had filched from him on his way out the door, then sought out the most comfortable part of a hayloft for his bed. Such, he'd supposed, was the lot of a man who had squired for the lord of Blackmour.

That lord would have found the tale vastly amusing.

Jason found the kink in his neck and his rapidly stuffing nose anything but.

He sneezed again as he rode into the bailey unchallenged. Guardsmen who would have demanded any other man's name merely gaped at him and weakly waved him past. Jason knew he should have been amused. After all, 'twas seldom that a man of a score and five had such a fiercesome reputation without having done much to deserve it.

It wasn't that he was a poor swordsman. Even he, modest though he considered himself to be, was well aware of his ability. One could not be the son of Robin of Artane and not have had some small talent for swordplay granted him. But whatever mastery he had of his blade, he had paid for himself by time spent in the lists.

He also didn't mind that the souls about him suspected him of all manner of dark habits. He had been first page, then squire, then willing guest of Christopher of Blackmour for most of his life. Some of the mystery surrounding the man had been bound to have cloaked Jason as well. He knew the true way of things, so idle gossip and charms spat out in haste when he passed didn't trouble him.

What did trouble him, though, was the fact that he'd finally found a purpose for which his soul burned, a cause so just and noble that it drove sleep from him at night, and here he was still unable to pursue it. Obstacle after obstacle had been placed in his path—lately and most notably the task of finding his brother and delivering a message from their father.

Jason scowled. It was his father's ploy, of course, to keep him from his course. But it would serve Robin naught. Jason was determined. Never mind that his course was one his father had forbidden him to pursue and one his former master had counseled him against.

But what else was he to do with himself? His eldest brother, Phillip, had estates aplenty and the burden of someday inheriting their father's title to harrow up his mind and try his soul. His other brother Kendrick burned like a flame, driving himself from conquest to conquest, as if he sought to force a dozen lifetimes into the one he would be allotted. Jason had no stomach for the tidiness of Phillip's life or the incessant roaming of Kendrick's. But he did have the stomach for a bit of crusading. A goodly bit. A bit that might take him out of England for years and give purpose to his life.

That it might also brighten up his reputation was nothing to sneeze at either.

But he sneezed just the same, all over a guardsman, who hastily backed away as if Jason had been spewing curses at him instead of the contents of his nose.

Jason scowled at the man and continued on his way toward the stables. At least his path there was clear—and likely only because his sire hadn't been able to find a way to thwart him so far from home. No doubt he would find more distractions awaiting him in France, should he by any chance find Kendrick, discharge his duty, then sail to the continent before he was too old to hoist a sword. But he would never have the chance to set foot on yonder shore if he didn't finish his business on the current shore, which was, of course, why he found himself chasing the king's court from London north, following his brother's erratic trail, and sleeping in haylofts with inadequate bedding.

The only positive thing to come of his journey so far was that he hadn't found the king at a monastery, as was often his custom. Jason knew he'd have trouble enough with the king's courtiers and whatever clergy he found himself surrounded by without scores of monks trying to exorcise the demons from him as well.

He dismounted in front of the stables and found a cringing stableboy at his side. He handed the lad his reins, knowing that no one would dare abuse his horse or pilfer his saddlebags. He would likely find them in the usual place—well away from any living soul.

Jason looked about him but found no sign of his brother in amongst the horseflesh. Perhaps Kendrick was romping out in the fields with some fair wench, crushing flowers and hearts beneath his heel with equal abandon.

The thought of flowers made his nose begin to twitch, so he decided to leave the fields for a later time and concentrate his search first on the castle itself. He crossed the courtyard and climbed the steps into the great hall.

He made himself known to the highest ranking of Henry's aides present there. The man was a foreigner of indeterminate origin, so Jason tried first French, then Latin. After receiving baffled, unhelpful shrugs in response to both, he gave up and excused himself with a bow. Obviously, he would have to search on his own.

He looked about him but saw no sign of his unruly brother. That meant nothing. Kendrick could have been anywhere, in any guise, stirring up any kind of trouble. That he was even rumored to be at court came as something of a surprise. Kendrick made no secret of his loathing of the king's flaws. Henry had an inordinate fondness for anything or anyone who had not sprung from English soil, and he seemed determined to beggar the country entertaining his entourage and building his monuments in London. Jason could only assume Kendrick was here to flatter the king into giving him, or selling him at a reduced price, some bit of land Kendrick had taken a fancy to.

Either that or Kendrick had been instructed by their father to lead Jason on a merry chase for as long as possible—likely in hopes that Jason would regain his good sense before he rushed off to do something foolish in France.

Damn them both.

Jason considered investigating bedchambers but thought better of it. Interrupting his brother whilst at his favorite labors was more than even he could stomach at present. But a solar might not be so perilous. After all, what havoc could possibly be wreaked in a woman's solar?

Jason climbed the stairs and started down the passageway, looking for a likely door. He hadn't taken a handful of paces before he saw a woman standing outside a door with her head bowed. Her hand was pressed against the wood, as if she couldn't quite bring herself to push the door open. She wasn't a servant; that much he could see by her clothing. Then why did she wait without?

He approached, heralding the like with a mighty sneeze stifled in the crook of his elbow. He dragged his sleeve across his face, immediately relinquishing the idea of making any kind of agreeable impression. He looked at the woman but could not see her very well. The place where she stood was filled with the deepest shadows in the passageway.

"My lady?" he said politely.

She did not lift her bowed head to look at him. She was silent for a moment, then acknowledged him with a soft "my lord."

"Do you require aid?"

"Aid?" she asked. "Nay, my lord, but I thank you for the offer."

Jason approached, then realized that the door was not closed, but rather slightly ajar. He could hear voices inside, and they were passing unpleasant in their tone.

"I could not believe my eyes."

"Nor could I! And the saints only know how long he'd been talking to her yesterday."

"Why would he pass time with her? Nothing could make up for the ugliness of her visage."

"Aye, and not that she had time to lift her skirts—"

"And not that he would have accepted *that* offer, even if he'd kept his eyes closed—"

Another voice spoke, a voice that sent chills down Jason's spine though he had never in his life been frightened by the sound of a woman speaking.

"She must be stopped."

Jason looked at the woman standing next to him. Did they speak of her? All he could see was the top of her head, so he couldn't judge by her expression if that were the case. But he could well imagine her not wanting to go inside and listen to any more of that rot—even if it had naught to do with her.

"Do you require something inside there?" he whispered.

She did not look up, even at that. "I thought to fetch my stitchery, but I daresay there isn't a need for that now."

"No doubt your gear will keep," Jason agreed, fully intending to wish her good fortune, bid her farewell, and then continue his search.

But two things stopped him.

One was that he'd heard his brother's name begin to be bandied about inside the solar. And the second was the woman who stood before him, cloaked in shadows, listening to the drivel being spewed inside that solar as if she needed to hear it. He stood not two paces from her but suddenly felt as if they two stood alone in the world. It was all he could do to breathe normally.

Who was this woman?

She stepped back from the door and pulled the hood of her cloak up around her face. And the moment was gone.

"I thank you for your kindness, my lord," she said. "I'm sure my things will be safe enough."

Jason had his doubts about that, but he also had no desire to enter the solar to find out. He was also beginning to wonder if he might need to break his fast soon. Obviously, he was faint from hunger and from the sneezes that threatened to overwhelm him at every turn. He had no ties to the woman before him. There was no good reason to feel as though the last thing he should do was walk away from her. By the saints, he had no idea what she even looked like! He shook his head to clear it. The sanest thing he could do was turn tail and flee.

Aye, that was wise. But he could not leave her where she was, not with the talk that was going on inside that solar.

"Might I es . . . ah—*ahchoo*—" he said with a mighty sneeze. He dragged his sleeve across his face and tried to regain his dignity. "Might I escort you to wherever you're going?" he said again. Perhaps the sunshine would burn his illness—and his sudden madness—from him before it overcame him completely.

"There's no need," the woman protested.

"My mother would be disappointed in me if I showed such a lack of courtesy," he said. "And who am I to disappoint her?"

"Very well," the woman said with a soft sigh. "But it won't be far. I'm only to go to the barbican gates."

Jason bowed to her, then followed her down the passageway.

"Whom go you to meet?" he asked as they reached the bottom of the stairs.

"No one of consequence," she said, her quiet voice almost lost in the bustle of the hall.

"A handsome knight come to woo you?" he asked lightly.

"I should think not," she said with half a laugh. "Nay, 'tis but a friend I made yesterday in the most unlikely of ways who offered to rescue me from a day passed inside the walls."

And given that her alternative would have been sitting in a solar with a handful of poisonous serpents, he could well understand her desire to accept the deliverance.

They left the great hall and crossed the bailey. Jason tried to steal looks at the woman beside him, but her cloak too thoroughly shadowed her face. He wondered why she chose to go about thusly, especially in the heat of the sun. Perhaps she met a lover for a secret tryst and wanted no one to recognize her. But surely there were few enough people at Henry's temporary court here that she would instantly be known by her clothing and bearing alone.

He shrugged aside his questions, for they weren't vital ones. If she wanted to hide herself, 'twas her affair and not his. What he needed to do was discharge his obligation to her so he could be about his business.

Which was, he thought with a scowl, much like what he was doing with his damned brother he couldn't seem to find.

They walked through the barbican gate. The woman stopped and looked about her. Jason saw her shoulders sag, and immediately sympathy surged through him. Obviously, the invitation hadn't been a trustworthy one. And then he caught sight of a tall figure loitering under a tree some distance down the road.

There was something unsettlingly familiar about that shape, dressed as it was in nun's gear.

"Perhaps there?" Jason said, pointing toward the beginning of an orchard.

The woman paused, then made a sound that Jason could have almost mistaken for a laugh.

"Perhaps," she agreed, and started down the path.

Jason followed, scowling fiercely and cursing under his breath.

The nun straightened as they approached, then walked toward them with a slow and solemn gait.

"My lady," the nun said in a high, hoarse voice. "You came as you said you would."

"Aye," the woman said, sounding amused.

"And I see you've brought your fool with you," the nun said, hiding hairy arms by tucking them into opposite sleeves. "Off with you, dolt. We've a walk to accomplish today."

The woman next to Jason stiffened. Perhaps she thought him offended by the other's words. He wasn't. It wasn't the first time he'd been insulted by the soul before him.

Nor was he surprised to find a nun with a voice that was better suited to bellowing battle cries than chanting prayers. He folded his arms over his chest and glared at the object of his search.

Which was, of course, his brother.

In skirts.

Not that such was all that unusual. Kendrick wasn't the first man in their long and illustrious line to disguise himself as a sister of the cloth. Jason had never in the past—and he prayed fervently that he would never be compelled to in the future—lowered himself to dress as a woman.

Dire circumstances called for momentous actions, he supposed. He wondered what sorts of straits Kendrick found himself in at present to necessitate such a disguise.

Then he found himself distracted by a movement at his side. The woman turned to look at him, and her hood caught on a low branch. It was pulled away to reveal dark hair coiled around her head and a visage that Jason could not look away from.

She was beautiful.

Or at least she had been before the pox.

He smothered his surprise, then gave her his most gentle smile.

"My lady," he said, making her a little bow, "surely you don't intend to pass your afternoon with this oaf here. His mere presence will put you off your food, cause you great pains in the head, and give you horrible dreams. Better that you allow me to save you from this unsavory invitation."

He found himself quite suddenly sprawled on his backside and 'twas a certainty only Kendrick could have put him there.

"Come, Lianna," Kendrick said, offering her his arm. "Let us leave the refuse along the side of the road and be on our way."

"But, my lord—"

"It isn't 'my lord.' It's simply Kendrick. And that unwholesome bit of offal is my younger brother, Jason. He's likely come to torment me with some business I've no stomach for hearing today. See you how the sun shines and the birds sing. We should enjoy it, don't you think?"

Jason thought many things, first and foremost of which was that he really should kill his brother at his earliest opportunity. Perhaps he would invite Kendrick to a war where he could commit fratricide with more ease.

Contemplating that happy possibility was almost enough to get him to his feet with a smile. He rose just the same, brushed off his abused backside, and stared at the ridiculous pair walking away from him. The lady, Lianna, was a mystery he wished he had time to solve. Why did she find herself at court? And what, the saints pity the poor girl, was she doing befriending his randy brother, who could have had any and all of the most beautiful women in England or France tumbling into his bed at the mere hint of an invitation?

He paused, tempted to solve those mysteries.

But nay, he couldn't. He had business to accomplish. The mystery of his brother's whereabouts was solved. Jason had little doubt he could find Kendrick again easily. Only his brother would clothe himself as a nun and stride about with his hairy legs clearly showing under skirts that hit him just below the knee and a cloak that didn't fall to the middle of his forearm—and believe that such a disguise would deceive any but the most foolish of men.

Or women, if that was his purpose, which Jason suspected it might be.

He was momentarily tempted to follow them and force Kendrick to speak with him immediately, but he could already see himself using his fists on his brother, and it would be just his luck to have someone see him brawling with a nun. His reputation was black enough without that.

Nay, he would but wait for supper, then see to delivering his message.

Then he would be on his way to France.

# Three

***Lianna sat in the shadows and stared at the fire in the*** midst of the great hall. The smoke burned her eyes if she didn't blink often enough, but such was the price one paid for a roof over one's head, she supposed. In her sire's hall, the fires had been set into the wall, with flues to carry the smoke outside. Her father's people had thought him mad to do such a thing, but he had been convinced of the wisdom of it. And Lianna, her eyes now burning in the midst of the king's appropriated hall, heartily agreed with her sire's thinking.

But at least the smoke gave her a reason to let her eyes water, which they wanted to do just the same from the kindnesses she'd been shown that day.

She peered through the smoke at the king's table and tried to discern the goings-on there. Normally, she would have been sitting there as well, but tonight all the places had been given to lords of either importance or wealth—such as Kendrick of Artane.

Or of dark reputation, given who sat next to Kendrick.

She picked absently at her supper and contemplated the very unlikely turn her life had taken over the past two days. Apparently, giving her tongue free rein in the presence of—and, unfortunately, in the most unflattering ways *about*—one of the most sought-after men in the realm had amused him enough to turn him into something of a comrade-in-arms. She had passed a delightful day in his company, finding him to be nothing that his critics said he was and everything they said he was not. In Artane's second son, she had found a brother and a friend.

Now, *his* brother was a different tale entirely.

From the very moment she had heard Lord Jason's voice in her ear, she'd been unsettled. She'd tried not to show that, to walk as other women did, speak with levity, and carry herself as if she hadn't a care in her heart. She'd certainly had no intention of letting him know what his brief kindness, or the mere sound of his voice in the passageway, had wrought in her. And she'd done her best to forget him as she walked with his brother in the sunlight and heard that brother tell stories of Jason as if he'd been a harmless pup—which Lianna couldn't believe he was.

Not if the rumors were true.

But none of those rumors was foul enough to dissuade her from searching for him through the smoke in the hall and wondering if his visage was as beautiful as she remembered, or if perhaps the spell he'd cast on her had been completely undone by an afternoon passed in his brother's sparkling company. Indeed, she began to suspect that Kendrick had wrought a goodly work on her wits, for she could scarce remember what Jason looked like.

Or so she told herself.

Odd how it had never occurred to her that Kendrick's brother might be even more handsome than he.

But nay, she couldn't say that, for she was just certain she couldn't remember Jason's visage, or the deep whisper of his voice, or the way chills went through her just standing next to him.

She sighed and rested her chin on her fist. Perhaps she was more interested than she cared to admit. And since the hall was smokey enough that he would never see her gaping at him, why shouldn't she? She decided to allow herself that luxury as she peered at him and thought back on what Kendrick had told her.

Jason had been a pleasant, cheerful lad at one time: Kendrick had assured her of such as he'd told her stories of his family. And according to Kendrick, Jason was still cheerful, though Lianna could scarce believe it. Shadows hung about him like shrouds. The current grimness of his visage—what she could see of it from where she sat—warned any and all he would not be amenable to lighthearted conversation. She certainly had no intention of daring the like. Besides, she had just learned to speak freely and comfortably to his brother—and Kendrick was as open as a flower that begged you to come pluck it and savour its fragrance.

Jason of Artane was nightshade, deadly to those who dared partake.

And so beautiful she could scarce convince herself she shouldn't.

She stared at him thoughtfully and began to suspect that perhaps they might have more in common than she wanted to believe. He seemed to have no more stomach for the pleasantries of court than she. She squinted and marked Kendrick laughing with, flattering, and charming the king and his courtiers. She knew that he spoke several languages, for she had heard for herself as he imitated each of the king's foreigners in their own tongues in turn as they walked through the orchard. Those same souls might not have hung on his every word so fully had they but known what amusement Kendrick had had at their expense not a handful of hours before. Even so, there was not a man there at that high table who didn't laugh with

Kendrick or find himself being drawn into the talk.

Except Jason, who put his head down and plowed through his supper with the concentration of a body that hadn't had a decent meal in a fortnight.

And when he did lift his head, he looked bored to tears.

She couldn't help but feel a certain kinship with him in that regard.

"Lady Lianna?"

The voice startled her so badly she almost fell from her chair. She turned around to find Linet of Byford standing beside her, shifting uncomfortably.

"The lady of H-Harrow asks if you w-w-would not be more comfortable in our . . . c-c-circle," Linet said, stumbling badly over her words, "when the entertainments begin." She looked behind her to where Maud had already begun to set up her own little court. As if Maud had arranged it, the king stood and the tables began to be set aside to clear spaces for whatever amusements had been arranged.

Lianna was surprised by the invitation, and she couldn't help but wonder if Kendrick's arrival hadn't heralded more than just an afternoon's freedom from the prison of her visage. If these ladies were deigning to include her as well, who knew what might happen in the ensuing days?

The thought was truly staggering.

"Well," Lianna said, rising, "aye, I daresay I would. Thank you."

Linet looked as miserable as if she'd been banished to the kitchens, and that made Lianna pause. Did that bode ill for her? Was Linet dreading having to spend any more time than necessary in Lianna's company? Then why invite her for the remainder of the eve?

When she reached the circle, the others who waited only wore friendly expressions. A chair was placed on Maud's right, and Lianna was welcomed into it. When she was seated, she was handed a goblet of wine and offered a plate of sweets.

"You must forgive us," Maud said. "We have been less than friendly to you, and for that we are truly sorry. Aren't we, ladies?"

The others bobbed their heads obediently.

Maud looked back at Lianna. "Come, eat," she said, indicating the plate. "Drink. Take your ease with us. There will be fine minstrels to sing to us of heroic deeds. Will that please you?"

Maud smiled and Lianna tried to smile back. But something about Maud's smile disturbed her greatly, for it seemed to fashion itself about her mouth only. No vestige of warmth reached the woman's eyes.

Lianna wished quite suddenly that she'd refused the invitation, but 'twas far too late to leave at present. She looked about her desperately for a place to hide, but found only a wooden plate in one of her hands and a goblet of drink in the other.

So she buried her face in her cup to escape. When she found the brew to be quite nasty, she occupied her hands and her mouth with the sweets until they tasted just as noxious as the other, forcing her to drink more to get them down her throat.

Just as she thought she could bear no more, she looked up to find Kendrick of Artane standing there, frowning down at her thoughtfully.

And behind him, looking as harmless as a clutch of nettles, scowled his younger brother. He glanced at her, then suddenly and quite violently sneezed all over his brother's back.

Kendrick's curse was formidable.

"I need to speak with you," Jason said pointedly. "Turn yourself about."

"Why, so you can drench the front of me? I'll speak with you later. I've more important things to do at present." He made Maud and her companions a bow. "Ladies. My lady," he said, bowing to Lianna as well.

"The dancing begins," Maud said, jumping to her feet

as if she'd been launched there. "My lord, if you will allow me to be so bold?"

Kendrick inclined his head and led Maud off without so much as a murmur of protest, though he exchanged a brief, unpleasant look with his brother on the way by. Jason cursed, swept the women before him with a disgruntled glance, then sat down in Maud's vacated chair. He dragged his sleeve across his watering eyes, then looked with faint interest at Lianna's cup and plate.

"Finished?" he asked.

She had scarce managed an aye before he took the cup and tasted the last drop.

Then he suddenly went very still.

"I'll take that, my lord," said Adela, reaching forward.

Jason did not move. "Will you? I think not. Indeed, I might want some of this myself. Have you any more of this brew?"

"The king's finest," squeaked Linet. "Lady Harrow obtained it for us."

Lianna could not fathom why Jason looked suddenly so angry or why the women about her looked suddenly quite so pale.

Then she realized who sat with them, and his reputation gave her all the answer she needed. He was the Dragon's man, likely something of a dragon himself, and a fit of foul temper had overcome him. No wonder the women about her were so terrified. Indeed, Lianna suspected that she as well should be just as terrified, but somehow she wasn't. She put the plate on the floor and gave Jason her most dazzling smile, only realizing as she looked him full in the face that she shouldn't be doing the like, not with her visage.

But somehow she couldn't find the energy to hide. So she spoke boldly and wondered at her boldness, for it was certainly newfound.

" 'Tis but wine, my lord," she said, then she stopped, for she found that her tongue wasn't working properly.

Indeed, all of the sudden, she felt heartily and thoroughly sick.

"Too much wine," offered Linet.

"I daresay," Jason said darkly.

Lianna pushed herself to her feet, wondering desperately if she might make either the outside or a garderobe before she was violently ill.

"She's going to sick up her supper on my feet," Adela said with distaste. "Go elsewhere, Lianna. These are new slippers I'm wearing."

Lianna felt Jason's hands suddenly on her arms, but she pushed him away. She turned and stumbled toward the stairs, praying she could make the passageway. She could be sick there. But please, just not here in front of the king's company. Not here where she would be fodder for mockery.

She stumbled up the stairs, gained the garderobe by sheer willpower, then hung her head over the hole and wretched until she could scarce stand.

It took a lifetime to retreat to the passageway and several more to walk a handful of paces.

Her head felt as if someone had taken an axe to it, and her poor form no better. And then, quite suddenly, a blessed darkness began to descend.

"Lianna!" a deep voice called urgently from behind her.

But she could not turn, nor could she answer. She closed her eyes and slid happily down the slope toward blackness. The last thing she heard was a mighty sneeze, followed by a equally mighty curse.

She did not feel the arms that broke her fall.

# *Four*

***Jason knelt in the passageway with the lady Lianna of*** somewhere-yet-to-be-discovered in his arms and wondered why in the bloody hell she found herself at court with women who had likely poisoned her.

Perhaps she had no choice, and for that he pitied her. He'd been at Henry's court less than a day, and already he couldn't wait to escape. He couldn't stomach the thought of much more conversation that revolved around the perfect cut of a man's tunic, the proper color for hose, or how one might dress to best grace the latest of the king's building projects. What he wanted was a simple conversation about the feeding of swine, or whether the barley and hops might grow well in the north fields, or a discussion of the virtues of the keep's blacksmith.

Aye, he could scarce wait to take his leave. He would have, and that night, too, had it not been for the woman in his arms.

He'd seen her at supper, hiding in the shadows. He'd

watched her be drawn into the ladies' circle after supper and felt alarm sweep through him. Surely they would have no kindness for such a one as she. He'd followed Kendrick willingly, not only to hound his brother, but also to see what mischief the women were combining.

After his brother had made his nimble escape, Jason had decided to wait him out and keep watch over Lianna whilst he was doing it. Besides, it gave him somewhere to sit where the conversation might revolve around something besides men's garments.

He'd noticed almost immediately that Lianna had looked flushed, and he'd wondered what she'd been drinking. Tasting her wine had assured him 'twas more than simply the brew that had worked such a foul business on her.

And now, as he stared down into her poor, ravaged face, he could only hope she didn't pay the ultimate price for having trusted those who had given it to her.

Women Jason would see repaid for their misdeed, in time.

He dragged his arm across his running nose then swung Lianna up into his arms. He kicked at the first door he saw. It was opened none too quickly by a sleepy servant.

"Let me in," Jason growled.

"But, my lord," the woman squeaked, "this is the ladies' chamber. You cannot—"

"I can and I will," Jason said. He pushed past her, strode across the chamber, and jerked back the bedcurtains. He laid Lianna down and wondered if he shouldn't undress her as well. Her gown was soiled and would likely be better off in some pile of rags destined for the beggars.

He looked at the servants huddled behind him and chose the one who looked the least likely to harm Lianna further.

"Strip her," he commanded, "and dress her in clothing

she can wear abed comfortably. I will wait without." He looked at the other two servants. "Leave."

"But, my lord," protested one.

He merely gestured curtly toward the door, and the women quit the chamber without further comment. Jason followed them out, then pulled the door shut behind him. He leaned back against it and stared grimly at the wall facing him. Now that he had peace for thinking, he would have to decide on a course of action. He could only hope that Lianna had managed to vomit up all but the quickest of the poison.

He had just begun to consider what he might give her to aid her when he noticed a commotion to his left. There coming toward him were the women responsible for Lianna's distress, trailed by the servants he had tossed from the chamber. Jason simply could not believe they had innocently given her drink laced with death. Worse still was how they walked about so freely, as if they thought no one would think to question their actions.

"Move yourself," one woman said briskly. "And take that foolish girl inside with you. I'm certain her illness is but a ruse."

"What was in her wine?" Jason asked.

One of the other women made a sound of misery and slumped back against the wall. That was telling enough, he supposed.

"Something in her wine, my lord?" the first woman said evenly. "How could you think such a thing of us?"

Jason looked at the woman who faced him with such apparent lack of fear, and suddenly a name attached itself to the face. Maud of Harrow, who possessed a tongue more poisonous than an adder's. He should have known she would have been behind this.

"I have eyes," he said, "and I recognize the signs."

"Having brewed several unwholesome things yourself," the lady of Harrow said with a cold smile. "Along with casting spells and other such activities particular to your kind."

"Or so it is rumored," one of the other women agreed.

"Silence, Adela," Maud commanded. She turned back to Jason and smiled unpleasantly at him.

"I have many skills," he said with a shrug, silently marveling that she would so boldly accuse him of sorcery. "I daresay you wouldn't want to acquaint yourself with too many of them."

"You don't frighten me," Maud said, puffing herself up.

But it would seem that he frightened the rest of her rabbits, for the other three were near to collapse in the passageway.

"Perhaps I don't," Jason conceded. "But you don't know the extent of what I can do. Especially my talent for carrying tales to the king to ruin the lives of foolish, spiteful wenches possessing sharp tongues and few wits. Do you care for a performance of that one?"

Maud considered, then turned and, one by one, slapped three whimpering women smartly across their faces.

"On your feet, Linet. Come, Adela. Stand up, Janet, you fool! Let us be away. We'll sleep in the solar."

Jason waited, faintly satisfied, until they had stomped away before he turned and went back inside the chamber. The serving girl was covering Lianna with blankets.

But Lianna wasn't moving.

Jason hastened to the side of the bed. The servant looked up as he approached.

"I did as ye bid me, milord," she said. "But she's powerful ill."

"Aye," Jason said absently. "I daresay 'twas poison."

"Mayhap 'tis mostly gone from her."

"Let us pray that 'tis so," he said. "Fetch my brother, will you? I've an errand for him. I'll need several things from the healer, if the man can provide them."

"Aye, milord, as ye will."

Jason sent the woman on her way, then looked about

him for something to sit on. Finding a small stool, he pulled it near the bed, sat, and searched back through his own lessons at a healer's knee for what he should do at present. His lessons had been thorough, and most unusual, given from whom he'd had them. He smiled to himself at the thought. Perhaps the lady of Harrow had not spoken amiss after all. He could brew a love potion, cure warts and other afflictions, and slather on quite a salve of beauty, should circumstances require.

As well as spew out a variety of quite potent curses, which was enormously tempting at the moment.

But the saints pity him should he not be able to remember the simple herbs to aid the woman before him in ridding her body of what foul brew she'd ingested.

He contemplated that list of herbs for what seemed to him an inordinately long amount of time. He was on the verge of going to seek out Kendrick himself when the door opened and a torch entered the chamber, carried by none other than his yawning brother.

"Lianna, where are you? I know that to have called me to you as I was about to retire can only mean that you've one desire of me—"

Kendrick's yawn ceased abruptly when he saw who was laid out on the bed.

"What happened to her?" he said, coming to stand next to Jason.

"To Lianna?" Jason asked, looking up at his brother sourly. "To the woman you couldn't see fit to introduce to me?"

Kendrick looked at him blankly. "I was tormenting you. 'Tis my sworn duty as your elder brother to do so. Now, what happened to her? She was seemingly happy enough with the ladies. When I was summoned here, I thought perhaps she had a tryst in mind."

"With you? Poor girl, I should hope not," Jason said.

"Why not? Many women—"

“Aye, exactly. Perhaps this one has more sense than the ers.”

endrick flicked him smartly on the ear, then peered s shoulder. “Why are you here then? And see you e sleeps. What have you done, Jason? Bored her eeply that she must sleep to escape you?”

“Kendrick, you fool, she was poisoned!”

Kendrick gasped. “Nay! By whom?”

“By those who would have you, likely.”

“Stupid wenches. Surely no man is worth this—not even I.”

At least in that his brother was showing some sense. Jason reached for Lianna’s hand and held it between his own. Her flesh felt as if it were on fire. Jason looked up at his brother.

“Go fetch me herbs,” he said.

Kendrick blinked. “Are you brewing love potions for her now?”

“Healing ones, dolt.”

“One never knows, what with your teachers.”

“Berengaria is a fine healer.”

“Oh, aye,” Kendrick agreed, “she is that. I daresay her two accomplices might have a different tale to tell about her varied talents and whether or not she is of the witchly ilk. Though I must admit Phillip was no worse for the wear for his time spent in their company.”

Phillip, their older brother, had followed his bride on a merry chase, accompanied by none other than Berengaria of Artane, lately of Blackmour, and her two apprentices, one of whom had willingly gone north in search for—of course—the thumb-bone of a wizard.

Whether she had found it or not was something of a family secret.

Jason smiled faintly. “They were all that aided him in taming his bride, so I daresay he has no complaints. And now that you’ve convinced yourself my skills aren’t dark ones, go fetch me what I need.”

"I'm not at all sure your skills aren't dark ones," Kendrick said with half a laugh, "but I will fetch you what you require, then I will return and make certain that our lady's honor isn't compromised by having you loitering about her chamber alone with your own sour self."

Jason spat out his list at his brother, then rose and gave him a healthy shove toward the door.

"Shall I bring you anything else?" Kendrick asked from the doorway. "Something for your sneezes? Or can you spell yourself into good health?"

"Horehound," Jason said shortly. "It will serve me as well as the lady here. But be swift, for I would waste no more time in seeing to the rest of this poison."

"As you will," Kendrick said, turning to leave.

"And a lute," Jason added.

"Lute?" Kendrick echoed. "And where am I to find—"

"There are musicians aplenty. Filch one of theirs."

Kendrick sighed and left without further comment.

Jason stared after him and spared a fleeting thought for how he really should be following his brother out that door, down the stairs, and out the castle gates. He had a crusade to make, kings to woo, and a noble cause to righteously pursue.

None of which had anything to do with where he was at present or what poor service he felt compelled to render here.

Jason sat, bowed his head over Lianna's hand, and offered up the most humble prayer his black soul could muster. His other life would have to wait while he fought for this life here. He could only hope he had enough skill to save that life.

With the way she was breathing so unevenly, he wasn't sure he would manage it.

# Five

***Lianna was sure she had died.***

And by the sound of things, she was certain, though somewhat surprised, that she had actually been admitted straight to Heaven without having to spend any time doing penance in Purgatory.

Music surrounded her, music that sounded remarkably like that made by a lute. That was puzzling, to be sure, as she'd always been led to believe that choirs of angels would attend the entrance of any soul through those Eternal Gates. But perhaps she was lowly enough—and had barely sufficed as a entrant—to merit naught but a single instrument to welcome her home.

And then the chord went astray.

"Damn."

Lianna struggled to open her eyes. Perhaps she'd sinned more than she thought to merit naught but a lute and a lutenist who dared curse in such a place. Perhaps she was still on the outskirts of the Eternal City, trapped with those who were still seeking to make themselves presentable.

"You should have practiced more," said a deep voice.

Lianna did manage to open her eyes then, though the sight that greeted her was no less baffling than what she'd imagined.

"I did practice. I practiced a great deal. Father vowed the sweet sounds of a lute were the way to win a lady's heart. I practiced until my bloody fingers were bloody!"

"In between consorting with witches, warlocks, and other sorcerers of dubious origins, of course."

"Aye, well, that too."

Lianna blinked. She would have rubbed her eyes as well, but her hands were too heavy to lift. She looked blearily at the two great birds sitting not far from her, one with fair feathers and one with dark. The dark bird was tall and graceful, with a proud tilt to his head and shining dark eyes. He was also holding the lute and cursing now and again. The fair bird next to him opened his beak and snorted.

Did winged creatures snort? She puzzled that out for several moments, but could come to no useful decision on it.

"It isn't as if *you* practiced any," the lute-playing one grumbled.

"And as you might imagine, my bed has not suffered from my lack of it. You must have more than pitiful skills on a lute to keep and hold the attention of a woman, brother."

"I have more skills than that."

"As one sees from the flocks of women who fight each other to have you."

Flocks of women? He obviously meant flocks of female birds. Lianna struggled to make sense of what they said, but it was difficult. She listened to them toss insults at each other, with increasingly unpleasant curses attached, for quite some time before it occurred to her that fowl such as these were certainly not members of any angelic choir, nor were they likely to be accompanying that choir anytime soon. A slow, steady feeling of terror swept over her.

"Nay," she breathed, when she could manage to find the word.

The dark bird immediately fastened a piercing gaze upon her hapless self, as if he intended to make a meal of her.

She tried to focus on him, but he seemed to weave about greatly, as if either he could not remain still or she could not. After trying to divine the truth of it for several minutes, she gave herself over to the only truth she knew.

She hadn't gone to Heaven. Heaven could not produce lute-playing birds with such foul speech. There was only one place for such as she, and she had apparently traveled there without delay. She felt tears begin to slip down her cheeks.

"I've gone to Hell," she wept.

"What?" the dark one asked.

"Foul notes, foul words," she managed.

And at that, the fair-feathered bird tossed back his head, opened his beak, and roared out a laugh.

She watched as the dark bird reached out toward her. No doubt he intended to clutch her with that hand he had suddenly fashioned himself and carry her down with him to his fiery dungeon. The saints pity her, she was doomed.

Blackness engulfed her, and she knew no more.

***She woke, only realizing then that she had been asleep.*** She stirred, and her poor form set up such a clamor that she immediately ceased all movement save drawing in hesitant breaths. By the saints, what had befallen her? Had someone beaten her nigh onto death?

She lay still for several minutes, searching back through her memories for one of any sense. There were dreams aplenty, ones with large birds and rather pleasant strumming of a lute, but those were surely naught but madness. Had she been ill? She had very vivid memories of the pox and how her fever had raged. This was akin to that but somehow worse, as if every part of her had been assaulted by some foul thing.

She could make out the bedhangings above her. Heavy layers of blankets and furs covered her. She was abed, which was something in itself given that she'd passed the majority of her nights as a member of the king's entourage sleeping on a straw pallet on the floor. The chamber was light, but that was from daylight, not candlelight. She turned her head to the right, wondering if she might be able to see out the window. But what she found was enough to still her forever.

Jason of Artane sat on a stool not a handful of paces away.

He was leaning back against the wall, his head tipped to one side, sound asleep. Lianna could scarce believe her eyes. How had he found his way into her chamber? And what, by all the blessed saints of Heaven, was he doing sleeping here? She looked to his right to find a serving maid curled up on the floor, sound asleep as well. Interesting though that might have been, it surely did not merit any further notice. So she turned her attentions back to the man who slept sitting up on a stool, with his hands limp in his lap and his mouth open to admit the passage of a soft snore or two.

He was almost close enough for her to touch him.

Deadly nightshade that he was.

But he didn't look deadly at present. He looked innocent and harmless and at peace. He looked like a man who would draw a child onto his lap and tell it stories for the whole of the afternoon if asked. He looked like a man who would pull his lady wife into his arms, rest his chin atop her head, and tell her he was happy to face life with her beside him. He looked like the sort of man her father would have found no fault with.

He looked like a man on the verge of drooling.

That sort of catastrophe was seemingly enough to rouse him from slumber, for he straightened with a snort, smacked his lips a time or two, then opened his eyes. And a smile of such dazzling brightness crossed his features, she was near blinded by it.

And at that moment, she was firmly and irretrievably lost.

He dropped to his knees at her bedside. "The saints be praised," he said, looking at her with visible relief. "Can you speak?"

She swallowed. "Aye," she whispered.

He put his hand to her forehead, and she received another pleased smile as a result.

"Your fever is but a slight one, though I daresay you're still recovering from the fierce one you've already had." Then he looked at her and frowned. "Do you know who I am?"

"Jason de Piaget."

"Well done, though we certainly cannot thank my brother for an introduction. And you're the lady Lianna, though you needn't thank my brother for that either, for he was very closemouthed about you. I had to pry all I know of you from the servants."

She could only imagine what he'd heard. She managed a snort of disgust.

"Nay, my lady, they were very few, those tales, and surely pleasant enough," he said with another smile. "Now, tell me how you fair. Shall you have a drink? I daresay food is beyond you still, but a bit of watered-down wine might suit." He looked toward the servant. "Aldith?"

The servant sat up sleepily and rubbed her eyes. When she saw Lianna awake, she rose to her knees.

"The saints be praised."

"Aye," Jason agreed. "Fetch a bit of the king's finest, won't you, and water to go with it. If anyone forbids you, tell them I commanded it and they'll answer to me if they deny you."

"Aye, my lord," she said, and quickly rose to her feet and left the chamber.

Lianna watched him turn back toward her, and she could scarce believe that Jason of Artane, master of dark arts and other sundry unsavoury habits, was kneeling by her head and now reaching for her hand to hold it between his own.

Odder still that she had no desire to flee in terror.

Indeed, looking at his beautiful blue eyes and even more pleasing visage, she wondered why anyone would find him anything but a harmless pup.

"The wine will come," he said confidently.

She managed a smile. "You are unused to being gainsaid, I suppose."

"What is the use of a foul reputation if it serves you nothing?" He looked down at her hand. "You're trembling. I daresay you'll be weak for some time."

"What befell me? Was I beaten?"

He looked at her quickly, one eyebrow raised in surprise. "Beaten? Nay. Poisoned, rather."

"Poisoned?" she breathed.

"The wine you drank. I would imagine your solar companions were ill-pleased with the time you passed with Kendrick."

She thought back. "I remember having a very sour stomach."

"Aye, well, best to forget that night," he said, patting her hand. "You were gravely ill, and I feared the worst. The following days were little better."

It took a moment or two to realize what he had been telling her. Had he stayed with her the entire time? She looked at his face and noted several days' growth of beard there. How many days had it been? Vividly her dream of the two birds came back to her. Had those been Jason and Kendrick, keeping watch by her bed?

And then an even more horrifying thought occurred to her, one that made her turn her head away from Jason in shame.

He had seen her visage. Not only had he looked on it whilst she dreamed, he had been forced to gaze at it whilst she spoke to him as boldly as a harlot. She reached up with the hand he was not holding and pulled some of her hair over her face.

"Thank you, my lord," she said, and her voice sounded horribly choked, even to her ears. "I don't know how I can repay you for your aid."

He said nothing.

She could not bear to look at him to see how he reacted to her words. All she could do was pull her hand free of his and turn more fully away from him.

"I daresay I'm well enough now. You needn't stay any longer. Surely a servant can tend me."

He was silent. Indeed, he was silent for so long, she wondered if he were struggling to master his disgust before he quit the chamber. But she heard no movement. In truth, she could hear nothing but shame pounding in her ears. How bold she had been! More the fool was she.

Then he cleared his throat. "Do you, my lady, know of my former master?"

She frowned. Why ask such a foolish question? Who didn't know of him? Christopher of Blackmour had the very blackest of reputations, full of violence and evil. He could change his shape, weave foul spells, do all manner of things she had never wanted to hear about after the sun went down. He was a dragon who caught unwary travelers in his claws when he wasn't loping over his land in the shape of a ferocious wolf, devouring all who dared set foot on his soil.

And Jason of Artane had been his squire.

The saints only knew what he had learned at his master's knee.

"Aye," she managed finally. "I know of him."

"Well, if you knew him as I do, then you would judge me differently," he said.

She could only imagine how.

"Now, I will go, if you wish it, but I will not go unless you look me in the face and tell me to."

Ah, what kind of man was he to be so cruel? Had Blackmour taught him that as well? She could only shake her head in misery.

He was silent for a goodly while, then spoke again.

"Why do you hide your face?" he asked gently.

"Why do you think?" she cried out, then bit her tongue.

"Do you think me so poor a man as that?" he asked quietly. "So weak-minded? So vain? So hollow in my character that I look only for perfection? Obviously, you have confused me with my brother."

She couldn't stop a smile at that, but neither could she face him.

"If you knew my master as I do, you would realize that he made me into a man who judges not by the sight of his eyes, but rather one who has learned to look deeper and trust what his heart tells him. Now, you do not know me, and you have unfortunately passed already too much time with my cocksure sibling and must, therefore, be permitted a bit of doubt about my character given what you've seen of his. I must tell you, though, that I cannot leave—nay, I will not leave—until you look me full in the face and tell me to go."

It was the hardest thing she had ever done. Indeed, it took more courage than facing the king's company at dinner. It took more courage than passing hours in a solar, closeted with women who loathed her. It took almost as much courage as it had taken to press on after her parents had died. Indeed, she suspected it might require more, for 'twas not her past that she faced.

It was her future.

She couldn't have said why that thought had come to her, but the truth of it burned within her breast. It was the same feeling that had fair set her on fire the first time she'd heard Jason's voice in her ear. It was the feeling that she was facing her destiny.

If she could face him, that is.

So she took a deep breath, brushed the hair back from her face, and turned to look at him.

She couldn't see him, of course. Her eyes were too full of tears.

"Stay or go?" he asked neutrally.

Ah, but that was too much to ask. How could she bid him stay when it might be against his will? She shook her head.

"That was unfair, I suppose," he conceded. "Let me ask it thusly: I wish to stay, though perhaps you might wish me to leave and at least change the clothes I've been wearing for the past several days. I will only go if you cannot bear my presence any longer. Now, shall I stay?"

She was having trouble enough just looking at him without giving in to the almost overwhelming desire to hide her face. But she supposed he would kneel there all day until she gave him some kind of answer, and there was only one answer she could possibly give. So she took what courage was left to her—and it seemed to be increasing by the moment—and cleared her throat.

"Stay," she said, and she was almost surprised by the firmness in her tone.

He smiled and inclined his head. "As my lady wishes. Shall I play for you as well? Whilst we await your wine?"

"Aye," she said.

He hadn't but set fingers to the strings before the door burst open and Kendrick bounded into the chamber, his smile almost blinding in its sunniness.

"Ah, Lianna," he said, beaming down at her, "you're

awake! And none too soon. The saints only know what sorts of frightening sounds Jason has subjected you to whilst you slept. Actually, I was here to hear them, and I would not be lying to tell you they were foul ones indeed." He sat himself down on Jason's lap, completely obscuring his brother from her view. "You look much improved."

"Aye, I am," she croaked.

"Jason is too, if you'll notice. No more sneezing. But the spells he had to cast! The brews he brewed! 'Tis enough to leave any sensible soul trembling—"

Jason reached around and set his lute upon Lianna. "Hold that for me will you, lady? I have this large lump of refuse to remove from your chamber."

She watched in fascination as the brothers engaged in a friendly tussle, which became less friendly after but a moment or two, then seemed to escalate into an all-out war.

"Excuse us—*oof,*" Jason said as doubled over with Kendrick's fist in his belly.

"I'll return brief—*aargh,*" Kendrick said as he was propelled out the door thanks to Jason's hands at his throat.

They did pause in the doorway long enough to taste wine that Aldith had brought, then waved her inside and continued their exercises. Aldith crossed the chamber and smiled at Lianna.

"Ye're lookin' well, milady," she said. "And with two such handsome men to attend ye, how could ye not?"

How indeed, Lianna thought, bemused.

But even as she enjoyed that thought, she couldn't help but wonder in the back of her mind just who it had been to give her poison and why.

# *Six*

***Jason walked along the passageway and wondered, as ser-***vants scattered before him like leaves before a strong wind, if there ever might come a time in his life where he could walk about without frightening everyone he met. Then again, it might serve him. He could be quite an asset on the battlefield. All he would need do was have a herald call out his name and watch the enemy disappear. Surely the king might have a use for him thusly.

But such service would have taken him far from where he wanted to be. He paused before Lianna's door and bowed his head, resting his palm against the wood. That he remained at court of his own will was startling enough. That his noble crusade was seeming less noble and more foolish by the moment was what had driven him to leave a sleeping Lianna's side and pace about the inner bailey, trying to find either his reason or his wits.

Neither of which he seemed to possess any longer.

But when the door opened before him and a very unsteady, though garbed for walking, Lianna of a place no one would tell him stood there clutching the doorway for support, he thought that perhaps his wits and reason hadn't left him after all.

Staying at this woman's side seemed the wisest thing he'd ever contemplated doing.

And he was almost certain his father and his former master would have approved.

"Where go you?" he asked, suppressing the urge to pick her up and carry her back to bed before she could answer.

"To seek my stitchery," she said weakly. "I can lie abed no longer."

Jason frowned. "Surely you've no desire to sit and sew amongst such women as those."

She was silent for a moment, then she lifted her face and looked at him. "What would you have me do else, my lord? I cannot ever hide from them. If it is not them I must endure, it will be others like them."

Jason doubted she could find four more vicious women to subject herself to, but he refrained from saying so. For one thing, she was looking at him without hiding her visage. For another, she was standing there without a hooded cloak around her shoulders for use in hiding later. If she had found the courage to allow the court to see her and not shrink, who was he to gainsay her?

He stepped back a pace and made her a low bow. "As my lady wishes."

She was still too weak to be up. Jason watched her struggle for only a handful of paces before he put his arm around her and gave her little choice but to lean on him. Their pace was very slow. It gave him ample time to wonder if there was a way he could convince her to let him fetch her things. Surely she could sew just as well whilst she was abed.

When they reached the solar door, Lianna straightened. Jason let his arm fall away from her, but he did so reluctantly.

"Are you certain?" he asked softly. "Perhaps another day—"

She shook her head. "I am well enough." Then she looked at him and smiled faintly. "Thank you, my lord. For all your kindnesses to me."

"Jason," he said. "My name is Jason."

"Jason, then," she said, after only a slight hesitation.

"I'll wait for you here."

"But—"

"I'll wait for you here," he said, folding his arms over his chest. "And don't drink any of their bloody brews."

"Far better to drink yours?"

"The worst mine might do is make you fall in love with me," he said, fully meaning for it to come out teasingly, but somehow the words came out of his mouth and hung in the air, still. He stared down at Lianna and couldn't believe that he had revealed so much of his heart with a simple handful of words.

Or that such words had uncovered so much of his heart he hadn't yet been able to face.

She only stared at him for a moment or two in complete silence, then shut her mouth and struggled visibly to look unconcerned.

Jason took a deep breath. "I will," he said, trying desperately for a much lighter tone, "remain without should you need me."

"I vow I won't drink anything."

"Very wise."

She gave him the briefest of smiles before she turned and pushed her way unsteadily into the solar. Jason heard the conversation come to an abrupt halt. The feeling of malice that flowed from the chamber was enough to set his hair on end—and he was the one supposedly accustomed to consorting with all manner of evil-doers.

He immediately tossed aside his promise to remain out in the passageway. He pushed the door fully open, then leaned against the doorframe, where he had full view of the goings-on inside.

Maud of Harrow and her accomplices sat in a circle with their feet at a brazier like so many witches hovering over a pot of bubbling mixture destined to wreak havoc on some unsuspecting soul. Only they weren't watching their feet or their imaginary pot. Their eyes, to a woman, were trained upon Lianna.

And their glances were not friendly ones.

Well, all except Linet of Byford, who Jason had encountered more than once hovering by Lianna's door as if doing penance for her part in the tragedy.

"What are you doing here?" Maud said, her voice as quiet as a knife sliding between unresisting ribs.

"I came to fetch my stitchery," Lianna said, her words steady and sure.

Jason noted her change of plans, but he had no intentions of commenting on it. Even he would have found little to recommend an afternoon in the company of these women.

"Of course," Maud said, gesturing toward the corner with a smile an assassin would have been happy to call his own. "By all means, fetch it."

Lianna made her way carefully across the chamber and knelt down before a small trunk. Jason watched the other women and wondered at the tangible sense of anticipation that seemed to run through them. Had they some new barb to throw at Lianna before she quit the chamber? Surely they wouldn't dare with him standing right there.

And then he realized that Lianna was not moving. He looked over to find her kneeling before her trunk, still as stone.

A feeling of dread swept over him.

He pushed away from the wall, skirted the chairs, and crossed the little chamber to kneel down at Lianna's side. A very hasty look revealed things that would never be useful again. He reached out and lifted up threads that were none of them a quarter the length of his smallest finger. Needles were bent double, past ever being used again for their original purpose. Cloth was torn into strips. He fingered several of those tattered strips and could see that they had once been a tapestry in the making.

And on the top of all the destruction was a charred bit of wood that he could only assume had once been her tapestry frame. The rest had no doubt gone to feed some fire or other.

He wondered why it was that Lianna didn't break down and weep.

He watched as she gently pushed his hand aside, then dug through the ruins of her art. She pulled out a needle. It was bent, but not so thoroughly that it couldn't be saved. Jason watched Lianna finger it for several moments in silence. Then she looked up at him.

And to his surprise, one corner of her mouth seemed to be tipping up, as if it considered beginning a smile.

"They missed something," she remarked calmly.

Indeed, she spoke so calmly they might have been discussing something as unimportant as whether or not the garrison was exercising until past noon or before.

Jason swallowed past a very dry throat. "Did they?" he managed.

Lianna toyed with the needle for a moment or two, then held it up to the light. "Can you brew potions, Jason?"

He blinked in surprise. "I beg your pardon?"

She fixed him with a purposeful glance. "Potions, my lord. Can you brew them?"

He wondered if anything he might say could possibly lead to anything but him being carried off to some unwholesome dungeon and subsequently being put to death in an unpleasant way. But he also suspected he knew what Lianna was thinking, so he stroked his chin, as if he considered his answer.

"Aye," he said finally. "I've been trained to do the like."

Lianna stood, swayed, then steadied herself. She shuffled slowly over to where Linet sat, quivering, all amusement, however faint, gone from her expression.

"Could you brew a potion that would bring death?" Lianna asked.

"Aye, likely so."

Lianna moved to stand behind another woman. "This is the lady Adela. Could you brew up something to ruin whatever wits might remain her?"

"Surely."

She moved behind another woman. "Here is her sister, Janet, a woman of particular desires. Could you see to it that she rots from the inside out, that a man never wanted to lie with her again?"

He suspected Janet would acquire that particular affliction on her own soon enough, but there was no sense in ruining Lianna's play.

"Easily done."

Lianna moved to stand behind Maud of Harrow. Maud sat as stiff as a pillar on her chair, every muscle tensed, a look of absolute hatred on her face.

"What about," Lianna said quietly, "something to ruin a face? To ruin beauty? To take away the visage a woman holds most dear?"

"I could have caught the pox from you and done that," Maud snapped.

"Aye, but that would have been over and done with in a handful of weeks," Lianna said, leaning down close to Maud's ear. "I daresay my lord could find a way to ruin your visage over the course of months, leaving you ample time to mourn your loss." She looked at Jason. "Your thoughts, my lord?"

He lifted his eyebrows. "It could be done. And there could be a great amount of pain with it. Would that please you, my lady?"

Lianna paused, as if she considered, then she straightened and shrugged. "Why trouble yourself? Life will do it to her in time anyway. A woman cannot be so ugly on the inside and not have it seep out eventually. What think you?"

What he thought was that she was the most amazing woman he had ever met and he would be damned lucky if he could ever call her his.

Something he was finding he wanted very much indeed.

And then Maud moved.

Jason was on his feet, across the chamber, and standing between Maud and Lianna before Maud could get to her feet and whirl around to slap Lianna. Jason stared at Maud's upraised hand.

"Lianna," he said, "quit the chamber. I'll fetch your things and follow you."

He held Maud's gaze in the same way he'd held countless opponents, waiting for a twitch in her face or a blink of her eye that would signal her intent to strike first.

She dropped her hand, huffed disdainfully, then spun back around and flung herself down into her chair. Jason waited until Lianna was standing outside the door before he fetched her little trunk, then walked to the door himself. He looked back at the women seated there, then held each of their gazes in turn.

"I sincerely hope," he said quietly, "that you all reap the rewards of what you've sown."

And with that, he left the chamber and closed the door behind him.

Lianna was waiting for him, trembling. He smiled down at her.

"You were extraordinary," he said. "And I'm very sorry about your gear."

She laughed, a choked sound that seemed to go quite well with the tears coursing down her cheeks.

"Aye, well, when compared to the pox or poison, this seems a small thing." She paused. "I am glad you were there."

"You just wanted me for my foul reputation."

"It seemed a pity not to make use of it."

"I daresay there is more to you than meets the eye."

He was just giving thought to how he might go about discovering what that more was when he looked up and saw the very last person he wanted to see at present. He cursed under his breath. Kendrick's ability to ruin any and all of Jason's attempts at wooing a woman was nothing short of uncanny. Did his father have a hand in this as well? Jason glared at his brother.

"What do you want?"

Kendrick blinked innocently. "What mean you?"

"We're busy, as you can see. Be off with you."

Kendrick looked at him assessingly, as if he knew what Jason was planning.

"I thought," Kendrick said slowly, as if he considered something of deep import, "that you had business to be about. Crusading or some such rot."

Jason sensed Lianna looking up at him. He wondered what she would think if he took his fist and planted it solidly in his brother's mouth to stop any more witless words. At least he could do so now and have it accomplish something. He remembered vividly all the years he'd wanted to but couldn't.

"I've changed my mind," Jason growled.

"Ah," Kendrick said wisely. "You found something, well, *here* to change your mind, hmmm?"

"Shut up," Jason said. "Before you force me to see to that for you."

Kendrick looked as if he planned to say something else. Jason brushed past him, nodding to Lianna to come with him. He saw her inside her chamber and set her trunk down by the bed.

"We will seek out a fair and find you other things to stitch with. Or perhaps the king has a stitcher with thread and cloth to spare."

"His Majesty seems to have an abundance of clothing," she agreed.

"I will see what I can find, then return. Does that suit you?"

She sat down on the bed and looked up at him with a smile. "And I've no doubt you've business with your brother."

"You see too clearly," he said with a scowl. "Aye, I'll see to him, find things for you, then return." *And I'll find a guard for your door,* he added silently. He nodded to Lianna, left the chamber, closed the door, then rewarded his brother with a blow to the belly that should have silenced him for a goodly while.

Kendrick straightened with a grunt. "What was that for?"

"I'm thinking to woo her, you fool. I do not need your aid."

Kendrick grunted. "If she'll have you."

"Why wouldn't she?"

"Why indeed?"

"There's nothing amiss with me."

To his surprise, Kendrick clapped him with a friendly hand on the shoulder.

"To be sure, brother. But don't you realize who she is?"

"I was just in the process of trying to discover more about her," Jason said pointedly, "when you arrived with your bothersome self."

"Or what she's doing in the king's company?" Kendrick continued, as if he hadn't heard the slur.

Jason considered briefly, then shook his head. "She's not his lover. She couldn't be."

"She's his ward, dolt."

Jason blinked. "His ward?"

"Aye. She's Lianna of Grasleigh. Didn't you know?"

Grasleigh. *Grasleigh?* Jason felt the blood drain from his face. He remembered well hearing of Grasleigh's death, but he hadn't stopped to consider the daughter who had been left behind after the family's slaughter. And what a daughter—one who possessed almost as much wealth as his sire himself.

"You'll have trouble with the king," Kendrick said unhelpfully. "Doubt he'll want a third son for such as she."

Jason doubted it as well. He leaned back against the wall, wondering why he hadn't been quick enough to have found out who she was before Kendrick did him the honor of informing him.

Kendrick punched his arm. "Cheer up. We'll think of something."

"Thank you," Jason said faintly. "I think."

Kendrick laughed. "Your lack of faith in me wounds me. And when did you fall for her? I thought you were off to pursue your noble cause in France. Though I can understand why you would want her. She is quite remarkable."

"And she doesn't want you."

"You don't know that," Kendrick said with a glint in his eye.

Jason sensed a battle in the offing. At least that might take his mind off the devastating tidings he'd just received.

"She has two eyes," Jason said. "And a nose."

Well, that was enough to do it, Jason found. And as he brawled with his brother in the passageway, he considered how it was he might attain the impossible.

Such as a third son wedding with the richest heiress in England.

# *Seven*

***Lianna sat in a comfortable chair under a tree, enjoying*** the sunshine and poking through the basket of thread Jason had amassed for her over the past three days. At first she'd been too grateful to complain about the colors. Now, she had begun to suspect he'd chosen them with great care.

For they were mostly cheerful colors.

Not the colors of shadows.

Indeed, she suspected that fashioning a shadow or a dragon or anything else gloomy or grim with any of these things would be quite impossible. And that was enough to bring yet another smile to her lips, something that seemed to be happening with alarming regularity.

Especially since she wondered how such happiness could possibly last.

She looked at her companion, who sat on the ground with his back against the tree, plucking the strings of his filched lute and frowning over his fingerings. His blackened eye was healing nicely, and the cut on his lip had scabbed over well enough. She had thought to ask how he'd come by such injuries, but she'd already known the answer—given that she'd listened to him scuffle with his brother in the passageway. And she'd seen Kendrick's face later that day as well.

"You must have an interesting family," she said dryly.

Jason looked up. "Why do you say that?"

"The displays of brotherly affection I've seen between you and Kendrick. Remarkable, truly."

Jason shook his head with a smile. "We love each other well enough, I suppose. What you don't understand is that I've been the youngest all my life, and therefore the one least likely to come out the winner in any conflict."

"Do you all go about bloodying each other's noses regularly?"

"We're wrestling, my lady," he said solemnly. "Harmless encounters. And as I was saying, I always used to come out on the bottom of such friendly skirmishes."

"And then you grew."

"I grew," he agreed. "And my brothers grew fat and lazy. You can imagine why the temptation to best them now at every opportunity is almost overwhelming."

"Kendrick does not seem overplump to me. Has your other brother gone to fat?"

"Gone to seed is more like it," Jason said with a snort. "Nay, Phillip is not fat either, though he's become somewhat less tidy than he used to be. He used to shun wrestling for fear of mussing his clothes." Jason strummed thoughtfully. "I suppose that he's since worn enough of his children's meals to no longer care about the condition of his tunics. Happily for me," he said, looking up at her with twinkling eyes, "such slovenliness and weariness leave him ripe pickings for being vanquished. And Kendrick can be distracted with insults, leaving him vulnerable as well."

"Not that you need to rely on such tactics, of course," she said. "Being so intimidating yourself."

"What with my reputation and all," he agreed.

She nodded but found herself quite abruptly unable to speak further. Thinking on Jason and his brothers and what closeness they shared made her think on things she hadn't in months. A horrible longing for her family rose up and washed over her, a yearning so strong that all she could do was bow her head and bury it in her threads. A tear slid down her cheek and dripped onto her hand.

She heard some part of Jason creak as he drew closer to her. Blinking rapidly revealed that he was kneeling before her. His large, strong hands came to rest over hers.

"Lianna," he said softly, "what ails you? Are you unwell?"

She shook her head.

"The thread doesn't please you."

" 'Tis lovely," she managed.

"Then what?"

She blinked furiously and wanted to shout at him *what ails me is that being near you gives me a sense of home for the first time in almost a year, and you're too much a fool to notice that you're responsible for it!* She dragged her hand across her eyes to clear them, then glared at him—only to find that he was looking at her with an expression of surprise. And that made her want to slap the look straight from his face.

'Twas no wonder his family skirmished so often.

"Don't you have a crusade to attend to?" she asked shortly.

He studied her closely, wriggling his jaw a time or two as if he considered whether or not he should let it loose and speak.

"Well?" she demanded.

And then he laughed at her.

She growled and gave him a mighty shove. But apparently she was not up to the Artane standards of battle, for she found herself pulled right along with him. Her basket of thread went flying, and she found herself sprawled atop him, having left her dignity and her good sense behind her.

"Let me up, you fool," she said.

"Lianna of Grasleigh," he said, shaking his head in wonder, "you surprise me with your foul tongue. I suppose I should have known your true nature would show itself soon enough."

"If you seek to compliment me," she said, trying to pull away, "you're failing miserably!"

"Then what if I ask you to wed with me?"

It was as if someone had dumped a bucket of winter water on her, so startled was she. She looked down into his face so close to hers and could find nothing to say. He sat up, pushing her back to her knees. He got to his knees as well and took both her hands in his.

"Is the thought so horrifying?" he asked softly.

"Saints, nay," she breathed.

The smile he gave her was so brilliant, she could scarce look at him. She found that she was smiling in return, a smile so wide she felt that her face might split in two. And when he reached up and trailed his fingers over her cheek, she only spared a brief thought for the ruin of her face.

"You are beautiful," he said.

"Nay, no longer."

"Scars mark the passage of battle," he said simply. "I don't see them. I see a woman I love, a woman I want to mother my children, a woman I want by my side for the rest of my days. What are a few scars in comparison?"

"You, my lord, have a remarkable vision."

"And you, my lady—"

"Oh, by all the bloody saints, kiss her, won't you? I can scarce stomach any more of this drivel."

Lianna blinked and looked to her right. Who should be

standing there but Kendrick himself, dressed in normal garb. That was odd enough to merit attention.

"Where are your skirts?" she asked.

Jason laughed heartily, and Kendrick took a step closer, his fists at the ready.

"Nay," Lianna said, holding out her hand, "do not ruin his mouth until he's sealed his offer."

"Did you say him aye?" Kendrick asked.

Lianna looked at Jason. "Mine is not the will you must bend to yours."

"Best kiss her anyway, Jason," Kendrick advised. "It may be all you get."

"Thank you for that," Jason grumbled.

Lianna would have added her thoughts as well, but she found herself suddenly quite occupied, and overcome, by the miraculous event of Jason of Artane taking her face in his hands and kissing her.

And kissing her.

And kissing her yet again.

Indeed, though she was excruciatingly aware of Kendrick standing there making noises of impatience, Jason seemed to take no note of anything but her mouth. And her hair, which he was fingering into complete disarray.

And when he let her breathe again, she wondered if she would ever manage a normal breath again.

"By the saints," Kendrick said in disgust, "that was overdoing it, don't you think?"

"You needn't watch longer," Jason said pointedly.

"Ha," Kendrick replied. "Think you I would leave you alone with her now? The poor girl must have a chaperon, and who better than me to fill those shoes? Take your groping hands off the lass, there's a good lad. Come, my lady, and let me see you safely back to the keep. Your love can press his suit with the king whilst your virtue is still intact."

"Her virtue is safe with me!" Jason bellowed.

"Hrumph. I'll judge that for myself. And how is it you

intend to convince the king to give this prize to a bumbling clod such as yourself?"

"You were supposed to be giving it helpful thought," Jason snapped, helping Lianna to her feet. He gathered up her sewing and his lute, then nodded pointedly at her chair. "Carry that," he said to his brother.

Kendrick looked ready to protest but seemed to think better of it. Lianna soon found herself walking back to the castle flanked by two Artane brothers, who were fighting over her head as to how best win her hand. Jason was holding one of her hands, Kendrick the other. She wondered, as she noted the looks the guardsmen were giving them on their way through the barbican gates, if her reputation would be so ruined that it wouldn't matter who was offering to wed her.

Or perhaps when Maud and her ladies found out whose hands she was holding, she would be too dead for that to matter.

She was left in Kendrick's care while Jason went to stow her stitchery with his gear upstairs. Kendrick found her a place at the table, then sat next to her.

"He agrees with you?" he asked seriously.

The look of earnestness on his face was so surprising she smiled.

"Are you so concerned?"

"Of course. You deserve a happy home, Lianna."

"And you don't think he'll give it to me?"

He did smile then, a rueful smile. "Aye, I suppose he will. 'Tis difficult for me to think of my younger brother being able to do the like, but I suppose he's man enough now."

"But you'll forever look on him as a lowly squire fetching you this and that when you came to visit his master, aye?"

"He told you, then."

"The tortures were described in great detail," she agreed. "And I understand. I could never look at my younger brother that I did not see him as a lad of six or seven, hanging on my mother's skirts."

Kendrick nodded, then looked at her solemnly. "This will be difficult. Whether you'll admit it or not, your lands are vast. The king would prefer to make a more advantageous match for you, no doubt."

"Think you he can be convinced?"

"I've been studying his weaknesses for months. We'll strike at those and see if he cannot be persuaded—"

"By the saints, what filth have we here?"

Lianna blinked in surprise at the harsh voice that cut through their peaceful conversation like a dull knife ripping through linen. She looked at the man who was standing before their table, staring at Kendrick with nothing less than pure hatred.

"Sedgwick," Kendrick said flatly.

"I would call you *Artane,* but that is your brother's right, isn't it?" the other man said. "Have you any title? Ah, how foolish of me to have forgotten. The second son, the one with nothing to call his own but his father's charity."

Kendrick snorted. "William Artane—your memory fails you. My *father,* not my brother, is your father's liege-lord. He will be *your* liege-lord when drink and whoring send your sire to his early death. And then you will be master of Sedgwick, and all the luxury that entails, won't you?"

"At least I'll have a keep," William snarled.

"By my father's charity as well, so that makes you no better than I, does it?" Kendrick returned. "Cousin."

William turned his furious gaze on Lianna. "And who is this? Your latest whore?"

Kendrick rose.

"You're losing your skill, cousin," William said with an unpleasant laugh. "Is this all you could woo to your bed? This pock-marked, uninteresting by-blow of a kitchen lad?"

Lianna watched, open-mouthed, as Kendrick vaulted

over the table and planted his fist in William of Sedgwick's mouth. She watched them push, shove, and hurl insults for several moments before they both drew swords and began hacking at each other.

"By the saints," Jason said, skidding to a halt at her side, "what madness is this?"

"Sedgwick," she said. "He insulted Kendrick."

"What else did he say?" Jason demanded. "Kendrick wouldn't be using his blade for a mere insult to himself." He looked down at her. "Did he say aught to you?"

She winced. "Naught that I haven't heard before."

"Damn," he breathed. "I should have been here."

The herald suddenly bellowed the king's arrival.

"Could matters worsen?" Jason said tightly.

Lianna watched the events before her unfold with a dizzying sense of unreality. Jason sat next to her, clutching her hand under the table, as the king made his way to his place, sat, and demanded a recounting of the dispute.

She listened with growing distress as Kendrick bargained for a chance to see to William on the field. She was certain the king wouldn't allow it. But apparently His Majesty was either overtired or he thought it would make a public example to let the two fight it out, for he agreed.

And then the worst came.

"And to the winner?" the king asked, picking at his tabard. "What prize shall there be?"

"Besides life?" Kendrick asked.

The king looked at him dispassionately. "You fought over a woman. You must value more than just life for that."

"The woman, then," William said. "I'm in need of a wife."

Kendrick opened his mouth to speak, but the king was swifter and his edict was law.

"Lianna of Grasleigh to the one of you who can show

us you're canny enough to win your own life. Then perhaps you'll be worthy of her wealth."

Lianna wished with all her heart that she had a constitution that was prone to fainting, for she would have done it at that moment gladly and not found herself hale and sound and perfectly capable of understanding what had just transpired.

Two men were fighting each other for their lives.

And for her.

While the man she wanted sat next to her, cursing fluently and clutching her hand with enough strength to bruise it.

# Eight

*Jason stood on the edge of the field next to the woman of* his heart and cursed his brother's damned chivalry. And he cursed his own. Had he not been fool enough to trouble himself seeing to Lianna's bloody gear, he would have been in the great hall, ready and willing to avenge his lady for the insults paid to her by that great buffoon, his cousin, William of Sedgwick. Instead, where did he find himself?

Standing on the side of the field, wringing his hands like a woman.

Lianna fared no better, though she seemed to be able to keep herself from wringing her hands. They were clasped together before her so tightly that her knuckles were white. They matched perfectly the pallor of her face.

Jason moved and his mail squeaked. He really should find himself some kind of squire to see to that. Pity he never could find a lord willing to sacrifice his son to Jason's care. Perhaps in time Jason would find himself lord of an obscure keep and some poor lad would come to him then.

Though none of that would matter if he couldn't manage to discover a way to keep Lianna from either Kendrick or William's greedy hands—and he wasn't sure at the moment who would have been worse!

He fingered the hilt of his sword and gave himself over to furious thought. If William prevailed, he could demand a challenge to avenge his then-dead brother, and surely he would emerge the victor. He could worry about his grief over losing Kendrick later. He would have Lianna and repay Sedgwick for Kendrick's death with the same stroke.

Now, if Kendrick won, things would become stickier. How was it one went about challenging one's own brother for the right to a woman? And to the death? His father would surely find that less than pleasing. Then again, he supposed it had been done in the past. Mayhap it could be done in the future.

He heard the clash of metal on metal and realized that Kendrick and William were already at it. Swords, apparently, which gave Kendrick the advantage. Actually, it wouldn't have mattered what the weapon or the battlefield. Jason knew his brother's skill—and he knew what bumbling idiots Sedgwick produced. William would lose, and as his lifeblood drained from him, he would rage about the injustice of having grown up in a keep full of rats, with poor food, and lack of handsome women to bed. That his father was a fool, as his father had been before him, would never enter into the argument. The fault would have lain at Artane that no one there had sent help. Never mind that help would have been summarily rejected.

Jason watched Kendrick fight and found it less exciting than nauseating. His brother was skilled, so skilled that the sight of it should have been enough to give Jason pause. Kendrick had the advantage of five years more training, five years more warring, five years more life on the earth.

But he didn't have the advantage of a desperate desire to wed with Lianna of Grasleigh.

He looked at the field to find Kendrick had gone down on one knee.

But his brother rolled, came up, and cast himself back into the fray without a grunt or a curse. Jason had to admit that it was fascinating to watch the oaf fight, for he did it with the beauty of a dance.

A deadly dance, to be sure.

Time wore on. Jason wished desperately for a very long stick to shove down his back and relieve him of the itch that seemed to have lodged a hand's span below his ribs. The sun beat down on him, leaving him feeling rather like a meat pie, roasting in his mail.

And still the battle continued.

Jason yawned widely, wishing Kendrick would get on with the business at hand. It might have provided Kendrick with amusing entertainment for the morning, but Jason had things to see to.

William, in the end, went down. Kendrick stood over him with his sword at the other man's throat.

"Yield," Kendrick commanded.

"Never," William spat.

"Then die—"

"Nay! I yield, I yield!"

"Coward," muttered Jason. "Like his father before him."

Kendrick pulled his sword away, turned, and went to kneel before the king. Jason closed his eyes and prayed.

*Give me a miracle. Just one. I'll never cast another spell.*

"Kendrick!"

Jason scarce managed to stop Lianna before she bolted onto the field to save his fool brother, who was near to having himself slain by William of Sedgwick, who had come upon him suddenly from behind. Kendrick rolled, and William's stroke merely grazed him instead of impaling him.

The battle began again, but it was short-lived. With a negligent flick of his wrist, Kendrick sent William's sword flying from his hand. William found himself immediately surrounded and overcome by the king's men who swarmed onto the field.

Jason spared little time wondering what would happen to his cousin. He could have passed the rest of eternity rotting in hell and Jason wouldn't have cared. What concerned him was how he was going to keep his brother from taking Lianna to wife. Could a challenge possibly go wrong?

Kendrick had scarce opened his mouth to flatter Henry before Jason had stepped out into the field, quickly before Lianna could stop him, and strode across to kneel before the king.

"Your Majesty," Jason said, bowing his head, "I challenge Kendrick of Artane for his right to the lady of Grasleigh."

Where there had been low murmuring before, there was a deafening silence now.

Or perhaps that deafness came from the blood thundering in his ears.

Or the waves of Henry's displeasure that washed over him in a thunderous rush.

Jason couldn't tell and didn't dare lift his head to look.

"You, Lord Jason, are not who we would choose for our ward," the king announced in less-than-dulcet tones.

Jason kept his head down. "Artane blood runs through my veins as well, Majesty. I can be an asset and an ally to the crown in the north."

For which his father would blister his ears and likely his arse as well if he could manage it, but there were times a man said what he had to in order to have what he desired. He would be the king's man until it was in his best interest not to be. And with the growing discontent surrounding Henry's extravagant ways, that day could come sooner than Henry might wish.

But for now, he would give as much fealty as his honor would allow and fight his brother for the prize.

Assuming Henry would give him the chance.

It seemed to take the king an inordinate amount of time to come to a decision. Or perhaps he was trying to decide how best to kill Jason so no dark forces were loosed. Jason wasn't sure what the king was thinking, and he didn't dare look up to examine the king's expression.

A sudden and quite ferocious trumpet blast fair gave him a permanently crooked neck from jerking his head up so quickly. Apparently, leave had been granted for him to try to kill his brother.

"To the death, my liege?" Kendrick asked smoothly.

"It seems a pity," the king said thoughtfully, "to lose one of such a fine family."

Jason began to give thanks.

"But all in the name of chivalry, we suppose. Do what you must, my lords."

"Perfect," Jason muttered under his breath as he rose to his feet and looked at his brother.

"I'm bleeding," Kendrick said with what for him was a pout. "Be gentle."

"I'll cut off your head as tenderly as I know how," Jason replied.

"I daresay 'twould grieve our king to lose us both. I'll see that he loses the lesser of us, so his grief is not so heavy."

"I'll play your favorite ballad at your wake," Jason shot back. "And practice much beforehand, that your blighted spirit might not need flinch as you listen."

Kendrick lifted his sword. "A final chance to cry peace and save your wretched life."

"And watch you wed my beloved? I'd rather die."

"Death it is," Kendrick agreed with a regretful sigh.

"Yours."

"Nay, yours I'm afraid."

"You could only hope."

"Shall I use the right or the left?" Kendrick asked, studying his hands. "I believe I used to fight you using the left and yet I was still able to best you thoroughly."

"You'll find, my lord, that my skills are much improved. I'd use the right, were I you."

Kendrick smiled, an unpleasant baring of teeth. "No casting of spells, Jas. That wouldn't be sporting."

"I'll brew you a numbing draught to ease the pain as you expire," Jason promised. "Now, be about this business. I've a wedding to see to."

"But no raising of a ghostly ruckus when I take Lianna to wife," Kendrick warned, waving his sword at Jason. "I'll have your word on that now, before I send you to the afterlife."

"You'll be the one doing the haunting," Jason said, flexing the fingers of his free hand and wondering if knifing his brother suddenly would be considered poor manners. At least that way he wouldn't have to listen to any more of Kendrick's incessant chatter.

But then he remembered that such was one of Kendrick's ploys to throw him off guard. And he remembered it the heartbeat before his head almost came away from his neck. He looked at his brother in shock.

"You intend to kill me."

"The king commands it."

"He didn't!"

Kendrick shrugged and continued a very relentless and brutal assault. Jason cast a final look at Lianna before throwing up his sword to avoid another lethal swipe. Kendrick's blade screeched as it traveled the length of Jason's and was stopped by the hilt.

"Fight me or die," Kendrick growled.

"Whoreson," Jason spat.

He wished, absently, that he hadn't said that.

And he wondered, quite seriously, if that might be one of the last things he would regret saying.

# Nine

***Lianna of Grasleigh, now Lianna de Piaget, still of Gras-***leigh, rode next to her newly made husband and wondered just how his parents would take to her, given what it had cost to win her. She fretted, she worried, she twisted her reins in her hands and thought she might be ill. It wasn't just a matter of them acquiring a new daughter-in-law. There was the matter of the life-and-death battle she'd been the prize for not a se'nnight earlier. And the tremendously serious outcome of that battle.

That being the humiliation of one de Piaget brother by another before the king's court, of course.

"Are you well, wife?" came the question from the man beside her.

"Well enough, husband."

"You look nervous."

She looked at her husband of a se'nnight and smiled—nervously. "Will they blame me, do you think?"

"Blame you for what? My victory?"

"Nay, your brother's defeat."

"Does he look defeated?"

She looked to her left to find the aforementioned defeated one, Kendrick of Artane, smiling pleasantly at her. "Don't be fooled," he whispered conspiratorially. "I allowed Jason to win."

"Ha," Jason said scornfully. "Your memory fails you."

"I could not rob you of your love, Lianna," Kendrick continued. "I considered it my chivalric duty to let him win."

Jason snorted. "You've no reason to fear for his ego, my lady. He'll repeat the story for years and end it with you warning him of William's attempted treachery. Somehow he will come away smelling sweetly, and there will be no mention of him kneeling at my feet, weeping for mercy."

"I did not weep."

"Tears were coursing down your face."

"I was sweating."

"You were weeping. And begging. I could not in good conscience slay you."

Kendrick leaned closer to Lianna. "He feared his mother would take a switch to his behind for the deed. I daresay it isn't too late to annul your marriage to him. I am, as you might have noticed, still quite available."

Something whizzed past her nose and connected quite perfectly with Kendrick's. Perhaps there hadn't been much blood on the battlefield before the king, but there was certainly ample draining onto Kendrick's tunic now.

"Damn you," Kendrick snarled, trying to staunch the flow with his sleeve, "can you not fight like a man? Throwing fruit! Who ever heard of such a womanly tactic!"

Lianna found it rather practical at the moment, so she had no argument with it. Kendrick, however, gave his brother a look full of promise and spurred his horse on ahead.

"He's plotting your death," Lianna said wisely, having grown accustomed to the habits of her husband and his brother over the past pair of weeks.

"Aye, likely," Jason said serenely. He looked at her. "Are you happy, my lady?"

"Of course, my lord."

He looked at her for several moments in silence, then his smile faded to be replaced by a look of seriousness.

"Are you?" he asked quietly. "Happy with such a one as I? Henry could have wed you to a man with power and status. I am, as it happens, but the third son."

She shrugged. "What is power but wealth? I daresay you now have enough of that to satisfy any lust you might have for power."

"Aye," he said with a shiver. "Your father had enough of both, and to spare."

"And you wouldn't have known it to look at him. He was much more content discussing pigs than he was bits and baubles for his court clothes. I daresay you'll follow in his footsteps easily enough."

He looked startled enough that she wondered if she'd said aught amiss.

"Jason?"

He shook his head. "Idle thoughts."

"Tell me of them."

"Well, if you must know, the day I arrived at court, I was lamenting the foolishness of courtly conversation that focused on the cut of a tunic or the color of cloth. How much more, I thought, would I have rather been talking to the swineherd about the feeding of his charges, or discussing with the steward whether or not barley and hops might grow well in the north fields, or loitering in the blacksmith's hut to see him at his labors."

"My father would have been pleased with you," she said.

"I could only hope." He reached over for her hand and squeezed it. "If I'm ignorant of something, I'm not too proud to ask for aid. I'll try not to shame you or your sire's memory."

She nodded, but in truth she was thinking less about how he might shame her than she was about how blessed she had been to have found someone with whom she had found a home. For that alone, her father would have loved Jason of Artane. Or Jason of Grasleigh, as it was. The Falcon of Grasleigh, as he would be known. She wondered what he would think when they arrived at her father's keep and she showed him her father's coat of arms.

A falcon with a dragon pinned under its foreclaw. A falcon with its head thrown back in victory.

She could only hope he saw the humor in it she did.

They rode on in companionable silence for the rest of the day. As dusk fell, Lianna was startled to see several men bearing down on them. Jason and Kendrick immediately drew their swords, then Jason called a greeting and was answered in the same tone. Lianna looked at him in surprise.

"Who are they?"

"Our escort," he said. "I'm not surprised to see them, but I am surprised to see them so soon." He leaned on the pommel of his saddle and smiled at her. "What think you of a few days passed in the dragon's lair, my lady?"

Lianna smiled weakly. "These are Blackmour's men?"

"Aye, come to protect his little kit," he said, "and the kit's bride."

"Us?" she asked, feeling rather faint.

"Who else?" He looked at her closely. "Surely you don't fear Blackmour. He is the tamest of men, I assure you. He will merely want to inspect you, see that you have all your teeth, and check that your ears are formed well enough to suit him."

"And should I not suit him?"

"Seven maidens a day before breaking his fast," Jason said with a sigh, "or the occasional consumption of one newly wedded lady. I suppose, then, that if you don't please him, he'll have you for his morning nibble."

She considered her husband. "Your time will come, you know. I daresay you'll be twisting your reins into unrecognizable shapes as we near my home."

"I daresay," he agreed dryly.

"And I will do nothing to ease your suffering."

"Ah-ha," Kendrick called back at them, "you have made your bed, little brother, and see how she smoothes the sheets already. I fear you've met your match in this one."

"And gladly so," Jason said. He smiled at her. "My lord also has a fine chamber for guests with his second most comfortable goose-feather mattress—"

"Not that you've ever slept on it," Kendrick said loudly.

"He," Jason said with a glare at his brother, "will not be accompanying us to your hall, Lianna."

"You'll need someone to guard your back," Kendrick said, "from your lady, should you not show yourself well. 'Tis best I come and see to that. Now, can we be on our way? I've a mind to reach some kind of inn before the sun sets completely."

Lianna looked at Jason. "How much farther?"

"To Blackmour? At least four or five days. These lads have ridden hard to catch us. But I promise you a goodly rest there on that second most comfortable goose-feather mattress I spoke of. And I *have* passed a night or two on it—by myself," he threw at his brother. He smiled at Lianna. "You'll feel comfortable there. You'll see."

***It was indeed another five days of travel, but the road was*** pleasant and the weather fine. Lianna watched Blackmour's men with Jason and saw the respect they accorded him, even though he was much younger than they. She found that by the time they had reached the keep, she had even stopped taking Jason and Kendrick's barbs seriously. There had only been a minor skirmish or two, but Kendrick had very solicitously avoided damaging anything she might find useful.

For herself, she found that being wed to the Dragon's kit was more of a joy to her with each day that passed. He was kind and gentle, and he looked at her with love in his eyes.

What she did find curious, however, was that none of Blackmour's men made any mention of Jason's dark reputation. She had only jested of it once, and by the complete lack of expression on all the faces surrounding her, save Jason who had smiled, she decided that 'twas a subject better left undiscussed.

Except, of course, for the brief moment of privacy she'd had with her husband the morning before they'd arrived at Blackmour when he'd led her off into a small copse of trees for a private kiss or two. When she'd managed to gasp in a breath, she looked at him seriously.

"Have you cast spells?" she asked bluntly.

He blinked, then half of his mouth quirked up in something of an embarrassed smile. "One or two."

"Did they work?"

"We'll have to look at Maud in a year or two and see what's left of her."

She shuddered to think what sorts of torments he had left in place for the women who had dared harm her. Perhaps 'twas best not to know.

"Have you brewed potions?" she asked, determined not to be distracted.

"Aye."

"Studied dark arts?"

He paused. "In a manner of speaking."

"In a manner of speaking?"

He considered for a moment or two. "I have walked blindly into the darkness," he said finally, "and studied art there with my master."

"Have you indeed."

"Aye. Swordplay and such. When you meet him, you'll understand."

"Hrumph," she said, unconvinced. "I vow the only magics you've worked on me are best left for the privacy of our own tent."

"Then you don't think I brewed a potion to make you love me?" he asked, reaching up to tuck a bit of her hair behind her ear. "Or to make you wed with me?"

She pulled him to her and kissed him thoroughly. "Mayhap you brewed aught for me, but my heart was given the moment I saw you, and where my heart was given, my hand was destined to go. Or didn't you know that my father cast his own kind of spell and bound that upon me from an early age?"

"I'll thank him when next we meet, after you and I have spent a very long lifetime together."

"Aye, my beloved nightshade."

He laughed and pulled her close. "Is that how you think of me? What will your people say to that?"

"They'll think me enormously brave to partake of you," she said. "And isn't that your damned brother bellowing for us to return?"

He looked down at her and smiled fondly. "I love you, Lianna."

"And I you, my lord. Now, let us return before I propose a wrestle to silence him myself."

That had been the morning before and she'd found herself too nervous to do aught but give Kendrick a companionable flick on the ear in passing. Now, as she crossed over the enormously small and completely inadequate bridge that separated Blackmour's aerie from the rest of England, she wished she had brawled with her brother-in-law truly. The victory might have occupied her mind enough to cause her to forget her nervousness.

She dismounted in the courtyard. Well, she actually slid from her horse in something of a faint and found herself caught quite deftly by her husband, who set her on her feet as calmly as if he was accustomed to tending swooning wives daily.

They entered the hall, and Lianna soon found herself surrounded by a press of people, adults and children, who couldn't seem to get close enough to Jason. Children tugged at him, cast themselves into his arms, and wept at the sight of him. A handful of lordly men clapped him on the shoulder, and a pair of women greeted him with kisses and affectionate ruffles of his hair.

And then the throng parted.

The Dragon himself—and it could be no other—stood there, waiting with his arms crossed over his chest and a fierce look on his face.

Jason took Lianna's hand and pulled her with him. She didn't want to resist. Not truly. Somehow, though, her heels just seemed to dig into the rushes of their own accord. It was to no avail, of course, for she soon found herself standing far too close to Christopher of Blackmour for her comfort.

"My lord," Jason said, inclining his head.

"So," the Dragon said gruffly, "you found yourself a bride."

"I did, my lord."

"Bested that womanly brother of yours for her, I hear."

"That, too, my lord," Jason said, loudly enough to cover a mighty snort from said womanly brother.

"Let me see her," the Dragon said, "and tell her to stop quivering. I never devour brides until they've slept at least one peaceful night under my roof."

"Oh, Christopher," said one of the women with a sigh.

Lianna looked from the woman, who was shaking her head, then back to the Dragon himself, who seemed to be having trouble maintaining his frown. Perhaps he was tempted to let it disintegrate into something more fierce.

Jason was of no help to her. He stepped aside and placed her hand in the Dragon's talon without so much as a flinch. Lianna swallowed over the hideously dry place in her throat and did her best to stand tall.

"Blonde?" Christopher of Blackmour asked.

Lianna blinked. "I beg your pardon?"

"Dark-haired, my lord," Jason said dryly.

Blackmour grunted. "Her nose is crooked."

Lianna felt her nose with her free hand. It was, as it happened, her best remaining feature. "It most certainly is not," she said, frowning at her host.

"But surely those teeth are rotting."

"My second best feature," Lianna said stiffly, then she realized something that had escaped her attention whilst she was defending what beauty remained her.

Christopher of Blackmour was looking at her.

But he was not seeing her.

She felt her mouth slide open. She gaped at her husband's former master for several moments in silence whilst a pair of things that had never made sense to her suddenly became very clear.

Blackmour rarely left his keep, but the rumor had been because he was too busy practicing his dark arts to do so.

Jason had said his master had taught him to see with his heart, to look beyond what the eye normally was consumed by.

And why not, when his master was blind?

Lianna felt tears well up in her eyes and course down her cheeks before she could stop them.

Christopher of Blackmour sighed. "Now I've made her weep. Gillian, have you a cloth about you for this poor girl? Jason, see what my sweet lady wife has to give you for the tending of your bride. By the saints, this gruff business works so much better when your sire does it."

The woman who Lianna supposed was the lady Gillian snorted in a most unladylike manner. "You've grumbles enough of your own, my lord, and they work well enough. 'Tis but this lady's sweet heart that causes her tears, for I daresay she sees more quickly than most."

She smiled at Lianna, and Lianna found she had an entirely new well of tears to draw upon. What kind of woman was it, she wondered absently, who married a dragon and flourished under his wing?

She suspected 'twas the kind of woman she could only hope to one day become. She accepted Gillian's ministrations, then found herself swept up into a family circle that was so much like her own that it took her breath away.

But it didn't break her heart.

For such a family was now hers.

*It was a good deal later that she snuggled with her husband* on Blackmour's second finest goose-feather mattress. Having verified its luxury for herself, she could only agree with Jason's assessment of it. She sighed happily.

"This is lovely."

"Aye," he said, stroking her hair with his hand, "it is. I daresay I could not be happier than at this moment."

She lifted her head to look at him. The candlelight flickered softly over his face.

"I never would have guessed his secret," she said.

"He hides it well."

"And you keep it well."

Jason smiled gravely. "He made me the man I am. My gratitude knows no bounds. There is little I would not do for him."

"Or he for you." She made herself comfortable with her head on his shoulder. "I understand he has a present for you. A wedding gift."

"Surely not. What do I need? My own private steward, perhaps," he added with a snort, "to explain to me what I must know to run your father's lands."

"Nay, you'll have me. I served my father often thusly. Your gift is much more precious."

"What is it? And how is it you know of it and not I?"

"You were engaged in spirited discussion of your

brother's faults with your brother and his fists when Lord Christopher told me of it. And to answer your first question, he is sending you something to page."

Jason went very still. "A page?"

"Aye," she said, suspecting very clearly what it would mean to him. "His son, I believe. Surely you know him. Robin of Blackmour?"

Jason was silent for so long, she had to look at him. She leaned up on one elbow and brushed away the tears that had trailed down his temple to wet his hair.

" 'Tis a very great trust," she said quietly.

"From him," Jason said hoarsely, "and your sire as well. I am thoroughly humbled."

She smiled at him, then kissed him briefly. "I'll brew you a potion to bolster your courage."

He grunted at her. "The saints preserve me."

"I met your Berengaria, you know. And her helpers. Nemain and Magda were fighting over who could better teach me what I should know."

"The saints preserve us all," he said fervently.

She laughed and snuggled back down into his arms. "I understand now about your dark arts."

"Do you?"

"Aye. Gillian told me how you and Christopher had trained together, quite often in the dark. With swords, of course."

"Of course."

She paused. "And that is all, isn't it?" she asked suspiciously.

"Of course," he said lightly—and not at all convincingly.

"Jason de Piaget, if you haven't told me—"

But then she found herself pinned by her grinning husband and she was almost distracted enough to forget her suspicions.

Almost.

"I'll count Maud's warts," she warned him.

"You do that," he said with a laugh.

"I'll discover your secrets," she vowed. "All of them."

"May it take a lifetime," he said, bending his head to kiss her. "A very long lifetime with very long days of your constant and thorough scrutiny. Discover away, my love. I could not wish for more."

*It was very much later that Lianna had the chance to lie* next to her sleeping husband and give thought to the course her life had taken. Who would have known that from such shadows of death, bereavement, and danger at court, she would have come to such a place of light and beauty? She suspected she would be forever inadequate to the task of expressing a proper amount of gratitude for the blessings of family which were now hers. Perhaps a tapestry could be made, one of sunlight and sweet things that grew and flourished. Of course, there would be shadows here and there, for what life was without them?

Especially when one's husband was of the ilk to mutter the odd charm now and again under his breath. And the saints only knew what kinds of things he would put into the cooking pot when not watched closely.

But those were the kind of shadows she could live with, especially when she had Jason of Artane in trade.

She closed her eyes, smiling deeply.

She would begin her stitchery on the morrow.

As soon as it was light.

# An Interrupted Tapestry

Madeline Hunter

# One

***Giselle had ample time to practice swallowing her pride.***
She spent most of the afternoon doing so, while she paced Andreas von Bremen's luxurious hall. She came to know his carved furniture very well and memorized every image in the four tapestries adorning his walls.

Occasionally, she paused to gaze through the unshuttered windows at the yard surrounded by stables and storage buildings. Wagons kept arriving from the docks, carrying the products that secured Andreas's wealth. As a member of the Hanseatic League, the network of Germanic traders whose famous cogs plied the northern seas, Andreas von Bremen was no ordinary merchant.

Which was why she had come.

She strove to quell not only her pride but her growing resentment. In a way, it was Andreas's fault that she was here at all. For that reason alone, he might be more gracious and not keep her waiting so long. They had an old friendship, too. That should count for something, even if they had not spoken in four years.

Irritation spiked again, colored by disappointment and hurt. She itched to stride right out of this house.

She didn't. A deeper emotion kept her waiting.

Fear.

She had to see this through. Andreas was her only hope. If he refused her, she had nowhere else to turn, and her brother would be lost to her.

Boot steps on the stairs and voices speaking lowly penetrated the noise rolling in from the yard.

She swung around. Two men's bodies lowered into view as they descended from the upper level of the house.

The short one of middle years, the one wearing a richly tucked and embroidered robe and a hat festooned with drapery, did not interest her. The other one, the young one of commanding height and lean strength, with thick dark hair and beautiful blue eyes, riveted her attention.

Other than distant glimpses in the city, she had not seen him in a long time. She had forgotten how easy it was to smile whenever he arrived. Even now, despite her worries and pique, the old joy sparkled through her.

As he escorted his guest through the hall, Andreas became aware of her. He glanced over and the light of recognition flared.

Snatches of the men's low conversation reached her ears. They did not speak in English, or French, or even Andreas's language.

She suddenly realized who the other man was. The Venetian galleys had arrived in London a few days ago, and he must be one of the powerful traders from that city.

The Venetian took his leave. Andreas stood at the threshold, watching until the horse trotted through the gate.

He turned his attention to her.

"Giselle."

He did not say anything else, but just looked at her

with those blue eyes. The lights of his youth still sparked in them, but other, deeper ones did, too. At twenty Andreas had possessed good humor despite his natural reserve. Now, ten years later, his silence had grown more complex.

And dangerous. It made no sense, but she could not escape the sensation. As the pause stretched, she grew increasingly unsettled.

"My apologies, Giselle. My man said that a woman was here. He did not explain that it was you."

"You are very busy when you visit London. You could hardly ask your guest to wait while you spoke to me."

"That would have been difficult to explain, I will admit."

He smiled with wry amusement as he said it. Giselle realized that she had arrived during some very special trading.

It was rumored that Andreas had come to London to negotiate a new marriage. Not with an English family, it appeared. He was looking for a more ambitious match than that and had timed his visit to coincide with the galleys from Venice.

Years ago he had confided to her a mad dream of linking his family's network to that of a Venetian's. It appeared he was about to make the dream a reality.

Small wonder he had kept her waiting.

He moved two chairs to the windows on the side of the hall that faced the garden. He came back to her. "Please sit. I am happy to see you. It has been too long."

She hesitated. Something in his manner made her want to make a quick retreat. This was the Andreas she had known so well, but also an Andreas she had never met.

His hand almost touched her back as the other gestured to the chairs. With a phantom embrace, he guided her to the window.

A prickle of excitement and caution scurried up her spine.

They sat facing each other, their knees separated by an arm's span. Soft northern light gently illuminated the face that she knew well. Many times she had admired at close range the square jaw and straight, feathering eyebrows. None of the details had changed, but the countenance had. Youthful softness used to mute its chiselled severity but no longer did. Mature precision revealed the intelligent, shrewd mind of the man who owned it.

Despite the change, for an instant it was like old times. They might have been sitting together in her own home, by her windows, during one of his visits to the city. When he was younger and his trading brought him to London, he did not live in this grand house, but in hers, as a guest and friend of her brother, Reginald.

The joy sparkled again, reminding her of how much she had enjoyed his company back then.

It had been thus from the first time Reginald brought him home and announced that he would use the tiny, spare chamber that jutted out over the street. She had looked at Andreas's astonishingly handsome face that day and immediately seen warmth in his eyes despite his cool manner. They had formed a quick bond during that first visit. Over the years the connection had grown deep and steady and full of unspoken understanding.

And then, abruptly, four years ago, Andreas had severed the link to Reginald, the house, and her.

Remembering that insult made the joy disappear.

"You are looking well, Giselle. You are as beautiful as ever."

The Andreas she had known had never flattered her. It appeared that with his success and wealth he had assumed courtly airs.

It did not help that at twenty-eight she was no longer as beautiful as ever. The first bloom of youth had passed, and she knew it.

"It is kind of you to say so. You also appear well, and happy in your success. I always knew that you would rise high in the Hanse." She could not keep her gaze from drifting over the deep green garment he wore. Its cut and fabric spoke of his ascending status, just as her worn, mended blue gown revealed how debased her own had become.

Her gaze moved back up and met his. Her breath caught as the years fell away. She might have been seeing him at her threshold, so familiar was what passed between them. The instant bond, the promise of a quiet intimacy—it flashed through her with an intense, vital reality, just as it had when they had been friends.

No, it was not quite the same. Those reunions had never made her uncomfortable, and this one did. Something new simmered in the familiarity. As if a gauzy veil had been lifted, certain aspects of her reaction sharpened and demanded her attention. A sly, alluring disturbance wound its way around her other emotions.

She had intended to beg for his help, but his manner provoked her, and she decided to change her approach. There was no point in pleading in the name of a dead friendship. She would speak in a language he would understand and respect.

"I have not only come to visit, Andreas."

"No, I expect that you have not."

He sounded resigned. She thought that took some gall. After all, *she* had not dropped *his* friendship.

"I am in need of money. I will repay it," she said.

His gaze shifted to the garden out the window. The old Andreas completely disappeared. Suddenly she was speaking with a stranger who had heard petitions like hers before. Too often.

The humiliation of what she was doing overwhelmed her. She gritted her teeth and forged on.

"I need one hundred pounds."

He kept looking at the garden. "Your brother sent you, didn't he? It was cowardly of him not to come himself and to use you in this way."

"He did not send me. This was my decision."

"The hell it was." His gaze snapped back to her. "Since this is about trade, I must respond as a trader. I regret to say that I must refuse you. There is no way that this loan will be repaid, and I would be a fool to make it."

His abrupt denial astonished her. Her heart wanted to sink down to her toes.

"It will be repaid. If you doubt my word—"

"One hundred pounds is a great sum. You have not seen that much in the last five years combined. You may promise to repay it with an honest heart, but your brother never will."

"It is my promise, not my brother's. I will pledge property as surety. Our house is not worth that much, but there is also a small farm in Sussex, and together they should secure this debt."

A bit of curiosity passed in the gaze piercing her. "Are you saying that the farm and the house are chartered to you?"

"No, but—"

"Then they are not yours to pledge and of no value to this discussion."

She could not believe his cold indifference. Panic began beating in her heart. She was going to fail. She would not be able to save Reginald.

Andreas appeared angry with her. That made her own ire spike. He had probably agreed to such things often before and with people he knew less well. And if not for him, she would not be in this situation.

"Since you are convinced that my word will not do and that my brother will not honor my pledge of the property, let us make this an outright sale. I see that your love of tapestries has not abated." She gestured to the rich hangings adorning the hall's walls. "I still have mine. You often admired it and told me yourself that it was worth at least a hundred pounds. I will sell it to you now."

It sickened her to say it. That tapestry, woven of silk

and brought back from a crusade by an ancestor, was the only thing of value that she owned.

It would break her heart to give it up. Losing it would finally obliterate her small hold on a life she had once led. She would never let go of it to save herself, but now, faced with the need to save her brother, she had no choice.

She thought that she saw Andreas's expression soften. She was sure that he would agree. Instead, he turned his attention once more to the garden.

"I cannot buy it, Giselle."

"My attachment to it is long over, if that is your concern."

"A man does not buy what he already owns. Reginald pledged that tapestry as surety against a loan years ago. The loan was not repaid."

Shock numbed her for a ten count. Then fury crashed into her stunned mind—fury at Reginald and fury at this man sitting here in his damnable self-possession.

How dare her brother pledge her property. Bad enough that Reginald had depleted their meager wealth with ventures always ruined by unforseen misfortune. Bad enough that he had left tallies all over London to pay for garments he could not afford and wine long ago drunk. To have procured coin by using the tapestry was an inexcusable betrayal of their heritage.

Andreas knew what that weaving meant. He should have never agreed to such a thing. He only had because he coveted the tapestry.

She rose, barely controlling the anger trembling through her. "I can see that I have wasted my time and yours. I have nothing else to sell except my virtue, and I am sure that a great man like you will not consider that worth one hundred pounds." She almost spit the words and did not care that her tone sounded bitter and sarcastic and imperious.

His gaze, full of sharp alertness, swung to her. The old warmth and connection entered it, along with that other, frightening intensity that had so unsettled her today.

She had intended to make a grand retreat, but suddenly she could not move.

"Actually, Giselle, the pledge of your virtue is the only one that I might consider."

"You insult me, Andreas."

"You raised the possibility, my lady. Not I."

She dragged the remnants of her dignity around her like a shredded cloak. "I apologize for intruding on your household. It was a mistake. I knew that my brother and I were no longer of use to you, but I had not realized just how proud and arrogant you had become. I see now that you despise us. Good day to you."

Somehow she tore herself away from his blue eyes and his irritating, compelling presence and retreated with all of the nobility that she could muster.

*Andreas threw open the window shutters beside his bed.* His chamber was at the top of the tall house, under the steep pitch of the roof. It was neither the largest nor the most comfortable chamber, but it was the one he had chosen for himself. From this window he could look down on the rooftops of London and peer into gardens and streets.

He peered now and saw the small blue dot moving on the lane alongside the house next to his. Giselle's stride spoke of her indignation even at this distance. He watched as she turned onto a lane parallel to his, and he waited each time she disappeared behind a house for her to show again.

It had been a surprise to see her in the hall. A wonderful surprise. It had been all he could do not to drag Signore Alberti out to his horse and send him off at once.

He smiled ruefully at his reaction. So much for time dulling a youthful fascination.

Giselle's tiny figure finally became obscured. Andreas

pictured her entering the house that her brother could no longer afford to maintain, and moving around the furnishings that were remnants of a life much grander than they now lived. On the wall across from the hearth the silk tapestry would be hanging, a banner of Giselle's belief that their lost nobility would one day be restored.

Every year that passed made that less likely. Andreas knew their current situation very well. He might have ceased visiting that house, but he had never lost sight of Giselle.

He fixed his gaze on a spot of distant garden visible between the edges of two buildings. He waited for the blue dot to appear there. The wind was right, and if she played her lute he would hear it today.

"Did Signore Alberti still appear amenable?"

Andreas glanced back to his youngest brother, who also served as his clerk and assistant. Stefan was meticulously unpacking parchments from a wooden chest. "Yes, he did, Stefan."

"It will be a great alliance, and I hear that his daughter is most lovely."

"So it is said."

"It is an ambitious plan for you to attempt to join the power of the Hanse with that of Venice."

It *was* ambitious, but if it worked his family and the Alberti would form a trading network more vast than any ever known. The entire world, from Eire to the Far East, would know their names.

He had first gotten a glimmer of the possibilities of this union when he was no more than a youth. With the death of his father, who did not trust Venetians, he had begun considering it more seriously. When his wife passed away three years ago, the means to achieve it had been placed in his hands. Signore Alberti was also an ambitious man, but would only form the alliance if the head of Andreas's family bound himself, literally, to the Alberti and Venice.

"Some say it is too bold and contrary to tradition," Stefan said.

"Tradition can be a cage. If some men do not reach between the bars, nothing ever changes."

Andreas kept his sight on that bit of garden, waiting, suddenly not caring much about Signore Alberti and this bold, ambitious dream.

When he had seen Giselle in the hall, he had briefly, stupidly, let himself think that she had understood after all. That she had come because she understood. He had assumed that they would talk of it, finally, and—and what? He wasn't really sure.

Instead, she had been distant and officious and spoken only of money and loans. He had barely contained his disappointment and sense of insult. In his vexation, he had given back what he got.

He had imagined a reunion with her many times, but never the one that they had just had.

"Should I be drawing up a preliminary contract?" Stefan asked. "Obviously, there will be many changes and negotiations, but if we make the first document it will be to your advantage."

"Yes, you should probably do that."

He pictured her sitting in his hall, the sunlight glowing off the coppery tones of her deep red hair. She had been so close and so beautiful that it made him ache. She had appeared unsettled and embarrassed, and he had thought—well, he had thought wrong.

Of course he had. He had never revealed his hunger for her. Until today. That had been clumsy and hard and an impulsive reaction to her haughty manner.

He kept watching for her, regretting what he had said, how he had said it, and how he had treated the whole episode.

Finally, the blue dot appeared. It sat on a bench under a tree. Moments later, the vague trickling of a lute's notes rose and receded on the capricious breeze.

Images of their meeting moved through his mind. He forced himself to see them without the rancor he had felt in the hall.

If she had come to him at all, she must need the money very badly. If she had offered to sell the tapestry, she must be desperate.

"Stefan, carry a message to Alberti. Tell him that a sudden matter of trade means that I cannot visit him tomorrow, but that I will contact him when I am again available, and well before the galley leaves."

"Are you sure? He might misunderstand."

"Bring the amber and gold necklace I bought in Novgorod. Say it is for his daughter. He will know its value and will not misunderstand. Beneath all of his silk and Venetian superiority, he is a merchant."

# Two

***Shortly after dawn the next day, Andreas walked down*** the lane toward Giselle's house. Tucked in his tunic were the pledges that Reginald had made. They were his excuse to go and see her, but he hoped that they would speak of other things.

It had been years since he had trod this street, but the old emotions assaulted him all the same, like spiritual echoes from his youth. The joy and expectation. The promise of peace and serenity. As a young man he only visited London for several months in any year, but the walks from the docks to this house had been full of anticipation, such as a man feels when returning home.

Peace and serenity did not wait for him this time. Noise and confusion poured out of Giselle's home. Neighbors loitered by their doors and hung out windows to watch the spectacle unfolding on her doorstep.

As Andreas walked toward the disturbance, two local

tailors passed him, carrying a long, heavy bench. With an adroit step, he blocked their path.

"Why are you taking that?"

The men set down their burden. One pulled a tally out of his tunic. "There's four rich garments Reginald owes us for. This is hardly compensation, but one gets what one can at such times."

Andreas looked down the lane to Giselle's house. A crowd of merchants and craftsmen surrounded the entrance, pushing and jostling to get in.

"Return the bench," he said.

"We are within our rights."

"That remains to be seen. Return the bench, or no member of the Hanse will patronize your shop."

Andreas continued to the house. The tailors began shuffling after him, hauling the bench back.

He waited patiently at the edge of the crowd. Eventually, he was noticed. Men moved aside. Some did because they knew him and wanted to stay in his good graces. Others did, he knew, because of his garments and size. London was a city that respected wealth and strength, in that order.

He stepped into the crowded hall. An amazing sight waited for him.

Waving tallies and pledges, men shouted demands for payment. Others had taken matters into their own hands and were stripping the house of its possessions. Loud thumps on the stairs heralded a bed board being dragged down from an upper chamber. Two merchants of high standing were bickering over the few pieces of silver plate propped on a high shelf.

Giselle stood near the wall that displayed the silk tapestry, looking like a warrior maiden from the old myths. Her red hair streamed down her body, and her blue eyes flared a deadly challenge. She clasped her brother's sword high by her shoulder, ready to bring it down on any man who approached.

Andreas walked over to her. "Do you plan to kill them all?"

"Only the ones who try to steal what is mine."

"What has caused this?"

"They claim to have tallies from Reginald."

"Your brother has been leaving such things with merchants for years. Why are they all here to collect today?"

She kept her fierce gaze on a knot of men who were waiting for her to weary so they could claim the prize that she guarded. "My brother has disappeared. His long absence has been noticed."

That would do it. Fearing no payment at all, every tradesman to whom Reginald owed money would try to grab something before nothing was left. Since Reginald had been liberal in his pledges and miserly in his payments, half of London would arrive before evening.

Andreas stepped between Giselle and the agitated merchants. They all immediately shifted their attention from her to him.

Reaching into his tunic, he retrieved a stack of parchments and held them high.

"I have pledges from the owner of this property that are more than four years in the waiting. If any man has an older claim, present it now. Otherwise, mine take precedence, and I doubt that there is anything in this house that these parchments do not cover."

An outburst of objections greeted his announcement. He threw the pledges on the hall's long table and allowed the others to paw through them to check his claims. A few men held older documents, and Andreas spent the next hour negotiating which of the house's furnishings they could take in payment.

Finally, the little swarm drifted away. Andreas watched as the long bench departed once again, only this time with two representatives of the Templars. Their claim had not been older than his, but a wise man did not argue such details with those particular money lenders.

A hollow silence fell on the house. Andreas gazed around the hall where he had spent many contented days as a young man. He had served as his father's clerk, just as Stefan now served as his, and his father had insisted that he take his board at an English home when trading brought them here. On his first visit he had met Reginald at a tavern, and decided that living with a young nobleman would be more fun than staying with an old merchant. It had been a good way to learn the language and the customs and to form friendships based on more than coin.

There were objects missing from the house that had not been taken today. Over the last four years, many things had been sold. Barely enough remained to give the impression of aristocratic status.

The tapestry made all the difference. It was a hanging such as a king might own. Covered with vines and flowers and woven of red and gold silken threads, it glowed on its wall. Even its flaw, where a subtle change in colors indicated the weaving had been interrupted near the top, did not detract from its glory.

He remembered Giselle telling him the story behind that interruption. Supposedly, the woman who made it had been given in marriage to a man she did not love, and thus had been separated for years from the man she wanted. Later, when the first husband died, she had returned to both the weaving and the lover of her youth.

Giselle still stood in front of the tapestry, and her eyes still blazed. Now the anger was directed at only one person. Him.

She let the sword fall. It clattered to the plank floor as she bore down on the table. One by one, she lifted the pledges and examined them. As the last fell from her hand, she shot him a look of scathing disdain.

"Damn you, Andreas."

* * *

***She could not believe her brother's recklessness. She had*** known that he borrowed money, but he had never told her how precarious their situation was.

She stared in fury at the pledges Andreas had brought.

The loans had been made in the customary way. Reginald had sold items at one price and promised to buy them back at a higher one. If the surety was not rebought, it was forfeit.

Andreas owned everything. The furniture. The house itself. Reginald had even pledged their father's ring. One parchment indeed included her tapestry.

"I thought you were his friend." She grabbed some pledges and threw them at him. They floated through the air. "A friend does not do this. A friend does not lure a man onto the path to ruin."

"I lured him nowhere."

"You had him join you in that first scheme. You showed him the riches to be gained. You—"

"He begged to be included in that trading venture, and he saw good profit. If he had not gotten greedy and assumed that he was shrewder than any other man, if he had known his limitations in such things and not decided to instigate his own plans—"

"His ideas were good. Bad luck haunted him, that is all."

"There is always the chance of bad luck. Reginald never thought of the risks and was too quick to gamble everything. He had no head for trade. I told him that, Giselle, many times."

"Did you tell him that as he signed away this house to you? My father's ring?"

He just looked at her, completely unmoved.

She forced some composure on her livid indignation. Reginald had left her in a dreadful place. She needed coin for his sake, and now she had discovered that she possessed almost nothing to sell in order to get it.

"There is the property in Sussex at least," she muttered, more to herself than Andreas.

"He sold that. Years ago."

Her breath left her. She thought she would faint. That poor farm had been the only land left to them after their father was disseised for joining Simon de Montfort's rebellion. It had been Reginald's hold on the past, just as the tapestry had been hers.

What had her brother been thinking?

She knew the answer to that. He had explained it often enough. Just one big success was all it would take. One investment in one major trading venture and they would have the wealth and the means to reestablish themselves.

Only the grand plans always hit snags. Bad weather, bad timing, bad goods—bad luck, as Reginald would later explain.

She sank down on the bench beside the table. The only bench, since the other had been taken by the Templars. Discouragement spread from her heart to her whole being, making her unbearably weary.

"So, you have come with your pledges, too, Andreas. Just like the other vultures. You are a shrewd merchant indeed to make these loans to my brother. It is all yours. I will arrange to vacate the house by evening."

"If my goal had been to see you homeless, I would have taken the property years ago. I do not require that you leave this house."

"I will not accept anyone's charity. I will not be an object of pity."

"It is not charity to receive help from a friend."

She glanced at the pledges littering the floor. "I can see the sort of help that you give friends."

He bent down and collected the parchments. "I broke with your brother for good reason. That my friendship with you ended, too, was an unfortunate consequence.

You came asking for my help yesterday, so there is no reason to refuse it today."

He sat beside her on the bench. He set the pledges aside in a neat stack. "As to these debts, we will find a way to settle them that does not leave you impoverished."

Her gaze snapped to the strong hand resting atop the pledges. Her spirit jolted out of its numbness. She instantly became very aware of his size and masculinity. His presence warmed her shoulder. It seemed as though she could feel his breath on her hair.

"Have you come to buy the tapestry?"

"I will not buy it, nor is it yours to sell. We will find another way."

She had no other way. She had nothing else of value to give him. Except, as she had said at their meeting yesterday, her virtue.

She remembered his response to that. That must be the other way he alluded to.

She stared at the table, mortified. Not only by the implications, but also by the fact that the notion did not entirely disgust her.

That dismayed her. She could not look at him.

"You used to offer me ale as soon as I entered this house, Giselle. Am I no longer worthy of your hospitality?"

He spoke quietly, in the voice that she knew from their past. A strange excitement thickened her throat, and she had difficulty responding.

"Those men drank the ale and ate what food was here. I have nothing to offer you."

She felt his attention on her, as if he studied her very closely. It made the odd spell he cast get heavier.

"Then let us go to the tavern at the crossroads. We can discuss your situation while we have some food and drink."

She agreed with relief. She wanted to have other people around, and the tavern would be crowded. Maybe if they sat across from each other at a table, instead of side-by-side like this, almost touching, she would not find herself so confused and alert, as if a hidden part of her was waiting for something to happen.

***The serving girl brought tumblers of ale and a stack of*** small meat pies. Giselle eyed the food with the greedy glint of someone who had not eaten her fill in a long time.

Andreas subtly pushed the pies toward her. He turned his gaze on the noisy men at the next table so that she would not be embarrassed by having him notice her hunger.

It knotted his heart to see that glint. She was his lady, and he did not like seeing her suffering such base needs.

He would kill Reginald this time.

He knew when the pies had dulled the worst of it. He turned his attention back to her just as she brushed her hands of crumbs.

"You are enjoying your visit to London, Andreas? It has been profitable?"

"Profitable enough."

"Your reserve always masked deeper thoughts, and I can see that has not changed. That was a Venetian merchant at your house yesterday, wasn't it?"

"I often trade with them."

She smiled slyly. "Do you plan a very special trade this time?"

He did not respond to that.

"Always quiet. Always discreet. That is you, Andreas. I remember you once telling me of your ideas about the Hanse and Venice. So, now you have built your family's power enough to make it true. It sounded like a boy's mad dream, but maybe I always knew that you would make it happen."

Her courteous banter irritated him. He did not want to talk about this. "Where is your brother?"

Her face fell, and she hesitated before answering. "I do not know. He has left before. Normally, he tells me where he is going, but he did not this time. It has been ten days."

"Do you think he fled the realm? It is not unusual when borrowing from Peter to pay Paul brings a man to ruin."

"My brother would never run away from his debts and leave me to reckon with the consequences."

*The hell he wouldn't.*

His expression must have spoken the silent words, because her eyes glinted with belligerent lights.

"He has not left the realm, I tell you. In fact, a messenger came from him two days ago."

"Then where is he? What message did he send you?"

She bit her lower lip and occupied her hands with brushing pie crumbs into a little pile. "The message was not exactly from him."

Andreas knew her expressions very well. He had learned to read her moods and worries years ago. He had memorized the nuances that revealed joy and sadness, dreams and disillusionments. Rarely, however, had he seen what he saw now.

She was afraid.

"Tell me, Giselle."

"A man came. Reginald is being held by brigands, who will kill him if I do not pay a ransom. I asked where Reginald is now, but he refused to say. I am to have the coin in five days, when the man will come for it or send word of where to bring it." She blurted the explanation with annoyance and, it seemed to Andreas, also a bit of relief.

"Am I correct that the amount he demanded was one hundred pounds?"

She nodded. "It is such a huge sum. I tried to get it from some merchants who Reginald knows, but they would not help me. Small wonder. They were there today, with their tallies and pledges. In seeking that coin, I brought all of London down on our heads."

"Your brother's extravagance and carelessness brought the city down on you."

"Stop blaming him. He is in danger. He might be killed. I will not sit here and listen to you speak badly of him." She scooted to the end of the bench and began to rise.

Andreas caught her wrist.

She resisted his hold, but he did not let go. He was not about to let her face this alone, but he also held on because the feel of her frail bones and warm skin entranced him.

He had never before touched her.

He knew that for a fact, because he had wanted to—ached to—many times.

Her indignant gaze met his. Her vexation slipped away, and astonishment took its place. They stayed like that for a long count, her half risen and him grasping, keeping her in place. During that deep pause the noise of the tavern was obscured by a spiritual silence in which all that existed was their connected flesh and gazes.

He would have gladly spent eternity in that stillness.

It affected her as much as him. He knew it as he looked into her eyes. This touch had been too long in coming. Too long denied.

The silent admission of that seemed to surprise her.

"Sit, Giselle."

Flustered, she obeyed. He reluctantly released her. She tightened herself into a noble, formal column and kept her gaze on the table.

"You said that the man gave you five days. How many has it been thus far?"

"This is the third. It took one to learn that no London lender would help me, and I wasted yesterday at your house."

"I think that we should try to find your brother. He may even be in the city."

"If we do find him, then what? We attack with swords and lances and rescue him?"

"I do not think it will come to that."

He suspected they would find Reginald hale and fit and not in danger at all.

This story sounded like a ploy. Reginald had finally come to the end of the rope he had been climbing down for years. No one would lend to him, but they might take pity on a desperate, beautiful sister trying to save his life.

"I will look for Reginald, Giselle. If he is truly in danger, or if I cannot find him by the fifth day, I will give you the money to pay the ransom."

She appeared to agree to it. At least, she did not disagree. She just sat there, staring at the table planks, distraught and resigned and vulnerable. And afraid.

Her fear was not just for Reginald. Her quick glances said that their reaction to that touch occupied her concerns now, too.

He pushed the last meat pie closer to her and called for more ale.

Maybe he would not kill Reginald. Perhaps he would thank him.

# Three

*"If I knew where he was, I'd be taking what he owes me* out of his hide, not settling for a few bits of bent, pitted plate."

John Hastings pointed his greasy, fat finger derisively at the two cups lying on the scales in his counting room. As one of the few merchants with a pledge older than Andreas's, John had been allowed to remove the cups from Giselle's house.

He went back to tearing the flesh off the joint of lamb in front of him. His hat formed a long beak in front, and its tip kept touching the meat. The table groaned with an abundance of food. He appeared intent on consuming it all.

Giselle fumed at the way he dismissed the remaining pieces of plate that she had carried from her ancestral home. "The silver exceeded the amount of the tally," she reminded him. "Your own scale proves it."

John shot Andreas an exasperated glance with his pale,

owl eyes. It was obvious that he resented having a woman participating in this conversation.

Giselle did not care that one of London's leading citizens found her too outspoken. This was the fifth merchant they had visited today, and it appeared he would be no more help than the others. One of her precious five days was leaching away, and she was getting more worried by the minute.

"She is correct, John. You can have no complaints on the payment."

"You know damn well I am not speaking of that measly old tally, Andreas. Reginald cost me ten times that silver, and I'll never see it now. There should be laws against such things."

"There are," Giselle snapped. "Usury is a sin, and you have now reaped the rewards."

The owl eyes pierced her. "I do not speak of tallies and pledges. I was stupid enough to join your brother in a partnership to bring in timber from Norway. Four years ago, it was, and I've not seen a stick of wood nor a bit of coin from it yet." He turned his annoyance on Andreas. "I only agreed because he said you were behind it. We all knew how you lived in that house back then—"

Andreas interrupted. "Do you have any ideas of who might know what has become of him?"

John pondered that while he clawed at the meat. "About a year ago he got involved with a trader from Genoa who came to London, a bastard son of the Comini family. Sandro, his name was. I never learned for sure what they cooked up. If Reginald crossed one of those traders from the south, he is probably at the bottom of the sea."

"Is this Sandro still in London?"

John scoffed. "He left after two months and never came back. However, since the galleys are here, you might ask the Venetian, Narni, about him. Narni's nephew married a woman of the Comini, so he might know about Sandro.

You waste your efforts, though. I still say the knave just ran away."

"My brother is no knave, you gluttonous, discourteous—"

Andreas cut her off with polite farewells. Taking her arm, he hauled her out to the lane.

"We had better speak with this Narni," she said.

"I will. You are going home."

"I told you in the tavern that I am coming with you. He is *my* brother."

Arms crossed over his chest, he assumed a pose of displeasure. "You did not tell me that you intended to insult every man we spoke with."

"I only gave back what I got."

"You have been getting the truth, which is why I did not want you with me. I will take you home now, so that you do not have to hear more of it."

"I am not going home. I am going to find out if this Narni knows who holds my brother."

"Then behave yourself, or I will turn you over my knee later. I trade with these men, and if you speak to Narni the way you just did to John, it will take me years to regain his favor."

The walk to the galleys was a long one. Andreas kept touching her as he guided her through the crowds. His hand took her arm when the bodies got thick. His fingers occasionally tapped her shoulder to remind her it was time to turn down another lane. Courteous and protective, there was nothing insinuating about any of it.

She noticed every single time, however. The warm pressure would jolt her out of her worries. For an instant she would be totally alive and vividly aware of the handsome man at her side.

The long walk gave her time to think about what she had learned today. No one could say where Reginald was, but all those merchants had known her brother very well—

better than she had. The image they had revealed was not a good one.

She had been blind to her brother's faults and had found excuses for his behavior. She debated whether she had done that because she wanted to believe his dreams.

They were hers, too, after all.

People and wagons crowded the area by the docks. The visits by the Venetian galleys always created a mercantile chaos. Workers swarmed everywhere, unloading the holds of their wares. Vendors of food and drink added to the confusion.

Lost in her reflections about Reginald, Giselle absorbed the noise through a daze. Wagons rolled past, people shouted, and the smells of food and dung filled the breeze.

Suddenly, almost everything on the street froze. The head of a horse came toward her, growing quickly in size. The sounds of wheels penetrated her ears and then those of shouts.

The world swirled. Colors flashed. She flew.

She found herself up against a shed, surrounded by a masculine wall. She peered out of her sanctuary and saw a wagon hurtling past while its driver fought to regain control over the galloping horse that pulled it.

The sanctuary tightened. The scent of the man who held her filled her head, and the comforting warmth of his protection absorbed her shock.

She looked up.

Andreas's face was very close to hers. The earlier annoyance was gone from his expression. All the warmth of their past was in the way he looked down at her, and the old joy sparkled in response. The dangerous intensity of the last two days was there, too, however.

He appeared very handsome. Compellingly so. He had the kind of face that one stared at. She never had before, but when he had sat in her house or garden, she could look all she wanted and not even notice that she did so.

Without any movement, his protective hold became an

embrace. She could not find the voice to object. It felt good being in his arms. Safe and deliciously risky, all at once.

"That was close," he said.

His quiet voice, so close that his breath warmed her cheek, made her skin tingle from her scalp to her breasts. "Thank you. If you had not grabbed me, I would have been trampled. I was lost in my thoughts and did not see the danger until it was too late."

He broke the embrace but not the touch. With his arm resting along the back of her waist, as if it had a right to now, he guided her toward one of the largest galleys.

"He used you, didn't he? Reginald used your name, without your permission, to lend legitimacy to his plans. That is what John meant, and that first merchant we spoke with, Harold, alluded to that, too."

She voiced the suspicions that had been distracting her. The intimacy that the danger had created permitted such frankness. There had been so much of the old Andreas in the way he held her, even if the physical connections were completely new.

He did not respond. She guessed that doing so would reflect badly on her brother. It touched her that he wanted to spare her.

"It was terrible of Reginald to do that. Small wonder that you broke with him upon hearing of it."

"That is one of the reasons."

"There are others? Tell me now, so that I do not receive more sad surprises as I listen to these men."

"No man whom we will meet knows the rest of it." He began handing her up the gangway to the long, sleek ship. "Do not speak when we are with Narni, Giselle. He will accept your presence because these Venetians understand family bonds very well, but he will find any intrusion on your part impertinent."

* * *

***Andreas did not have to wait like the other merchants*** crowding the galley's deck. A clerk recognized him, rattled out an effusive greeting in his foreign tongue, and disappeared into the cabin.

It had been thus with every man today. They had been received because of Andreas's power, not her aristocratic blood. The English merchants had tripped over themselves to make Andreas happy. Giselle had almost heard their minds calculating their good fortune that a powerful member of the Hanseatic League had decided to visit, ask a favor, and thus place himself in their debt.

It seemed that even the richest Venetian traders regarded Andreas the same way. Signore Alberti wanted a marriage alliance and, as the clerk soon announced, Signore Narni would see them at once.

Signore Narni was as skinny as John had been fat. Short and wizened, with closely cropped white hair under his satin scull cap, he appeared far too old to be making long journeys on his galley. Despite his small stature, however, danger emanated from him. The eyes of a hawk peered out from his wrinkled face.

Giselle thought of John's words, about a man who crossed these traders ending up at the bottom of the sea.

Andreas donned armor of inscrutable reserve as soon as they entered the cabin. Neither merchant displayed deference in their greetings, but both showed respect. Andreas spoke in Narni's language, and Narni responded in Andreas's.

Andreas introduced her, and Narni switched to English out of courtesy for her. "I did not expect you for two days, Andreas."

"I will be back then. This visit is on another matter."

"So long as the salt in your ship's hold is still mine and not diverted to Alberti to win his daughter's hand, I can wait two days."

He bid them sit in lovely, carved chairs and arranged his sapphire brocade robe into satin folds as he settled into a third one. He offered wine poured by his servant into bejewelled silver cups. Another servant passed a plate of dried figs and nuts.

Giselle barely managed not to gawk. This merchant lived more luxuriously in his galley's cabin than most barons did in their castles.

"What is this other matter?" Narni asked.

"Lady Giselle's brother, Reginald, is missing. We have been told that a year ago he had some dealings with Sandro Comini. We are wondering if you know about this?"

"I can tell you about Sandro. An impatient young man and a great trial to his father. He got it into his head to form a *commenda* contract. No man in Genoa would back him, so he decided to look farther afield. He came here."

Andreas must have noticed her curiosity. "A *commenda* is a way of financing trade, Giselle. The project is backed by a man of wealth, and another makes the journey. It is common south of the Alps."

"Except that no man south of the Alps would risk his coin on Sandro's plan," Narni explained. "Furs from Russia and the Baltic, I think it was. He had a ship, but he had never sailed those waters and knew no traders in Novgorod or Riga." He smiled knowingly at Andreas. "Nor would the Hanse appreciate such incursions in their arena. So, Sandro came to London to find his *commenda.* It was said that he paired up with a wealthy young nobleman, who brought together several other barons to provide the money. The lady's brother, perhaps."

"Perhaps," Andreas said. "When did Sandro return to Genoa?"

"Never. Perhaps his ship wrecked. Or maybe those Baltic pagans sold him into slavery. His father prays for his return, but without much hope."

"Did you hear any name attached to this venture?"

Narni's eyes narrowed to slits as he searched his memory. Giselle did not doubt that if any name had been given, at any time, this man would remember it.

"Does the name Wolford mean anything to you? I recall hearing it amidst the talk about Sandro, and it sounds English."

Giselle's heart flipped, and not with relief. She had been desperate for any tidbit of information, but she could have done without hearing this morsel.

If Reginald was mixed up with Wolford, he might be dead already.

# Four

***It was a long walk back to the house. Andreas revelled in*** every moment of it.

It did not matter that a worried frown marred Giselle's forehead. He took ridiculous joy in merely walking beside her and shameful pleasure that her distraction gave him excuses to touch her shoulder or arm as he guided her through the lanes.

He bought some food on the way so she would feel obliged to invite him to share it with her, and thus prolong the day. When they arrived at her house in the early evening, she seemed to accept that he would not leave and went up to her chamber to wash.

A low, weary groan drifted down to him, followed by a barely muffled curse.

He went up to see what the problem was.

Giselle stood in her little chamber. The boards and ropes of her bed lay strewn on the floor. An upturned bucket rested in a damp corner.

"I had forgotten that those men took apart the bed," she muttered, giving one of the boards a little frustrated kick.

*Come sleep at my house.* He almost said it. God knew he wanted to. Over the years he had learned to forget how much he wanted her, but this day had unleashed the old desire. It burned low in his awareness, constantly, a fierce point of heat in danger of roaring out of control and consuming him. *Come sleep at my house, with me. Let me hold you all night.*

Somehow he swallowed the impulse to blurt it, but he admitted that soon it would be said anyway. He was not a youth anymore. He no longer had the time or patience for hopeless fascinations and half measures.

Giselle picked up the pail. "I must go and get some water, since they spilled that, too. I will return soon."

"I will rebuild the bed while you are gone."

He worked at it while she went to fetch water at the city fountain. As he set the boards together with their pegs, he remembered that during his first visit to this house there had been a woman servant who did chores like hauling water. By his third visit, however, she was gone.

Giselle returned just as he was tightening the bed's ropes. He heard her enter the other chamber and then come back out and into her own.

"At least the straw did not get wet," she said, feeling the stuffed cloth heaped near the corner.

He helped her set the mattress on the ropes. She began to pour water from the pail into a chipped crockery bowl set on a tiny table. "Thank you for your help, Andreas. I put some water in your chamber, if you want to wash."

*His chamber.* He did want to wash, since the day had been warm and busy, but he wasn't sure that he wanted to do it there.

He walked the few steps into the house's other upper room, the one Reginald used, and crossed to the tiny addition on its far end where space had been stolen over the street.

Giselle had opened the shutters that looked out on the lane, and the muted sounds of families joining for meals wafted in. It still contained the simple bed and the wide shelf set on stacked stones that served as a table. There was not much room for anything else.

Except dreams. Glorious dreams of riches and of daring trading schemes. Hot dreams of carnal sensuality, in which Giselle always appeared.

How often had he laid on this bed in the still of the night and listened to the sounds of the house, stretching to hear her breathing beneath Reginald's snores?

He stripped off his tunic and undergarment. He sloshed water over his shoulders and torso to cool his body of all the heat that the day and his thoughts had raised.

He heard her breathing, and for a moment he assumed that a nostalgic memory from his nights here had entered his head. Then he realized that the sound was real and nearby.

Turning his head, he saw her at the low, narrow doorway to Reginald's room. The moisture of her own washing still dampened her brow, and some wet hairs clung to the sides of her face.

She did not realize that his attention was on her. He caught the way she observed him, how her gaze slowly traveled over his nakedness. Four years ago she would have quickly retreated if she came upon him wearing nothing but hose and boots, but she had not this time.

The appreciative, womanly lights in her eyes sent his desire flaring.

She realized he had noticed her watching him and flustered. Blushing, she looked in his eyes and opened her mouth to speak.

He looked straight back, and her words died.

A heavy silence stretched with them standing there, watching each other. Each moment pounded with the mutual acknowledgment they had established in the tavern, that he was a man and she was a woman and something other than friendship now drew them together.

It could no longer be denied. He would not *let* it be denied. The power of what pulled between them set his teeth on edge. He barely resisted striding across the small space and grabbing her.

She held a small linen cloth, old but clean and neatly mended. He reached out his hand to her. Her eyes widened, and she stepped back, as if she feared he was beckoning her to come to him.

He let her know that was exactly what he was doing.

She averted her gaze and blushed deeper yet. "I forgot to leave a linen for you." She threw the towel at him, as if she dared not take the step necessary to place it in his hand. "I will go down and prepare the meal. The evening is fair, and we can eat in the garden."

***"You are very quiet, Giselle."***

Andreas did not worry that she would take the observation as a rebuke for being discourteous. Giselle had never required chatter of him, nor he of her. Some of their most pleasant hours together had been spent in silence.

She picked at the cooked fowl that he had bought on their way back from the galley. Sweet smells of flowers and herbs filled the air of her garden, and the gentle light of evening played off the dark golds and coppers of her hair.

He had not really minded her silence or her continued distraction. It had meant that he had lots of time to just look at her. A few of her glances suggested that what had happened upstairs occupied part of her mind, but he knew that bigger worries preyed on her.

"What are we going to do now?" she finally asked. "If Wolford is involved—"

"If he is, at least we know where we stand. Where is this Wolford to be found?"

"His castle is south, near the coast, but he has a small manor in Essex, not far from London."

"If he has your brother, it is probably close by. I will ride to his manor in Essex tomorrow and learn if Reginald is there."

"You cannot ride into Wolford's gate and accuse him of abducting Reginald. If you anger him, your body will never be found. He and his brothers are little more than thieves. Everyone knows that their men openly rob travelers. They probably took my brother off the road and think there is a rich family to pay a ransom."

Andreas doubted the explanation would be such simple brigandage. "I will not accuse Wolford of anything. I will offer to sell him goods and then learn what I need to know. If he has Reginald, he will be glad to hear that the ransom will be paid."

She shrugged her acceptance of the plan, but her distraction did not lift.

"I blame myself. I should have seen where Reginald was headed and said something. Instead, I just trusted and believed."

"He was your brother. That is normal."

She shook her head. "I saw the furnishings sold. I knew that every month there were more grocers and food stalls where I was not welcome. I kept excusing the evidence. I did not want to accept that no great plan would reverse things and that our fall was permanent. Reginald has been deceiving himself about the truth of that, and I gladly joined in."

He would have given anything not to see her face that. The quiet dignity with which she let her illusions die touched him more than any outpouring of tears could.

The admission appeared to lighten her mood, however. She looked at him and smiled with warm familiarity. "Come with me. I want to show you something."

He joined her as she strolled over to the tree in the garden's near corner. The bench where she sometimes played her lute was under it. She sat down and patted the place beside her in invitation.

"Look there. Between those two roofs. That is the top of your house there. It is three lanes over, but from this spot in the garden, it is visible."

"So it is."

"I was surprised that you bought one in this ward. Normally members of the Hanse live in that enclave near the river, near where the Hanse stores its staples. But then you always said that a trader should live among the people in the city where he made his second home."

"I found this ward familiar, and I liked the house."

She cocked her head and peered toward the distant roof. "I always knew when you came to London, because that window up there would open only then. There was that long period three years ago when it stayed closed, and I thought perhaps you would never return. But then, one day, the shutters were flung wide once more."

"That was after my wife died. There were many matters to settle in Bremen, and I did not make long journeys for a long time."

"I was sorry to hear about your loss. When I visited yesterday, I should have asked you about it, instead of thinking only of my own troubles."

"It was three years ago. What grief there was is long past."

"I still should have asked. Tell me what happened."

"She died in childbirth. The babe was dead in her womb."

"Oh, Andreas, I am so sorry. To have finally been blessed with a child, and then to lose them both—"

"The child was not mine, Giselle."

She leaned back against the tree trunk behind the bench. He could not see her face with her angled away like that, but he felt her as if he embraced her, as he had near the galleys.

A long pause beat between them. Not a peaceful, contented silence. He sensed her studying him and heard questions forming.

"Why did you stop coming here, Andreas? That you bought your own house made sense. It was long overdue. But why did you not even visit?"

There was no easy answer to that, so he said nothing.

"You said today that there were other reasons, besides my brother using your name in his ventures. I want to know what they were."

"No, you do not. Trust me on this."

"I do want to know. I remember the last night you spent in this house. I could tell that you were angry with Reginald, but we also spoke more honestly that night than ever before. Do you remember telling me about your wife? You had been married for three years, but that was the first time you ever spoke to me about her. I felt very close to you and went to sleep knowing that I had a true friend in you. And then you left the next morning, and I never spoke with you again. It hurt me deeply that you would discard my friendship so easily."

He turned to see her. She looked like a flaming flower glowing in the shadowed twilight under the leaves. "Not so easily. Do not accuse me of such callousness."

"Then why?"

He debated whether to tell her. If he didn't, what pulsed between them would never be more than a tantalizing possibility, because she would continue blaming him for the last four years.

"Did you not think it odd that Reginald was not with us that night, Giselle?"

"He sometimes went away from the house when you visited. And, as I said, I suspected that you were angry with him."

"But this time he did not return until morning."

"He said that he got besotted and fell asleep in a tavern."

"He lied. He left you alone with me on purpose."

She went very still. "What are you saying?"

"When I arrived in London that time, Reginald was desperate for money. He had committed to some venture that would make his fortune, he was sure, but did not have the silver he had promised. He asked it of me, but he had come to me too often, and it already strained our friendship. I could see he was on the path to ruin, and this venture was no sounder than the others."

"So you refused him? Did you assume that I would hold that against you? You should have known that I would have understood."

"Giselle, when I refused him, he offered to sell the only thing of value he had left."

"What was that?"

He saw her suspecting the answer before he spoke it. "You."

# Five

*"He offered you as my leman, Giselle."*

Her hands flew to her face. She covered her mouth and closed her eyes to try to contain her shock.

When that did not help, she jumped up and ran away into the garden.

Seeking its farthest corner, she leaned against the wall. Holding herself with crossed arms, she tried to calm a shame and humiliation so devastating that she shook.

It had been a day of disheartening revelations, but this was the worst.

The danger that Reginald faced from whomever held him would be nothing compared to what waited for him with her. When she got her hands on him—

And Andreas—saints, she would never be able to look at him again.

Boot steps approached. Horrified, she turned to face the wall.

"I told you that you would not want to hear it, Giselle."

"You should have said that you had grown bored with us. You should have said that our foolish grasping at past glory was pitiful, and you could no longer bear such pretense."

"It has become clear that you concluded I thought those things. I decided that I did not want you thinking of me that way any longer."

"Why not?"

"You know why not."

"I don't. Your lying would have spared my hearing that my brother tried to make me a whore—and to a man who did not even want one." Acknowledging *that* part of it made her face burn. "Small wonder that you broke the friendship and never came back here after Reginald insulted you like that."

He came up behind her. She could feel him all along her back.

His hands closed on both of her shoulders, and he turned her around.

"You misunderstand. Reginald did not insult me. He tempted me."

She felt her face burn hotter. She kept her gaze on the ground while she tried to reconcile what he was saying with what she remembered of that night. There had been new colors to their friendship. New tones. A heightened intimacy. The air had contained a heavy anticipation, and their bond a luring excitement.

In fact, she had felt much the same as she had since she visited him yesterday. That night, however, she had not comprehended the reason for the changes.

Then again, perhaps she had but denied it. Andreas had been a married man, and she was saving her virtue for a knight or lord, for a marriage that would help them regain their place.

"Are you saying that you made this bargain with Reginald?"

"I refused his offer. But when he left that night, I knew

that he was counting on desire vanquishing my honor, since I knew he would not object. I should have left, too, but I could not. Perhaps I was secretly hoping for a sign from you that you were agreeable. More likely I foresaw that those would be the last hours I would spend with you and could not give them up."

She could not ignore what he was saying. If she had been agreeable, he might not have been so honorable, despite his intentions. He was speaking frankly of what he had been broaching all day with those touches and looks. "My ignorance of Reginald's offer must have been awkward for you."

"Torturous would be a better word."

That made her laugh. It dulled her embarrassment enough that she ceased wanting to be swallowed by the ground. "More bad luck for Reginald. He betrayed his honor and mine, lost a good friend, and did not even get the money."

No, not bad luck. Bad judgment.

"The next day, I gave him the money. But I also told him we would not meet again. I suspected that he would try to coerce you the next time he was in trouble. I ended our friendship to preserve my honor and your dignity."

She did not want to believe this of her brother, but she could imagine it all happening. She could see Reginald, smiling and charming, suggesting this bargain to Andreas, convincing himself that it was not so shameful as it seemed.

"My brother is such a fool. I have been learning that to my sorrow today, but this story—he did not know you well, despite the years of friendship."

The last of twilight was fading, but she saw the slow way he smiled. She saw the way he looked at her, with all of the warmth of the old Andreas, but also the exciting danger of the new one.

He laid his palm on her face and stroked his fingers into the hair behind her ear. Her cheek and neck and scalp tingled from his firm touch. He tilted her face so that he could see it and so she had to see his.

"You keep misunderstanding. He knew me very well, Giselle. My marriage was not a warm one and was typical of the family alliances that traders make. When my wife died, I mourned her. I even mourned the child. But mostly I felt anger that being faithful to her and my honor had kept me from having the woman I wanted."

His expression mesmerized her. It was that of a man who had decided not to make the same sacrifice again. The veils of his reserve had been falling since she met with him yesterday, and now they were all gone.

His confidences made everything very clear. She understood the new intensity now. He had wanted her back then, and he was helping her now because he wanted her still. And she had agreed to certain things in accepting his aid.

She realized that she did not mind that obligation. His touch had her weak-kneed, and the way he looked at her left her breathless.

He stroked her lips with his fingertips, and she could not control her reactions. They streaked through her, shamelessly out of control. Her heart filled with the joy he had so often inspired. Her spirit yearned for the special intimacy they had once shared. Her body responded forcefully, suddenly eager for more of the touches and embraces that he had given her today.

He kissed her, and there was no part of her left to object.

The kiss left her helpless. She had never guessed that such a small physical connection could create such sweetness, such thrilling excitement. She did not want it to end.

It didn't. It went on and on, the one kiss becoming many. Delicious, stimulating sensations slid through her whole body, awakening a determined craving that obscured every other thought. He pulled her into a tight embrace, and she held him too, so grateful for the closeness that her heart ached, so desperate for more connection that she grew frantic.

Kisses on her ear, her neck, the skin above her gown. Luring kisses, possessive ones. Kisses full of breath that titillated her skin. Masterful kisses that demanded abandon.

Finally, a new kiss. A nip on her lip, requesting something. A quiet, verbal command to open her mouth when she did not understand.

The invasive tenderness shocked her. Undid her. It changed her responses from pleasure to need. It insinuated rights to other invasions and other possessions.

His embrace did, too. Supportive and gentle, it was still an embrace of power. With firm caresses, he touched her in ways that left her gasping and pressing against him and hoping for more.

His kiss returned to her ear while his hand caressed the front of her waist, rising in seductive strokes to the base of her breasts.

"Tell me that you want this, Giselle," he said lowly. "Promise me that you do."

She could barely talk at all.

"Tell me."

"I want this, Andreas."

He responded with a new kiss, fevered, and hard. A new caress, as his hand rose to her breast. A new closeness, as his knee pushed between her thighs, to press the moisture and ache torturing her.

The way that he touched her breasts raised unbearable pleasure. She lost awareness of everything except an intensifying hunger. She wanted him to kiss her harder, touch her more, tease her forever.

A sound abruptly disturbed the frantic bliss. A noise broke through her besotted senses.

A voice called Andreas's name.

They froze and turned their heads toward the sound. A

man stood at the doorway to the house. He quietly called for Andreas again.

*"Ich bin hier,"* Andreas called back.

His embrace loosened. He brushed her lips with his and glanced to the man again. "That is my brother, Stefan. He knew that I came here this morning."

"You should find out why he is looking for you."

"I suppose I must."

As they walked to the house, Andreas's arm slid down her back and across her waist until, when they approached Stefan, he was not touching her at all.

They spoke in their native tongue, and she understood none of it. She heard the name *Alberti,* however.

Andreas sent Stefan away and pulled her back into his arms. "I must go. A trader's clerk has arrived at my house with a gift, and I should see him."

She accepted it with a calm that surprised her. Her heart fell a little, and the joy dimmed a bit, but not enough to make her regret what had just happened.

Of course the negotiations with Signore Alberti would continue. It was the way of such things. She had no illusions that she could hold on to Andreas. But in this garden he had been hers alone, as he had been years ago.

"I will come and see you tomorrow before I go to Essex," he said, giving her a final kiss.

"I will be ready to ride when you come."

"I must refuse to let you accompany me this time, Giselle. From what you have said, Wolford is no John Hastings."

"I will not enter his manor, but I am coming to Essex. If something has happened to Reginald already, I want to know at once. If he is safe, I want to know that, too. I will not wait here in London while this unfolds."

***Giselle lingered in the garden after Andreas left. She did*** not contemplate what had happened but simply basked in the magical mood that their embrace had created. She marvelled at the way her whole being remained flushed with wonder and surprise long after his departure.

Finally, regretfully, she relinquished her hold on the spell, and its on her, and entered the house.

Only moonlight guided her, but its eerie glow showed the table and bench in the hall, and the one remaining stool. The shelf that once displayed the silver plate formed a harsh, black gash on the white wall. The whole chamber appeared as so many voids, all lacking the objects that held memories and made a home. The house had been reduced over the years to little more than a structure, and this morning's losses had stripped it further.

At least the tapestry remained. It burned like a brilliant flower in a barren wasteland. Its reds and golds absorbed the vague light and then threw it back, increased a hundredfold. The flowing, organic vines defied the rest of the chamber's angular practicality.

Normally, the sight of it gave her comfort, but not tonight. It was no longer hers, for one thing. She also knew now that the tapestry would never serve the purpose in her life that she had assumed.

In her youth it had hung in her family's hall, and as a girl she learned the story of how it had come to them, its ancient age, and the story attached to its flaw. It had moved her profoundly when, on her fifteenth birthday, her father said it was hers, to be brought to her new home when she married the lord he had just chosen for her.

There had been no marriage, of course. The rebellion against King Henry had interrupted those plans. When the war was over her father was dead, and she and Reginald lost their patrimony. The man who had taken their home had been kinder than necessary and accepted her word that the tapestry was hers. He had allowed them to remove a few other things, too.

Things like the plate and the iron candleholders—none of which remained.

The tapestry had hung here for ten years, waiting to be the great luxury that set her dowry apart when Reginald found the coin to arrange a marriage for her. That had been the goal of all his grand plans, or so he had always explained. A marriage to a landed lord was the surest way to begin reestablishing the family. She had wasted the best years of her life sitting in this house, believing it would happen.

From what Andreas had said, however, it appeared that Reginald had given up on that idea long ago.

She had been slowly accepting reality all day, and now she swallowed the bitter conclusion. There would be no dowry. Ever. No husband at all, let alone a landed lord. No secure place.

The cold truth of that lodged in her soul like a lump of lead. Her eyes began misting, but she wiped them furiously with her hand. She would not weep over her stupidity.

Her strength cracked despite her efforts. The tears flowed faster than she could brush them away.

What a foolish dreamer she had been, living in a cloud. She was lucky that the whole city had not laughed at her outright when she walked down the lanes.

Suddenly, the tapestry struck her as ugly. Its vines appeared ensnaring, and its flowers monstrous.

She turned to the stairs, feeling old and painfully wise.

She wished that she were back in the garden, in Andreas's arms, where for a lovely few moments she had tasted what it meant to be young and beautiful and desired. She wished that he was here to hold her, as he had near the docks, in an embrace of protection and friendship.

# *Six*

***"If I have not returned by today's nightfall, do not grow*** concerned."

"And if you have not returned by tomorrow's nightfall?"

"In that event, you might call for the sheriff."

Andreas's light tone did not mask the dark implications of what he said. Confronting Wolford would be dangerous. Even if that knave did not hold Reginald, he might decide that Andreas von Bremen would make an attractive hostage.

Giselle watched as Andreas removed Reginald's sword from its scabbard and tested its weight and feel. She had insisted on bringing it with them, but its glinting edge and point only sharpened her worry.

"Have you used one before?"

"Of course."

"Are you skilled with it?"

He shrugged.

"Then perhaps you should not take it."

"If I look too much a merchant, they may not see a man, but a chicken to be plucked."

She turned away from the hard image Andreas cut as he raised and lowered the sword to accustom himself to it.

She looked out the window of her chamber. Andreas had taken two of them on the top level of the inn. From here she could see most of the little town and the fields beyond that stretched to the horizon.

The journey here had been pleasant and happy. Andreas had brought an extra horse for her, and they had ridden side-by-side through the beautiful summer morning. They had spoken of many things, but not the ones that mattered.

There had been no mention of Reginald or of the ordeal waiting. Nor had there been conversation about last night or what had occurred in the garden. That passion might have never happened.

Except that thoughts of it had never left her mind. Or his, she suspected. The memories existed in the looks he gave her and the gentle protection he showed. There was no mistaking that their friendship and bond had changed—forever.

The sound of steel on steel made her turn. Andreas was returning the sword to its scabbard. He reached into a bag that he had carried up from his horse and withdrew a small purse. "There is coin in here for your meals, and if you need it for anything else."

He began to throw it toward the bed but stopped, and dropped it on the hearthstone instead.

"You are leaving now?"

He nodded.

She branded her mind with the sight of him, standing tall and strong, clasping the sword in his hand. Of course he would be safe. He was twice as clever as any brigand and, she suspected, twice as dangerous when he chose to be. A man did not rise in the Hanse if he was stupid or careless or weak.

"I find myself regretting that I involved you in this, Andreas. It was not fair to you."

"You have honored me by asking for my help, Giselle."

"No, I have endangered you."

"There will be little danger, I am sure."

She wasn't sure at all. Her stomach churned, and her mind filled with images of violence.

He must have seen her worry. He laid the sword on the bed and extended his arm to her.

She ran to the sanctuary of his embrace.

"Kiss me, my lady, so that I know you do not regret what started between us last night."

*Started.* That implied a finish. After this day her debt to him would be much greater than any loan made thus far.

The warmth of his arms made that obligation insignificant. The subtle excitement that had stirred in her all night and all morning spun a little faster. She wished that he was not leaving and that she could nestle in this security for hours.

Even if there were no debts, no danger, and no need for his help, she would want a finish. She had made that decision last night while she laid on her bed in the silent house, thinking about him.

She raised her head and kissed him, so he would know that there were no regrets.

The promise of what waited for them was in that kiss, in his embrace, and in the look he gave her as he left the chamber.

***"I do not understand why Wolford was so accommodating,*** but I am glad that he was. The chamber he gave me was very small and barely fit for a servant. And his board is not to my liking, either. Too much fish and his wine was sour."

Reginald waited until they were out of sight of Wolford's manor before speaking. He rode the extra horse that Andreas had optimistically brought and appeared none the worse for his imprisonment. His rich garments were soiled, but their gold embroidery and his blond hair sparkled so brilliantly in the light of the evening sun that a bit of dirt hardly mattered.

"He was agreeable because I promised to come back with the money within three days," Andreas said.

"I had made the same promise, but he was not agreeable with *me*."

"The difference may be that he believes I will indeed bring it."

Reginald's brow puckered. "A fine thing, when a man accepts a merchant's word over a fellow knight's."

Andreas barely resisted the urge to wipe Reginald's frown away with his fist. Reginald kept missing life's lessons, even to the point of death.

The frown left of its own accord, and Reginald's easy smile returned. "This is my sister's doing, isn't it? Your being here."

"You left her nowhere else to turn. There is hell to pay back in London, Reginald. If fate had not brought me to England now, Wolford would be eating you for dinner tomorrow."

"He never would have killed me. It was just a ruse on his part to get the money."

Andreas thought of the swarthy, angry lord with whom he had just negotiated. Reginald would have probably been laughing and joking to the end and been astonished as hell when the sword actually fell.

As they rode back to the town, they spoke of old times and pointless things. Andreas could see private worries growing in Reginald's mind despite their aimless conversation. They were reflected in his blue eyes and on his precise features and in the way he kept scratching the scalp beneath his golden hair.

"I am thinking that I should not return to London right away," he said as they entered the town. "It would make more sense for me to go elsewhere and procure the coin to pay those tradesmen."

"How would you do that?"

"I have a few plans afoot. Once they come together—"

"And your sister? Will you take her with you?"

"I would like to, but I don't see as I can. She will be better contented in London anyway."

"How will she eat? Where will she live?"

"Everyone likes her, and once she explains that I will return soon and pay the tallies, no one will put her out or let her starve. You can explain that to her when you are back in London, and she will understand."

"Well, she is here in this town, so *you* can explain it to her."

Reginald's face fell. "It will embarrass her to see me. I can guess the bargain she made with you, and—"

"Do not insult her. Do not forget that I am the one who still has the sword."

Andreas led the way to the inn and around the back to its stables.

"It would be best if I just leave," Reginald explained. "I do not care for long farewells. Women always weep so."

"Get off the horse, Reginald."

"I truly think that it would be better—"

"Off."

Looking too much like a petulant youth, Reginald dismounted. Andreas gestured him into the long shadow beneath the stable's eaves.

"If you are determined to leave, so be it. There is a ship's master in the Cinque Ports named Paul Knowles. He is always looking for swords to guard his cargo."

Reginald laughed indulgently. "Hardly fitting for me, Andreas. The lowest man at arms can do that duty."

"It is an honest living, but choose as you prefer. There are two other things that I want to settle with you, however. You have given Giselle the fright of her life, forced her to beg for money to save you, and now you intend to leave her to fend for herself. You will go up to her, and you will apologize for all of it."

None too happy, Reginald nodded his agreement on that part. "What is the second thing?"

"This."

Andreas swung his fist and crashed it into Reginald's charming, perfect face.

*When Giselle saw Andreas and Reginald ride down the* lane together, her heart lifted with relief that bordered on ecstasy.

She watched them from her window until they disappeared around the inn. She was grateful that Reginald was safe, but it was Andreas who absorbed her attention.

It took them a long time to come up to her. She paced impatiently, until finally she heard boots trudging up the wooden steps.

Reginald entered, smiling, confident, and handsome. His manner both reassured and irked her. He might be returning from a night at a tavern. Except for a new swelling under one eye, he appeared hale and fit.

Before he closed the door, she saw Andreas entering the chamber across the landing.

She joined her brother in an embrace. "Thank the saints that you are unharmed."

"It was churlish of Wolford to play such a game and give you such distress."

"The whole world knows that Wolford is a knave, so his demanding this ransom could not have surprised you."

"He and I got along well before. I thought he favored me and am disappointed in him."

"There are limits to any man's favor, Reginald."

"Still, I will never forgive him for making you humble yourself to procure the coin."

She did not miss that Reginald was making this Wolford's fault alone. It had always been thus with him, and probably always would be.

She looked up at the brother who had been the champion of her childhood and the measure of men in her youth. She saw him very clearly, for the first time. She envied him his childish belief in the future and in his rights. She would always love him, but she could never lie to herself about him again.

She told him what had transpired at the house. "What do we do now, Reginald?"

He gently extricated himself from her arms. "I must leave and make my fortune, Giselle. If I return to London I might be imprisoned, and how can I make it right if that happens?"

"You will take service and live by your sword?" That was something, at least. He had always resisted that option.

"It would be humiliating to do so, as I have often told you. I should be giving service, not taking it. However, if it isn't England . . . Flanders, perhaps . . ."

A shadow slid into her heart.

"It won't be for long, Giselle. You will see. I will be back before winter and make things right. Those pledges and tallies will wait until then."

They wouldn't wait. She had just explained that.

"Of course, if it is the only way, brother, that is how it must be."

"If I cannot return soon, I will send for you."

"I will come when you do."

He took her hands in his. Squeezing them, he smiled so warmly that she almost believed in him again. "I should go at once, while there is still light. Andreas will get you back to London. He will take care of you."

He appeared a tad sly as he said the last part.

She narrowed her eyes on him. "I will take care of myself while you are gone, Reginald."

He released her and patted her cheek. "Of course you will. You are a good girl."

She wanted to smack him. She itched to upbraid him for the bargain he had once offered Andreas and for assuming she had struck a similar one now.

Except that, in a way, she had.

Gazing at him, it did not matter. Reginald was leaving her. Suddenly, the years of love meant more than the recent discoveries. Nostalgic memories saddened her more than the truths she had learned.

She would let the old illusions live for a few more moments, until she gave them up forever.

Taking his face in her hands, she filled her memory with the sight of him and let her heart cry.

His smile cracked. His face fell. Swallowing hard, he stepped back. "I should be going."

Her eyes misted as he walked to the door.

He stopped. He stood there, with his back to her.

"I am sorry, Giselle."

He left.

# *Seven*

***She waited by the window for Reginald to appear on his*** horse down below. She stayed there, in the creeping silence and shadows of the night, as he rode away. From her high position she was able to keep him in sight as he galloped over the fields.

Finally, the deepening dusk absorbed him.

She blinked, and he disappeared completely.

She did not turn away from the window, but she knew she was not alone in the chamber. She had not heard Andreas enter, but she felt him behind her, close enough to offer invisible support.

"How did you get him out?"

"I convinced Wolford that I would bring the money in three days. It was not a ransom, but the amount Reginald had convinced him to invest in Sandro's scheme. Reginald had neglected to explain that the chance for great profit also meant the chance for great loss."

She narrowed her eyes on the distant spot where she

had last seen her brother. "I am never going to see him again, am I?"

"I think you will find him on your threshold someday. He always relied on you more than you did him."

"So, you bought his life. One hundred pounds is a large sum, even for you."

"It is a gift, and not to you, but to Reginald." He reached around and placed the stack of pledges on the sill. "However, the previous debts must be settled now."

She looked down at his hand lying upon those parchments. He was very close now, warming her shoulder and back.

Didn't he know that she was his even without those pledges? That settling them had little to do with what would happen?

"I want to burn these, Giselle. I do not want these debts standing between us. I do not want you obligated to me."

She smiled. It seemed he did know, after all. "Burn them, then."

"If I do, others will make claims on the house and property. You will lose it all."

"I have already lost it all."

"You must know that I would never actually take the house."

"I do know that, but I would prefer that notions of charity and debt not shadow our friendship. Burn them. If you are willing to take the loss, so am I."

He moved away, and she turned to see him bending to the low fire that had been lit to remove the evening chill. The parchments joined the flame, making it rise.

Andreas watched the debts disappear. He continued gazing into the hearth long after the fire had died back down.

She went over to him and saw his pensive expression. "What are you thinking?"

His arm embraced her shoulders then slid down to hold her more closely. "I am thinking that a good man would leave now and use the other chamber tonight."

A good woman would insist that he use the other chamber. She had no obligations to him now. No excuses.

But his embrace already had her blood pulsing faster and her body warming. Memories of last night, of the incredible physical pleasure, swam through her head until the pleasure returned as a real sensation.

He turned so that they faced each other, and the embrace pressed her to him. "I am also thinking that I am tired of being good where you are concerned. I desire you too much."

She was tired of being good, too. Tired of saving herself for the husband who would never come and for the future that had been a girlish dream. Her past had just disappeared on the horizon, and her future was for tomorrow. The present was here and now. For the next few hours this chamber and Andreas were her whole world.

His gaze and touch stirred delicious excitements, and she did not want to fight them. She did not care about anything but holding this man who made her feel alive and beautiful and safe. The warmth of his embrace dulled the heartache about Reginald and obscured her fears about the new life waiting in London.

Even the knowledge that she could not hold onto him became insignificant as the desire poured out of them both, changing the air. If anything, knowing that she could not have him forever made her want this even more.

The first kiss came slowly. Too slowly. He gave her time to change her mind. Impatiently, she rose on her toes and met him halfway, so the kiss was as much hers as his.

The new Andreas kissed her, but so did the old one. The way his mouth took hers, gently but demanding, and the way his arms dominated her, totally but carefully, contained the friendship of years and the passion of last night. He made her feel precious, something that he valued highly but was determined to possess.

Their bodies pressed so closely that they could not get closer. Kisses, wonderful kisses, heated her lips and skin and neck. Like a spiral of magic, the desire tightened and rose, pulling her to its center, making her senses swirl. She lost hold on her restraint and spun, spun, in the heady excitement.

She loved the way he held her. Touched her. His rough palm, warm and male and careful, on her face. His controlling arm across her back. His claiming caresses through her garments, pressing her hip and waist and thighs and back. She loved the gentle intimacy of his breath on her skin and hair and the alarming intimacy of his invasive kiss. Her body and soul wanted more of both, and the impatience returned. Their closeness wasn't enough; their kisses weren't enough.

Soundlessly, she cried her acceptance of the ascending madness. *Yes*, her mind chanted. *Yes*, her body demanded. *Yes*, her heart sang.

"Yes," her voice whispered when he held her head with both of his hands and asked a question with his eyes that needed no words.

He lifted her and carried her to the bed. Thrills of desire and fear slid down her body in tantalizing streaks.

He sat on the edge of the bed and began undressing her. "You should not be afraid. I know that you are still a maid. I am not going to hurt you."

Small pauses interrupted his words, as if he had to think to find the right ones in English. It reminded her of how he spoke the language when she first met him. The evidence that he had lost his smooth command of his English sent tenderness streaming out of her heart.

"I am not afraid." That was a lie. A delicious fear trembled through her, made more exciting by the closeness of his hands. He dragged the lacing of her gown down her body, level by level, until the narrow cloth of her robe parted to her hips, revealing her shift.

He laid his palm flat on her stomach. Its rough warmth

seemed to permeate all through her loins, as if he touched her womb. His caress rose up her body, creating a path of arousal. When it passed over her breast, her heart rose to her throat.

"I saw your body once. The second time I stayed at your house. I passed your little chamber while you were washing, and the door was ajar. I wanted you so much that I could not move."

His memory provoked one of her own. One of her standing by her washstand years ago, with her shift falling around her hips, and the strong sense that someone had paused by her door. A shocking excitement had pounded through her, and she also had been unable to move.

"I knew you were there, I think. I wanted you to look at me like that, I think."

What else had she wanted? What else had she pretended did not exist?

She looked at his face, handsome and shadowed in the dim light. For ten years her heart had filled with sweet longing as it did now whenever she saw him or thought of him.

She had called it friendship.

His hand covered her breast, gently but possessively. It was a claim of sorts. His expression hardened subtly. She knew there was no turning back.

She welcomed the kiss that demanded new rights. Caresses on her breast teased her toward abandon. He laid beside her, so that the intimacy of their embrace extended their whole lengths. A wonderful madness took possession of her, so that she knew only gratitude when he slid off her garments and exalted in a shocking glory when he looked at her naked body.

Desperate hunger and incredible sensations ruled her. She wanted . . . everything. A closeness that even his hand on her body did not satisfy. An entwining that surpassed their long embrace.

With fingers that would not obey her, she fumbled at

his garments, eager to feel the body under them. He broke their eternal kiss long enough to strip them off. The intimacy of holding him then, of having his naked warmth sealing her side and his skin beneath her hands, left her breathless.

That strong, wonderful hand stroked her whole body while he looked at her and kissed her breasts, her stomach, her thighs. He spoke lowly in his native tongue, but she understood the meaning if not the words. Desire and praise and tenderness were in his tone and his touch, and her own arousal developed layers of emotion in response.

He licked the tip of one breast. An arrow of amazing pleasure shot completely through her, making her arch in surprise. He used his mouth to transform that one arrow into a stream of sensation that flowed to a new hunger and desperation low and deep in her body. He slowly palmed the other breast, and she grew more frantic.

He spoke again, a quiet command, but it was his caress on her thighs that told her what he wanted. She parted her legs, and the vulnerable act alone jolted her passion to new heights. His touch sent her reeling. The pleasure became crazed and furious and centered on the soft, hidden place that he stroked and probed.

When he moved on top of her she clutched him to her, embracing him with her arms and thighs, holding his strength to her entire body. She did not mind the gentle pain at first and only gasped in shock when a sharper one brought an onslaught of glaring clarity.

She blinked and looked up at the face and shoulders above her and absorbed the profound sensation of being connected in ways that nothing could ever undo.

The tightness of his muscles and expression revealed his forced control. Passion lit his eyes, but so did a beautiful warmth. He kissed her carefully and spoke quietly in her ear.

He gazed down and must have seen her incomprehension. "I said that . . ." He paused, searching for his English amidst his body's distractions. "I said that I have wanted you from the first time I saw you."

He moved, and she did not mind the pain. It became submerged in a fullness of pleasure and joy that her heart could barely contain. The passion found her again, too, richer than before, deeper and drenched with happiness. When their joining turned less careful and then furious, she opened to the power of it all, holding him to her breast as his thrusts touched her womb and her soul.

He did not leave the bed afterward. The second chamber remained unused. He tucked her under the sheet and into his embrace and fell asleep beside her.

She stared at the night through the window, unable to sleep herself. This new experience, of lying beside him for hours, moved her in new ways. When they made love she had wanted to sing. Now she wanted to weep.

They had called it friendship for years, and tonight he had called it desire. She now knew the real name of the emotion in her own heart, however.

Love.

She was glad that she admitted that. It made the joy bittersweet, but wonderfully so. She was grateful that she had been given the gift of loving a man.

She would lose everything else, even him, but this love was hers to keep forever. She would never be impoverished.

# Eight

*"I will need a fresh horse, Stefan. Also, take this to the* counting house and retrieve one hundred pounds from the trading account that they hold for me."

Stefan's mouth pursed as he accepted the note. "Can I assume that these funds do not go to Alberti?"

"You can assume what you like."

"You must go and see him today. You said that you would two nights ago, and he expects you. You cannot leave the city again and have him wondering . . . that is, he may have heard about this woman of yours."

Andreas pulled on his boots and swallowed his inclination to remind Stefan of his place. The disadvantage of having a brother as your clerk was that he felt free to speak boldly. "Whatever he has heard, he will not care. Our arrangements are really about a trading network, not a marriage. He understands that. Everyone understands that."

Even Giselle understood that. Not once had she mentioned his marriage negotiations, although surely she knew of them. All of London probably knew, and Narni had referred to it in her presence.

Of course she had not spoken of it. What could she say? What could either of them say? It was the way of the world. If she had married, it would have been about land, not ships, but it would have been the same.

As he finished dressing in clean garments, he thought about the years ahead, when he would be bound to one woman but hungering for another. He had already lived that life once. It appeared that it was to be his fate forever.

He went to the window and looked down on the city. He peered at the spot of garden several lanes over. The next time he came to London she would not be sitting there. The breeze would not carry the sounds of her lute.

Where would she be instead? Her future was precarious. Burning those pledges had been a gallant but selfish gesture. A necessary one, however, for both their sakes. He had not wanted her owing him anything, least of all her body.

Thoughts of that body, of her warmth and beauty, filled his head. He closed his eyes and experienced again the raging desire and delirious pleasure. But the memory that had stayed with him ever since, that he could not get out of his mind, was the way she looked as she woke in the morning, and the burst of joy that had saturated him when she smiled and snuggled closer.

He would take care of her. He would buy her a different house and arrange an income for her. He would explain it was not payment, that he was not keeping her. He would make her understand that he could not leave her destitute, in the name of their old friendship and not because of last night.

And whenever he visited London, he would once more walk down a lane with the heart of a man who was truly coming home.

"I will return for the coin soon, Stefan. You had better

pay two swordsmen to accompany me as well. With that much money, I may need some protection on the road."

*He found Giselle in her hall, standing on a stool in front* of the tapestry.

"Help me get this down."

"Why?"

"You burned the pledge that included it, and no one else had one on it. That means it is still mine. I want you to sell it for me, so that I can give you the money to bring Wolford."

"I said that will be a gift to Reginald."

She began heaving the iron bar from the wall. He reached up to take its weight in his own hands.

"I know you said that, but in truth the gift is to me. One more debt. One more obligation." She busied herself with sliding the tapestry's looped braids off the bar. "I would prefer to pay the sum myself. I gave myself to you with a pure heart, and I am glad I did. However, after you marry again, my memory of that bed will be all that I keep of you. I do not want what happened to be tainted in the years ahead by any thoughts that I . . . whored. Can you understand that?"

He could, too well.

"Do you know someone who will buy it and give me what it is worth?"

He rolled the tapestry and folded it into thirds. Made of silk as it was, it easily formed a compact bundle. "I know of a man who will be happy to buy it."

"Not you, Andreas. Please, do not—"

"Not me."

He kissed her, then carried the tapestry out of the house. Giselle's resolve to sell it had told him everything he needed to know.

She had told him that last night had been all that he

thought it had been, and that she wanted to preserve its memory.

She had told him that she would not lie with him in adultery.

Of course she wouldn't.

She had also told him that she would face the future on her own. She was not going to let him take care of her.

***"One hundred pounds? You are a madman, or else you*** think I am England's biggest fool." John Hastings struck an insulted pose, crossing his thick arms over his chest. He nodded toward the tapestry spread out on his table. "Without the flaw, maybe thirty pounds, but with that interruption you will be lucky to see half that much."

"There is a poignant story attached to that flaw. The woman who wove it was given in marriage to a man she did not love. The weaving remained unfinished until her husband died and she returned to her girlhood love."

"Oh, horses' turds. Traders always come up with sweet tales to explain bad goods. I'll give you twenty, and only because you are a friend."

"The lady who owns it was told it is worth a hundred, so that is the price."

"What idiot told her such a thing?"

*An idiot who wanted her to believe she owned something of great value so that she would think she had some security.* Andreas began folding the tapestry. "A pity that you do not favor it. I will find another merchant who appreciates its age and quality."

"I hope you are not angry, Andreas. It is very lovely, just not worth such a high sum. Surely you know that."

"I am not angry at all. Our friendship will continue as before. When I next visit London, I will be sure to come see you. I should be back before winter. I expect to bring in a shipment of flax soon, as well as some furs."

John's lids lowered. His mouth twitched. "What kind of furs?"

"Sables from the Rus. They are rare and fetch astonishing prices with the nobility."

"That is what I heard that worthless fool Reginald was going to bring in with Sandro. No one ever saw a single pelt."

"I am not Reginald."

Andreas continued slowly folding the tapestry. John uncrossed his arms and casually paced around the table.

"Have you arranged the sale of these furs?"

Andreas lifted the tapestry and shook it in front of John's face to remove the wrinkles.

He laid it down on the table and smoothed it with his hand.

"I have been so occupied that I have not had time to strike a bargain with any London merchant yet. Well, it can wait until I come back. There are many men who will want such a cargo."

He began to roll up the tapestry.

John's hand descended to stroke the silk, stopping him.

"It really is a very lovely weaving," John said. "Most artful. Very unique. I find myself growing fond of it."

"Did I mention the story attached to the interruption?"

"Yes. Touching. I am so moved that I might buy it for myself. How much did you say?"

"One hundred pounds. If you keep it yourself, I might offer to buy it back from you someday. That is how much I favor it, and I am pleased to see that you appreciate its beauty."

"It is really magnificent. I must have it. Of course, if you should ever want to buy it back, I would be hard-pressed to refuse a good friend. I would be even harder-pressed to refuse a partner in a fur trade."

Andreas smiled. "It sounds as though the bargain is struck, John."

He waited while John retrieved the silver from the hiding places where he kept his coin. A long time later Andreas tied the heavy chest to the back of his horse.

He sent word to Giselle that he would leave at once to deliver the money.

From his place in the saddle, he could see some of the masts of the ships at the docks. Moored among them would be the long, low, sleek galleys of the Venetians.

He gazed in that direction, not moving his horse.

A future he had planned and built for years waited on one of those galleys. A dream beckoned that he had constructed as a youth and then pursued as a man. It was a magnificent dream, in which wealth was the least of the rewards. The achievement itself would be the true prize, and the fame would be the enduring legacy.

The chest pressed against his back, reminding him of Giselle. Memories of their lovemaking flooded his mind. The image of her face, aglow with trusting passion, hung in front of him.

He turned his horse, fully aware of what he would be giving up.

Before he returned to his house to fetch the fresh mount and the guards, he stopped at a Venetian galley moored at the docks, in order to finally visit with Signore Alberti.

# Nine

*Giselle sat on the carved bench with her back pressed to* the edge of the table behind her. She gazed at the wall across the chamber. The tapestry had hung there for so long that now, even after three days, it startled her to see only plaster and timbers instead of silken vines of red and gold.

She was not thinking about the tapestry, however. Her eyes might fix on that wall, but her head was elsewhere, in a different chamber. She was looking up at the face of a man she had known for years, as passion stripped her heart and laid bare a hidden love.

Andreas had filled her thoughts since he walked out of the house carrying the tapestry. Filled her soul. The warmest happiness accompanied those images and memories, but a poignant nostalgia was creeping in already.

He absorbed her so completely that it did not startle her to find him standing at the threshold. She had not heard his steps approach. He was simply there suddenly, and it was right and natural that he should be.

The joy sparkled, as it had so many times. Only now she understood what it meant.

He came over and sat beside her, so that the two of them faced the blank wall.

"It is done?" she asked.

"Wolford is appeased. We even dined together. Reginald was right. His wine is sour." He gestured to the wall. "You should not have sold it. It was not necessary, and I know what it meant to you."

It *had* been necessary. "I find that I do not miss it. In fact, I think I am glad that it is gone. I have been sitting here, waiting to be sad, but instead whenever I see that empty spot my heart rises instead of falls. It is the oddest reaction. Almost triumphant."

"It is a very odd reaction. That tapestry wove you to your heritage and place. It was a banner proclaiming who you should be."

"I never thought of it that way, but perhaps you saw more clearly than I did. Maybe I thought of that interruption as the years I lived here in London and of the continuation as the future when my family would be restored. I know that will never happen now, and I am glad to let that expectation die. It feels good to be free of it."

He took her hand in his. "I am relieved if you do not grieve for it."

"The tapestry?"

"The expectation."

"I grieve for nothing. I should, but I don't. I should be afraid, too, but I'm not." She turned her attention from the wall to him. His own gaze rested on their hands, but his handsome profile attracted hers. "I have been thinking these last two days about what I will do now. I have realized that I have several choices and that my situation is not very dire at all."

"It will be some months before the others realize I will not be taking the property. It will not be until I return that anyone demands to see the pledges, to learn if they still stand. You do not have to do anything right away."

"All the same, I must consider my future."

"What choices do you see?"

She crooked her leg up on the bench so she faced him and could enjoy watching his thoughtful gaze resting on their connected hands. "Well, I have a kinsman in the north, east of York, who is my father's cousin. They broke with each other because of the rebellion, but I can go there. I am his blood, and he would give me a place, I'm sure."

"I do not like that choice. This kinsman will marry you off to some small landowner to be free of the cost of you. Also, York is far from London, or any port."

Far from the England that he visited was what he meant. It touched her that it mattered to him, but in the years ahead it no longer would. She suspected that desire faded quickly once fulfilled. He had wanted her for ten years, but two years hence he probably would not think of her much anymore.

She would be the one who remembered.

"There also is Lady Agatha. She spends many months here in her London house and has always been a friend to me. She guessed my situation, I think, and has several times asked me to join her household to help educate her daughters."

"You mean that she has asked you to be a servant."

"Not truly a servant."

"Most *truly* a servant, no matter where you sleep or if you take your board at her high table. But without the freedom of a servant, since you will be tied to that hearth by your blood and need. Better to go serve in a tavern, where the pay is in coin and your life is your own."

His reaction annoyed her. These choices she had discovered during the last days' contemplation had given her hope and confidence. Andreas appeared determined to belittle them.

"I do not approve of these options that you have found," he said.

"That is obvious."

"You must find another."

"There is no other."

His head turned. The way he looked at her made her heart flutter.

She knew what he was thinking.

"At least, there is no other that is respectable," she said quietly.

He reached out, and with great care slowly brushed some errant hairs away from the sides of her face. "That is not true. There is one other choice that is respectable enough. You could marry me."

His words stunned her. She could not move, not even to blink. She just stared at him as his hands gently grazed her cheeks.

It was an astonishing proposal. Tempting and mesmerizing. Reckless and impossible. In the silence of her daze, her heart filled with the purest, lovely emotion and then fell with excruciating pain, all in one instant.

He was being as impractical and foolish as Reginald.

"Signore Alberti . . ."

"I have told him that my marriage to his daughter will not happen."

"But the trading alliance . . ."

"It was too ambitious. My pride wanted it, and for all the wrong reasons. Alberti and I will continue to be friends and to enrich each other."

This new proposal of marriage was being made for all the wrong reasons, too. She turned her face away from his gaze and touch.

"Look what I have done. I came to you with my problem, and now you feel obligated enough that you will put aside an alliance that you have been planning for years.

This is very kind of you, Andreas, but you do not have to do it. I knew in that chamber that a marriage was impossible, and I did not give myself with that expectation."

"I am not being kind. I am being selfish. I want you for myself. I do not make this offer under obligation, but with the excitement of a boy. I do not want you living with some kinsman and maybe given to some other man. I do not want you with Lady Agatha, at a house where I am not welcome because my trade is scorned as base. I want you in my home in Bremen and with me on my ship when I journey back here. When I walk down a lane to my house, I want your arms and body waiting for me, and your eyes filling with their warm lights when I enter through the threshold. All the Venetian gold in the world cannot purchase any of that, Giselle."

"The excitement of a boy quickly dims, Andreas. The luster of Venetian gold never does."

His fingers closed on her chin and turned her face back so she had to look at him. "I could have settled the marriage negotiations with Alberti months ago, Giselle. His agent was in Hamburg, and it could have all been done there, by proxy. I insisted on coming here to meet with him personally, however. I think my heart secretly knew what it really wanted and was hoping that something would happen to bring you and me together again before I committed myself. And something did. I will thank God for Reginald's recklessness until the day I die."

He stunned her again. Aching hope almost left her speechless. Her love wanted to grab hold of a future with him. If she had still been a girl, ignorant of the world, she would gladly surrender to that emotion. Her heart wanted to. Cried to.

"Your family will hate me. I am impoverished."

"There are many ways to be impoverished, and lacking property and coin is only one of them."

"It is the one that matters in marriage. I have nothing to bring you."

"You bring me the woman whom I have loved for years. If you also bring me the chance that I will have your love in return, that is enough."

Love. He had been alluding to that, but there it was, casually stated, as if they had spoken of it many times before.

Maybe they had. Not in words, but in the joy that accompanied his returns and in the quiet hours by the hearth or in her garden. And in the soulful passion that they had shared in that Essex bed.

His gaze mesmerized her. Lights of warmth and passion, of the old Andreas and the new, burned in them. So did the determination of a man who had decided to take what he wanted.

Her heart was so full she thought it would burst. "You already have my love in return, Andreas. And not only the love of a friend."

He pulled her into his arms, surrounding her, claiming her.

She had not been doing well keeping her hope contained, and now it overflowed. He kissed her and it became a flood, carrying away her misgivings.

His embrace warmed her like a toasty hearth on a winter day. She shed her worries and fears like so many garments that had protected her from the chill. His kisses gave excitement and love and safety all at once. The bliss filled her so completely that tears blurred her eyes.

He noticed and kissed at a line of wetness on her cheek. "What is this?"

"Happiness. Joy at learning that you love me as I love you."

"I told you that night that I have loved and wanted you since the first time I saw you."

"You said nothing of love."

"Didn't I? Well, I discovered that my English is not so good at such moments. I have had little practice in speaking of love in any language, and I was very distracted that night." He rose and held out his hand. "Come up to bed with me. I promise to speak the words correctly this time."

She took his hand and rose on her toes to kiss him. "If I am to live in Bremen, maybe you should teach them to me in your language."

He caressed her face. "*Ich liebe dich.* I love you."

"*Ich liebe dich.*"

"*Meine Liebe.* My love." He kissed her cheek. "*Meine Freundin.*"

"*Meine Freundin?*"

"My friend."

As Andreas led her to the stairs, he looked to the wall where the tapestry used to hang. Giselle had said that she was glad it was gone, but that would pass. She would not mind when he bought it back from John Hastings. He had planned to do that anyway, but it would be essential now.

The tapestry with the interrupted weaving belonged in their home.

# Dragonswan

Sherrilyn Kenyon

# One

*Richmond, Virginia*

***"Be kind to dragons, for thou art crunchy when roasted*** and taste good with ketchup."

Dr. Channon MacRae paused in her note-taking and arched a brow at the peculiar comment. She'd been staring at the famous Dragon Tapestry for hours, trying to decipher the Old English symbolism, and in all this time no one had disturbed her.

Not until now.

With her most irritated look, she pulled her pen away from her notepad and turned.

Then she gaped.

No annoying, irreverent little man here. He was a tall, mind-blowingly sexy god who dominated the small museum room with a presence so powerful that she wondered how on earth he had entered the building without shaking it to its foundations.

Never in her life had she beheld anything like him or the seductive smile he flashed at her.

Good grief, she couldn't take her eyes off him.

Standing at least six feet five, he towered over her average height. His long black hair was pulled back into a sleek ponytail, and he wore an expensively tailored black suit and overcoat that seemed at odds with his unorthodox hair yet perfectly fitting with his regal aura.

But the most peculiar thing of all was the tattoo covering the left half of his face. A faded dark green, it spiraled and curled from his hairline to his chin like some ancient symbol.

On anyone else such a mark would be freakish or strange, but this man wore it with dignity and presence—like a proud birthright.

Yet it was his eyes that captivated her most. A rich, deep, greenish-gold, they were filled with such warm intelligence and vitality that it left her completely breathless.

His grin was both boyish and roguish and framed by inviting dimples that enchanted her. "Rendered you speechless, eh?"

She loved the sound of his voice, which was laced with an accent she couldn't quite place. It seemed a unique blending of the British and Greek. Not to mention, deep and provocative.

"Not quite speechless," she said, resisting the urge to smile back at him. "I'm just wondering why you would say such a thing."

He shrugged his broad shoulders nonchalantly as his golden gaze dropped to her lips, making her want to lick them. Worse, his prolonged stare sent a rush of desire coiling though her.

Suddenly, it was so extremely warm in this little glass room that she half expected the gallery windows to fog up.

He folded his hands casually behind his back, yet he seemed coiled for action, as if he were ready and alert to take on anyone who threatened him.

What a strange image to have . . .

When he spoke again, his deep voice was even more seductive and enticing than it had been before, almost as if it were weaving some kind of magical spell around her. "You had such a serious frown while you were staring at the tapestry that it made me wonder what you would look like with a smile in its place."

Oh, the man was beguiling. And just a little too cocksure of his appeal, judging by his arrogant stance. No doubt he could get any woman who caught his eye.

Channon swallowed at the thought as she glanced down at her tan corduroy jumper and her hips, which were not the fashionable, narrow kind. She'd never been the type of woman who drew the notice of a man like this. She'd been lucky if her average looks ever garnered her a second glance at all.

Mr. Do-Me-Right-Now must have lost a bet or something. Why else would he be speaking to her?

Still, there was an air of danger, intrigue, and power about him. But none of deceit. He appeared honest and, strangely enough, interested in her.

How could that be?

"Yes, well," she said, taking a step to her left as she closed her pad and slid her pen down the spiral coil, "I don't make it my habit to converse with strangers, so if you'll excuse me . . ."

"Sebastian."

Startled by his response, she paused and looked up. "What?"

"My name is Sebastian." He held his hand out to her. "Sebastian Kattalakis. And you are?"

*Completely stunned and amazed that you're talking to me.*

She blinked the thought away. "Channon," she said before she could stop herself. "Shannon with a C."

His gaze burned her while a small smile hovered at the edges of those well-shaped lips and he flashed the tiniest bit of his dimples. There was an indescribable masculine aura about him that seemed to say he would be far more at home on some ancient battlefield than locked inside this museum.

He took her cold hand into his large, warm one. "So very pleased to meet you, Shannon with a C."

He kissed her knuckles like some gallant knight of long ago. Her heart pounded at the feel of his hot breath against her skin, of his warm lips on her flesh. It was all she could do not to moan from the sheer pleasure of it.

No man had ever treated her this way—like some treasured lady to be quested for.

She felt oddly beautiful around him. Desirable.

"Tell me, Channon," he said, releasing her hand and glancing from her to the tapestry. "What has you so interested in this?"

Channon looked back at it and the intricate embroidery that covered the yellowed linen. Honestly, she didn't know. Since she'd first seen it as a little girl, she'd been in love with this ancient masterpiece. She'd spent years studying the detailed dragon fable that started with the birth of a male infant and a dragon and moved forward through ten feet of fabric.

Scholars had written countless papers on their theories of its origin. She, herself, had done her dissertation on it, trying to link it to the tales of King Arthur or to Celtic tradition.

No one knew where the tapestry had come from or even what story it related to. For that matter, no one knew who had won the fight between the dragon and the warrior.

That was what intrigued her most of all.

"I wish I knew how it ended."

He flexed his jaw. "The story has no ending. The battle between the dragon and the man lives on unto today."

She frowned at him. He appeared serious. "You think so?"

"What?" he asked good-naturedly. "You don't believe me?"

"Let's just say I have a hefty dose of doubt."

He took a step forward, and again his fierce, manly presence overwhelmed her and sent a jolt of desire through her. "Hmmm, a hefty dose of doubt," he said, his voice barely more than a low, deep growl. "I wonder what I could do to make you believe?"

She should step back, she knew it. Yet she couldn't make her feet cooperate. His clean, spicy scent invaded her head and weakened her knees.

What was it about this man that made her want to stand here talking to him?

Oh, to heck with that. What she really wanted to do was jump his delectable bones. To cup that handsome face of his in her hands and kiss his lips until she was drunk from his taste.

There was something seriously wrong here.

*Mayday. Mayday.*

"Why are you here?" she asked, trying to keep her lecherous thoughts at bay. "You hardly look like the type to study medieval relics."

A wicked gleam came into his eyes. "I'm here to steal it."

She scoffed at the idea, even though something inside her said it wouldn't be too much of a stretch to buy that explanation. "Are you really?"

"Of course. Why else would I be here?"

"Why else, indeed?"

Sebastian didn't know what it was about this woman that drew him so powerfully. He was involved in grave matters that required his full attention, yet for the life of him, he couldn't take his gaze from her.

She wore her honey-brown hair swept up so that it cascaded in riotous waves from a silver clip of old Welsh design. Several strands of it had come free of the clip to dangle haphazardly around her face as if the strands had a life of their own.

How he longed to set free that hair and feel it sliding through his fingers and brushing against his naked chest.

He dropped his gaze down over her lush, full body and stifled his smile. Her dark blue shirt wasn't buttoned properly and her socks didn't match.

Still, she drove him crazy with desire.

She wasn't the kind of woman who normally drew his interest, and yet . . .

He was beguiled by her and her crystal blue gaze that glowed with warm curiosity and intelligence. He longed to sample her full, moist lips, to bury his face in the hollow of her throat where he could drink in her scent.

Gods, how he yearned for her. It was a need borne of such desperation that he wondered what kept him from taking her into his arms right now and satisfying his curiosity.

He'd never been the kind of man to deny himself carnal pleasures—especially not when the beast inside him was stirred. And this woman stirred that deadly part of him to a dangerous level.

Sebastian had only come into the museum to get the lay of it for tonight and to find out where they housed the tapestry. He hadn't been looking for a woman to pass the lonely night with until he could return home where he would be . . . well, lonely again.

However, he still had hours before he could leave. Hours that he would much rather spend gazing into her eyes than waiting in his hotel room.

"Would you care to join me for a drink?" he asked.

She looked startled by his question. But then he seemed to have that effect on her. She was nervous around him, a bit jumpy, and he longed to set her at ease.

"I don't go out with men I don't know."

"How can you get to know me unless you . . ."

"Really, Mr. Kat—"

"Sebastian."

She shook her head at him. "You are persistent, aren't you?"

She had no idea.

Suppressing the predator inside him, Sebastian put his hands in his pockets to keep from reaching out to her and scaring her off. "I'm afraid it's ingrained in me. When I see something I want, I go after it."

She arched a brow at that and gave him a suspicious look. "Why on earth would you want to talk to me?"

He was aghast at her question. "My lady, do you not own a mirror?"

"Yes, but it's not an enchanted one." She turned away from him and started away.

Moving with the incredible speed of his kind, Sebastian pulled her to a stop.

"Look, Channon," he said gently. "I fear I have bungled this. I just . . ." He stopped and tried to think of the best way to keep her with him for a while longer.

She looked to his hand, which still gripped her elbow. He reluctantly let go, even though every part of his soul screamed for him to hold her by his side, regardless of the consequences. She was a woman with her own mind. And the first law of his people ran through his head: Nothing a woman gives is worth having unless she gives it of her own free will.

It was the one law not even he would break.

"You what?" she asked softly.

Sebastian drew a deep breath as he fought down the animal part of himself that wanted her regardless of right or laws, the part of him that snarled with a need so fierce that it scared him.

He forced a charming smile to his lips. "You seem like a very nice person, and there are so few of you in this world that I would like to spend a few minutes with you. Maybe some of it might rub off."

Channon laughed in spite of herself.

"Ah," he teased, "so you *can* smile."

"I can smile."

"Will you join me?" he asked. "There's a restaurant on the corner. We can walk there, in plain sight of the world. I promise, I won't bite unless you ask me to."

Channon frowned lightly at him and his quirky humor. What was it about him that made him so irresistible? It was unnatural. "I don't know about this."

"Look, I promise I'm not psychotic. Eccentric and idiosyncratic, but not psychotic."

She still wasn't completely sure about that. "I'll bet the prisons are full of men who have told women that."

"I would *never* hurt a woman, least of all you."

There was such sincerity in his voice that she believed him. Even more convincing, she didn't feel any inner warnings, no little voice in her head telling her to run.

Instead, she was drawn to him and felt a most peculiar kind of serenity in his presence, almost as if she were supposed to be with him. "Down the street?"

"Yes." He offered her his arm. "C'mon. I promise I'll keep my fangs hidden and my mind control to myself."

Channon had never done anything like this in her life. She was a woman who had to know a guy for a long time before she'd even consider a date.

Yet she found herself pulling on her coat and placing her hand in the crook of his arm, where she felt a muscle so taut and well formed that it sent a jolt through her.

By the feel of that arm, she could tell his fashionable black suit and overcoat hid one incredible body.

"You seem so different," she said as he walked her out of the room. "Something about you is very Old World."

He opened the glass door that led to the museum's foyer. "*Old* being the operative word."

"And yet you're very modern."

"A Renaissance man trapped between cultures."

"Is that what you are?"

He cast a playful sideways look to her. "Honestly?"

"Yes."

"I'm a dragon slayer."

She laughed out loud.

He scoffed. "Again you don't believe me."

"Let's just say it's no wonder you said you wanted to steal the tapestry. I suppose there's not much call for slaying a mythological beast, especially in this day and age."

Those greenish-gold eyes teased her unmercifully. "You don't believe in dragons?"

"No, of course not."

He tsked at her. "You are so skeptical."

"I'm practical."

Sebastian ran his tongue over his teeth as a sly half-smile curved his lips. A practical woman who didn't believe in dragons yet studied dragon tapestries and wore a misbuttoned shirt. Surely there wasn't another soul like her in any time or place. And she had the strangest effect on his body.

He was already hard for her, and they were barely touching. Her grip on his arm was light and delicate, as if she was ready to flee him at any moment.

That was the last thing he wanted, and that surprised him most of all.

A reclusive person, he only interacted with others when his physical needs overrode his desire for solitude. Even then, those encounters were brief and limited. He took his lovers for one night, making sure they were as well sated as he, then he quickly returned to his solitary world.

He'd never dawdled with idle conversation. Never really cared to get to know more about a woman than her name and the way she liked to be touched.

But Channon was different. He liked the cadence of her voice and the way her eyes sparkled when she talked. Most of all, he liked the way her smile lit up her entire face when she looked at him.

And the sound of her laughter . . . He doubted if the angels in heaven could make a more precious melody.

Sebastian opened the door to the dark restaurant and held it for her while she entered. As she swept past him, he let his gaze travel down the back of her body. He hardened even more.

What he wouldn't give to have her warm and naked in his arms so that he could run his hands down her full curves, nibble the flesh of her neck, and hold her to him as he slowly slid himself deep inside her while she writhed to his touch.

Sebastian forced himself to look away from Channon and to speak to the hostess. He sent a mental command to the unknown woman to sit them in a secluded corner. He wanted privacy with Channon.

How he wished he'd met her sooner. He'd been in this cursed city for well over a week, waiting for the opportunity to go home, where if not the comfort of warmth, he at least had the comfort of familiarity. He'd spent his nights in this city alone, prowling the streets restlessly as he bided his time.

At dawn, he would have to leave. But until then, he intended to spend as much time with Channon as he could, letting her company ease the loneliness inside him, ease the pain in his heart that had burned him for most of his life.

Channon followed the hostess through the restaurant, but all the while she was aware of Sebastian behind her—aware of his hot, predatorial gaze on her body and the way he seemed to want to devour her.

But even more unbelievable was the fact that she wanted to devour *him.* No man had ever made her feel so much like a woman or made her want to spend hours exploring his body with her hands and mouth.

"You're nervous again," he said after they were seated in a dark corner in the back of the pub.

She glanced up from the menu to catch sight of those greenish-gold eyes that reminded her of some feral beast. "You are incredibly perceptive."

He inclined his head toward her. "I've been accused of worse."

"I'll bet you have," she teased back. Indeed, he had the presence of an outlaw. Dangerous, dark, seductive. "Are you really a thief?"

"Define the term *thief*."

She laughed even though she wasn't quite sure if he was joking or serious.

"So tell me," he said as the waitress brought their drinks, "what do you do for a living, Shannon with a C?"

She thanked the waitress for her Coke, then looked to Sebastian to see how he would deal with her occupation. Most men were a bit intimidated by her job, though she'd never been able to figure out why. "I'm a history professor at the University of Virginia."

"Impressive," he said, his face genuinely interested. "What cultures and times do you specialize in?"

She was amazed he knew anything about her job. "Mostly preNorman Britain."

"Ah. Hwæt wē Gār-Dena in geār-dagum Þēod-cyninga Þrym gefrūnon, hū ðā æÞhelingas ellen fremedon."

Channon was floored by his Old English. He spoke it as if he'd been born to it. Imagine a man so handsome knowing a subject so dear to her heart.

She offered him the translation. "So. The Spear-Danes in days gone by and the kings who ruled them had courage and greatness. We have heard of those princes' heroic campaigns."

His inclined his head to her. "You know your *Beowulf* well."

"I've studied Old English extensively, which, given my job, makes sense. But you don't strike me as a historian."

"I'm not. Rather, I'm a sort of reenactor."

That explained the way he looked. Now his presence in the museum and knightly air of authority made sense to her.

"Is your study of the Middle Ages what had you in the museum today?" he asked.

She nodded. "I've studied the tapestry for years. I want to be the person who finally unravels the mystery behind it."

"What would you like to know?"

"Who made it and why? Where the story of it comes from. For that matter, I would love to know how the museum got it. They have no record of when they acquired it or from whom it was purchased."

His automatic answers surprised her. "They bought it in 1926 from an anonymous collector for fifty thousand dollars. As for the rest, it was made by a woman named Antiphone back in seventh-century Britain. It's the story of her grandfather and his brother and their eternal struggle between good and evil."

His gaze was so sincere that she could almost believe him. In a strange way, it made sense, since the tapestry had no ending.

But she knew better. "Antiphone, huh?"

He shook his head. "You just don't believe anything I tell you, do you?"

"Why, kind sir," she said impishly with a mock English accent. " 'Tis not that I don't believe you, but as a historian I must align myself with fact. Have you any proof of this Antiphone or transaction?"

"I do, but I somehow doubt you would appreciate my showing it to you."

"And why is that?"

"It would scare the life out of you."

Channon sat back at that, unsure of how to take it. She didn't really know what to make of the man sitting across from her. He kept her on edge all the while he lured her toward his danger. Lured her against all her reason.

They remained quiet as their food was placed on the table.

While they ate, Channon studied him. The candlelight in the pub danced in his eyes, making them glow like a cat's. His hands were strong and callused—the hands of a man who was used to hard work—yet he had the air of wealth and privilege, the air of a powerful man who made his own rules.

He was a total enigma, a walking dichotomy who made her feel both safe and threatened.

"Tell me, Channon," he said suddenly, "do you like teaching?"

"Some days. But it's the research I like best. I love digging through old manuscripts and trying to piece together the past."

He gave a short half laugh. "No offense, but that sounds incredibly boring."

"I imagine dragon-slaying is much more action-oriented."

"Yes, it is. Every moment is completely unpredictable."

She wiped her mouth as she watched him eat with perfect European table manners. He was definitely cultured, yet he seemed oddly barbaric. "So, how do you kill a dragon?"

"With a very sharp sword."

She shook her head at him. "Yes, but do you call him out? Do you go to him . . . ?"

"The easiest way is to sneak up on him."

"And pray he doesn't wake up?"

"Well, it makes it more challenging if he does."

Channon smiled. She was so drawn to that infectious wit of his. Especially since he didn't seem to notice the women around them who were ogling him while they ate. It was as if he could only see her.

As a rule, she stunk at this whole male-female thing. Her last boyfriend, a D.C. correspondent, had educated her well on every personal and physical flaw she possessed. The last thing she was looking for was another relationship in which she wasn't on equal terms with the man.

For her next love interest, she wanted someone just like her—a historian of average looks whose life revolved around research. Two comfortable peas in a pod.

She wasn't looking for some hot, mysterious stranger who made her blood burn with desire.

*Channon, would you listen to yourself and what you're saying! You are insane not to want this man!*

Perhaps. But things like this never happened to her.

"You know," she said to him, "I keep having this really weird feeling that you're going to take me someplace later and tie me up naked so that your friends can come laugh at me."

He arched a brow at her. "Does that happen to you often?"

"No, never, but this night has the makings for a *Twilight Zone* episode."

"I promise no Rod Serling voice-overs. You're safe with me."

And for some reason that made absolutely no sense whatsoever, she believed him.

Channon spent the next few hours having the dinner and conversation of her life. Sebastian was incredibly easy to talk to. Worse, he set her hormones on fire.

The longer they were together and the more laughs they shared, and the more incredible he seemed.

She glanced at her watch and gasped. "Did you know it's almost midnight?"

He checked his watch.

"I hate to cut this short," she said, placing her napkin on the table and sliding her chair back, "but I have to go or I'll never get a taxi out of here."

He placed his hand lightly on her arm to keep her at the table. "Why don't you let me drive you home?"

Channon started to protest, but something inside her refused. After the evening they had spent together, she felt oddly at ease with him. There was an aura about him that was so comforting, so open and welcoming.

He was like a long lost friend.

"Okay," she said, relaxing.

He paid for their food. Then he helped her up and into her coat and led her from the restaurant.

Channon didn't speak as they made their way toward his car down the street, but she felt his magnetic, masculine presence with every single cell of her body.

Though not a social butterfly by any account, she'd had plenty of dates in her life. She'd had a number of boyfriends and even a fiancé, but none of them had ever made her feel the way this stranger did.

Like he fit some missing part of her soul.

*Girl, you are crazy.*

She must be.

Channon paused as they neared his sporty gray Lexus. "Someone travels in style."

Winking devilishly at her, Sebastian opened the car door. "Well, I would turn into a dragon and fly you home, but something tells me you would protest."

"No doubt. I imagine the scales would also chafe my skin."

"True. Not to mention, I once learned the hard way that they really do call the military out on you. You know, fighter jets are hard to dodge when you have a forty-foot wingspan." He closed her door and walked to his side of the car.

She laughed yet again, but then she'd been doing that most of the night. Goodness, she *really* liked this man.

Sebastian got into the car and felt his body jerk the instant they were locked inside together. Her feminine scent permeated his head. She was so close to him now that he could almost taste her.

All night long he had listened to the dulcet sound of her smooth Southern drawl, watched her tongue and lips move as he imagined what they would feel like on his body, imagined her in his arms while he made love to her until she cried out from pleasure.

His attraction to her stunned him. Why did he have to feel this now, when he couldn't afford to stay in her time and explore more of her?

Cursed Fates. How they loved to tamper in mortal lives.

Pushing the thought out of his mind, he drove her to the hotel where she was staying.

"You don't live here?" he asked as he parked in the lot.

"Just here for the weekend to study the tapestry." She unbuckled her seat belt.

Sebastian got out and opened her door, then walked her to her room.

Channon hesitated at the door as she looked up at him and the searing heat in his captivating eyes. The man was so hot and sexy in the most dangerous of ways.

She wondered if she would ever see him again. He hadn't asked for her number. Not even her email.

Damn.

"Thank you," she said. "I had a really good time tonight."

"I did, too. Thanks for joining me."

*Kiss me.* The words rushed across her mind unexpectedly. She really wanted to know what this man felt like against her.

To her amazement, she found out as he pulled her into his arms and covered her lips with his.

Sebastian growled at the feel of her as he fisted his hands against her back. He clutched her to him as every fiber of his body burned and ached to possess her. Her tongue swept against his, teasing him, tormenting him.

She brushed her hand against the nape of his neck, sending chills all over his body, making him so hard for her that he throbbed painfully. He closed his eyes while he let all of his senses experience her. Her mouth tasted of honey, and her hands were soft and warm against his skin. She smelled of woman and flowers, and he thrilled at the sound of her ragged breathing as she answered his passion with her own.

*Take her.* The animal inside him stirred with a fierce snarl. It snapped and clawed at the human part of him, demanding he cede his humanity to it. It wanted her.

He was almost powerless against the onslaught, and his hands trembled from the force of holding himself back. He growled from the effort of it.

Channon moaned at the fierce feel of his powerful arms locked around her. She was pressed so tight against his chest that she could feel his heart pounding against her breasts.

His intensity surrounded her, filled her, made her burn with volcanic need. All she could think of was stripping his clothes off him and seeing if his body really was as spectacular as it felt.

He pressed her back against her door, pinning her to it as he deepened his kiss. His warm, masculine scent filled her senses, overwhelming her.

He kissed his way from her lips and down across her cheek, then he buried his lips against her neck. "Let me make love to you, Channon," he breathed in her ear. "I want to feel your warm, soft body against mine. Feel your breath on my naked skin."

She should be offended by his suggestion. They barely knew each other. Yet no matter how hard she tried to talk herself out of this, she couldn't.

Deep inside, she wanted the same thing.

Against all reason—all sanity—she ached for him.

Never in her life had she done anything like this. Not once. Yet she found herself opening the door to her room and letting him in.

Sebastian breathed deeply in relief as he struggled for control. He'd never come so close to using his powers on a woman. It was forbidden for his kind to interfere with human freewill unless it was in defense of their lives or someone else's. He'd bent that rule a time or two to serve his purposes.

Tonight, had she refused him, he held no doubt he would have broken it.

But she hadn't refused him. Thank the gods for small favors.

He watched her as she set her key card on the dresser. She hesitated and he felt her nervousness.

"I won't hurt you, Channon."

She offered him a tentative smile. "I know."

He cupped her face in his hands and stared into those celestial blue eyes. "You are so beautiful."

Channon held her breath as he pulled her to him and recaptured her lips. None of this night made sense to her. None of her feelings. She clung to Sebastian as she sought for an explanation why she had let him into her room.

Why she was going to make love to him. A stranger. A man she knew nothing about. A man she would like as not never see again.

Yet none of that mattered. All that mattered was this moment in time—holding him close to her and keeping him here in her room for as long as she could.

She felt his hands free her hair to cascade down her back. He slid her coat from her shoulders, and she let it fall to the floor. Running his hands up her arms, he pulled back to stare down at her with hungry eyes. No man had ever given her such a look. One of fierce longing, of total possession.

Scared and excited, she helped him from his overcoat. His eyes dark with unsated passion, he removed his jacket and tossed it aside without care that it would be wrinkled later. So much for his impeccable suit. It thrilled her that she meant more to him than that.

He loosened his tie and pulled it over his head.

His eyes softened as she moved to unbutton his shirt. He caught her right hand in his and nibbled her fingertips, sending ribbons of pleasure through her, then he led her hand to his buttons and watched her intently.

Hot and aching for him, Channon worked the buttons through the buttonholes of his shirt. She trailed her gaze after her hands, watching as she bared his skin inch by slow, studied inch. Oh, good heaven, the man had a body that had been ripped from her dreams. His muscles were tight and perfect and covered by the most luscious tawny skin she'd ever seen. Dark hairs dusted his skin, making him seem even more like a predator, even more dangerous and manly.

Channon paused at the hard abs that held several scars. She traced her hand over them, feeling his sharp intake of breath as her fingers brushed the raised, lighter skin. "What happened?"

"Dragons have sharp talons," he whispered. "Sometimes I don't get out of the way quickly enough."

She placed her hand over one really nasty-looking scar by his hipbone. "Maybe you should fight smaller dragons."

"That wouldn't be very sporting of me."

She swallowed as he removed his shirt and she saw his unadorned chest for the first time. He was scrumptious. She ran her palm over his taut, hard pecs, delighting in the way they felt under her hands. She ran her fingers up his chest and across his lean, hard shoulder, which was tattooed with a dragon. "You do like dragons, don't you?"

He laughed. "Yes, I do."

Sebastian was doing his best to be patient, to let her get used to him. But it was hard when all he really wanted to do was lay her down on the bed and relieve the fierce ache in his loins.

He nibbled at her neck as he unfastened the buttons on her jumper and let it fall to the floor. She stood before him wearing nothing but her shoes and her misbuttoned shirt. It was the sexiest thing he'd ever seen in his four hundred years of living. "Do you always button your shirts like this?"

She looked down and gasped. "Oh, good grief. I was in a hurry this morning and—"

He stopped her words with a kiss. "Don't apologize," he whispered against her lips. "I like it."

"You're a very strange man."

"And you are a goddess."

Channon shook her head at him as he picked her up in his arms and moved with her toward the bed. She placed her hands over his muscles, which were taut from his strain. The feel of them made her mouth water. He laid her gently on the mattress, then ran his hands down her legs to her feet so he could remove her shoes and socks and toss them over his shoulder.

Her heart pounding, Channon watched as he nibbled his way over her hip to her stomach. He moved his hands to her shirt and slowly unbuttoned it, kissing and licking every piece of her skin that he bared.

She moaned at the sight and feel of his mouth on her, at the way he seemed to savor her body. Spikes of pleasure pierced her stomach as her body throbbed and ached for him to fill her.

She wanted him inside her so much that she feared she might burst into flames from the fire tearing through her body.

Sebastian felt her wetness on his skin as he slid himself against her. His body screamed for hers, but he wasn't through with her yet. He wanted to savor her, to commit every inch of her lush body to his memory.

What he felt for her amazed him. It was unlike anything he'd ever experienced. On some strange level she gave him peace, sanctuary. She filled the loneliness in his battered heart.

He buried his face in her neck while her hardened nipples teased the flesh of his chest and her hands roamed over his back. "You feel so good under me," he whispered as he soaked her essence into him.

Channon took a deep, ragged breath. His words delighted her.

He nuzzled her neck, his whiskers softly teasing her flesh while his hand skimmed over her body to touch the burning ache between her legs. She hissed at the pleasure of his fingers toying with her and arched her back against him as he slowly dragged his mouth from her neck to her breast. His tongue swept against the hardened tip, making her tingle and throb.

She bit her lip as a wave of fear went through her. "I want you to know that I don't normally do this sort of thing."

He lifted himself up on his arms to look down at her. He pressed his hips between her legs so that she could feel the large bulge of him while his expensive wool pants slightly chafed her inner thighs. The hot feel of him there was enough to drive her wild with need.

"If I thought you did, my lady, I wouldn't be here with you now." His gaze intensified, holding her enthralled. "I see you, Channon. You and the barriers you have around you that keep everyone at a distance."

"And yet you're here."

"I'm here because I know the sadness inside you. I know what it feels like to wake in the morning, lost and lonely and aching for someone to be there with me."

Her heart clenched as he spoke the very things that really were a part of her. "Why are *you* alone? I can't imagine a man so handsome without a line of willing women fighting behind him."

"Looks aren't all there is in this world, my lady. They are certainly no protection against being alone. Hearts never see through the eyes."

Channon swallowed at his words. Did he mean them? Or was this all some lie he was telling her to make her feel better about what she was doing with him? She didn't know.

But she wanted to believe him. She wanted to comfort the torment she saw in his hungry eyes.

He pulled away from her and removed his shoes and pants. Channon trembled as she finally saw him completely naked. Like a dangerous, dark beast moving sinuously in the moonlight, he was incredible. Absolutely stunning.

Every inch of him was muscled and toned and covered by the most scrumptious tanned skin she'd ever beheld. The only flaws on his perfect body were the scars marking his back, hips, and legs. They really did look like claw and bite marks from some ferocious beast.

When he rejoined her on the bed, she pulled the tie from his hair, letting it fall forward to surround his sinfully handsome face.

"You look like some barbaric chieftain," she said, running her hand through the silkiness of his unbound hair. She traced the intricate lines of the tattoo on his face.

"Mmm," he breathed, taking her breast in his mouth.

Channon held his head to her as his tongue teased her. Ripples of pleasure tore through her.

She ran her hands down his muscled ribs, then along his arms and shoulders as she drifted through a strange hazy fog of pleasure. Something strange was happening to her. With every breath he expelled, it was like his touch intensified. Multiplied. Instead of one tongue stroking her, she swore she could feel a hundred of them. It was as if her skin was alive and being massaged all over at once.

Sebastian hissed as his powers ran through him. Sex always heightened the senses of his breed. The intensity of physical pleasure was highly sought by his people for the elevation it gave them and their magic. The beauty of it was that the surge of power usually lasted a full day, and in the case of truly great sex, two days.

Channon was definitely a two-day high.

He looked into her eyes to see her gaze unfocused and wild. His powers were affecting her, too. The physical stimulation to a human was even greater than it was to his breed.

He knew the moment she lost herself to the ecstasy of his sorcerer's touch. Her barriers and inhibitions gone, she threw her head back and cried out as an orgasm tore through her. "That's it," he whispered in her ear. "Don't fight it."

She didn't. Instead, she turned toward him and grabbed feverishly at his body. Sebastian groaned as he obliged her eagerness.

She sought out every inch of his flesh with her hands and mouth. He rolled over and pulled her on top of him, where she straddled his waist, letting him feel her wetness on the hollow of his stomach. He knew she was past the ability to speak now and a part of him regretted that. She was all need. All hot, demanding sex.

Her eyes wild and hungry, she took his hands in hers and led them to her breasts as she slid herself against his swollen shaft. She leaned forward to drag her tongue along the edge of his jaw as she nibbled her way to his lips.

She kissed him passionately, then pulled back. "What have you done to me?" she asked hoarsely, her words surprising him.

"It's not exactly me," he said honestly. "It's something I can't help."

She moaned and writhed against him, making his body burn even more. "I need you inside me, Sebastian. Please."

He wasted no time obliging her. Rolling her over, he curled his body around hers as they lay with her back to his front. He draped her leg over his waist.

He tucked her head beneath his chin and held her close as he drove himself deep inside her sleek wetness. He growled at the warm, wet feel of her while she leaned her head back into his shoulder and cried out.

Channon had never felt anything like this. No man had

ever made love to her in such a manner. Her right hip was braced against his inner thigh while he used his left knee to hold her left leg up so that he had access to her body from behind her. She didn't know how he managed it, but his strokes were deep and even, and they tore through her with the most intense pleasure she had ever known. He was so hard inside her, so thick and warm.

And she wanted more of his touch. More of his power.

He slid his hand down over her stomach, then lower until he touched her between her legs. She hissed and writhed as pleasure tore through her while his fingers rubbed her in time to his strokes. And still it felt as if a thousand hands caressed her, as if she were being bathed all over by his touch, his scent.

Out of her mind with ecstasy, she met him lush stroke for lush stroke. Her body felt as if it held a life of its own, as if the pleasure of her was its own entity. She needed even more of him.

Sebastian was awed by her response to him. No human woman had ever been like this. If he didn't know better, he'd swear she was part Drakos. She dug her nails into the flesh of the arms he had wrapped around her, and when she came again she screamed out so loudly, he had to quickly put a dampening spell around them to keep others from hearing her.

His powers surging, he smiled wickedly at that. He loved satisfying his partner, and with Channon he took even more delight than normal.

She rolled slightly in his arms, capturing his lips in a frenzied kiss.

Sebastian cupped her face as he quickened his strokes and buried himself even deeper in her body. She felt so incredibly good to him. So warm and welcoming. So perfect.

He held her close against him as his heart pounded and his groin tightened even more. The feel of her, the taste of her, cascaded through his senses, making him reel, making him ache, yet at the same time soothing him.

The beast in him roared and snapped in satisfaction while the man buried himself deep in her and shook from the force of his orgasm. With the two parts of him sated and united, it was the most incredible moment of his entire life.

Channon groaned as she felt his release inside her. Still wrapped around her, he pulled her even closer to his chest. She heard his ragged breathing and felt his heart pounding against her shoulder blade. The manly scent of him filled her head and her heart, making her want to stay cocooned by his body forever.

Slowly, the throbbing pleasure faded from her and left her weak and drained from the intensity of their love-making.

When he withdrew from her, she felt a tremendous sense of loss.

"What did you do to me?" she asked, turning onto her back to look at him.

He kissed his way across her collarbone to her lips. "I did nothing, *ma petite*. It was all you."

"Trust me, I've never done that before."

He laughed softly in her ear.

She smiled at him and dropped her gaze to the small gold medallion he wore around his neck. Odd, she hadn't noticed it before.

She traced the chain with her fingers, then took it into her hand. It was obviously quite old. Ancient Greek if she didn't miss her guess. The gold held a relief of a dragon coiled around a shield. "This is beautiful," she breathed.

Sebastian looked down at her hand and covered her fingers with his. "It belonged to my mother," he said, wondering why he spoke of it. It was something he'd never shared with anyone else. "I don't really remember her, but my brother said she told him to give it to me so that I would know how much she loved me."

"She died?"

He nodded. "I was barely six when . . ." His voice trailed off as his memories of that night scorched him. Inside his head he could still hear the screams of the dying and smell the fires. He remembered the terror and the arms of his brother, Theren, pulling him to safety.

He'd always lived with the horrors of that night close to his heart. Tonight, with Channon, it didn't seem to hurt quite so much.

She ran her hand over the markings on his face. "I'm sorry," she whispered, and inside his heart, he could feel her sincerity. "I was nine when my mother died of cancer. And there's always this little piece of me that wishes I could hear the sound of her voice just one more time."

"You're without family?"

She nodded. "I grew up with my aunt, who died two years ago."

He felt her ache inside his own heart and it surprised him. He hated that she was alone in the world. Like him. It was a hard way to be.

Tightening his arms, he let his body comfort her.

Channon closed her eyes as he ran his tongue around and into her ear, sending chills over her. She leaned into his arms and pulled him close for another scorching kiss. A tiny part of her wanted to beg him not to leave her in the morning. But she refused to embarrass herself.

She'd known going into this that tonight would be all they would ever have. Yet the thought of not seeing him again hurt her more than she could fathom. She literally felt that losing him would be like losing a vital part of herself.

Sebastian knew he should leave now, but something inside him rebelled.

It wasn't much longer until dawn. He still had to retrieve the tapestry and return home.

But right now, all he wanted was to spend a little more time holding this woman, keeping her in the warm shelter of his arms.

"Sleep, Channon," he whispered as he sent a small sleeping spell to her. If she were awake and looking at him, he would never be able to let her go.

Immediately, she went limp in his arms.

Sebastian ran his fingers over the delicate curve of her cheek as he watched her. She was so beautiful by his side.

He clenched his hand against her silken curls and took a deep breath in her hair. Her floral scent reminded him of warm summer days of shared laughter and friendship. Her bare hips were nestled perfectly against his groin, her lower back against his stomach. Her smooth legs were entwined with his masculine ones. Gods, how he ached to keep her here like this.

He felt himself stirring again. He felt the need within him to take her one more time before he upheld his obligation.

*You must go.*

As much as he hated to, he knew he had no choice.

Sighing in regret, he withdrew from the warmth of her and crept from the bed, still amazed by the night they had shared. He would never forget her. And for the first time in his life, he actually considered coming back here for a while.

But that was impossible.

His kind didn't do well in the modern world, where they were easily hunted and found. He needed wide-open spaces and a simpler world where he could have the freedom and solitude he needed.

Clenching his teeth against the pain of necessity, he dressed silently in the dark.

Sebastian stepped away from the bed, then paused.

He couldn't leave like this, as if the night had meant nothing to him.

Pulling his mother's medallion from his neck, he placed it around Channon's and kissed her parted lips.

"Sleep, little one," he whispered. "May the Fates be kind to you. Always."

Then, he shimmered from her room and out into the dark night. Alone. He was always alone.

He'd long ago accepted that fact. It was what had to be.

But tonight he felt that loneliness more profoundly than he had ever felt it before.

As he rounded the hotel's building and headed toward his car, he collided with a middle-aged woman who was walking, huddled from the cold, in a worn jacket. She wore the faded uniform of a waitress and the old shoes of a woman who had no choice but to be practical.

"Hey," he said as she started past him. "Do you have a car?"

She shook her head no.

"You do now." He handed her the keys to his Lexus and pointed it out to her. "You'll find the registration in the glove box. Just fill it out and it's yours."

She blinked at him. "Yeah, right."

Sebastian offered her a genuine smile. He'd only bought the car to use while he'd been trapped in this time period. Where he was going, there was no need for it.

"I'm serious," he said, nudging her toward it. "No strings attached. I took a vow of poverty about fifteen minutes ago, and it's all yours."

She laughed incredulously. "I have no idea who you are, but thank you."

Sebastian inclined his head and waited until the woman had driven off.

Cautiously, he stepped into the alley and looked around to make sure there were no witnesses. He called forth the powers of Night to shield him from anyone who might happen by, then he shifted into his alternate form. The power of the Drakos rushed through him like fire as the ions in the air around him were charged with electrical energy—electrical energy that allowed him to shed one form and shift into another.

In his case, his alternate form was that of a dragon.

Spreading his bloodred wings out to their full forty-foot span, he launched himself from his hind legs and flew into the sky, careful to stay below radar level this time.

Sebastian had one last thing to do before he could return to his time. Yet even as he headed back to the museum, he couldn't shake the image of Channon from his mind.

He could still see her asleep in the bed, her hair spread out around her shoulders. He could still feel the texture of the honey-laced strands in his palm.

His dragon form burned with need, and he yearned to return to her.

Not that he could. One-night stands with humans were all he dared. The risk of exposure was too great.

Sebastian crossed town in a matter of minutes and landed on the roof of the museum. He summoned the electrical field that allowed the molecules of his body to transform from animal to human and flashed back into his man form.

With a flick of his hand, he dressed himself all in black, then shimmered from the roof into the room that held the tapestry.

"There you are," he said as he saw Antiphone's work again. Sadness, guilt, and grief tore through him as he recalled his baby sister's gentle face.

After he'd sold this tapestry, he had never wanted to see it again.

But now he had to have it. It was the only way to save his brother's life. Not that he should care. Damos had never given a damn about him.

After all the things Damos had done to break him, Sebastian still couldn't turn his back on his brother and let the man die. Not when he could help it.

"I'm a bloody fool," he said disgustedly.

He willed the tapestry from the museum case into his hand. Then he folded and tucked it carefully into a black leather bag to protect it.

As he began to shimmer from the room back to the roof, an odd burning started in the palm of his left hand.

"What the . . . ?"

Hissing from the pain, he dropped the case and pulled off his glove. Sebastian blew cool air across his hot skin and frowned as a round geometric design appeared in his palm.

"No," he breathed in disbelief as he stared at it.

This wasn't possible, yet there was no denying what he saw and felt. Worse, there was a presence inside him, a tickling in the depth of his heart that made him curse even louder.

Against his will, he was mated.

# *Two*

***This was a nightmare. The absolute*** **worst** ***kind of night-***
mare.

It was wrong. It had to be.

Sebastian left the museum immediately, all the while debating his next step. On the building's roof, he paused. He needed to take the tapestry back to Britain of a thousand years earlier. He was sworn to it. He'd destroyed Antiphone's future, and now the fate of his brother was in his hands.

But the mark . . .

He couldn't leave his mate here while he went home. Nor could he stay in this time period where the danger of being inadvertently struck by an electrical charge was so strong—that was his one Achilles' heel.

Because he relied on electrical impulses to change forms, any kind of outside electrical jolt could involuntarily transform him. It was why his kind avoided any time period after Benjamin Franklin, the so-called Satan of his people.

But Arcadian law demanded he protect his mate.

At any cost.

Centuries of war had left the Drakos branch of the Arcadians virtually extinct. And since Sebastian hunted down and executed the evil animal Drakos, their kind would make it a point to track and kill his mate should they ever learn of Channon's existence.

She would be dead and it would be all his fault.

Should she die, he would never mate again.

"Mate, my bloody hell," he muttered. He looked up at the clear, full moon above. "Damn you, Fates. What were you thinking?"

To mate a human to an Arcadian was cruel. It happened only rarely, so rarely that he'd never even considered the possibility of it. So why did it have to happen now?

*Leave her.*

He should. Yet if he did, he would leave behind his only chance for a family. Unlike a human male, he was only given one shot at this. If he failed to claim Channon, he would spend the rest of his exceptionally long life alone.

Completely alone.

No other woman would ever again appeal to him.

He would be doomed to celibacy.

*Oh bloody, damned hell with that.*

There was no choice. At the end of three weeks, the mark on her human hand would fade and she would forget he'd ever existed. The mark on his Arcadian hand was eternal, and he would mourn her for the rest of his life. Even if he went back for her later, it would be too late. After the mark faded, his chance was over.

It was now or never.

Not to mention the small fact that during the three weeks she was marked by his sign, Channon would be a magnet to the Katagaria Draki who wanted him dead.

For centuries, he and the animal Katagaria had played a deadly game of cat and mouse. The Katagaria routinely sent out mental feelers for him, just as he did for them. Their psychic sonar would easily pick up his mark on Channon's body, allowing them to hone in on her.

And if one of them were to find his mate alone without a protector . . .

He flinched at the image in his mind.

No, he had to protect her. That was all there was to it.

Closing his eyes, Sebastian transformed himself into the dragon and went back to Channon's hotel, where he shifted forms again and entered her room as a man.

He was about to break nine kinds of laws.

He laughed bitterly. So what else was new? And why should he care? His people had banished him long ago. He was dead to them. Why should he abide by their laws?

He didn't care about them.

He cared for nothing. For no one.

Yet as he stared at Channon lying asleep in the moonlight, something peculiar happened to him. A feeling of possessive need tore through him. She was his mate. His only salvation.

For whatever twisted reason, the Fates had joined them. To leave Channon here unprotected would be wrong. She had no idea the kind of enemies who would do anything to have him, enemies who wouldn't hesitate to hurt her because she was his.

Sebastian lay down by her side and gathered her into his arms. She murmured in her sleep, then snuggled into him. His heart pounded at the sensation of her breath against his neck.

He looked down and saw her right palm, which bore the same mark as his left hand, laying upright by her cheek. He'd waited an eternity for her.

After all these centuries of empty loneliness, dare he even dream of having a home again? A family?

Then again, dare he not?

"Channon?" he whispered softly, trying to wake her. "I need to ask you something."

"Hmm?" she murmured in her sleep.

"I can't remove you from your time period unless you agree to it. I need you to come with me. Will you?"

She blinked open her eyes and looked up at him with a sleepy frown. "Where are you taking me?"

"I want to take you home with me."

She smiled up at him like an angel, then sighed. "Sure."

Sebastian tightened his arms around her as she fell back to sleep. She'd said yes. Joy ripped through him. Maybe he had done his penance after all.

Maybe, for once, he could have his one moment of respite from the past.

Holding her close, Sebastian stared out the window and waited for the first rays of dawn so that he could pulse them out of her world and into one beyond her wildest imagination.

***Channon felt a strange tugging in her stomach that settled*** into a terrible queasiness. What on earth?

She opened her eyes to see Sebastian staring down at her. He wore an intriguing mask of black and red feathers that made the gold of his eyes stand out even more prominently. It reminded her of a *Phantom of the Opera* mask as it only covered his forehead and the left side of his face where his tattoo was.

She'd never considered masks sexy before, but on him, mmm, baby.

Even more inviting than that, he wore black leather armor over a chain mail shirt—black leather armor covered in silver rings and studs that was laced down the front. The laces had come untied, leaving an enticing gap where she could see his tanned skin peeping through.

Ummm, hmmm.

Smiling, she started to speak until she realized she was

on the back of a horse. A really, really *big* horse.

Even more peculiar, she was dressed in a dark green gown with wide sleeves that flowed around her like some fairy-tale princess garment.

"Okay," she breathed, running her hand along the intricate gold embroidery on her sleeve. "It's a dream. I can cope with a dream where I'm Sleeping Beauty or something."

"It's not a dream," he said quietly.

Channon laughed nervously as she sat up in his lap and glanced around. The sun was high above as if it were well into the afternoon, and they were traveling on an old dirt road that ran perpendicular to a thick, prehistoric-looking forest.

Something was wrong. She could feel it in her bones, and she could tell by the stiffness of his body and his guarded look. He was hiding something. "Where are we?"

"The where of it," he said slowly, refusing to meet her gaze, "isn't nearly as interesting as the *when* part."

"Excuse me?"

She watched the emotions flicker in his eyes, but the most peculiar one was a fleeting look of panic, as if he were nervous about answering her question. "Do you remember last night when I asked if I could take you home with me and you said sure?"

Channon frowned. "Vaguely, yes."

"Well, honey, I'm home."

An ache started in her head. What was he talking about? "Home? Where?"

He cleared his throat and still refused to meet her gaze. The man was definitely hedging. But why?

"You said you like research, right?" he asked.

Her stomach knotted even more. "Yes."

"Consider this a unique research venture then."

"Meaning what?"

His jaw flexed. "Haven't you ever wished you could

go back to Saxon England and find out what it was really like before the Normans invaded?"

"Of course."

"Well, your wish is granted." He looked at her and flashed an insincere smile.

Okay, the guy was not Robin Williams, and unless she was missing something really important from last night, she didn't conjure him from a bottle. If he wasn't a genie . . .

She laughed nervously. "What are you saying?"

"We're in England. Or rather we're in what will one day soon become England. Right now, this kingdom is called Lindsey."

Channon went completely still. She knew all about the medieval Saxon kingdom, and this . . . this was not possible. No, there was no way she could be here. "You're joking with me again, aren't you?"

He shook his head.

Channon rubbed her forehead as she tried to make sense of all this. "Okay, you have slipped me a mickey. Great. When I sober up from this you do realize I will call the cops."

"Well, it'll be about nine hundred years before there are cops to call, about a hundred more years after that before you have a phone. But I'm willing to wait if you are."

Channon clenched her eyes shut as she tried to think past the throbbing ache in her skull. "So you're telling me that I'm not dreaming and I'm not drugged."

"Correct on both accounts."

"But I'm in Saxon England?"

He nodded.

"And you're a dragon slayer?"

"Ah, so you remember that part."

"Yes," she said reasonably, but with every word she spoke after that, her voice crescendoed into mild hysteria.

"What I don't remember is how the hell I got *here!*" she shouted, sending several birds into flight.

Sebastian winced.

She glared at him. "You told me there wouldn't be any Rod Serling voice-overs, yet here I am in the middle of a *Twilight Zone* episode. Oh, and let me guess the title of it, *Night of the Terminally Stupid!*"

"It's not as bad as all that," Sebastian said, trying to decide the best way to explain this to her. He didn't blame her for being angry. In fact, she was taking all this a lot better than he had dared hope. "I know this is hard for you."

"Hard for me? I don't even know where to begin. I did something I've never done in my life and then I wake up and you tell me you have supposedly time-warped me into the past, and I'm not sure if I'm insane or delusional or what. Why am I here?"

"I . . ." Sebastian wasn't sure what to answer. The truth was pretty much out of the question. *Channon, I practically kidnapped you because you are my mate and I don't want to be alone for the next three to four hundred years of my life.*

No, definitely not something a man told a woman on their first date. He would have to woo her. Quickly. And win her over to wanting to stay here with him.

Preferably before a dragon ate one of them.

"Look, why don't you just think of this as a great adventure. Instead of reading about the history you teach, you can live it for a couple weeks."

"What are you? Disney World?" she asked. "And I can't stay here for a couple weeks. I have a life in the twenty-first century. I will be fired from my job. I will lose my car and my apartment. Good grief, who will pick up my laundry?"

"If you stayed here with me, it wouldn't be a problem. You'd never have to worry about any of that again."

Channon was aghast at him. *Oh, God, please let this*

*be some bizarre nightmare*. She had to wake up. This could not possibly be real.

"No," she said to him, "you're right. I wouldn't have to worry about *any* of that in Saxon England. I'd only have to worry about the lack of hygiene, lack of plumbing, Viking invasions, being burned at the stake, lack of modern conveniences, and nasty diseases with no antibiotics. Good grief, I can't even get a Midol. Not to mention, I'll never find out what happens next week on *Buffy!*"

Sebastian let out an elongated, patient breath and gave her an apologetic look that somehow succeeded in quelling a good deal of her anger.

"Look," he said quietly, "I'll make a deal with you. Spend a few weeks with me here, and if you really can't stand it, I'll take you home as close to the departure time as I can manage. Okay?"

Channon still had a hard time grasping all this. "Do you swear you're not playing some weird mind game with me? I really am *here*, in Saxon England?"

"I swear it on my mother's soul. You are in Saxon England, and I can take you back home. And no, I'm not playing mind games with you."

Channon accepted that, even though she couldn't imagine why. It was just a feeling she had that he would never swear on his mother's soul unless he meant it.

"Can you really take me back to the precise moment I left?"

"Probably not the precise moment, but I can try."

"What do you mean, *try?*"

He flashed his dimples, then turned serious. "Timewalking isn't an exact science. You can only move through the time fields when the dawn meets the night, and only under the power of a full moon. The problem is on the arrival end. You can try to get someplace specific, but you have only about a ninety-five percent chance of success. I might get you back that day, but it could also be a week or two after."

"And that's the best you can do?"

"Hey, just be grateful I'm old. When an Arcadian first starts time-walking, we only have about a three percent chance of success. I once ended up on Pluto."

She laughed in spite of herself. "Are you serious?"

He nodded. "They're not kidding about it being the coldest planet."

Channon took a deep breath as she digested everything he'd told her. Was any of this real? She didn't know, any more than she knew whether or not he was being honest about returning her. He was still very guarded. "Okay, so I'm stuck here until the next full moon?"

"Yes."

Oh, good grief, no. Had she been the kind of woman to whine, she'd probably be whining. But Channon was always practical. "All right. I can handle this," she said, more for her benefit than his. "I'll just pretend I'm a Saxon chick and you . . ." Her voice trailed off as she recalled what he'd said about time-traveling. "Just how old are you?"

"My people don't age quite the same way humans do. Since we can time-walk, we have a much slower biological clock."

Oh, she really didn't like the way he said *humans,* and if he turned fangy on her, she was going to stake him right through the heart. But she would get back to that in a minute. First, she wanted to understand the age thing. "So you age like dog years?"

Sebastian laughed. "Something like that. By human age, I would be four hundred sixty-three years old."

Channon sat flabbergasted as she looked over his lean, hard body. He appeared to be in his early thirties, not his late four hundreds. "You're not joking with me at all, are you?"

"Not even a little. Everything I have told you since the moment I met you has been the honest truth."

"Oh, God," she said, breathing in slowly and carefully

to calm the panic that was again trying to surface. She knew it was real, yet she had a hard time believing it. It boggled her mind that people could walk through time and that she could really be in the Dark Ages.

Surely, it couldn't be this easy.

"I know there has to be more of a downside to all this. And I'm pretty sure here's where I find out you're some kind of vampire or something."

"No," he said quickly. "I'm not a vampire. I don't suck blood, and I don't do anything weird to sustain my life. I was born from my mother, just as you were. I feel the same emotions. I bleed red blood. And just like you, I will die at some unknown date in the future. I just come equipped with a few extra powers."

"I see. I'm a Toyota. You're a Lambourghini, and you can have really awesome sex."

He chuckled. "That's a good summation."

Summation, hell. This was unbelievable. Inconceivable. How had she gotten mixed up with something like this?

But as she looked up at him, she knew. He was compelling. That deadly air and animal magnetism—how could she have even hoped to resist him?

And she wondered if there were more men out there like him. Men of power and magic. Men who were so incredibly sexy that to look at them was to burn for them. "Are there more of you?"

"Yes."

She smiled evilly at the thought. "A *lot* more?"

He frowned before he answered. "There used to be a lot more of us, but times change."

Channon saw the sadness in his eyes, the pain that he kept inside. It made her hurt for him.

He looked down at her. "That tapestry you love so much is the story of our beginning."

"The birth of the dragon and the man?"

He nodded. "About five thousand years before you were born, my grandfather, Lycaon, fell in love with a woman he thought was a human. She wasn't. She was born to a race that had been cursed by the Greek gods. She never told him who and what she really was, and in time she bore him two sons."

Channon remembered seeing that birth scene embroidered on the upper left edge of the tapestry.

"On her twenty-seventh birthday," he continued, "she died horribly just as all the members of her race die. And when my grandfather saw it, he knew his children were destined for the same fate. Angry and grief-stricken, he sought unnatural means to keep his children alive."

Sebastian was tense as he spoke. "Crazed from his grief and fear, he started capturing as many of my grandmother's people as he could and began experimenting with them—combining their life forces with those of animals. He wanted to make a hybrid creature that wasn't cursed."

"It worked?" she asked.

"Better than he had hoped. Not only did his sorcery give them the animal's strength and powers, it gave them a life span ten times longer than that of a human."

She arched a brow at that. "So you're telling me that you're a werewolf who lives seven or eight hundred years?"

"Yes on the age, but I'm not a Lykos. I'm a Drakos."

"You say that as if I have a clue about what you mean."

"Lycaon used his magic to 'half' his children. Instead of two sons, he made four."

"What are you saying?" she asked. "He sliced them down the middle?"

"Yes and no. There was a byproduct of the magic I don't think my grandfather was prepared for. When he combined a human and an animal, he expected his magic would create only one being. Instead, it made two of them. One person who held the heart of a human, and a separate creature whose heart was that of the animal.

"Those who have human hearts are called Arcadians. We are able to suppress the animal side of our nature. To control it. Because we have human hearts, we have compassion and higher reasoning."

"And the ones with animal hearts?"

"They are called Katagaria, meaning miscreant or rogue. Because of their animal hearts, they lack human compassion and are ruled by their baser instincts. Like their human brethren, they hold the same psychic abilities and shape-shifting, time-bending powers, but not the self-control."

That didn't sound good to her. "And the other people who were experimented on? Were there two of them, too?"

"Yes. And we formed the basis of two societies: the Arcadians and the Katagaria. As with nature, like went with like, and we created groups or patrias based on our animals. Wolf lives with wolf, hawk with hawk, dragon with dragon. We use Greek terms to differentiate between them. Therefore dragon is drakos, wolf is lykos, etcetera."

That made sense to her. "And all the while the Arcadians stayed with the Arcadians and Katagaria with Katagaria?"

"For the most part, yes."

"But I take it from the sound of your voice that no one lived happily-ever-after."

"No. The Fates were furious that Lycaon dared thwart them. To punish him, they ordered him to kill the creature-based children. He refused. So, the gods cursed us all."

"Cursed you how?"

A tic started in his jaw, and she saw the deep-seated agony in his eyes. "For one thing, we don't hit puberty until our mid-twenties. Because it is delayed, when it hits, it hits us hard. Many of us are driven to madness, and if we don't find a way to control and channel our powers we can become Slayers."

"I take it you don't mean the good vampire slayer kind of slayer that kills evil things."

"No. These are creatures that are bent on absolute destruction. They kill without remorse and with total barbarism."

"How awful," she breathed.

He agreed. "Until puberty, our children are either human or animal, depending on the parents' base-forms."

"Base-forms? What are those?"

"Arcadians are human so their base-forms are human. The Katagaria have a base-form of whatever animal part they are related to. An Ursulan would be a bear, a Gerakian would be a hawk."

"A Drakos would be a dragon."

He nodded. "A child has no powers at all, but with the onset of puberty, all the powers come in. We try to contain those who are going through it and teach them how to harness their powers. Most of the time we succeed as Arcadians, but with the Katagaria this isn't true. They encourage their children to destroy both humans and Arcadians."

"Because we have vowed to stop them and their Slayers, they hate us and have sworn to kill us and our families. In short, we are at war with one another."

Channon sat quietly as she absorbed that last bit. So that was the eternal struggle he'd mentioned yesterday. "Is that why you are here?"

This time the anguish in his eyes was so severe that she winced from it. "No. I'm here because I made a promise."

"About what?"

He didn't answer, but she felt the rigidness return to his body. He was a man in pain, and she wondered why.

But then she figured it out. "The Katagaria destroyed your family, didn't they?"

"They took everything from me." The agony in his voice was so raw, so savage.

Never in her life had she heard anything like it.

Channon wanted to soothe him in a way she'd never

wanted to soothe anyone else. She wished she could erase the past and return his family to him.

Seeking to distract him, she went back to the prior topic. "If you're at war with each other, do you have armies?"

He shook his head. "Not really. We have Sentinels, who are stronger and faster than the rest of our species. They are the designated protectors of both man and were-kind."

Reaching up, she touched his mask that covered the tattoo on his face. "Do all Arcadians have your mark-ings?"

Sebastian looked away. "No. Only Sentinels have them."

She smiled at the knowledge. "You're a Sentinel."

"I *was* a Sentinel."

The stress on the past tense told her much. "What hap-pened?"

"It was a long time ago, and I'd rather not talk about it."

She could respect that, especially since he'd already answered so much. But her curiosity about it was almost more than she could bear. Still, she wouldn't pry. "Okay, but can I ask one more thing?"

"Sure."

"When you say long ago, I have a feeling that takes on a whole new meaning. Was it a decade or two, or—"

"Two hundred fifty-four years ago."

Her jaw dropped. "Have you been alone all this time?"

He nodded.

Her chest drew tight at that. Two hundred years alone. She couldn't imagine it. "And you have no one?"

Sebastian fell silent as old memories surged. He did his best not to remember his role of Sentinel. His family.

He'd been raised to hold honor next to his heart, and with one fatal mistake, he had lost everything he'd ever cared for. Everything he'd once been.

"I was . . . banished," he said, the word sticking in his throat. He'd never once in all this time uttered the word aloud. "No Arcadian is allowed to associate with me."

"Why would they banish you?"

He didn't answer.

Instead, he pointed in front of them. "Look up, Channon. I think there's something over there you'll find far more interesting than me."

Seriously doubting that, Channon turned her head, then gaped. On the hill far above was a large wooden hall surrounded by a group of buildings. Even from this distance, she could make out people and animals moving about.

She blinked, unable to believe her eyes. "Oh my God," she breathed. "It's a real Saxon village!"

"Complete with bad hygiene and no plumbing."

Her heart hammered as they approached the hill at a slow and steady speed. "Can't you make this thing move any faster?" she asked, eager to get a closer view.

"I can, but they will view it as a sign of aggression and might decide to shoot a few arrows into us."

"Oh. Then I can wait. I don't want to be a pincushion."

Sebastian remained silent and watched her as she strained to see more of the town. He smiled at her exuberance as she twisted in the saddle, her hips brushing painfully against his swollen groin.

After the night they had shared, it amazed him just how much he longed to possess her again, how much his body craved hers.

He still couldn't believe he'd told her as much as he had about his past and people, yet as his mate, she had a right to know all about him.

*If* she would be his mate.

He still hadn't really made up his mind about that.

The kindest thing would be to return her and let her go. But he didn't want to. He missed having someone to care for and someone who cared for him.

How many times had he lain awake at night aching for a family again? Wishing for the comfort of a soothing touch? Missing the sound of laughter and the warmth of friendship?

For centuries, his solitude had been his hell.

And this woman sitting in his lap would be his only salvation.

If he dared . . .

Channon bit her lip as they entered the bailey and she saw real, live Saxon people at work in the village. There were men laying stone, rebuilding a portion of the gate. Women with laundry and foodstuffs walking around, talking amongst themselves. And children! Lots of Saxon children were running around, laughing and playing games with each other.

Better still, there were merchants and music, acrobats, and jongleurs. "Is there a festival going on?"

He nodded. "The harvest is in and there's a celebration all week long to mark it."

She struggled to understand what the crowd around them said.

It was incredible! They were speaking Old English!

"Oh, Sebastian," she cried, throwing her arms around him and holding him close. "Thank you for this! Thank you!"

Sebastian clenched his teeth at the sensation of her breasts flattened against him. Of her breath tickling his neck.

His groin tightened even more, and it took all his human powers to leash the beast within. He felt the ripping inside as he set the two halves of him against each other.

It was a dangerous thing he did, but for both their sakes, it was a necessary action. Especially since both halves of him wanted the same thing—they wanted the Claiming where Channon would entrust herself to him, the ceremony that would bind them together for eternity. It wasn't something to be taken lightly. She would have to give up everything to be with him. Everything. And he wasn't sure if he could ask that of her.

It would be unfair to her, and he definitely wasn't worth such a sacrifice.

He saw the happiness in Channon's eyes and smiled at her.

But his smile faded as he looked around the town and saw all the innocent lives that would end if something went wrong.

Bracis had shown a rare streak of intelligence when he had set up this exchange. Sebastian was forbidden by his Sentinel oath to transform into his dragon form or to use his powers in any way that could betray his heritage to the humans. To the innocent, he must always appear human.

Bracis had sworn that the Katagaria would come in as humans to make the exchange and then leave peacefully. Unfortunately, Sebastian had no choice except to trust them.

Of course, Bracis knew the extent of Sebastian's powers, and the Katagari male would be an absolute idiot to cross him. And though the beast could be stupid, Bracis wasn't *that* stupid.

As soon as they reached the stable, Sebastian helped Channon down, then dismounted behind her. He pulled his hauberk lower so that no one could see just how much he craved the woman before him.

Channon watched as Sebastian removed his huge broadsword from his horse and fastened it to the baldric at his waist. She had to admit the man looked delectable like that, so manly and virile.

The chain mail sleeves fell from the shoulders of the leather armor, clinking ever so slightly with his movements. The laces of the hauberk were open, showing a hint of the hairs on his chest, and all too well she remembered her hours of running her fingers and mouth over that lush skin.

And as she stared at the small scar on his neck, she ached to trace it with her tongue. This man had a body and aura that should be cloned and made standard equipment for all men. Prideful and dangerous, it made every female part of her sit up and pant.

*Stop that!* she snapped at herself. They were in the middle of town and . . .

And she had other people to study.

*Yeah right.* Like they were really more interesting than Sebastian.

He adjusted his sword so that the hilt came forward and the blade trailed down his leg, then pulled a leather bag from the saddle. A youth ran up to take his mount.

"What day is today?" he asked the boy in Old English.

"It be Tuesday, sir."

Sebastian thanked him and gave him two coins before relinquishing his horse to the boy's care.

He turned toward her. "You ready?"

"Absolutely. I've dreamed of this my whole life."

Channon held her breath as he led her through the bustling village.

Sebastian looked behind him to see Channon as she tried to watch everything at once. She was so happy to be here.

Maybe there was hope for them after all. Maybe bringing her here hadn't been a mistake.

"Tell me, Channon, have you ever eaten Saxon bread?"

"Is it good?"

"The best." Taking her hand, he pulled her into a shop across the dirt road.

Channon breathed in the sweet smell of baking bread as they entered the bakery. Bread was lined up on the wooden counter and in baskets on tables all over the room. An older, heavyset woman stood to the side, trying to move a large sack across the floor.

"Here," Sebastian said, rushing to her side. "Let me get that."

Straightening up, she smiled in gratitude. "Thank you. I need it over there by my workbench."

Sebastian hefted the heavy sack onto his shoulder.

Channon watched, her mouth watering as his hauberk lifted and gave her a flash of his hard, tanned abs. His broad shoulders and toned biceps flexed from the strain. And when he placed the sack on the floor by the bench, she was gifted with a nice view of his rear covered by his black leather pants.

Oh yeah, she'd love a bite of that.

"Now what can I do for you gentle folks?" the woman asked.

"What looks good to you, Channon?"

Was that a trick question or what?

Forcing herself to look at something other than Sebastian, she attempted to find a substitute to sink her teeth into. "What do you recommend?" she asked, trying out her Old English. She'd never used it before in conversation.

To her amazement, the woman understood her. "If you're in the mind for something sweet, I just pulled a honey loaf from the oven."

"That would be wonderful," Channon said.

The woman left them alone. Sebastian stood back while she examined the different kinds of bread in the shop.

"So what's in the bag?" she asked, indicating the black one Sebastian had removed from his horse.

"It's just something I need to take care of. Later."

Again with the hedging. "Is that why you came back here?"

He nodded, but there was something very guarded in his look, one that warned her this topic was quite closed.

The woman returned with the bread and sliced it for them. While Channon ate the warm, delicious slice, the woman asked Sebastian if he would help her move some boxes from a cart outside into the back of her shop.

He left his bag with Channon, then went to help.

Channon listened to them in the other room while she ate the bread and drank the cider the woman had also given her. Her gaze fell to the black bag and curiosity got the better of her. Leaning over, she opened it to see what it contained. Her breath left her body as she saw the tapestry inside.

He really had stolen it. But why?

The old woman came in, brushing her hands on her apron. "That's a good man you got there, my lady."

Blushing at being caught in her snooping, Channon straightened up. At the moment, she wasn't so sure about that. "Is he still unloading the cart?"

The woman motioned her to the back, then took her to look out the door. In the alley behind the shops, she saw Sebastian playing a game with two boys who were wielding wooden swords and shields against him while pretending to be warriors fighting a dragon. The irony of their game wasn't lost on her.

She took a minute to watch him laughing and teasing them. The sight warmed her heart.

The Sebastian she had come to know was a man of many facets. Caring, compassionate, and tender in a way she'd never known before. Yet there was a savage undercurrent to him, one that let her know he wasn't a man to be taken lightly.

And as she watched him playing with the children, something strange happened to her. She wondered what he would look like playing with his own children.

With their children . . .

She could see the image so plainly that it scared her.

"Why do you wear a mask?" one of the boys asked him.

"Because I'm not as pretty as you," Sebastian teased.

"I'm not pretty," the little boy said indignantly. "I'm a handsome boy."

"Handsome you are, Aubrey," a middle-aged man said as he moved a keg through the back door of the building across the way. The man looked to Sebastian.

He gaped widely, then wiped his hand on his shirt and moved to shake Sebastian's arm. "It's been a long time since I seen one of you. It's an honor to shake your arm, sir."

The boys paused in their play. "Who is he, grandfather?"

"He's a dragon slayer, Aubrey, like the ones I tell you about at night when you go to sleep." The man indicated Sebastian's mask and sword. "I was just your age when they came to Lindsey and slew the Megalos."

She wondered if Sebastian was one of the ones who had come that day.

As if sensing her, Sebastian turned his head to see her in the doorway. "If you'll excuse me," he said to the man and boys, then made his way toward her.

Sebastian could tell by Channon's face that something was troubling her. "Is something wrong?"

"Were you one of the ones who fought the Megalos?"

He shook his head as pain sliced through him. If not for his banishment, he would have been here that day. Unlike the other Sentinels, he had to fight the Katagaria alone. "No."

"Oh."

"Is something else wrong? You still don't look happy."

She met his gaze levelly. "You stole the tapestry from the museum," she said in modern English so no one else would understand her. "I want to know why."

"I had to get it back here."

"Why?"

"Because it's the ransom for another Sentinel. If I don't give them the tapestry on Friday, they will kill him."

Channon scowled at that. "Why do they want the tapestry?"

"I have no idea. But since a man's life was at stake, I didn't bother to ask."

Suddenly, she remembered what he'd said last night about the tapestry. *"It was made by a woman named Antiphone back in seventh-century Britain. It's the story of her grandfather and his brother and their eternal struggle between good and evil."*

On their way into town, he'd said it was the story of *his* grandfather.

"Antiphone is your sister?"

"*Was* my sister. She died a long time ago."

By the look on his face she could tell the loss was still with him.

"Why was her tapestry in the museum?"

"Because . . ." He took a deep breath to stave off the agony inside him, agony so severe that it made his entire being hurt.

He felt the tic working in his jaw as he forced himself to answer her question. "The tapestry was with her when she died. I tried to return it to my family, but they wanted nothing to do with me. I couldn't stand having it around me, so I took it into the future where I knew someone would preserve it and make sure it was honored and protected as she should have been."

"You plan on taking it back after all this is over with, don't you?"

He frowned at her astuteness. "How did you know?"

"I would say I'm psychic, but I'm not. I just figured a man with a heart as big as yours wouldn't just steal something without making amends."

"You don't know me that well."

"I think I do."

Sebastian clenched his teeth. No, she didn't know. He wasn't a good man. He was fool.

If not for him, Antiphone would have lived. Her death had been all his fault. It was a guilt that he lived with constantly. One that would never cease, never heal.

And in that moment he realized something. He had to let Channon go. There was no way he could keep her. There was no way he could share his life with her.

If anything should ever happen to her . . .

It would be his fault, too. As his mate, she would be prime Katagari bait. Even though he was banished, he was still a Sentinel, and his job was to seek and destroy every Slayer he could find.

Alone he could fight them. But without his patria to guard Channon while he fulfilled his ancient oath, there was always a chance she would end up as Antiphone had.

He would sooner spend the rest of his life celibate than let that happen.

*Celibate! No!*

He squelched the rebellious scream of the inner Drakos. For the next three weeks, he would guard her life with his own, and once his mark was gone from her, he would take her home.

It was what *had* to be done.

***After they left the bakery, they spent the afternoon brows-*** ing the stalls and sampling the food and drink.

Channon couldn't believe this day. It was the best one of her entire life. And it wasn't just because she was in Saxon Britain, it was because she had Sebastian by her side. His light teasing and easy-going manner wrapped around her heart and made her ache to keep him.

"Beg pardon, my lord?"

They turned to find a man standing behind them while they were watching an acrobat.

"Aye?" Sebastian asked.

"I was told by His Majesty, King Henfrith, to come and ask for the honor of your company tonight. He wishes to extend his full and most cordial hospitality to you and to your lady."

Channon felt giddy. "I get to meet a king?"

Sebastian nodded. "Tell His Majesty that it would be my honor to meet with him. We shall be along shortly."

The messenger left.

Channon breathed nervously. "I don't know about this. Am I dressed appropriately?"

"Yes, you are. I assure you, you will be the most beautiful woman there." Then, her gallant champion offered her his arm. Taking it, she let him lead her through town to the large hall.

As they drew near the hall's door, she could hear the music and laughter from inside as the people ate their supper. Sebastian opened the door and allowed her to enter first.

Channon hesitated in the doorway as she looked around in awe. It was more splendid than anything she'd ever imagined.

A lord's table was set apart from the others, and there were three women and four men seated there. The man with the crown she assumed was the king, the lady at his right, his queen, and the others must be the daughters and sons or some other dignitaries perhaps.

Servants bustled around with food while dogs milled about, catching scraps from the diners. The music was sublime.

"Nervous?" Sebastian asked her in modern English.

"A little. I have no idea what Saxon etiquette is."

He lifted her hand to his lips and kissed her fingers, causing a warm chill to sweep through her. "Follow my lead, and I will show you everything you need to know to live in my world."

She cocked her brow at his words. There was something hidden in that. She was sure of it. "You are going to take me home at the next full moon, right?"

"I gave you my word, my lady. That is the one thing I have never broken, and I most assuredly would not break my oath to you."

"Just checking."

A hush fell over the crowd as they crossed the room and neared the lord's table.

Channon swallowed nervously. But she was there with the most handsome man in the kingdom. Dressed in his black armor and mask, Sebastian was a spectacularly masculine sight. The man had a regal presence that promised strength, speed, and deadly precision.

He stopped before the table and gave a low, courtly bow. Channon gave what she hoped was an acceptable curtsy.

"Greetings, Your Majesty," Sebastian said, straightening. "I am Sebastian Kattalakis, a Prince of Arcadia."

Channon's jaw went slack with that declaration. A prince? Was he for real or was it another joke?

He turned to her, his features guarded. "My lady, Channon."

The king rose to his feet and bowed to them. "Your Highness, it has been a long time since I've had the privilege of a dragon slayer's company. I owe your house more than I can ever repay. Please, come and be seated in honor. You and your lady-wife are welcomed here for as long as you wish to stay."

Sebastian led Channon to the table and sat her to his right, beside a man who introduced himself as the king's son-in-law.

"Are you really a prince?" she whispered to Sebastian.

"A most disinherited one, but yes. My grandfather, Lycaon, was the King of Arcadia."

"Oh my God," Channon said as pieces of history came together in her mind. "The king cursed by Zeus?"

"And the Fates."

*Lycanthrope*, the Greek word for werewolves, vampires, and shape-shifters, was taken from Lycaon, the King of Arcadia. Stunned, she wondered what other so-called myths and legends were actually real.

"You know, you are better than the Rosetta stone to a historian."

Sebastian laughed. "Glad to know I have some use to you."

More than he knew—and it wasn't just the knowledge he held. Today was the only day she could recall in an exceptionally long time when she hadn't been lonely. Not once. She'd enjoyed every minute of this day and didn't really want it to end.

She looked forward to spending the next few weeks with Sebastian in his world. And deep inside where she best not investigate was a part of her that wondered if, when the time came, she'd be able to leave him.

How could a woman give up a man who made her feel the way Sebastian did every time he looked at her?

She wasn't sure it was possible.

Sebastian cut and served her from the roast of something she couldn't quite identify. Thinking it best not to ask, she took a bite and discovered it was quite good.

They ate in silence while others finished their meals and started dancing.

After a time, Channon glanced to Sebastian and noticed his eyes seemed troubled. "Are you all right?" she asked.

Sebastian ran his hand over the uncovered portion of his face. He felt ill inside. The harmony between his two halves had been disrupted by his inner fighting over Channon, and the pain of it was almost more than he could stand.

The Drakos wanted her regardless, but the man in him refused to see her endangered. The struggle between the two sides was so severe that he wondered how he was going to make it for the next three weeks without doing permanent damage to one or the other of his halves.

It was this kind of internal struggle that caused the madness in their youth. And if he didn't restore the balance soon, his powers would be permanently scarred.

"Jet lag from the time-jump," he said.

Forcing the dragon back into submission, he didn't speak to Channon while she ate. He allowed her the time to experience the life and beauty of this time without intruding on her.

Gods, how he ached to make her stay here. He could take her right now and bind her to him for the rest of his life. It was fully within his power.

But he couldn't do that to her. The man in him refused to claim her against her will. It had to be her choice. He would never accept anything less than that.

Channon frowned as she noted the seriousness in Sebastian's eyes. "Are you sure you're all right?" she asked.

"I'm fine. Really."

She still didn't buy that. The musicians paused and the crowd clapped for them. As she applauded the musicians and dancers, Channon became aware of something on her hand. Frowning, she studied her palm. "What in the world?"

Sebastian swallowed. Up until now he'd used his powers to shield her from the marking. But his powers were weakening . . .

She tried to rub it off. "What is this?"

He started to tell her the truth, but it wedged in his throat. She didn't need to know that. Not right now. He didn't want to destroy the fun she was having by interjecting such a serious topic. "It's from the time-jump," he lied. "It's nothing major."

"Oh," Channon said, dropping her hand. "Okay."

The musicians started up again. Sebastian excused himself from her.

Channon frowned. Something in his demeanor concerned her.

He walked too deliberately with his spine rigid and his shoulders back.

Following after him, she watched as he left the hall and went outside. He rounded the side of the hall and headed toward a small well.

Channon stayed back while he pulled water from the

well, then removed his mask and splashed the water over his face.

"Sebastian?" she asked softly, moving to his side. "Tell me what's wrong with you."

Sebastian raked his gloved hands through his hair, dampening it. "I'm okay, really."

"You keep saying that, but . . ."

She placed her hand on his arm. The sensation of her touch rocked him so fiercely that he wanted to growl from it. His body reacted viciously as desire tore through him.

The dragon snarled and circled, demanding her. *Take her. Take her. Take her.*

No! He would not cost her her life. He would not endanger her.

"I shouldn't have brought you here, Channon," he said as he turned his powers inward to harness the Drakos. "I'm sorry."

She smiled at him. "Don't be. It's not turning out so badly. It's actually kind of nice here."

He shut his eyes and turned away. He had to. The beast inside was snarling again. Salivating.

*Claim her.*

It wanted total possession.

*And so did the man.*

His groin tightened even more, and he wondered how much longer he could keep that part of him leashed.

Channon saw the feral look in his eyes as he raked a ravenous look over her. Her body reacted to it with a desire so powerful that it stunned and scared her. She wanted him to look at her like that. Forever.

His breathing ragged, he cupped her face in his hands and pulled her close for a fierce kiss. Channon moaned at the raw passion she tasted as she surrendered her weight to him.

She wrapped her arms around his neck and felt his muscles bunch and flex. Images of last night tore through her. Again she could see his naked body moving in the moonlight and feel him deep and hard inside her.

Sebastian growled at the taste of her, at the feel of her tongue sweeping against his. Out of his mind with the passion, he pinned her against the wall of the gate.

He wanted her no matter the consequences, no matter the time or place.

Channon felt his erection as he held her between him and the wall. As if magnetized, her hips brushed against him. She wanted to feel him inside her again. She wanted nothing between them except bare skin.

"What is it you do to me?" she breathed.

Sebastian pulled back as her words penetrated the haziness of his mind. Still, all he could smell was Channon. Her scent spun around his head, making him even dizzier. He dipped his head for her lips, then barely caught himself.

Hissing, he forced himself to release her. If he kissed her again, he would take her here in the yard like an animal, without regard to her humanity, without regard for her choice.

Claiming was a special moment, and he refused to sully it like the Katagari. No, he wouldn't take her like this. Not out here where anyone could see them. He would not let the Drakos win.

"Channon," he whispered. "Please, go back inside."

Channon started to refuse, but the steeliness in his body kept her from it. "Okay," she said.

She paused at the corner of the hall and looked back at him. He was now leaning over the well with his head hung low. She didn't know what was wrong, but she was sure it wasn't good.

"Ha, take that!"

Channon turned at the sound of a child laughing. She saw the two boys with wooden swords who had been fighting Sebastian earlier. They ran across the yard.

"I will kill you, nasty dragon," one boy cried as they ran into a forge where the blacksmith cursed and chased them out, telling the tallest that he should be home eating.

She shook her head. Some things never changed, no matter the time period. Curious about what else reminded her of home, she crossed the yard.

*Sebastian breathed deeply, trying to summon his powers* back to him. This was not good. If he stayed around Channon, by the time Friday arrived, he wouldn't be able to face the Katagaria trio.

He had to have his powers back, intact and strong, which meant that he would either have to claim her or find some place safe for her to stay so that he could get distance from her.

Because if he didn't, they would both die.

"Bas?"

Sebastian looked around the yard, trying to find the source of that whispered call. It was a nickname no one had used in centuries.

Gold flashed to his right. To his shock, Damos appeared, then collapsed on the ground. Like a wounded animal, his brother held himself on all fours with his head hung low.

Unable to believe his eyes, Sebastian went to him. "Damos?"

Damos lifted his head to look at him. Instead of the hatred and disgust he expected to see, Sebastian saw only pain and guilt. "Did you get the tapestry?"

Sebastian couldn't answer as he saw his brother's face again. The two of them were almost identical in build and looks. The only real difference was in their hair color. Sebastian's hair was black while Damos's was a dark reddish-brown.

And as Sebastian looked into those eyes that were the same color as his own, the past flashed through his mind.

*"You're nothing but a cowardly traitor. You've never been worth anything. I wish it had been you they tore*

*apart. If there were any justice, it would be you lying in the grave and not Antiphone."* The cruel words echoed in his head, and even now he could feel the bite of the whip as they delivered the two hundred lashes to his back.

Battered and bloody, Sebastian had been dumped in a cesspit and left there to die or survive as he saw fit.

He'd crawled from the pit and somehow found his way into the woods, where he'd lain for days floating in and out of consciousness. To this day, he wasn't sure how he'd survived it.

"Bas!" Damos snapped, wincing from the effort as he pushed himself slowly to his feet. He staggered, and against his will, Sebastian found himself helping his brother to the well where he propped him.

Damos's long reddish-brown hair was lank and clotted with blood and snarls. His face was battered and his clothes torn. "You look like hell."

"Yeah, well, it's hard to look good when you're being tortured."

Sebastian knew that firsthand. "You escaped?"

He nodded. "Where's the tapestry?"

"It's safe."

Damos locked gazes with him. "Were you really going to trade it for me?"

"I brought it here, didn't I?"

Tears gathered in Damos's eyes as he looked at him. "I am so sorry for what I did to you."

Sebastian was stunned. So, Damos did know what an apology was.

"The Katagaria told me what happened that day, how they tricked you." Damos placed his hand against the scar on Sebastian's neck that Sebastian had received while trying to save Antiphone's life. "I can't believe you survived them. And I can't believe you did this for me."

"Not like I had anything better to do."

Damos hissed and placed his hand to his eyes. "Those damned feelers. They're trying to find me."

Sebastian went cold. Without his powers, he couldn't sense the feelers, but if they were sending them out for Damos, then they would find . . .

Channon!

His heart pounding, he ran for the hall.

***Channon wished she had her notepad to take notes on*** everything she saw. This was just incredible!

Enchanted, she walked idly past the stalls and huts, looking inside to see families eating and spending the evening together.

"You look lost."

She turned at the voice behind her. There were three men there, handsome all and quite tall. "Not lost," she offered. "Just out for a bit of fresh air."

The blond man appeared to be the leader of the small group. "You know, that can be quite dangerous for a woman alone."

Channon frowned as a wave of panic washed over her. "I beg your pardon?"

"Tell me, Acmenes." The blonde spoke to the tall brunette beside him. "Why do you think an Arcadian would bring a human woman through time?"

Panic gone, sheer terror set in, especially since the man was speaking in modern English.

She tried to head back to Sebastian, but of the third man caught her. He grabbed her right hand and showed it to his friends. "Because she's his mate."

The one called Acmenes laughed. "How precious is this? An Arcadian with a human dragonswan."

"No," the brunette said, "it's better. A lone Sentinel with a human mate."

They laughed cruelly.

Channon glared. She might look harmless, but she'd been on her own for quite some time, and as a woman alone, she'd learned a few things.

Tae Kwon Do was one of them. She caught the man holding her with her elbow and twisted out of his grasp. Before the others could reach her, she ran for the hall.

Unfortunately, the Katagaria moved a lot faster than she did and they grabbed her before she could reach it.

"Let her go." Sebastian's voice rolled across the yard like dangerous thunder as he unsheathed his sword.

"Oh no," Acmenes said sarcastically. "This is the best of all. A Sentinel who has *lost* his powers."

Channon's heart clenched at their words.

Sebastian's smile was taunting, wicked. "I don't need my powers to defeat you."

Before she could blink, the Katagaria attacked Sebastian.

"Run, Channon," Sebastian said as he delivered a staggering blow to the first one who reached him.

Channon didn't go far. She couldn't leave him to fight the men alone. Not that he appeared to need any help. She watched as they attacked him at once and he deftly knocked them back.

"Um, Acmenes," the youngest Katagari said as he picked himself up from the ground and panted. "He's kicking our butts."

Acmenes laughed. "Only in human form."

In a brilliant flash, Acmenes transformed into a dragon. The crowd that had gathered at the start of the fight shrieked and ran chaotically for shelter.

Channon stumbled back.

Standing at least twenty feet high, Acmenes was a terrifying sight. His green and orange scales shimmered in the fading daylight while his blue wings flapped. He slung his spiked tail around, but Sebastian flipped out of the way.

The other two flashed into dragon form.

Sebastian held his sword tightly in his hands as he faced them. Even if he still held his powers unsevered, he wouldn't have been able to transform. Not while in the middle of a human village. It was forbidden.

*Damn you, Fates.*

"What's the matter, Kattalakis?" Acmenes asked. "Won't you breech your oath to protect your humans?"

Bracis laughed. "He can't, brother, his powers are too fragmented. He's powerless to stop us."

Acmenes shook his large, scaled head and sighed. "This is so anticlimactic. All these years you've chased us, and now . . ." He tsked. "To comfort you as you die, Sebastian, know that your dragonswan will be as well used by all of us as your sister was."

Raw agony ripped through Sebastian.

Over and over, he saw his sister's face and felt her blood on his skin as he held her lifeless body in his arms and wept.

"Kill him," Acmenes said. Then he turned toward Channon.

The dragon beast inside Sebastian roared with needful vengeance. He'd been unable to save Antiphone, but he would never let Channon die. Not like that.

Ceding his humanity, he let loose his shields. His change came so swiftly that he didn't even feel it. All he felt was the love in his heart for his mate, the animal desperation to keep her safe regardless of law or sense.

Channon froze at the sight of Sebastian's dragon form. The same height as Acmenes, his scales were bloodred and black. He looked like some fierce, terrifying menace, and she searched for something to remind her of the man he'd been two seconds ago.

She found none of him.

What she did see terrified her.

Acmenes swung about to face Sebastian as he savagely attacked the other two dragons. Fire shot through the village as they fought like the primeval beasts they were.

Then, to her horror, she saw Sebastian kill the dragon on his left with one sharp bite. The one on his right stumbled away from him in wounded pain, then took to the skies.

Acmenes reached for her, but Sebastian tackled him. The force of them hitting the ground shook it. They fought like men, slugging at each other, and yet like dragons, as their tails coiled and moved trying to sting one another.

She cringed as both dragons were wounded countless times by their fighting, but neither would pull back. She'd never seen anything like it. They were locked in the throes of a blood feud.

Acmenes hefted his body and threw Sebastian over his head, then rolled to his monstrous feet. He stumbled as he tried to reach the sky, but before he could leap, Sebastian caught him through the heart with his tail.

"Dragon!"

Now armed and prepared, the men of the village came running back to do damage to the creatures who had invaded them.

At first Channon thought they came to help Sebastian, until she realized that they intended to attack him.

Without thought, she went to him. "Run, Sebastian," she said.

He didn't. He turned on her with frightening eyes, and in that moment she realized the man she knew was not in that body.

The dragon snarled at her as the crowd attacked him. Throwing his head back, he shrieked.

To her shock, he didn't attack the people.

Instead, he grabbed her in his massive claw and took flight.

Channon screamed as she watched the ground drift far away from her. She had no idea where he was taking her, but she didn't like this. Not even a little bit.

"Sebastian?"

Sebastian heard Channon's voice. But it came from a distance. He could only vaguely remember her.

Vaguely recall . . .

He shrieked as something flew past his head. Looking behind him, he saw Bracis coming for them.

And with the sight, his human memories came flooding back.

*"Sebastian, help us. We're trapped by the Slayers."*

*"I can't, Percy. I can't leave Antiphone."*

*"She's safe in the hills. We are in the open, unprotected. Please, Sebastian. I'm too young to die. Please don't let them kill me. I know you can beat them. Please, please help me."*

And so he had heeded the mental distress call and gone to protect his young cousin and brother, never knowing Percy's cry for help had been a trick, never knowing that Percy had deliberately summoned him from the cave.

He'd found his cousin barely alive and learned too late they had forced Percy to call for him.

By the time he'd returned to the cave where he'd left his sister hiding, the Slayers were gone.

And so was his sister's life.

Devastated on a level he'd never known existed, he'd refused to speak up in his own defense when his people had banished him.

He'd offered no argument at all against Damos's insults.

He should never have left Antiphone unprotected.

Now he looked at the woman he held cradled in his palm.

*Channon.*

The Fates had entrusted this woman to him, just as his brother had entrusted Antiphone to him.

He would not let Bracis have her. This time, he would see her safe. No matter what it cost him, she would live.

Sebastian headed for the forest.

Channon held her breath as they landed on the ground in a small clearing.

"Hide." The word seemed to sizzle out of Sebastian's dragon mouth.

She went without question, running into the trees and underbrush, looking for someplace safe. The forest was so thick that she quickly lost sight of the dragons. But she could hear them as they fought. She could feel the ground under her shake.

Grateful for the green dress, she found a clump of bushes and crawled into them to wait and to pray.

***Sebastian circled around Bracis, enjoying the moment, en-***joying the feel of the dragon blood coursing through his veins. For two hundred and fifty years he had dreamed of this moment. He had dreamed of drinking from the fount of vengeance.

Now the moment was upon him.

Bracis was the last of the Slayers left from that day. One by one, Sebastian had hunted them all down. He had hunted them through time and even space itself.

"Are you ready to die?" Sebastian asked his opponent.

Bracis attacked. Sebastian caught him with his teeth and clamped down on the Katagari's shoulder. He tasted the blood of the beast as Bracis shredded at his back with his claws.

Sebastian barely felt it. But what he did feel was the fear inside Bracis. It swelled up with a pungent odor so foul that it made Sebastian laugh.

"You may kill me," Bracis rasped. "But I'm taking you with me."

Something stung Sebastian's shoulder. Snarling, he jerked his head around to see the dagger protruding from his back. But it wasn't the steel that stung; it was the poison that coated the blade. Dragon's Bane.

Roaring from the pain of it, he turned back and finished Bracis off quickly by breaking his long, scaled neck.

He stood over the body of his enemy, staring at it blankly. After all this time, he'd wanted more out of the kill. He'd expected it to release the agony in his heart, to relieve his guilt.

It didn't.

He felt nothing except disappointed by it. Cheated.

No. In two hundred and fifty years only one thing had ever given him a moment's worth of peace.

Suddenly, a scream tore through the woods.

Channon.

Sebastian reared up to his full twenty foot height, searching for her through the trees with his dragon sight and senses.

He heard nothing more. His heart pounding, he ran for the woods where she'd vanished. With every step that closed the distance between them, all his feelings rushed through him. He relived every moment of Antiphone's death.

The guilt, the fear, the raw agony.

Under the onslaught of his human feelings, the dragon inside him receded again, leaving only the man. The man who had been crushed that day. The man who had sworn over his sister's grave to never let another person into his heart.

The same man who had looked into a pair of crystal blue eyes over dinner one night and had seen a future inside them that he wanted to live. A future with laughter and love. One spent in quiet serenity with a woman standing beside him to keep him strong and grounded.

Leaves and brambles tore at his flesh, but he paid no attention to them.

Like Antiphone, he'd left Channon alone to face an untold nightmare.

Left her to face . . .

He came to a stop as he caught sight of her.

Frowning, Sebastian struggled to breathe. His vision was so blurry from the poison that he wasn't sure he could trust it.

He blinked and blinked again. And still it stayed before his eyes. Channon stood with a sword in her hand, and it was angled at Damos's throat.

"Bas, would you please tell her I'm not a Katagari."

Channon glanced over her shoulder to see Sebastian standing naked in the woods. Human once more, he was pale and covered in sweat.

"Let him go."

By the sound of Sebastian's voice, she knew the man she held hadn't been lying to her. He was one of the good guys.

The instant she saw Sebastian stumble, she dropped the sword she'd taken from this stranger.

Channon ran to his side. "Sebastian?"

He was shaking in her arms. Together, they sank to the ground and she held his head in her lap.

"I thought you were dead," he whispered, running his hand over her forearms. "I heard you scream."

The man she'd cornered knelt beside them. "I startled her. I was trying to help you with Bracis. I sent out a feeler for your essence and it led me to her. You didn't tell me you were mated."

Channon ignored the man as Sebastian's body temperature dropped alarmingly.

Why was Sebastian trembling so? His wounds didn't look that severe. "Sebastian, what's wrong with you?

"Dragon's Bane."

Channon frowned as the man cursed. What was Dragon's Bane?

"Sebastian," he said forcefully, taking Sebastian's face in his hands and forcing him to look up at him. "Don't you dare die on me. Damn you, fight this."

"I'm already dead to you, Damos," he said, his voice ragged as he turned away from him. "You told me to die painfully."

Sebastian closed his eyes.

Channon saw the grief in Damos's eyes as her own tore through her. This couldn't be happening. She wanted to wake up.

But it wasn't a nightmare, it was real.

Damos looked at her, his greenish-gold eyes searing her

with power and emotion. "He's going to die unless you help him."

"What can I do?"

"Give him a reason to live."

Her hand started to tingle where the mark was. Channon scowled as it began to fade. "What the . . . ?"

"We're losing him. When he dies, your mark will be gone, too."

The reality of the moment hit her ferociously. Sebastian was going to die?

No, it couldn't be.

"Sebastian?" she said, shaking him. "Can you hear me?"

He shifted ever so slightly in her arms.

She wouldn't let him go like this. She couldn't. Though they had only known each other one day, it felt as if they'd been together an eternity. The thought of losing him crippled her.

"Sebastian, do you remember what you said to me in the hotel room? You said, 'I'm here because I know the sadness inside you. I know what it feels like to wake in the morning, lost and lonely and aching for someone to be there with me.' "

She pressed her lips against his cheek and wept. "I don't want to be alone anymore, Sebastian. I want to wake up with you like I did this morning. I want to feel your arms around me, your hand in my hair."

He went limp in her arms.

"No!" Channon cried, holding him close to her heart. "Don't you do this to me, Sebastian Kattalakis. Don't you dare make me believe in knights in shining armor, in men who are good and decent, and then leave me alone again. Damn it, Sebastian. You promised to take me home. You promised not to leave me."

The mark faded from her palm.

Channon wept as her heart splintered. Until that moment, she hadn't realized that against all known odds, against all known reason, she loved this man.

And she didn't want to lose him.

She pressed her wet cheek to his lips. "I love you, Sebastian. I just wished you'd lived long enough for us to see what could become of us."

Suddenly, she felt another tingle in her palm. It grew to a burning itch. It was followed by a slow, tiny stirring of air against her cheek.

Damos expelled a deep breath. "That's it, little brother. Fight for your mate. Fight for your dragonswan."

Channon looked up as Damos doffed his cloak, then wrapped it around Sebastian's body.

"Is he going to live?"

"I don't know, but he's trying to. The Fates willing, he will."

# Three

***Channon bathed Sebastian's fevered brow while she*** prayed for his survival and whispered for him to come back to her.

After they had stabilized Sebastian, Damos had taken them to a small village in Sussex where humans and Arcadians lived and worked together. She learned that though Arcadians could only time-jump during a full moon, they could use their magic to make lateral jumps from one place to another in the same time frame any time they wanted to.

It didn't really make sense to her, but she didn't care. At the moment, all that mattered to her was the fact that Sebastian was still fighting his way back from death.

It was long after midnight now. They were alone in a large room where the only light came from three candles set in an iron fixture against the wall. Sebastian lay draped in a sheet on an ornate bed that bore the images of dragons and wheat and was shielded from drafts by shimmery white drapes.

The sounds of the night drifted in from the open window while she waited for some sign that he would wake up.

None came.

At some point before dawn, exhaustion overtook her and she curled up by his side and went to sleep.

"Channon?"

Channon felt as if she were floating, as if she had no real form at all.

Suddenly, she stood in a summer field with wildflowers all around her. She was dressed in a sheer, white gown that left her all but bare. There was a medieval castle in the distance, highlighted against the horizon. It reminded her of one of the manuscript pages she studied.

None of it seemed real until she felt strong arms wrap around her.

Glancing over her shoulder, she looked up to find Sebastian behind her. Like her, he was practically naked, dressed only in a pair of thin white pants. The breeze stirred his dark hair around his handsome face, and he flashed those killer dimples. Her heart soaring, she turned in his arms, reached up, and placed her marked palm over his Sentinel tattoo. "Am I dreaming?"

"Yes. This was the only way I could reach you."

She frowned. "I don't understand."

"I'm dying."

"No," she said emphatically, "you're still alive. You came back to me."

The tenderness on his face as he looked at her made her heart pound. "In part, but I still lack the strength I need to wake."

He sat down on the ground and pulled her down with him. "I missed you today."

So had she, in a way that made no sense whatsoever to her, but then feelings seldom do. The entire time he'd been unconscious, she had felt as if a vital part of her was gone.

Now, in the circle of his arms, leaning back against him, she felt right again. She felt whole and warm.

Sebastian took her hand into his and used his thumb to toy gently with her fingers.

"I can't lose you," she whispered. "I've spent hours thinking of my life at home. It was lonely and empty. I had no one to laugh with."

He placed his lips against her temple and kissed her tenderly. Then he cupped her head in his hands and leaned his forehead against her. "I know, love. I've spent my life alone in caves, my only company the sound of the wind outside. But the only way I can fight my way back to you is to regain my powers."

"Regain them how? How did you lose them?"

She felt his lips moving against her skin as he whispered the words while he nuzzled her. It was wonderful to have him holding her again. "I was using them against myself. I set the dragon and the human inside me at odds."

His touch burned through her. She didn't want to live another day without feeling him by her side, without seeing that devilish smile and those deep dimples.

In short, she needed this man.

"Why did you do that?" she asked.

He pulled back and kissed her fingertips. "To protect you."

"From what?"

"Me," he said simply.

Channon stared up at him, baffled by his words. He would never hurt her. She knew that. Even in his true dragon form he had done nothing but protect her. "I don't understand."

He ran his thumb over her palm, tracing the lines of her mark. Chills swept up her arm, tightening her breasts as she watched him.

When he met her gaze, she saw his sorrow. "I lied to you when you asked me about the mark on your hand. Part of the curse of my people is that we are only designated one mate for our entire existence, a mate we don't choose."

Channon frowned. Damos had refused to speak to her when she asked him what he meant when he had called her Sebastian's mate. He'd told her it was for Sebastian to do.

Sebastian kissed her marked palm. "The moment we Arcadians and Katagaria are born, the Fates choose a mate for us. We spend the rest of our lives trying to find our other half. Unlike humans, we can't have a family or children with anyone other than our mate. If we fail to find our other half, we are doomed to live out our lives alone.

"As a human, you have the freewill to love anyone. You can love more than once. But I can't. You, Channon, are the only woman in any time or place who I can love. The only woman I can ever have a family with. The only woman I will ever desire."

She remembered Plato's theory about the human race being two halves of the same person—the male and female who were separated by the gods. Now she realized Plato's theory was based on the reality of Sebastian's people, not hers.

"So what do you need to regain your powers?"

He fingered her lips and stared at her with desperate need. She knew he was still holding himself back, still keeping himself from kissing her.

"You have to claim me as your mate," he said quietly. "Sex regenerates our powers. It heightens them. I was trying so hard to keep from forcing you into the Claiming that I buried them too deeply. There is a delicate balance in all Arcadians and Katagaria between the human and animal half. I was fighting myself so hard to protect you that I ruptured the balance."

"It can only be repaired by Claiming me?"

He nodded.

"And this Claiming, what is it exactly?"

He traced the line of her jaw, making her burn from the inside out. "When you Claim me, you acknowledge me as your soulmate. The ceremony is really quite simple. You place your marked palm over mine and then you take me into your body. You hold me there and say, 'I accept you as you are, and I will always hold you close to my heart. I will walk beside you forever.' "

"And then?"

"I repeat the words back to you."

That seemed just a little too easy to her. If that was all there was to it, why had he fought it so hard? "That's it?"

He hesitated.

Inwardly, she groaned. "I know that look," she said, pulling back slightly from him. "Any time you're not telling me the whole truth you get that look."

He smiled at her and planted a chaste kiss on her cheek. "All right, there is something more. When we join, my natural instinct will be to bond you to me."

That still didn't sound so bad. "Bond me how?"

"With blood."

"Okay, I don't like this part. What do you mean *with blood?*"

He dropped his hands and leaned back on them to watch her. "You know how humans will bind themselves together as blood brothers?"

"Yes."

"It's basically the same thing—but with one major difference. If you take my blood into you, our mortal lives are completely conjoined."

"Meaning we will become one person?" she asked.

"No, nothing like that. Do you remember your Greek myths at all?"

"Some of them."

"Do you remember who Atropos is?"

She shook her head. "Nope, not a clue."

"She is one of the Moirae, the Fates. She's the one who assigns our mates to us at birth, and if we chose to bond with that mate, her sister Clotho, who is the spinner of our lives, combines our life-threads together. At the end of a normal life Atropos will cut the thread and cause a death. But if we are bonded together and our threads are one, then she can't cut one without the other."

"We die together."

"Exactly."

Wow, that was a big commitment. Especially for him. "So you will have a human life span."

"No. My thread is stronger. You will have an Arcadian life span."

She blinked at that. "Are you saying I could live several hundred years?"

He nodded. "Or we could both die tomorrow."

"Whoa. Is there anything else?" she asked, curiously. "Will I also get some of your powers? Mind control? Time-walking?"

He laughed at her. "No. Sorry. My powers are tied to my birth and my destiny. Bonding only extends to our life-threads."

Channon smiled as she rose up on her knees, between his legs. She crouched over him, forcing him to lean back farther on his arms as she hovered over him. She bit her lip as she stared at his handsome face, at those lips she was dying to taste.

"So, what you're offering me is a gorgeous, incredibly sexy man who is completely devoted to me for the next few centuries?"

"Yes."

She smiled even wider. "One who can never stray?"

"Never."

She forced him to lie back on the ground as she straddled his waist and leaned forward on her arms so that her face was just a few inches above his. She felt his hard erection through his pants, pressing against her core. How she wanted him. But first she wanted to make sure she understood all the consequences.

"You know," she said, "it's real hard to say no to this. What downside could there possibly be?"

He shifted his hips under hers, making her burn for him as he tucked a stray piece of her hair back behind her ear. Still, he didn't touch her, and she knew he was leaving it all up to her now.

"The Katagaria who want me dead," he said seriously. "They will never cease coming for us, and because I am banished, it will only be the two of us to fight them off. Our children will be Arcadian and not human, and they, too, will have to battle the Katagaria. But most important, you will have to remain here in the Middle Ages."

"Why?"

"Because of the electricity in your time period. Arcadians who are natural animals such as hawks, panthers, wolves, bears, and such can live in your world. If they are accidentally changed, their animal forms are small or normal enough to hide from humans."

"But if you become a dragon, then we have a Godzilla movie."

"Exactly. And in your time period, there are plenty of tasers and electrical devices that can completely incapacitate me. No offense, but I don't relish being someone's science experiment. Been there, done that, and sold the T-shirt for profit."

She sat up straight, still straddling him, as she digested all of this.

The man offered her the deal of a lifetime.

Sebastian watched her carefully. It was taking all his restraint to keep his hands off her when all he wanted to do was make love to her. He'd told her everything. Now it was up to her, and he trembled with the fear that she would leave him.

She took his hands in hers and held them to her waist. "Our babies will be normal, right?"

"Perfectly normal. They will age like human children

with the only exception being that they won't be teenagers until their twenties."

"And that's a drawback?"

He laughed.

"Oh, by the way, you're no longer banished."

Sebastian scowled. "What?"

"While they were torturing Damos, the Katagaria admitted that they had tricked you so they could get the tapestry from Antiphone. But she refused to let them have it."

"Why? What was so important about it?"

"Unfortunately nothing, but they believed that it contained the secret for immortality. It seems Katagaria legend had it that the granddaughter of their creator had placed his secrets into the work she'd created to honor him. They captured Damos, thinking he had it, and when they found out you alone knew where it was, they arranged the bargain with you."

"My sister died for no reason?"

"Sh," she said, placing her hand over his lips. "Just be glad the truth is out and the tapestry is safe. Damos wants to make the past up to you."

Sebastian couldn't believe it. After all this time, his banishment was lifted?

That meant a real home for Channon where she would be safe. A home where their children would be safe.

Channon laid her body down over his and breathed him in. "Which means you're no longer alone, Sebastian. You don't really need me."

"That's not true. I need you more than I've ever needed anything else. My heart was dead until I looked into your eyes."

He cupped her face in his hands. "I want you to Claim me, Channon," he said fiercely. "I want to spend the rest of my life waking up with you in my arms and feeling your hair in my palm."

She choked as he used her words. He'd heard her. "I want you, too."

Laughing, he rolled over with her, pinning her to the ground and letting her feel every hard, wonderful inch of his body.

They kissed each other in a frenzied hurry as they helped one another out of their clothes.

Channon pulled back as their naked bodies slid against each other. "Does it count if we do this in a dream?"

"This isn't really a dream. It's an alternate place."

"You know, you scare me when you talk like that."

He smiled at her. "I have much to teach you about my world."

"And I am willing to learn it all." Channon kissed those delectable lips as she wrapped her bare legs around his. She felt his erection against her hip, and it made her burn with need.

"Are you sure about this?" he asked, nibbling his way along her jaw. "You'll be giving up all your future *Buffy* episodes."

She drew her breath in sharply between her teeth as she thought it over. "I have to tell you, it's a hard decision to make. Watching Spike prance around and be all Spikey, versus a couple hundred years of making love to a Greek god." She clucked her tongue. "What is a woman to do?"

She moaned as he ran his tongue around her ear and whispered, "What can I do to sway your verdict?"

"That's a real good start right there." She sighed as her body erupted into chills and he dipped his head to torment her breast with his hot mouth. "I guess I'll just have to find another pastime to television watching."

"I think I can help you with that." He rolled over again to place her on top of him.

The intensity of his stare scalded her.

"Tradition demands you be in charge of this, my lady. The whole idea behind the Claiming is that the woman places her life and her trust into the hands of her mate.

Once you accept me, the animal inside me will do whatever it takes to keep you safe."

"Like when you turned into a dragon in front of all those people?"

He nodded.

She smiled. "You know it's a pity I didn't know you in third grade. There was this bully—"

He cut her words off with a kiss.

"Mmm," she breathed. "I like that. Now, where were we?"

She nibbled her way down his chin to his chest.

Sebastian growled as she found his nipple and teased it with her tongue and lips. He felt his powers surging again, felt the air around them charging with the force of it.

Channon felt it, too. She moaned as the energy moved around her body, caressing her.

Sebastian held his left hand up. The mark in his palm glowed and shimmered. Looking into his eyes, Channon covered his mark with hers and laced her fingers with his.

Heat engulfed her entire body as she felt something hot and demanding rush through her. She saw the beast in his eyes and the man as he breathed raggedly.

It was the sexiest thing she'd ever beheld.

Arching her back, she lifted her hips and took him deep into her body.

They moaned in unison.

She watched Sebastian's face as she slowly ground herself against him. "Um, I forgot the words."

He laughed as he lifted his hips, driving himself so deep into her that she groaned. "I accept you as you are."

"Oh," she breathed, then remembering what she was doing, she repeated his words. "I accept you as you are."

"And I will always hold you close to my heart."

"Umm, hmmm. I will most definitely hold you close to my heart."

"I will walk beside you forever."

She placed her hand on his chest, over his heart. "I will walk beside you forever."

His eyes turned eerily dark. He reached up with his free hand and cupped her cheek. His voice was a deep, low growl, a cross between the voice of the dragon and the voice of the man. "I accept you as you are, and I will always hold you close to my heart. I will walk beside you forever."

He'd barely finished the words before his teeth grew long and sharp and his eyes darkened to the color of obsidian.

"Sebastian?"

"Don't be afraid," he said as he bared his fangs. "It's the dragon wanting to bond with you, but I have control of it."

"And if I want to bond with you?"

He hesitated. "Do you understand what you're doing?"

Channon paused with him inside her and locked gazes with him. "I've lived alone all my life, Sebastian. I don't want to do it another day."

He sat up, keeping them joined.

Channon hissed at how good he felt as she wrapped her free arm around his waist and he pulled her against him with his.

She lifted her hips, then dropped herself down on him.

"That's it, love, claim me as yours." Sebastian let her ride him slowly as he waited for more of his powers to return. He needed to be in total control for this.

Their marked hands still joined, he held her close to him so that he could feel her heart beating in rapid time to his.

When he was certain his powers were perfectly aligned, he leaned his head forward and sank his teeth gently into her neck.

Channon shivered at the feeling of his hot breath and teeth on her, but oddly enough, there was no pain at all. Instead, it was an erotic pleasure so intense that her entire body exploded into a sensation of colors and sound. Her head fell back as she felt the strength of him moving through her, the smell of him engulfing her. It was electrifying and terrifying.

Her sight grew sharper and clearer, and she felt her teeth elongate.

Growling, she knew instinctively what she was supposed to do. She clutched feverishly at his shoulders, pulling herself up in his arms. Then she leaned forward and sank her teeth into his shoulder.

For an instant, time stood still with them locked together. Channon couldn't breathe as her body and mind joined his in a place she'd never known existed. It was just the two of them. Just their hearts beating, their bodies joining.

Sebastian hissed as he felt their bonding. The air around them sizzled and spun as they came together in an orgasm so intense, so powerful, that they cried out in unison.

Panting and weak from it, he kissed her lips, holding her to him as he felt her teeth recede.

"That was incredible," she said, still clutching him to her.

He smiled. "Too bad it's a one-time thing."

"Really?"

He nodded. "You're fully human again. Except you have a long life ahead of you."

She bit her lip and gave him a hot, promising look. "And my own pet dragon."

"Aye, my lady. And you can pet him any time you want."

She laughed at him. "You know, since the moment I saw you, I keep having this strange feeling that all of this is just some weird dream."

"Well, if it is, I don't want to wake up."

"Neither do I, my love. Neither do I."

# Epilogue

*Two years later*

***Channon left the podium, her heart pounding in triumph.*** Every historian in the room had been left completely speechless by the paper and research she had just delivered to them. She'd done the one thing she'd always wanted to do.

She'd solved the mystery of the tapestry, which now hung back in the museum.

"Brilliant research, Dr. Kattalakis," Dr. Lazarus said, shaking her hand as she left the podium. "Completely ground-breaking. This takes us into a whole new area."

"Thank you."

She tried to step past him, but he cut her off.

"How ever did you find those answers? I mean that *Book of Dragons*, you said it was from the Library of Alexandria. How did you ever find it?"

She looked past his shoulder to see Sebastian leaning

against the wall with his arms folded across his chest, waiting patiently for her. Dressed all in black, he cut a fearsome pose.

Still, she missed seeing him in his armor. Something about the mail over those luscious muscles . . .

She needed to get back home. Real soon.

She returned her attention to Dr. Lazarus and his questions.

The *Book of Dragons* had been her birthday present from Sebastian last year. He said he'd swiped it the day before the fire that burned the ancient library. With that book and Antiphone's tapestry, she had been able to concoct an entire mythology based on his people that was guaranteed to keep any "experts" from ever discovering the truth of the Draki people.

The Arcadian Draki were safe from human curiosity.

"The book was found in an estate sale. I've handed it over to the Richmond Museum." She patted his arm. "Now, if you'll please excuse me?"

She sidestepped him.

But before she could reach Sebastian, Dr. Herter stopped her. "Have you reconsidered coming back to work?"

She shook her head. "No, sir. I told you, I'm retired."

"But after that paper you just delivered—"

"I'm going home." She handed him the pages in her hand. "Publish it and be happy."

Dr. Herter shook his gray head at her. "The Myth of the Dragon. It's a brilliant piece of fiction."

She smiled. "Yes, it is."

As soon as she reached her soulmate, Sebastian wrapped his arms around her and drew her close. "I don't know if you helped us or hurt us with that."

"We can't let the humans know of you. This way, no one will question the tapestry anymore. It's preserved as you originally wanted, and the academic community can stop nosing around for the truth."

She looked up and saw him staring at the tapestry on the museum's wall. Anytime he thought of his sister, he always looked so incredibly sad. "It's a pity the Fates won't let you guys change the past."

He sighed. "I know. But if we try, they make us pay for it tenfold."

She hugged him tightly, then pulled back so they could leave.

"Well," he said, draping his arm over her shoulders as he walked her out of the museum, "tonight's the full moon. Are you ready to go home?"

"Absolutely, Sir Dragon-Knight. But first . . ."

"I know," he said with a long-suffering sigh, "it's the *Buffy* marathon torture that you always put me through whenever we visit here."

She laughed. He'd been very patient with her on their infrequent visits to her time period, where she caught up on all her favorite shows. "Actually, I was thinking there is one thing I do miss most when we're in Sussex."

"And that is?"

"Whipped cream loincloths."

He arched a brow at that, then smiled a wicked smile that flashed his dimples. "Mmm, my lady, I definitely like the way your mind works."

"Glad to hear it, because you know what they say?"

"What's that?" he asked as he opened the door for her.

"Be kind to dragonswans, for thou art gorgeous when naked and taste good with Cool Whip."

# Into the Dreaming

Karen Marie Moning

For my sister Laura, whose talent for shaping unformed clay extends to far more than that which can be fired in a kiln.

May your gardens ever bloom in lush profusion,
May your peach jam and pecan chicken always taste like heaven,
May the artistry inside your soul always find expression,
And may you always know how loved you are.

*His hard, wet body glistened in the moonlight as he emerged from the ocean. Brilliant eyes of stormy aquamarine met hers, and her heart raced.*

*He stood naked before her, the look in his eyes offering everything, promising eternity.*

*When he cupped one strong hand at the nape of her neck and drew her closer to receive his kiss, her lips parted on a sigh of dreamy anticipation.*

*His kiss was at first gentle, then as stormy as the man himself, for he was a man of deep secrets, a man of deeper passion, her Highlander.*

*One hand became two buried in her hair, one kiss became a second of fierce and fiery desire, then he swept her into his arms, raced up the castle steps, and carried her to his bedchamber . . .*

Excerpted from the unpublished manuscript
*Highland Fire* by Jane Sillee

# *One*

*928*
*Not quite Scotland*

***It was a land of shadows and ice.***

Of gray. And grayer. And black.

Deep in the shadows lurked inhuman creatures, twisted of limb and hideous of countenance. Things one did well to avoid seeing.

Should the creatures enter the pale bars of what passed for light in the terrible place, they would die, painfully and slowly. As would he—the mortal Highlander imprisoned within columns of sickly light—should he succeed in breaking the chains that held him and seek escape through those terrifying shadows.

Jagged cliffs of ice towered above him. A frigid wind shrieked through dark labyrinthine canyons, bearing a susurrus of desolate voices and faint, hellish screams. No sun, no fair breeze of Scotland, no scent of heather penetrated his frozen, bleak hell.

He hated it. His very soul cringed at the horror of the place.

He ached for the warmth of the sun on his face and hungered for the sweet crush of grass beneath his boots. He would have given years of his life for the surety of his stallion between his thighs and the solid weight of his claymore in his grip.

He dreamed—when he managed to escape the agony of his surroundings by retreating deep into his mind—of the blaze of a peat fire, scattered with sheaves of heather. Of a woman's warm, loving caresses. Of buttery, golden-crusted bread hot from the hearth. Simple things. Impossible things.

For the son of a Highland chieftain, who'd passed a score and ten in resplendent mountains and vales, five years was an intolerable sentence; an incarceration that would be withstood only by force of will, by careful nurturing of the light of hope within his heart.

But he was a strong man, with the royal blood of Scottish kings running hot and true in his veins. He would survive. He would return and reclaim his rightful place, woo and win a bonny lass with a tender heart and a tempestuous spirit like his mother, and fill the halls of Dun Haakon with the music of wee ones.

With such dreams, he withstood five years in the hellish wasteland.

Only to discover the dark king had deceived him.

His sentence had never been five years at all, but five *fairy* years: five hundred years in the land of shadow and ice.

On that day when his heart turned to ice within his breast, on that day when a single tear froze upon his cheek, on that day when he was denied even the simple solace of dreaming, he came to find his prison a place of beauty.

* * *

*"My queen, the Unseelie king holds a mortal captive."*

The Seelie queen's face remained impassive, lest her court see how deeply disturbing she found the messenger's news. Long had the Seelie Court of Light and the Unseelie Court of Dark battled. Long had the Unseelie king provoked her. "Who is this mortal?" she asked coolly.

"Aedan MacKinnon, son and heir of the Norse princess Saucy Mary and Findanus MacKinnon, from Dun Haakon on the Isle of Skye."

"Descendent of the Scottish king, Kenneth McAlpin," the queen mused aloud. "The Unseelie king grows greedy, his aim lofty, if he seeks to turn the seed of the McAlpin to his dark ways. What bargain did he strike with this mortal?"

"He sent his current Hand of Vengeance into the world to bring death to the mortal's clansmen yet bartered that if the mortal willingly consented to spend five years in his kingdom, he would spare his kin."

"And the MacKinnon agreed?"

"The king concealed from him that five years in Faery is five centuries. Still, as grandseed of the McAlpin, I suspect the MacKinnon would have accepted the full term to protect his clan."

"What concession does the king make?" the queen asked shrewdly. Any bargain between fairy and mortal must hold the possibility for the human to regain his freedom. Still, no mortal had ever bested a fairy in such a bargain.

"At the end of his sentence, he will be granted one full cycle of the moon in the mortal world, at his home at Dun Haakon. If, by the end of that time, he is loved and loves in return, he will be free. If not, he serves as the king's new Hand of Vengeance until the king chooses to replace him, at which time he dies."

The queen made a sound curiously like a sigh. By such cruel methods had the Unseelie king long fashioned his deadly, prized assassin—his beloved Vengeance—by capturing a mortal, driving him past human limits into madness, indurating him to all emotion, then endowing him with special powers and arts.

Since the Unseelie king was barred entrance to the human world, he trained his Vengeance to carry out his orders, to hold no act too heinous. Mortals dared not even whisper the icy assassin's name, lest they inadvertently draw his merciless attention. If a man angered the Unseelie king, Vengeance punished the mortal's clan, sparing no innocents. If grumblings about the fairy were heard, Vengeance silenced them in cruelly imaginative ways. If the royal house was not amenable to the fairy world, Vengeance toppled kings as carelessly as one might sweep a chessboard.

Until now, it had been the Unseelie king's wont to abduct an insignificant mortal, one without clan who would not be missed, to train as his Vengeance. He went too far this time, the Seelie queen brooded, abducting a blood grandson of one of fair Scotia's greatest kings—a man of great honor, noble and true of heart.

She would win this mortal back.

The queen was silent for a time. Then, "Ah, what five hundred years in that place will do to him," she breathed in a chill voice. The Unseelie king had named the terms of his bargain well. Aedan MacKinnon would still be mortal at the end of his captivity but no longer remotely human when released. Once, long ago and never forgotten, she'd traversed that forbidden land herself, danced upon a pinnacle of black ice, slept within the dark king's velvet embrace . . .

"Perhaps an enchanted tapestry," she mused, "to bring the MacKinnon the one true mate to his heart." She could not fight the Unseelie king directly, lest the clash of their magic too gravely damage the land. But she could and would do all in her power to ensure Aedan MacKinnon found love at the end of his imprisonment.

"My queen," the messenger offered hesitantly, "they shall have but one bridge of the moon in the sky. Perhaps they should meet in the Dreaming."

The queen pondered a moment. The Dreaming: that elusive, much-sought, everforgotten realm where mortals occasionally brushed pale shoulder to iridescent wing with the fairy. That place where mortals would be astonished to know battles were won and lost, universes born, and true love preordained, from Cleopatra and Marc Antony to Abelard and Heloise. The lovers could meet in the Dreaming and share a lifetime of loving before they ever met in the mortal realm. It would lay a grand foundation for success of her plan.

"Wisely spoken," the queen agreed. Rising from her floral bower with fluid grace, she raised her arms and began to sing.

From her melody a tapestry was woven, of fairy lore, of bits of blood and bone, of silken hair from the great, great-grandson of the McAlpin, of ancient rites known only to the True Race. As she sang, her court chanted:

*Into the Dreaming lure them deep*
*where they shall love whilst they doth sleep*
*then in the waking both shall dwell*
*'til love's fire doth melt his ice-borne hell.*

And when the tapestry was complete, the queen marveled.

"Is this truly the likeness of Aedan MacKinnon?" she asked, eyeing the tapestry with unmistakable erotic interest.

"I have seen him, and it is so," the messenger replied, wetting his lips, his gaze fixed upon the tapestry.

"Fortunate woman," the queen said silkily.

* * *

***The fairy queen went to him in the Dreaming, well into*** his sentence, when he was quite mad. Tracing a curved nail against his icy jaw, she whispered in his ear, "Hold fast, MacKinnon, for I have found you the mate to your soul. She will warm you. She will love you above all others."

The monster chained to the ice threw back his dark head and laughed.

It was not a human sound at all.

# *Two*

*Present day*
*Oldenburg, Indiana*

***Jane Sillee had an intensely passionate relationship with*** her postman.

It was classic love-hate.

The moment she heard him whistling his way down her walk, her heart kicked into overtime, a sappy smile curved her lips, and her breathing quickened.

But the moment he failed to deliver the acceptance letter extolling the wonders of her manuscript, or worse, handed her a rejection letter, she hated him. *Hated* him. Knew it was his fault somehow. That maybe, just maybe, a publisher had written glowing things about her, he'd dropped the letter because he was careless, the wind had picked it up and carried it off, and even now her bright and shining future lay sodden and decomposing in a mud puddle somewhere.

*Just how much could a federal employee be trusted, anyway?* she brooded suspiciously. He could be part of some covert study designed to determine how much one tortured writer could endure before snapping and turning into a pen-wielding felon.

"Purple prose, my ass," she muttered, balling up the latest rejection letter. "I only used black ink. I can't *afford* a color ink cartridge." She kicked the door of her tiny apartment shut and slumped into her secondhand nagahide recliner.

Massaging her temples, she scowled. She simply had to get this story published. She'd become convinced it was the only way she was ever going to get him out of her mind.

Him. Her sexy, dark-haired Highlander. The one who came to her in dreams.

She was hopelessly and utterly in love with him.

And at twenty-four, she was really beginning to worry about herself.

Sighing, she unballed and smoothed the rejection letter. This one was the worst of the lot and got pretty darned personal, detailing numerous reasons why her work was incompetent, unacceptable, and downright idiotic. "But I *do* hear celestial music when he kisses me," Jane protested. "At least in my dreams I do," she muttered.

Crumpling it again, she flung it across the room and closed her eyes.

Last night she'd danced with him, her perfect lover.

They'd waltzed in a woodland clearing, caressed by a fragrant forest breeze, beneath a black velvet canopy of glittering stars. She'd worn a gown of shimmering lemon-colored silk. He'd worn a plaid of crimson and black atop a soft, laced, linen shirt. His gaze had been so tender, so passionate, his hands so strong and masterful, his tongue so hot and hungry and—

Jane opened her eyes, sighing gustily. How was she supposed to have a normal life when she'd been dreaming about the man since she was old enough to remember dreaming? As a child, she'd thought him her guardian angel. But as she'd ripened into a young woman, he'd become so much more.

In her dreams, they'd skipped the dance of the swords between twin fires at Beltane atop a majestic mountain while sipping honeyed mead from pewter tankards. How could a cheesy high-school prom replete with silver disco ball suspended from the ceiling accompanied by plastic cups of Hawaiian Punch compare to that?

In her dreams, he'd deftly and with aching gentleness removed her virginity. Who wanted a Monday-night-football-watching, beer-drinking, insurance adjuster/frustrated wannabe-pro-golfer?

In her dreams he'd made love to her again and again, his heated touch shattering her innocence and awakening her to every manner of sensual pleasure. And although in her waking hours, she'd endeavored to lead a normal life, to fall for a flesh-and-blood man, quite simply, no mere man could live up to her dreams.

"You're hopeless. Get over him, already," Jane muttered to herself. If she had a dollar for every time she'd told herself that, she'd own Trump Tower. And the air rights above it.

Glancing at the clock, she pushed herself up from the chair. She was due at her job at the Smiling Cobra Café in twenty minutes, and if she was late again, Laura might make good on her threat to fire her. Jane had a tendency to forget the time, immersed in her writing or research or just plain daydreaming.

*You're a throwback to some other era, Jane,* Laura had said a dozen times.

And indeed, Jane had always felt she'd been born in the wrong century. She didn't own a car and didn't want one. She hated loud noises, condos, and skyscrapers and loved the unspoiled countryside and cozy cottages. She suffered living in an apartment because she couldn't afford a house. Yet.

She wanted her own vegetable garden and fruit orchard. Maybe a milking cow to make butter and cheese and fresh whipped cream. She longed to have babies—three boys and three girls would do nicely.

Yes, in this day and age, she was definitely a throwback. To cave man days, probably, she thought forlornly. When her girlfriends had graduated from college and rushed off with their business degrees and briefcases to work in steel-and-glass high-rises, determined to balance career, children, and marriage, Jane had taken her BA in English and gone to work in a coffee shop, harboring simpler aspirations. All she wanted was a low-pressure job that wouldn't interfere with her writing ambitions. Jane figured the skyrocketing divorce rate had a whole lot to do with people trying to tackle too much. Being a wife, lover, best friend, and mother seemed like a pretty full plate to her. And if—no, she amended firmly—*when* she finally got published, writing romance would be a perfect at-home career. She'd have the best of both worlds.

*Right, and someday my prince will come . . .*

Shrugging off an all-too-familiar flash of depression, she wheeled her bike out of the tiny hallway between the kitchen and bedroom and grabbed a jacket and her backpack. As she opened the door she glanced back over her shoulder to be sure she'd turned off her computer and ran smack into the large package that had been left on her doorstep.

*That* hadn't been there half an hour ago when she'd plucked her mail from the sweaty, untrustworthy hands of the postman. Perhaps he'd returned with it, she mused; it *was* large. It must be her recent Internet order from the online used bookstore, she decided. It was earlier than she'd anticipated, but she wasn't complaining.

She'd be blissfully immersed in larger-than-life heroes, steamy romance, and alternate universes for the next few days. Glancing at her watch again, she sighed, propped her bike against the doorjamb, dragged the box into her apartment, wheeled her bike back out into the hall, then shut and locked the door. She knew better than to open the box now. She'd quickly progress from stealing a quick glance at the covers, to opening a book, to getting completely lost in a fantasy world.

And then Laura would fire her for sure.

*It was nearly one in the morning by the time Jane finally* got home. If she'd had to make one more extra-shot, one-half decaf, Venti, double-cup, two-Sweet-n-Low, skim with light foam latte for one more picky, anorexic bimbo, she might have done bodily harm to a customer. Why couldn't anyone drink good old-fashioned coffee any-more? Heavy on the sugar—*loads* of cream. Life was too short to count calories. At least that's what she told herself each time the scale snidely deemed her plump for five-foot, three and three-quarter inches.

With a mental shrug, she scattered thoughts of work from her mind. It was over. She'd done her time, and now she was free to be just Jane. And she couldn't wait to start that new vampire romance she'd been dying to read!

After brushing her teeth, she slipped out of her jeans and sweater and into her favorite nightie, the frilly, romantic one with tiny daisies and cornflowers embroidered at the scooped neckline. She tugged the box near her bed before dropping cross-legged on the plump, old-fashioned feather ticks. Slicing the packing-tape seal with a metal nail file, she paused and sniffed, as an irresistibly spicy scent wafted from the box. Jasmine, sandalwood, and something else . . . something elusive that nudged her past feeling dreamily romantic to positively aroused. *Great time to read a romance,* she thought ruefully, *with no man to attack when the love scenes heat up*. Untouched except in her dreams, her hormones tended to simmer at a constant gentle boil.

With a wry smile, she dug past the purple Styrofoam peanuts and paused again when her hands closed on rough fabric. Frowning, she tugged it free, sending peanuts skittering across the hardwood floor. The exotic scent filled the room, and she glanced at the closed casement window, bemused by the sudden sultry breeze that lifted strands of her curly red hair and pressed her nightie close to her body.

Perplexed, she placed the folded fabric on her bed, then checked the box. No postmark, no return address, but her name was printed on the top in large block letters, next to her apartment number.

"Well, I'm not paying for it," she announced, certain a hefty bill would shortly follow. "I didn't order it." Darned if she was paying for something she didn't want. She had a hard enough time affording the things she did want.

Irritated that she had no new books to read, she plucked idly at the fabric, then unfolded it and spread it out on the bed.

And sat motionless, her mouth ajar.

"This is *not* funny," she breathed, shocked. "No," she amended in a shaky whisper, "this is not *possible*."

It was a tapestry, exquisitely woven of brilliant colors, featuring a magnificent Highland warrior standing before a medieval castle, legs spread in an arrogant stance that clearly proclaimed him master of the keep. Clad in a crimson and black tartan, adorned with clan regalia, both his hands were extended as if reaching for her.

And it was *him*. Her dream man.

Taking a deep breath, she closed her eyes, then opened them slowly.

It was still him. Each detail precisely as she'd dreamed him, from his powerful forearms and oh-so-capable hands to his luminous aqua eyes, to his silky dark hair and his sensual mouth.

How she would have loved living in medieval times, with a man like him!

Beneath his likeness, carefully stitched, was his name. "Aedan MacKinnon," she whispered.

***Mortals did not bide captivity in Faery well—they did*** not age and time stretched into infinity—and Aedan MacKinnon was no exception. It took a mere two hundred years of being imprisoned in ice, coupled with the king's imaginative tortures, for the Highlander to forget who he'd once been. The king devoted the next two centuries to brutally training and conditioning him.

He educated the Highlander in every language spoken and instructed him in the skills, customs, and mores of each century so that he might move among mankind in any era without arousing suspicion. He trained him in every conceivable weapon and manner of fighting and endowed him with special gifts.

During the fifth and final century, the king dispatched him frequently to the mortal realm to dole out one punishment or another. Eradicating the mortal's confounded sense of honor had proven impossible, so the king utilized dark spells to compel his obedience during such missions, and if the conflict caused the mortal immeasurable pain, the king cared not. Only the end result interested the Unseelie king.

After five centuries, the man who'd once been known as Aedan MacKinnon had no recollection of his short span of thirty years in the mortal realm long ago. He no longer knew that he was mortal himself and did not understand why his king was banishing him there now.

But the king knew he owned his Vengeance only once he had fulfilled all the terms of the original agreement—the agreement the Highlander had long ago forgotten. In accordance with that agreement, the king was forbidden to coerce him with magic or instruction of any kind: Vengeance was to have his month at Dun Haakon, free of the king's meddling.

Still, the king could offer a few suggestions . . . suggestions he knew his well-trained Vengeance would construe as direct orders. After informing Vengeance—to whom time had little meaning—that the year was 1428, refreshing his knowledge of the proper customs of the century, and giving him a weighty pouch of gold coin, the Unseelie king "suggested," choosing his words carefully:

"Your body will have needs in the mortal realm. You must eat, but I would suggest you seek only bland foods."

"As you will it, my liege," Vengeance replied.

"The village of Kyleakin is near the castle wherein you'll reside. It might be best that you go there only to procure supplies and not dally therein."

"As you will it, my liege."

"Above all else, it would be unwise to seek the company of female humans or permit them to touch you."

"As you will it, my liege." A weighty pause, then, "Must I leave you?"

"It is for but a short time, my Vengeance."

Vengeance took a final look at the land he found so beautiful. "As you will it, my liege," he said.

*Jane studied the tapestry, running her fingers over it,* touching his face, wondering why she'd never thought to try to create a likeness of him before. What a joy it was to gaze upon him in her waking hours! She wondered where it had come from, why it had been delivered to her, if it meant he *really* existed out there somewhere. Perhaps, she decided, he'd lived long ago, and this tapestry had been his portrait, handed down from generation to generation. It looked as if it had been lovingly cared for over the centuries.

Still, that didn't explain how or why it had been sent

to *her*. She'd never told anyone about the strange recurring dreams of her Highlander. There was no logical explanation for the tapestry's arrival. Baffled, she shook her head, scattering the troubling questions from her mind, and gazed longingly at his likeness.

Funny, she mused, she'd been dreaming about him for forever, but until now she had never known his last name. He'd been only Aedan and she only Jane.

Their dream nights had been void of small talk. Theirs had been a wordless love—the quietly joyous joining of two halves of a whole. No need for questions, only for the dancing and the loving and, one day not too far off, babies. Their love transcended the need for language. The language of the heart was unmistakable.

*Aedan MacKinnon.* She rolled the name over and over in her mind.

She wondered and wished and ached for him, until at last, she rested her cheek against his face, curled up, and tenderly kissed his likeness. As she drifted into dreams—in that peculiar moment preceding deep sleep that always felt to Jane like falling—she thought she heard a silvery voice softly singing. The words chimed clearly, echoing in her mind:

*Free him from his ice-borne hell*
*And in his century you both may dwell.*
*In the Dreaming hast thou loved him*
*Now, in the Waking must thou save him.*

And then she thought no more, swept away on a tide of dreams.

# *Three*

*1428*
*Isle of Skye*

***When Jane awakened there was a kitten draped across*** her neck, napping. Paws buried in her curly hair, it kneaded and purred deliriously, its tiny body thrumming with pleasure.

She blinked, trying to wake up. *Had there been a kitten in the box, too?* she wondered, petting its silky belly, feeling terribly guilty for failing to notice it earlier. How had it breathed in the box? Poor thing must be starved! She thought she might have some tuna in the pantry to give the little tyke. Stretching gingerly, she lifted the tiny creature off her neck and rolled over onto her side.

And shrieked.

"L-l-*lake!*" she sputtered. "There's a lake in my bedroom!" Three feet away from her. Deep blue and gently lapping at the shore. The shore that she'd been sleeping on.

Stunned, she sat up, performing a frantic mental check. Bedroom, gone. Apartment, gone. Tapestry, gone. Kitten, here. Nightie—

Gone.

"I am *so* not in the mood for an inadequacy dream," Jane hissed.

Purple flowery stuff. Here. Castle. Here.

*Castle?*

She rubbed her eyes with the heels of her palms. The kitten mewed and gave her an insistent head-butt, demanding more belly rubbing. She clutched the tiger-striped kitten and gaped at the castle. It looked very much like the castle she visited in her dreams, except this castle was in near ruin; a mere quarter of it stood undamaged.

"I'm still sleeping," she whispered. "I'm just dreaming that I woke up, right?" She would have been only mildly surprised had the kitten bared pearly teeth and cheekily replied.

But it didn't, so, cradling its tiny body, she rose and started walking toward the castle, wincing as her bare feet padded across stones. She tried to imagine herself some dream clothes and shoes, but it didn't work. *So much for controlling one's subconscious,* she thought. As she gazed at the portion of the castle still intact—a square central tower abutted by one wing that sported a smaller round tower—her gaze was caught by a dark flutter atop the walls. As she watched, the flutter became a shirt, the shirt a shoulder, the shoulder a man.

*Her* man.

She stood motionless, gazing up.

***Vengeance could not fathom what had driven him to climb*** to the top of the tower. He'd intended to sit in the hall of the strange castle, eating only enough to survive, gazing at nothing, waiting to return to his king, but moments ago he'd felt an overwhelming compulsion to go outside. Being outside, however, was disconcerting—no cool shadows and ice but riotous color and heat—so he'd climbed instead to the walk atop the tower, where he felt less besieged by the foreign landscape.

And there she stood—the lass.

Bare as she'd been fashioned.

Something low in his gut twisted. Mayhap the cold, hard bread he'd eaten, he decided.

Distantly, he acknowledged her beauty. Flames of curly red hair framed a delicate porcelain face, tumbled down her back, and fell in ringlets over her breasts . . . breasts full and high and pink-tipped.

Legs of alabaster and rose; slender of ankle, generous of thigh. More shimmering red curls where they met. For a moment, he suffered an inexplicable inability to draw his gaze higher.

But only for a moment.

She clutched a tiny kitten to her breasts, and he had another strange moment, considering the wee beastie's lush perch, assailed by a vague and distant recollection.

It eluded him.

Unseelie females were icy creatures, with thin limbs and chill bodies.

Yet this woman didn't look icy. Nor slim. But full and generously rounded and soft and . . . warm.

*It would be unwise to seek out the company of female humans or permit them to touch you,* his king had ordered.

Vengeance turned his back and left the tower walk.

***Jane's mouth opened and shut a dozen times while he stood*** at the top of the tower gazing down at her. He'd disappeared without a word. As if he didn't even know her! As if they hadn't been dream lovers for nearly forever!

As if she wasn't even standing there in all her glory, which—if one believed the love words he'd whispered in her dreams—was considerable.

*Well,* Jane Sillee thought irritably, *if he thinks this is a dream breakup, he's got another thought coming.*

# Four

***It was a little difficult to convincingly stomp into a castle*** nude, even in a dream.

One fretted about things like cellulite and what one's bare foot might stomp upon.

So Jane succeeded only, despite her righteous ire, in slinking into the castle, looking rather uncertain and, if her nipples were a weathervane, noticeably chilled.

He was sitting before the empty hearth, staring into it. She gazed at the fireplace wistfully, longing for a fire. It might be summer outside, but it was cold within the damp stone walls. Ever chivalrous in her dreams, he would surely accommodate her slightest wish and build a fire.

It occurred to her then that she'd never been cold in one of her dreams before. She filed the thought away for future consideration. There was something very odd about this dream.

"Aedan," she said softly.

He didn't move a muscle.

"Aedan, my love," she tried again. Perhaps he was in a bad mood, she thought, perplexed, although he'd never been in a bad mood in any of her dreams before, but she supposed there was a first time for everything. Was he angry at her for something? Had she popped in after committing some dream transgression?

He still didn't move or respond.

"Excuse me," she said not so sweetly, circling around in front of him, using the love-starved kitten as a shawl of sorts, feeling suddenly insecure, wondering what to cover, her breasts or her . . . Well, maybe he wouldn't look down.

He looked down.

When she lowered the mewing kitten, he looked up.

"That's not fair," she said, blushing. "Lend me your shirt." This was not unfolding like one of her dreams at all. Ordinarily, she didn't mind being nude with him because they were either making love in bed, or in a pile of freshly mown hay, or in a sweet, clear loch, or on a convenient table, but now he was fully clothed, and something was way off-kilter. "Please." She extended her hand.

When he shrugged, stood up, and began unlacing his linen shirt, her breath caught in her throat. When he raised one arm over his head, grabbed the nape of his shirt in a fist, and tugged it over his head, she swallowed hard. "Oh, *Aedan*," she breathed. Gorgeous. He was simply flawless, with supple muscles rippling in his arms, his chest, and his taut abdomen. She'd kissed every smooth ripple in her dreams. The sheer, visceral beauty of her Highlander hit her like a fist in the stomach, making her knees weak.

"I know not why you persist in addressing me by that appellation. I am Vengeance," he said, his voice like a blade against rough stone.

Jane's mouth popped open in an "O" of surprise. "Vengeance?" she echoed blankly, round-eyed. Then, "This *is* a dream, isn't it, Aedan?" It was quite different from her usual dream. In her dreams everything was soft-focus and fuzzed around the edges, but now things were crystal clear.

A little too clear, she thought, frowning as she glanced around.

The interior of the castle was an absolute mess. Grime and soot stained the few furnishings, and cobwebs swayed from the rafters. There was no glass in the windows, no draperies, no sumptuous tapestries, no luxurious rugs. A lone rickety chair perched before a dilapidated table that tilted lopsidedly before an empty hearth. No candles, no oil globes. It was spartan, gloomy, and downright chilly.

He pondered her question a moment. "I doona know what dreams are." There was only existing as he had always known it. Shadows and ice and his king. And pain sometimes, pain beyond fathoming. He'd learned to avoid it at all cost. "But I am not who you think."

Jane inhaled sharply, hurt and bewildered. Why was he denying who he was? It was him . . . yet not him. She narrowed her eyes, studying him. Sleek dark fall of hair—same as in her dreams. Chiseled face and sculpted jaw—same. Brilliant eyes, the color of tropical surf—not the same. Frost seemed to glitter in their depths. His sensual lips were brushed with a hint of blueness, as if from exposure to extreme cold. Everything about him seemed chilled; indeed, he might have been carved from ice and painted flesh tones.

"Yes, you are," she said firmly. "You're Aedan MacKinnon."

An odd light flashed deep within his aquamarine eyes but was as quickly gone. "Cease with that ridiculous name. I am Vengeance," he said, his deep voice ringing hollowly in the stone hall. He thrust his shirt at her.

Eagerly, she reached for it, intensely unsettled, needing clothing, some kind of armor to deflect his icy gaze. As her hand brushed his, he snatched his back, and the shirt dropped to the floor.

Doubly hurt, she stared at him a long moment, then

stooped and placed the kitten on the floor, where it promptly twined about her ankles, purring. Fumbling in her haste, she swiftly slipped the shirt over her head and tugged it down as far as it would go. The soft fabric came nearly to her knees when she rose again. The neck opening dropped to her belly button. She laced it quickly, but it did little to cover her breasts.

His gaze seemed quite fixed there.

Taking a quick deep breath, she skirted the amorous kitten and stepped toward him.

Instantly, he raised a hand. "Stay. Doona approach me. You must leave."

"Aedan, don't you know me at all?" she asked plaintively.

"Verily, I've ne'er seen you before, human. This is my place. Begone."

Jane's eyes grew huge. "Human?" she echoed. "Begone?" she snapped. "And go where? I don't know *how* to leave. I don't know how I got here. Hell's bells, I'm not certain I really *am* here or even where here is!"

"If you won't leave, I will." He rose and left the hall, slipping into the shadows of the adjoining wing.

Jane stared blankly at the space where he'd been.

***Jane studied the lake a long moment before dipping her*** finger in, then licking it. The tiger-striped kitten sat back on its haunches, twitching its wide fluffy tail and watching her curiously.

Salt. It was no lake she was surrounded by, but the sea. *What sea?* What sea abutted Scotland? She'd never been good with geography; she was lucky she could find her way home every day. But then again, she mused, never before in one of her dreams had she bothered to wonder about geography—more evidence that this dream was strikingly abnormal.

Jane dropped down cross-legged on the rocky shore,

shaking her head. Either she'd gone completely nuts, or she was having her first-ever nightmare about her dream lover.

As she sat, rubbing her forehead and thinking hard, the soft syllables of a rhyme teased her memory. Something about saving him . . . about being in his century.

*Jane Sillee, you've finally done it,* she chided herself, *you've read one too many romance novels*. Only in books did heroines get swept back in time, and then they usually ended up in medieval—*oh!*

Lurching to her feet, she spun back toward the castle and took a long, hard look at her surroundings. To the left of the castle, some half-mile in the distance, was a village of thatch-roofed, wattle, and daub huts, with tendrils of smoke curling lazily skyward.

A very medieval-looking village.

She pinched herself, hard. "Ow!" It hurt. She wondered if that proved anything. "It's not possible," she assured herself. "I *must* be dreaming."

*Free him from his ice-borne hell and in his century you both may dwell. In the Dreaming hast thou loved him now, in the Waking must thou save him.* The rhyme, elusive a few moments ago, now resurfaced clearly in her mind.

"Impossible," she scoffed.

*But what if it isn't?* a small voice in her heart queried hopefully. What if the mysterious tapestry had somehow sent her back to medieval times? Accompanied by pretty clear instructions: that if she could save him, she could stay with him. In *his* century.

What century was that?

Jane snorted and shook her head.

*Still,* that small voice persisted with persuasive logic, *there are only three possibilities: You're dreaming. You're crazy. Or you're truly here. If you're dreaming, nothing counts, so you may as well plunge right in. If you're crazy, well, nothing counts either, so you may as well plunge right in. If you're really here, and you're supposed to save him, everything counts, so you'd better hurry up and plunge right in.*

"I'm crazy," she muttered aloud. "Time-travel, my ass."

But the small voice had a point. What did she have to lose by temporarily suspending disbelief and interacting with her surroundings? Only by immersing herself in her current situation might she be able to make any sense of it. And if it were a dream, eventually she'd wake up.

But heavens, she thought, inspecting the landscape, it all seemed so *real*. Far more real than any of her dreams had ever been. The dainty purple bell-shaped flowers exuded a sweet fragrance. The wind carried the tang of salt from the sea. When she stooped to pet the kitten, it felt soft and silky and had a wet little nose. If she was dreaming, it was the most detailed, incredible dream she'd ever had.

Which made her wonder how detailed and incredible making love with Aedan in this "dream" might be. That was incentive enough right there to plunge in.

Her stomach growled insistently, yet another thing that had never happened in one of her dreams. Resolutely, she turned back toward the castle. The kitten bounded along beside her, swiping at the occasional butterfly with gleeful little paws, then scurrying to catch up with her again.

She would keep an open mind, she resolved as she stepped inside the great hall. She would question him, find out what year it supposedly was, and where she supposedly was. Then she would try to discover why he didn't know her and why he thought he was "Vengeance."

Aedan sat again, as he had before, staring into the empty fireplace. Clad in loose black trousers, boots, and a gloriously naked upper torso, he was as still as death.

When she perched on the chilly stone hearth before him, his eyes glittered dangerously. "I thought you left," he growled.

"I told you, I don't know how to leave," she said simply.

Vengeance considered her words. Had his king deliberately placed the female human there? If so, why? Always before when his king had sent him into the mortal realm, Vengeance had been given precise instructions, a specific mission to accomplish. But not this time. He knew not what war to cause, whose ear to poison with lies, or whom to maim or kill. Mayhap, he brooded, this was his king's way of testing him, of seeing if Vengeance could determine what his king wanted of him.

He studied her. There was no denying it, he was curious about the human. She was the antithesis of all he'd encountered in his life; vibrant, with her flaming hair and curvy body. Pale porcelain skin and rosy lips. Eyes of molten amber fringed by dusky lashes and slanted upward at the outer corners. She had many facial expressions, lively muscles that pulled her lips up and down and many which ways. He found himself wondering what she would feel like, were he to touch her, if she was as soft and warm as she looked.

"Would you mind building me a fire?" she asked.

"I am not cold. Nor do you look cold," he added, his gaze raking over her. She looked far warmer than aught he'd seen.

"Well, I am. Fire. Now, please," she said firmly.

After a moment's hesitation, he complied with her command, layering the bricks, making swift work of it, never taking his gaze from her. He felt greatly intrigued by her breasts. He could not fathom what it was about those soft plump mounds beneath the worn linen that so commanded his attention. Were they on his own body, he would have been appalled by the excess fatty flesh, yet gazing upon her, he found his fingers clenching and unclenching, desirous to touch, perhaps cup their plump weight in his hands. For a mere human, she had a powerful presence. He considered the possibility that—wee as she was—she might be quite dangerous. After all, there were things in Faery minute of stature capable of inflicting unspeakable pain.

"Thank you," she said, rubbing her hands together before the blaze that sputtered in the hearth. "Those are peat bricks, aren't they? I read about them once."

"Aye."

"Interesting," she murmured thoughtfully. "They don't look like I thought they did." Then she shook her head sharply and focused on him again. "What is the name of this castle?"

"Dun Haakon," he replied, then started. Where had that name come from? His king had told him naught about his temporary quarters.

"Where am I?"

More knowledge he had no answers for: "On *Eilean A Cheo*."

"Where?" she asked blankly.

" 'Tis Gaelic for 'misty isle.' We are on the Isle of Skye." Mayhap it was knowledge his king had taught him long ago, he decided. There, silent until needed. His king had oft told him he'd prepared him for any place, any time.

Jane took a deep breath. "What year is it?"

"Fourteen hundred twenty-eight."

She inhaled sharply. "And how long have you lived here?"

"I doona live here. I am to remain but one passing of the moon. I arrived yestreen."

"Where *do* you live?"

"You have many questions." He reflected for a moment, and decided there was no harm in answering her questions. He was, after all, Vengeance. Powerful. Perfect. Deadly. "I live with my king in his kingdom."

"And where is that?"

"In Faery."

Jane swallowed. "Fairy?" she said weakly.

"Aye. My king is the Unseelie king. I am his Vengeance. And I am perfect," he added, as if an afterthought.

"That's highly debatable," Jane muttered.

"Nay. 'Tis not. I am perfect. My king tells me so. He tells me I will be the most feared warrior ever to live, that the name of Vengeance will endure in legend for eternity."

"I'm quaking," Jane said dryly, with an aggrieved expression.

He looked at her then, hard. Her hair, her face, her breasts, then lower still, his gaze lingering on her smooth bare legs and slender ankles. "You are not at all what I expected of humans," he said finally.

*Go with it,* she told herself. *Since none of this makes any sense, just run with what he's told you and see where it leads.* "You aren't what I expected of a fairy," she said lightly. "Aren't you supposed to have sparkly little wings?"

"I doona think I am a fairy," he said carefully.

"Then you're human?" she pressed.

He looked perplexed, then gave a faint shake of his head.

"Well, if you're not a fairy and you're not human, what are you?"

His brows dipped and he shifted uncomfortably but made no reply.

"Well?" she encouraged.

After a long pause he said, "I will be needing my shirt back, lass. You may find clothing in the round tower down the corridor." He pointed behind her. "Go now."

"We're not done with this conversation, Aedan," she said, eyes narrowing.

"Vengeance."

"I'm not going to stop asking questions, *Aedan*. I have oodles of them."

He shrugged, rose, and wandered over to the window, turning his back to her.

"And I'm hungry, and when I get hungry I get grumpy. You do have food, don't you?"

He remained stoically silent. A few moments later he heard her snort, then stomp off in search of clothing.

*If you're not a fairy and you're not human, what are you?* Her question hung in the air after she'd left, unanswered. Unanswerable.

Verily, he didn't know.

# *Five*

***She was a demanding creature.***

Vengeance ended up having to make three trips into Kyleakin to acquire those things the lass deemed "the bare necessities." It was abundantly clear that she had no plans of leaving. Indeed, she intended to loll in the lap of luxury for the duration of her stay. Because he wasn't certain if his liege had arranged her presence as part of some mysterious plan he'd chosen not to impart, and because he'd been told to reside at the castle until summoned, it seemed he must share his temporary quarters. He was greatly uneasy and just wished he knew what was expected of him. How could he act on his king's behalf if he knew not why he was there?

On his first foray into Kyleakin—the only trip made of his own volition while she'd been occupied rummaging through trunks in the round tower—he'd purchased naught but day-old bread so they both might eat that eve. Although he found the heat and colors of the landscape chafing, he was relieved to escape her disconcerting presence and foolishly believed procuring food might silence her ever-wagging tongue.

When she discovered he'd "gone shopping" without informing her, she'd tossed her mass of shining curls and scowled, ordering him to procure additional items. The second time he'd spent a fair amount of the gold coin his liege had given him purchasing clean (so mayhap they were a bit scratchy and rough, but *he* didn't even need them to begin with) woolens, meat, cheese, fruit, quills, ink, and three fat, outrageously costly sheets of parchment—the parchment and quills because she'd proclaimed she was "a writer" and it was imperative she write every day without fail. At first he'd been puzzled by her bragging that she knew her letters, then he realized it was, like as not, a rare achievement for a mere mortal. He imagined he knew many more letters than she, and if she still needed to practice them, she was a sorry apprentice indeed.

Unimpressed with the results of his second expedition, she'd sent him back a *third* time, with a tidy little list on a scrap of parchment, to find more parchment, coffee beans or strong tea, a cauldron, mugs, eating tools, a supply of rags and vinegar for cleaning, *soft* woolens, down ticks, wine, and "unless you wish to fish the sea yourself," fresh fish for the useless furry beastie.

Vengeance, being ordered about by a wee woman. Fetching food for a mouse-catcher.

Still, she was a mesmerizing thing. Especially in the pale pink gown she'd dug out of one of the many trunks. Her eyes sparkled with irritation or as she listed her demands, her breasts jiggled softly when she gestured, then she turned all cooing and tender as she stooped to scratch the beastie behind its furry ears.

Making him wonder what her slender fingers might feel like in his hair.

He was unprepared for one such as she and wondered

why his king had not forewarned him that humans could be so . . . intriguing. None that he'd e'er encountered in his past travels had been so compelling, and his king had e'er painted them as coarse, sullen, and stupid creatures, easily manipulated by higher beings like Vengeance.

He'd not yet manipulated the smallest portion of his current circumstances, too busy being ordered about by her. *Build me a fire, give me your shirt, buy me this, buy me that. Hmph!* What might she demand next? He—the formidable hand of the fairy king's wrath—was almost afraid to find out.

*"Kiss me."*

"What?" he said blankly.

"Kiss me," she repeated, with an encouraging little nod.

Vengeance stepped back, inwardly cursing himself for retreating, but something about the fiery lass made him itch to flee to the farthest reaches of the isle. At her direction, he'd fluffed several heavy down ticks on the sole bed in the keep. She was happily spreading it with soft woolens and a luxurious green velvet throw he'd not intended to buy. He'd been coerced into taking it by the proprietor, who'd been delighted to hear a woman was in residence at Dun Haakon and had eagerly inquired "Be ye the new laird and lady of Dun Haakon?" Scowling, he'd flung coin at the shopkeeper, snatched up the bedclothes, and made haste from the establishment.

He was beginning to resent that his king had given him no orders. There, in his dark kingdom, Vengeance knew who he was and what his aim. Here, he was lost, abandoned in a stifling, garish world he did not understand, surrounded by creatures he could not fathom, with not one word of guidance from his liege.

And now the wench wanted him to do something else. Precisely what, he wasn't certain, but he suspected it boded ill for him. She was a creature greatly preoccupied with her physical comforts, and down that path—so his king oft said—lay weakness, folly, and ruin. Vengeance had few physical needs, merely food, water, and the occasional hour of rest.

"Kiss me," she said, making a plump pucker with her lips. She gave the velvet coverlet a final smoothing. "I think it might help you remember."

"What exactly is a kiss?" he asked suspiciously.

Her eyes widened and she regarded him with amazement. "You don't know what a kiss is?" she exclaimed.

"Why should I? 'Tis a mortal thing, is it not?"

She cocked her head and looked as if she were having a heated internal debate. After a moment she appeared to reach a decision and stepped closer to him. Stoically, he held his ground this time, refusing to cede an inch.

"I merely want to press my lips against yours," she said, innocence knitted to a disarming smile. "Push them together, like so." She demonstrated, and the lush moue of her mouth tugged something deep in his groin.

"Nay. You may not touch me," he said stiffly.

She leaned closer. He caught a faint scent, something sweet and flowery on her fiery tresses. It made him want to press his face to her hair, inhale greedily, and stroke the coppery curls.

He leaned back. Fortunately, the lass was too short to reach his face without his cooperation. Or a step stool.

"You are so stubborn," she said, with a gusty sigh. "Fine, let's talk then. It's pretty clear we have a *lot* to talk about." She paused, then, "He doesn't know what kisses are," she muttered to herself, shaking her head. "*That's* never happened in my dreams before." Perching on the end of the bed, her feet dangling, she patted the space beside her. "Come. Sit by me."

"Nay." When the kitten jumped daintily onto the bed and spilled across the velvet coverlet, he scowled at it. "You or that bedraggled mop of fur—I'm fair uncertain which is more useless. At least the beastie doesna prattle on so."

"But the beastie can't kiss either," she said archly. "And it's not bedraggled. Don't insult my kitten," she added defensively.

"You attribute high value to these kisses of yours. I scarce believe they are worth much," he said scornfully.

"That's because you haven't kissed me yet. If you did, you'd know."

Vengeance moved, in spite of his best intentions, to stand at the foot of the bed between her legs. He stared down at her. She scooped up the kitten and pressed her lips to its furry head. He closed his eyes and fought a tide of images that made no sense to him.

"Perhaps you're afraid," she said sweetly.

He opened his eyes. "I fear nothing."

"Then why won't you let me do something so harmless? See? The kitten survived unscathed."

He struggled with the answer for a moment, then said simply, "You may not touch me. 'Tis forbidden."

"Why not, and by whom?"

"I obey my king. And 'tis none of your concern why."

"I think it is. I thought you were a man who thought for himself. A warrior, a leader. Now you tell me you follow orders like some little puppet."

"Puppet?"

"An imitation of a real person fashioned of wood, pulled this way and that by its master. You're nothing but a servant, are you?"

Her delicate sneer cut him to the quick, and he flinched angrily. Who was she calling a servant? He was Vengeance, he was perfect and strong and . . . *Och, he* was *his king's servant.* Why did that chafe? Why did he suffer the odd sensation that once he'd not been anyone's serf but a leader in his own right?

"Why do you obey him?" she pressed. "Does this king

of yours mean so much to you? Is he so good to you? Tell me about him."

Vengeance opened his mouth, closed it again, and left the room silently.

"Where are you going?" she called after him.

"To prepare a meal, then you will sleep and leave me in peace," he growled over his shoulder.

*Jane ate in bed, alone but for the kitten. Aedan brought* her fish roasted over an open fire and a blackened potato that had obviously been stuffed in the coals to cook, accompanied by a similarly charred turnip, then left in silence. No salt. No butter for the dry potato. Not one drop of lemon for the fish.

Warily, she conceded that she was probably not dreaming—the fare had never been so unpalatable in one of her dreams. And upon reflection, she realized that although she'd attended many dream feasts, she'd never actually eaten anything at any of them. Now, she choked it down because she was too emotionally drained to attempt cooking for herself over an open fire. Tomorrow was another day.

The tiger-striped kitten, whom she'd christened Sexpot (after apologetically peeking beneath her tail) because of the way the little tyke sashayed about as if outrageously pleased with herself, hungrily devoured a tender fish filet, then busied herself scrubbing her whiskers with little spit-moistened paws while Jane puzzled over her situation.

She'd been astonished to discover Aedan had no idea what a kiss was, but the more she thought about it, the more sense it made.

Aedan not only didn't know he was Aedan, he didn't remember that he was a *man,* hence he didn't recall the intimacies of lovemaking!

She wondered if that made him a virgin of sorts. When they finally made love—and there was no doubt in her mind that they would, one way or another, even if she had to ambush and attack him—would he have any idea what it was all about? How strange to think that she might have to teach him, he who'd been her inexhaustible dream tutor.

He certainly hadn't liked being provoked, she mused. He'd grown increasingly agitated when she'd mocked him for obeying his king and had visibly bristled at the idea of being a mere servant. Still, despite such promising reactions, he had a formidable shell that was going to be difficult to penetrate. It would help if she knew what had happened to him. She needed to make him talk about his "king," and find out when and how they'd met. Were there indeed a "fairy king," perhaps the being had enchanted him. The idea taxed Jane's credulity, but, all things considered, she supposed she couldn't suspend disbelief without suspending it fully. Until she reached some concrete conclusions about what was going on, she would be unwise to discount any possibilities.

Whatever had happened to him, she had to undo it. She hoped it wouldn't take too long, because she wasn't sure how long she could stand watching her soulmate glare at her with blatant distrust and dislike. Withholding kisses. Refusing to let her touch him.

*You have one month here with him, no more,* a woman's lilting voice whispered.

Sexpot stopped grooming, paw frozen before her face. She arched into a horseshoe shape and emitted a ferocious hiss.

"Wh-what?" Jane stammered, glancing about.

*Cease with your absurd protestations that this place is not real. You* are *in the fifteenth century, Jane Sillee. And here you may stay, if you succeed. You have but one full cycle of the moon in the sky to make him remember who he is.*

Jane opened her mouth, closed it, and opened it again, but nothing came out. Sexpot suffered no such problem, growling low and long. Gently smoothing the spiked hairs on the kitten's back, Jane wet her lips and swallowed. "That's impossible, the man will hardly speak to me! And who are you?" she demanded. *I'm talking to a disembodied voice,* she thought, bewildered.

*I'm not the one who doesn't know. Worry about him.*

"Don't be cryptic. Who are you?" Jane hissed.

There was no reply. After a few moments, Sexpot's back no longer resembled a porcupine's, and Jane realized that whoever had spoken was gone.

"Well, just what am I supposed to do?" she shouted angrily. A month wasn't a whole lot of time to figure out what had happened to him and to help him remember who he was. She'd like to know who was making up the rules. She had a bone or two to pick with them.

Aedan appeared in the doorway, glancing hastily about the chamber. Only after ascertaining she was alone and in no apparent danger did he speak. "What are you yelling about?" he demanded.

Jane stared at him, framed in the doorway, gilded by a shaft of silvery moonlight that spilled in the open window, his sculpted chest bare, begging her touch.

She was suddenly stricken by two certainties that she felt in the marrow of her bones: that as the woman had said, she truly was in the fifteenth century, and that if she didn't help him remember, something terrible beyond her ability to imagine would become of him. Would he live and die the icy, inhuman creature he'd become? Perhaps turn into something even worse?

"Oh, Aedan," she said, the words hitching in her throat. All her love and longing and fear were in his name.

"I am *Vengeance*," he snarled. "When will you accept that?"

When he spun about and stalked from the chamber, Jane sat for a long time, looking around, examining everything anew, wondering how she could have thought for even a moment that she might be dreaming. The reason everything had seemed so real was because it *was* so real.

She fell back onto the bed and stared at the cobwebby ceiling through the shimmer of silent tears. "I won't lose you, Aedan," she whispered.

***Hours later, Vengeance stood at the foot of the bed, watch-***ing her sleep. He'd passed a time of restless slumber on the floor in the hall and awakened intensely agitated. His rest had not been of the kind he'd known in Faery—an edgy, mostly aware state of short duration. Nay, he'd fallen into deep oblivion for far longer than usual, and his slumbering mind had gone on strange journeys. Upon awakening, his memory of those places had dissolved with the suddenness of a bubble bursting, leaving him with the nagging feeling that he'd forgotten something of import.

Troubled, he'd sought her. She was sprawled on her back, pink gown bunched about her thighs, masses of fiery curls about her face. The kitten of which she seemed strangely fond—and it was too stringy to be palatable over a fire, nor was it capable of useful labor, hence her interest in it baffled him—was also sprawled on its back and had managed to insinuate itself into her hair. Its tiny paws curled and uncurled while it emitted a most odd sound. A bit of drool escaped its thin pink lips.

Cautiously, Vengeance lowered himself onto the bed. The lass stirred and stretched but did not awaken. The kitten curled itself into a circle and purred louder.

Gingerly, Vengeance plucked up a ringlet of her hair and held it between his fingers. It shimmered in the moonlight, all the hues of flame: golden and coppery and bronze. It was unlike aught he'd seen before. There were more colors in a simple hank of her hair than had been in the entirety of his world until yesterday.

He smoothed the curl between his thumb and forefinger.

The kitten opened a golden eye and stared at Vengeance's dark hand.

It did not flee him, he mused, which confirmed he wasn't fairy; for 'twas well known that cats loathed fairies. On the other hand, it didn't attempt to touch him, which he supposed meant he wasn't human either, for the thing certainly flung itself at the lass at every opportunity.

*So what am I?*

Sliding his hand beneath her tresses, he sneaked a quick glance at her. Her eyes were still closed, her lips slightly parted. Her breasts rising and falling gently.

Two hands.

It felt. So. Good.

There certainly was a lot of touching going on in this place. Even the kitten seemed to crave it. And she—ah, *she* touched everything. Petted the beastie, stroked the velvety coverlet he'd procured in Kyleakin, and would have touched him a dozen times or more—he'd seen it in her eyes. *Kiss me,* she'd said, and he'd nearly crushed her in his arms, intrigued by this "pressing of the lips" she'd described. The mere thought of touching such warmth did alarming things to his body. Tentatively, he touched the tip of his index finger to her cheek, then snatched it away.

The kitten buried its pink nose in her hair. After a moment's pause, Vengeance did, too. Then rested his cheek lightly against it, absorbing the sensation against his skin.

*Why do you obey him? Is he so good to you?*

Vengeance tried to ponder that thought. His king was . . . well, his king. What right did Vengeance have to question whether his liege was good to him? It was not his place!

*Why not?* For the first time in centuries, unhampered by the constant coercion of the king's dark spells, an independent thought sprouted and thrust down a thick taproot in his mind. He had no idea whence such a blasphemous thought had come, but it had, and it defied his efforts to cast it out. Pain lanced through his head behind his eyes. Excruciating pressure built at his temples, and he clamped his hands to his ears as if to silence voices only he could hear.

*Aedan, come quickly, I have something to show you. Da brought me a baby pine marten!* A lass's voice, a lass who'd once been terribly important to him. A wee child of eight, about whom he'd fretted and tried to protect. *Mary, she'll be fine with the wee pet*, a man's voice said.

*But we're sailin' out on the morrow,* Mary protested. *'Tis wounded and might harm her without meanin' to.*

*Aedan has a way with the wee creatures, and he'll watch o'er his sister.*

"Aedan," he breathed, testing the sound of it on his tongue.

"Vengeance," he whispered after a moment.

Neither name fit him like skin on bones. Neither place he'd been—neither his land of ice nor this isle—felt like well-worn boots, broken in and suited to the heel.

He suffered a fierce urge to claw his way from his own body, so strange and ill-fashioned did it suddenly seem. In his king's land he knew who he was and what purpose he served. But here, och, here, he knew nothing.

Nothing but pain in places deep in his head and tingles in places deep in his groin.

Warily, he eyed the pale curves of her legs peeking from the hem of the gown. How smooth they looked . . . how warm.

He squeezed his eyes tightly shut, envisioning his beloved home with his king.

*Be ye the new laird and lady of Dun Haakon?* the shopkeeper queried brightly in his mind, obliterating his soothing image of ice and shadow.

"Nay," he whispered. "I am Vengeance."

# *Six*

***The villagers descended upon the castle at daybreak.***

Jane awakened slowly, feeling disoriented and vulnerable. She'd not dreamed of Aedan, and if she'd suffered any remnants of doubts that she was in the fifteenth century before she'd fallen asleep, they were gone now. She'd never slept through an entire night without at least one dream of her Highland love.

At first she wasn't certain what had awakened her, then the clamor of voices rose in the hall beyond the open door of the bedchamber. High-pitched and excited, they were punctuated by stilted, grudging replies in Aedan's deep burr.

Swiftly she performed her morning ritual of positive reinforcement by announcing brightly to the empty bedchamber, "It's today! What better day could it be?" She'd read somewhere that such small litanies were useful in setting one's mood, so she recited it each morning without fail. Yesterday was a memory. Tomorrow was a hope.

Today was another day to live and do one's best to love. In her estimation that was pretty much all a person could ask.

Kissing the drowsy kitten on the head, she slipped from the bed, quickly stripped off her wrinkled dress, then donned the simple yellow gown she'd unearthed yesterday while going through the trunks. She was looking forward to wearing it, because it was undeniably romantic with its low, laced bodice and flowing skirt. Coupled with the complete lack of undergarments in any of the trunks, she felt positively sinful. Ready for her man at any moment. How she hoped it would be today!

Casting a quick glance about the room, she narrowed her eyes thoughtfully. She was going to want a few more items from the nearby village, and soon, specifically a large bathtub and whatever medieval people used for toothpaste and soap. Lured by the hum of voices, she hurried from the bedchamber.

***Vengeance backed against the hearth like a cornered an-***imal. A dozen yammering villagers thrust baked goods and gifts at him and prattled nonstop about some legend and how delighted they were to have a MacKinnon back to watch over them. How they would serve him faithfully. How they planned to rebuild his castle.

Him—watch over them? He'd as soon sweep his hand and raze the room, leaving naught but bones and silence!

But he kept both his hands, and the fairy gifts of destructive power his king had given him, carefully behind his back, because he didn't know what the blethering hell his liege wanted. Rage simmered in his veins—rage at the villagers, rage at his liege—stunning him with its intensity. Then *she* sauntered in and some of the rage dissipated, ousted by discomfort of another sort, slightly more palatable but no less disconcerting.

She was a sunbeam flickering about the gloomy interior

of the hall. As he watched in tense silence, she smiled and spoke and took the villagers' hands in hers, welcoming the entire ragamuffin lot of them into what had been, for a blissfully short time, *his* quarters alone. How and when had he so completely lost control of himself and his environ? he wondered. Was control something the Fates leeched away slowly over a period of time, or a thing instantaneously nihilated by the mere appearance of a female? Enter woman—exit order.

And och, how they were smiling at her, beaming and adoring, clearly accepting her as their lady!

"She's *not* a MacKinnon," he snapped. Best he swiftly disabuse them of the foolish notion that he was laird and she lady.

All heads swiveled to look at him.

"Milord," one of them said hesitantly after a pained pause, " 'tis naught of our concern if ye've handfasted her or no. We're simply pleased to welcome ye both."

"Nor am *I* a MacKinnon," he said stiffly.

A dozen people gaped, then burst into uneasy laughter. An elderly man with silver hair, clad in russet trews and a linen shirt, shook his head and smiled gently. "Come," he beckoned, hastening from the hall into the adjoining wing.

Wholly irritated with himself for doing so, Vengeance sought the lass's gaze. He was so accustomed to obeying orders that making simple decisions, like whether or not to follow the elder, paralyzed him. He despised the confusion he felt, despised being left to his own devices. She stepped toward him, looking as if she planned to tuck her hand through his arm. Baring his teeth in a silent snarl, he spun around and followed the old man. Better his own decisions, he decided, then to rely upon *her*.

A few moments later, he stood in the round tower watching the elderly man remove dusty woolens draped over objects stacked behind an assortment of trunks near the wall. The elder seemed to be looking for one item in particular, and upon locating it, devoted much care to wiping it free of dust. Then he swiveled it about and propped it in front of him, where all could see.

Vengeance sucked in a harsh breath. The elder had uncovered a portrait of a dark-haired girl sitting between a man and a woman. The man bore an eerie resemblance to himself. The woman was a beauty with wild blond tresses. But the little girl—ah, merely gazing upon her filled him with pain. He closed his eyes, his breathing suddenly rapid and shallow.

*But you canna leave me, Aedan! Ma and Da hae gone sailin' and I canna bear to be alone! Nay, Aedan, dinna be leavin' me! I've a terrible feelin' you willna be comin' back!*

But this "Aedan," whoever he was, had had to leave. He'd had no choice.

Vengeance wondered who the man and child were and how he knew of them. But such thoughts pained his head so he thrust them from his mind. 'Twas none of his concern.

" 'Tis Findanus and Saucy Mary, with their daughter, Rose," the old man informed him. "They promised centuries ago that although the keep might be abandoned, one day a MacKinnon would return, the village would prosper, and the castle would be filled with clan again."

"I am *not* a MacKinnon," Vengeance growled.

The elder retrieved yet another portrait of three men riding into battle. Even Vengeance was forced to concede his resemblance to them was startling.

" 'Tis Duncan, Robert, and Niles MacKinnon. The brothers were killed fighting for Robert the Bruce more than a century ago. The keep has stood vacant since. The remaining MacKinnon resettled easterly, on the mainland."

"I am no kin of theirs," Vengeance said stiffly.

The lass who'd invaded his castle snorted. "You look

just like them. Anyone can see the resemblance. You're obviously a MacKinnon."

" 'Tis an uncanny coincidence, naught more."

The villagers were silent for a time, watching their elder for a cue. The old man measured him for several moments, then spoke in a tone one might employ to gentle a wild animal. "We came to offer our services. We brought food, drink, and materials to rebuild. We will arrive each morn at daybreak and remain as yer servants 'til dusk. We pray ye choose to remain with us. 'Tis clear ye are a warrior and a leader. Whatever name ye go by, we would be pleased to call ye laird."

Vengeance felt a peculiar helplessness steal over him. The man was saying that whether he was MacKinnon or not, they needed a protector and they wanted *him*. He felt a simultaneous disdain, a sense that he was above it all, yet . . . a tentative tide of pleasure.

He longed to put a stop to it—to cast the villagers out, to force the female to leave—but not being privy to his king's purpose in sending him there, he couldn't, lest he undermine his liege's plan. It was possible that his king expected him to submit to a fortnight of mortal doings to prove how stoically he could endure and demonstrate how well he would perform amongst them in the future. There was also the possibility that since he was his king's emissary in the mortal realm, he might have future need of this castle, and his king *intended* the villagers to rebuild it. He shook his head, unable to fathom why he'd been abandoned without direction.

"Oh, how lovely of you to offer!" the lass exclaimed. "How kind you all are! We'd *love* your help. I'm Jane, by the way," she told the elder, clasping his hand and smiling. "Jane Sillee."

Vengeance left the tower without saying another word. *Jane*. He rolled the name over in his mind. She was called Jane. "Jane Sillee," he whispered. He liked the sound of it on his lips.

His head began to pound again.

* * *

*"What's ailing him, milady?" Elias, the village elder,* asked after Aedan had departed and introductions had been made all around.

"He suffered a fall and took a severe blow to his head," she lied smoothly. "It may be some time before he's himself again. His memory has suffered, and he's uncertain of many things."

"Is he a MacKinnon from one o' their holdings in the east?" Elias asked.

Jane nodded, ruing the lie but deeming it necessary.

"I was fair certain, there's no mistakin' the look," Elias said. "Since the battle at Bannockburn, they've left the isle untended, busy with their holdings on the mainland. Long have we prayed they would send one of their kin to stand for us, to reside on the isle again."

"And so they have, but he was injured on the way here and we must help him remember," Jane said, seizing the opportunity offered, grateful that she now had co-conspirators. "Touch him frequently, although it may appear to unsettle him," she told them. "I believe it helps. And bring children around," she said, remembering how in her dreams Aedan had adored children. "The more the better. Perhaps they could play in the yard while we work."

"We? *Ye* needn't labor like a serf, milady," a young woman exclaimed.

"I intend to be part of rebuilding our home," Jane said firmly. *Our home*—how she liked the sound of that! She was gratified to see a glint of appreciation in the women's eyes. There were several approving nods.

"Also, I heard somewhere that familiar scents can help stir memories, so if you wouldn't mind teaching me to bake some things you think he might like, I'd be most appreciative. I'm afraid I'm not the best cook," she admitted. "But I'm eager to learn."

More approving nods.

Jane beamed. Her morning litany really did help: Today was turning out to be a fine day after all.

# *Seven*

***And so they settled into a routine with which Jane was*** pleased, despite Aedan's continued insistence that he was not a MacKinnon. Days sped by, too quickly for Jane's liking, but small progress was being made both with the estate and with the taciturn, brooding man who called himself Vengeance. Each day, Jane felt more at home at Dun Haakon, more at home with being in the fifteenth century.

As promised, each morning at daybreak, the villagers arrived in force. They were hard workers, and although the men departed in the late afternoon to tend their own small plots of land, the women and children remained, laboring cheerfully at Jane's side. They swept and scrubbed the floors; scraped away cobwebs; polished old earthenware mugs and platters, candlesticks, and oil globes; and aired out tapestries, hanging them with care. They repaired and oiled what furniture remained, stored beneath cloths saturated with the dust of decades.

Before long, the great hall sported a gleaming honey-blond table and a dozen chairs. The sole bed had been lavishly (and with much giggling by the women) covered with the plumpest pillows and softest fabrics the village had to offer. Sconces were reattached to the stone walls, displaying sparkling globes of oil with fat, waxy wicks. The women stitched pillows for the wooden chairs and strung packets of herbs from the beams.

The kitchen had fallen into complete rubble decades ago, and it would take some time to rebuild. After much thought, Jane decided it wasn't *too* risky to suggest the piping of water from a freshwater spring behind the castle and direct the construction of a large reservoir over a four-sided hearth, guaranteeing hot water at a moment's notice. She also sketched plans for counters and cabinets and a massive centrally located butcher's block.

In the meantime, Jane was learning to cook over the open fire in the great hall. Each afternoon the women taught her a new dish. Unfortunately, each evening, she ate it with a man who refused to eat anything but hard bread, no matter how she tried to tempt him.

Late into the twilight hours, Jane scribbled busily away before the fire, sometimes making notes, sometimes working on her manuscript, all the while peeking at Aedan over her papers and writing the future she hoped to have with him. She liked the laborious ritual of using quill and ink, the flames in the open hearth licking at her slippered toes, the hum of crickets and soft hooting of owls. She relished the complete absence of tires screeching, car alarms pealing, and planes flying overhead. In all her life, she'd never experienced such absolute, awe-inspiring stillness.

By the end of the first week of renovations, she'd begun to draw hope from Aedan's bewildered silence. Although he refused to speak to her, day by day, he participated a bit more in the repairs to the estate. And day by day, he seemed a bit less forbidding. No longer did she see disdain and loathing in his gaze, but confusion and . . . uncertainty? As if he didn't understand his place and how he fit into the grand scheme of things.

Jane intended to use her month as wisely as possible. She learned in her psychology courses at Purdue that attacking "amnesia" head-on could drive the person deeper into denial, even induce catatonia. So after much hard thought, she'd decided to give Aedan two weeks of absolutely no pressure, other than acclimating to his new environment. Two weeks of working, of being silently companionable, of not touching him as she so longed to do, despite the misery of being with him but forbidden to demonstrate her love and affection.

After those two weeks, she promised herself the seduction would begin. No more baths in Kyleakin in one of the village women's homes. She would begin bathing before the fire in the hall. No more proper gowns in the evening. She would wear lower bodices and higher hems.

And so, Jane bided her time, cuddled with Sexpot in the luxurious bed, and dreamed about the night when Aedan would lay beside her and speak her name in those husky tones that promised lovemaking to make a girl's toes curl.

*Aedan stood on the recently repaired front steps of the* castle and stretched his arms above his head, easing the tightness in his back. The night sky was streaked with purple. Stars twinkled above the treetops, and a crescent moon silvered the lawn. Every muscle in his body was sore from toting heavy stones from a nearby quarry to the castle.

Although he'd learned to avoid pain in the land of shadows, the current aches in his body were a strangely pleasurable sensation. He'd refused to participate in the repairs at first, withholding himself in silent and aloof censure, but much to his surprise, as he'd watched the village men work, he'd begun to hanker to lift, carry, and patch. His hands had itched to get dirty, and his mind had been eager to redesign parts of the keep that had been inefficiently, and in places, hazardously constructed.

Pondering the three commands his king had given, he'd concluded there was nothing to prevent him from passing time more quickly by working.

When on the third day he'd silently joined the men, they'd worked with twice the vigor and smiled and jested more frequently. They asked his opinion on many things, leading him to discover with some surprise that he *had* opinions, and, further, that they seemed sound. They accepted him with minimal fuss, although they touched him with disconcerting frequency, clapping him on the shoulder and patting his arm.

Because they weren't females, he deemed it acceptable.

When they asked the occasional question, he evaded. He completely ignored the lass who doggedly remained in the castle, leaving only to traipse off to the village, from whence she returned clean and slightly damp.

And fragrant smelling. And warm and soft and sweet looking.

Sometimes, merely gazing upon her made him hurt inside.

Vengeance shook his head, as if to shake thoughts of her right out of it. With each passing day, things seemed different. The sky no longer seemed too brilliant to behold, the air no longer too stifling to breathe. He'd begun to anticipate working each day, because in the gloaming he could stand back and look at something—a wall recently shored up, steps re-laid, a roof repaired, an interior hearth redesigned—and know it was his doing. He liked the feeling of laboring and rued that his king might deem it a flaw in his character, unsuitable for an exalted being.

And each day, when his thoughts turned toward his king, they were more often than not resentful thoughts. His king might not have bothered to inform him of his purpose at Dun Haakon, but the humans were more than willing to offer him ample purpose.

Purpose without pain.

Without *any* pain at all.

He had a blasphemous thought that took him by surprise and caused a headache of epic proportions that throbbed all through the night: He wondered if mayhap his king mightn't just forget about him.

# Eight

***Swiftly did one blasphemous thought breed another, the*** next more blasphemous, making the prior seem nearly innocuous. Swiftly did traitorous thought manifest itself in traitorous action.

It was on the evening of the eleventh day of his exile, when she was laying her meal on the long table in the great hall, that Vengeance began his fall from grace.

He'd labored arduously that day, and more than once his grip had slipped on a heavy stone. Furthering his unease, wee children from the village had played on the front lawn all afternoon. The sound of their high voices, bubbling with laughter as they chased a bladder-ball at the edge of the surf or teased the furry beastie with woolen yarns, had reverberated painfully inside his skull.

Now, he sat in the corner, far from the hearth, chewing dispiritedly on hard bread. Of late, he'd been eating loaf after loaf of it, his body starved by his daily labors. Yet no matter how much bread he consumed, he continued to lose mass and muscle and to feel lethargic and weak. He knew 'twas why his grip had slipped today.

Of late, when she spread the table with her rich and savory foods, his stomach roiled angrily, and on previous evenings, he'd left the castle and walked outdoors to avoid temptation.

But recently, indeed only this morning, he'd thought long and hard about his king's remark concerning sustenance and had scrutinized the precise words of his command.

*You must eat, but I would suggest you seek only bland foods.*

I would suggest.

It was the most nebulous phrase his liege had ever uttered. *I would suggest.* That was not at all how his king spoke to Vengeance. It made one think the king might be . . . uncertain of himself, unwilling, for some unfathomable reason, to commit to a command. And "bland." How vague was bland? An engraved invitation to interpretation, that word was.

After much meditation, Vengeance concluded for himself—a thing coming shockingly easier each day—that apparently his king had suffered some uncertainty as to how hard Vengeance might be laboring, so he'd been unable to anticipate what sustenance his body would require. Thus, he had "suggested," leaving the matter to Vengeance's discretion. As his king had placed such a trust in him, Vengeance resolved he must not return to his king weakened in body and risk inciting his displeasure.

When he rose and joined her at the table, her eyes rounded in disbelief.

"I will dine with you this eve," he informed her, gazing at her. Nay, lapping her up with his eyes. The tantalizing scent of roasted suckling pig teased his nostrils; the glorious rainbow hues of fiery-haired Jane clad in an emerald gown teased something he couldn't name.

"No bread?" she managed after an incredulous pause.

" 'Tis not enough to sustain me through the day's labors."

"I see," she said carefully, as she hastened to lay another setting.

Vengeance eyed the food with great interest. She served him generous portions of roast pork swimming in juices and glazed with a jellied sauce, roasted potatoes in clotted cream with chive, some type of vegetable mix in yet another sauce, and thin strips of battered salmon. As a finishing touch, she added several ladles of a buttery-looking pudding.

When she placed it before him, he continued to eye it, knowing he'd not yet gone too far. He could still rise and return to his corner, to his bread.

*I would suggest.*

He glanced at her. She had a spoon in her mouth and was licking the clotted cream from it. That was all it took. He fell upon the food like a ravening beast, eating with his bare hands, shoving juicy, deliciously greasy pork into his mouth, stripping the tender meat from the bones with his teeth and tongue.

*Christ, it was heavenly!* Rich and succulent and warm.

Jane watched, astonished. It took him less than three minutes to devour every morsel she'd placed on his plate. His aquamarine eyes were wild, his sensual mouth glistening with juices from the roast, his hands—oh, God, he started licking his fingers, his firm pink lips sucking, and her temperature rose ten degrees.

Elation filled her. Although he'd never admitted that he'd been ordered to eat only bread, she'd figured it out herself. Each night while she'd dined, he'd shot furtive glances her way, watching her eat, eyeing the food with blatant longing, and a time or two, she'd heard his stomach rumble.

"More." He shoved his platter at her.

Happily, she complied. And a third time, until he sat back, sighing.

His eyes were different, she mused, watching him. There was something new in them, a welcome defiance. She decided to test it.

"I don't think you should eat anything but old bread in the future," she provoked.

"I will eat what I deem fit. And 'tis no longer bread."

Her lips ached from the effort of suppressing a delighted smile. "I don't think that's wise," she pushed.

"I will eat what I wish!" he snapped.

*Oh, Aedan*, Jane thought lovingly, fighting a mist of joyous tears, *well done*. One tiny crack in the façade, and she had no doubt that a man of Aedan's strength and independence would begin cracking at an alarming rate now that it had begun. "If you insist," she said mildly.

"I do," he growled. "And pass me that wine. And fetch another flagon. I feel a deep thirst coming on." Centuries of thirst. For far more than wine.

***Aedan couldn't get over the pleasure of eating. Sun-***warmed tomatoes, sweet young corn drenched with freshly churned butter, roasts basted with garlic, baked apples in delicate pastry smothered with cinnamon and honey. There were so many new, intriguing sensations! The fragrance of heather on the autumn breeze, the salty rhythmic lick of the ocean when he swam in it to bathe each eve, the brush of soft linen against his skin. Once, when no one had been in the castle, he'd removed his clothing and stretched naked on the velvet coverlet. Pressed his body into the soft ticks. Pondered lying there with *her,* but then he'd caught a rash from the coverlet that had made the part of him between his legs swell up. He'd swiftly dressed again and not repeated that indulgence. Unfortunately, the rash lingered, manifesting itself at odd intervals.

There were unpleasant sensations, too: sleeping on the hard, cold floor whilst she curled cozily in the overstuffed bed with the beastie. The tension of watching the lass's ankles and calves as she sauntered about. The sickness he felt in his stomach when he gazed upon the soft rise of her breasts in her gown.

He'd seen much more than that, yestreen, when the audacious wench had tugged a heavy tub before the fire and proceeded to fill it with pails of steaming water and sprinkle it with herbs.

He'd not comprehended what she was doing until she'd been as naked and rosy-bottomed as when she'd arrived at the castle a fortnight past, and then he'd been too stunned to move.

Feeling strangely nauseous, he'd finally gathered his wits and fled the hall, chased by the lass's soft derisive snort. He'd warred with himself on the newly laid terrace, only to return a quarter hour hence and watch her from the shadows of the doorway where she couldn't see him. Swallowing hard, endeavoring to slow his breathing, to stop the thundering of his blood in his veins, he'd watched her soap and rinse every inch of her body.

When his hands were trembling and his body aching in odd places, he'd closed his eyes, but the images had been burned into his brain. Thirteen more days, he told himself. Less than a fortnight remained until he could return to his king.

But with each day that passed, his curiosity about her grew. What did she ponder when she sat before the hearth staring into the flames? Why had she no man when the other village women did? Why did she watch him with that expression on her face? Why did she labor so over her letters? Why did she want him to touch her? What would come of it, were he to comply?

And the most pressing question of late, as his thoughts turned less often to his king and more often to that puzzling pain between his legs or the hollow ache behind his breastbone:

*How long would he be able to resist finding out?*

# Nine

***"What are you writing?" Aedan asked casually, his tone*** implying that he cared not what she replied, or even if she did.

Although her heart leapt, Jane pretended to ignore him. They sat in chairs at catty-corner angles near the hearth in the great hall; she curled near a table and three bright oil globes, he practically inside the hearth atop the blaze. He'd been surreptitiously watching her across the space of half a dozen feet for over an hour, and his question was the first direct one he'd asked of her since her arrival at Dun Haakon that didn't concern castle matters. Concealing a smile, she continued writing as if she hadn't heard him:

> *He rose from the chair so abruptly that it toppled over, crashing to the floor. His aquamarine eyes glittering with desire, he ripped the sheaf of papers from her hands and threw them aside. He towered*

*over her, his intense gaze seeming to delve into her very soul. "Forget these papers. Forget my question. I want you, Jane," he said roughly. "I need you. Now." He began to strip, unlacing his linen shirt, tugging it over his head. He pressed a finger to her lips when she began to speak. "Hush, lass. Doona deny me. 'Tis no use. I will have you this night. You are mine, and only mine, for all of ever, then yet another day."*

*"Why another day?" she whispered against his finger, her heart hammering with nervousness and anticipation. She'd never been with a man before, only dreamed of it. And the dark Highlander standing before her was every inch a dream come to life.*

*He flashed her a seductive grin as he unknotted his plaid and let it slip down over his ~~taut buttocks~~ lean, muscular hips. Bracing his hands on the arms of her chair, he lowered his head toward hers. "Because not even forever with you will be enough to satisfy me, sweet Jane. I'm a greedy, demanding man."*

"I said what are you writing?" His voice was tight.

*His hard body glistened bronze in the shimmering light of dozens of oil globes. "I can't resist you, lass. God knows I've tried," he groaned, his voice low and taut with need. "I think about you day and night, I can't sleep for wanting you. 'Tis a madness I fear will never abate."*

Jane swallowed a dreamy sigh and paused, quill poised above the paper. She arched a brow at him, outwardly calm while inwardly melting. His eyes flashing in his dark face, he coiled tensely in his chair, as if he might leap up at any moment. And pounce. *Oh, if only!*

"Why do you care?" she said with a shrug, trying to sound nonchalant. She was sick of being patient. She knew that the presence of the villagers, the laboring with his hands on what had once been his home, and his nocturnal spying upon her in the bath were beginning to take a toll. She'd been wise to take a passive role for the past two weeks, but it was time to be more proactive. She had twelve days, and she was *not* going to lose him.

"You do nothing without purpose," he said stiffly. "I merely wish to know your purpose in practicing your letters so faithfully each eve."

Jane pressed her quill to parchment again:

*He tugged her up from the chair, crushing her body against the hard length of his own. Gazing into her eyes, he deliberately rocked his hips forward so she could feel his ~~huge cock~~ need. Hard and hot, ~~his impressive erection~~ he throbbed, pressing through the thin silk of her gown . . .*

Jane blew out a breath of pure sexual frustration—writing love scenes sure could be sheer torture for a girl with no man of her own—and placed the quill aside. Sexpot promptly jumped onto the small side table and attacked the feather, shaking it violently. Rescuing the quill before the kitten shredded yet another one, she hesitated before answering. She knew that one inadvertent misstep might drive him back into his rigid shell. He'd made it clear he would never permit her to touch him. She had to find a way to coax him to touch her.

"I'm not practicing my letters. I write stories."

"What kind of stories?"

Jane stared at him hungrily. He was so damned sexy sitting there. Only yesterday he'd taken to wearing a plaid for the first time since his arrival, saying it was cooler to work in. There he sat looking just like *her* Aedan, clad in crimson and black and no shirt. His upper body glistened with a faint sheen of sweat as he perched as close to the fire as he could get.

"You wouldn't understand any of it," she said coolly.

"Understand what?" he said angrily. "I understand many things."

"You wouldn't understand what I write about," she goaded. "I write about human things, things you couldn't possibly understand. Remember, you're not human," she pressed. "By the way," she added sweetly, "have you figured out yet what you actually *are?*" There, she thought smugly, he looked incensed. Her Aedan was a proud man and didn't like to be belittled. Over the past week he'd begun to display resentment toward anything resembling a direct order, which pleased her and made her suspect that he would defy her outright, were she to issue a firm command.

Anger and confusion warred behind his eyes. "I have been laboring with other humans. You doona know what I can and can't understand."

"*Never* read my stories," she said sternly. "They are private. It's none of your business, Aedan."

"So long as I am laird of this castle, everything is my—" He broke off with a stricken expression.

"Laird of this castle?" she echoed, searching his gaze. He hadn't even bothered to chastise her for calling him 'Aedan.'

He stared into her eyes a long moment, then said stiffly, "I meant that the villagers think I am, so if you're to live here, in what they think is my castle, you should abide by that perception, too. Or find another place to live, lass. That's all I meant," he snapped, then pushed himself angrily up from his chair. But at the doorway, he cast a glance over his shoulder so full of frustrated longing, so rife with desire, that it sent a shiver up her spine. It was plain to see that he was beginning to feel all the things he'd once felt, but couldn't understand them.

Much later, Jane scooped up her papers in one arm and Sexpot in the other. She knew *exactly* which scene of the manuscript she was working on to inadvertently leave lying about tomorrow.

# *Ten*

*The first time he kissed her slowly, brushing his lips lightly back and forth, creating a delicious sensual friction, until hers parted, yielding utterly. The second, deeper, even more intimately, and the third so possessively that it made her dizzy. His silky tongue tangled with hers. He fitted his mouth so completely over hers that she could scarcely breathe. If a kiss could speak, his was purring, "You are mine forever."*

*Subsequent kisses blended, wet and hot and intoxicating, one into another until her head was reeling. She trembled, burning with the scorching heat of desire.*

*She whimpered when he traced the curve of her jaw, down her neck to the top of her breast. His touch evoked a blend of lassitude and adrenaline that made her feel strong and weak at the same time. Soft and supple, yet close to aggression. Hot and needy and achy.*

*His aquamarine eyes promised lovemaking that would strip bare far more than her body. Gently slipping the sleeves of her gown from her shoulders, he bared her breasts to his hungry gaze. The chill air coupled with the molten promise in his eyes made her breasts feel tight and achy. When he lowered his dark head and captured a ~~pouty~~ nipple in his mouth, she whimpered with pleasure. When he buried his face between her breasts, slipping her gown down over her hips, she pressed ~~her honeyed womanhood~~ against him, clinging.*

*His lips seared her sensitive skin. He scattered light kisses across her tummy, nipping and nibbling, then dropping to his knees before her.*

*She could barely stand, her knees so weak with desire, and when his hot tongue pressed to her hotter flesh, lapping sweetly at her ~~passion juices~~ most private heat, she nearly screamed with the exquisiteness of it.*

***Jane stood in the doorway of the great hall, a smile curving*** her lips, watching Aedan. Fifteen minutes ago, she'd informed him that she was going to take a quick nap before beginning preparations for their evening meal. She'd headed for the bedchamber, conveniently leaving a few pages of her manuscript lying beside the hearth, as if forgotten.

He'd nodded nonchalantly, but his gaze had betrayed him by drifting to the parchment. Shortly after retiring to the bedchamber, she'd crept back to the hall. He was standing by the fire, reading so intently that he didn't even notice her standing in the shadows of the stone doorway, watching as his eyes narrowed and his grip tightened on the parchment. After a few minutes, he wet his lips and wiped beads of sweat from his forehead with the back of his hand.

"I feel quite rested now," she announced, striding

briskly into the hall. "Hey!" she exclaimed, feigning outrage that he was snooping. "Those are my papers! I told you not to read them!"

His head shot up. His eyes were dark, his pupils dilated, his chest rising and falling as if he'd run a marathon.

He shook the parchments at her. "What are these . . . these . . . *scribblings?*" Vengeance demanded in a voice that should have been firm but came out sounding hoarse. His chest felt tight, that heavy part of him betwixt his legs . . . *och, Christ, it hurt!* Instinctively, he palmed it through the fabric of his kilt to soothe it, hoping the pain would diminish, but touching it only seemed to make it worse. Appalled, he removed his hand and glared at her. She seemed to find the gesture quite fascinating.

Jane cornered him and tried to grab the papers from his hand, but he held them above his head.

"Just give them back," she snapped.

"I doona think so," he growled. He stood looking at her, her jaw, her neck. Her breasts. "This man you write of," he said tensely, "he has dark hair and eyes of my hue."

"So?" she said, doing her best to sound defensive.

" 'Tis *me* you write about," he accused. When she made no move to deny it, he scowled. " 'Tis in no fashion a proper woman might write—" He broke off, wondering what he knew of proper women when he knew naught of female humans but what he'd learned from her. He studied her, trying to think, which was immensely difficult with parts of his body behaving so strangely. His breath was too short and shallow, his mouth parched, his heart pounding. He felt intensely alive, all his senses stirring . . . demanding. *Starving for touch.* "This pressing of the lips of yours makes one feel as if one is"—he glanced back at the papers—"burning with the scorching heat of desire?" He, who'd long been cold, ached to feel such heat.

"Yes—if a man's any good at it," she said archly. "But

you're not a man, remember? It probably wouldn't work for you," she added sweetly.

"You doona know that," he snapped.

"Trust me," she provoked. "I doubt you have the right stuff."

"I doona know what this right stuff of yours is, but I know that I am formed like a man," he said indignantly. "I look as all the villagers do." He thought hard for a moment. "Verily, I believe I am more well formed than the lot of them," he added defensively. "My legs more powerful," he said, moving his plaid to display a thigh for her. "See? And my shoulders are wider. I am greater of height and girth, with no excess fatty parts." He preened for her, and it was everything she could do not to drool. More well formed? Sheesh! The man could drive the sales of *Playgirl* right through the roof!

"*What*ever," Jane said, purloining one of her teenage niece Jessica's most irritating responses, guaranteed to provoke, issued in tones that implied *nothing* he could say or do might interest her.

"You would do well to not dismiss me so lightly," he growled.

They stared at each other for a long tense moment, then he glanced back at the parchment. "Regardless of whether I'm human or no, 'tis plain from your writings that you wish me to do such things to you." His tone challenged her to deny it.

Jane swallowed hard. Should she pretend to order him not to? Should she concede? She was on tricky terrain, uncertain what would push his buttons just a teeny bit further. He was so close to falling on her like a ravening beast—and God, how she wanted him to! As fate would have it, her very indecision provoked him correctly. As she hesitated, nibbling on her lower lip, a thing she did often while thinking hard, his gaze fixed there. His eyes narrowed.

"You *do* wish me to," he accused. "Else you would have denied it outright."

She nodded.

"Why?" he asked hoarsely.

"It will . . . er, make me happy?" she managed lamely, twirling a strand of hair around her finger.

He nodded, as if that were a fine excuse. After a moment's hesitation he croaked, "You wish this now? At this very moment? Here?" He fisted his hands, half crumpling the parchment. His blasted voice had risen and dropped again like a green lad's. He felt incomparably foolish. Yet . . . also as if he faced a moment of ineluctable destiny.

Jane's throat constricted with longing as she gazed at him. She wanted him every bit as much as she needed to breathe and eat. He was necessary to the care and feeding of her soul. She nodded, not trusting herself to speak.

Vengeance stood motionless, his mind racing. His king had ordered that he not permit a human female to touch him. But he'd said nothing about *Vengeance* touching a human female. There was this thing inside him, this great gnawing curiosity. He wondered if there was such a thing as "burning with the scorching heat of desire," and if so, just how it might feel. "If I do this, you may not touch me," he warned.

"I can't touch you?" she echoed. "That's *so* ridiculous! Don't you wonder why your king made up that idiotic rule?"

"You will do as I demand. I will do this thing as you have written, only if you vow not to touch me."

"Fine," she snapped. *Anything* to get his hands on her. She'd cheerfully acquiesce to being tied to the bed, if she must. Hmmm . . . intriguing thought, that.

When he stepped forward, she tipped her head back and gazed up at him.

He glanced swiftly at the parchment, as if committing it to memory. "First, I am to brush my lips lightly across yours. You are to slightly part yours," he directed.

"I think we can play it by ear," she said, leaning minutely nearer, praying fervently that he wouldn't change his mind. She felt she might combust the moment he touched her, so long had she ached to feel his hands on her body.

He glanced back at the parchment with a look of alarm and confusion. "You mentioned naught of ears in your writing. Am I to do something with your ears, too?"

Jane nearly whimpered with frustration. Snatching the parchment from his hands, she said, "It's a figure of speech, Aedan. It means we'll figure it out as we go along. Just begin. You'll do fine, I promise."

"I'm merely trying to ascertain we both know our proper positions," he said stiffly.

*The hell with proper,* Jane thought, moistening her lips with her tongue and gazing up at him longingly. The last thing she wanted from him was *proper*. "Touch me," she encouraged.

Warily, he leaned closer.

Jane swayed forward, drawn like a magnet to steel. She wouldn't be satisfied until she was clinging to him like Saran Wrap. Although she was forbidden to out and out touch him, once he touched her, she certainly could press against him.

But still, he didn't move.

"Would you please just *start* already?"

"I am not quite certain I know what your 'most private heat' is," he admitted reluctantly. What was happening to him? he wondered. Complying with his demand, she was not touching him, but the tips of her breasts nearly brushed his chest, he could feel the heat of her body, and an alarming urgency flooding his.

"I'll help you find it," she assured him fervently.

"You're too short," he hedged.

It took Jane two seconds to retrieve the small footstool from beside the hearth, plop it down at his feet, and stand on it. It put them nose to nose, a mere inch apart.

She stared at him, heart thundering.

And he stared silently back.

Their breath mingled. His gaze dropped from her eyes to her lips. Back to her eyes, then lips again. He wet his lips, staring at her.

Jane kept her hands behind her back so she wouldn't touch him, knowing he'd use it as an excuse to leave. It was intensely intimate, such closeness without actually touching. And the way he was looking at her—with such raw hunger and heat!

A small sound escaped her. He answered in kind, then looked startled by his involuntary groan. Jane scarcely dared breathe, waiting for him to move that last tiny half inch. His dark, raw sexuality coupled with his innocence of lovemaking was an irresistibly erotic combination. The man was an expert lover, of that she had no doubt, yet it was as if it were his first time ever, and each touch would be an undiscovered country to him.

She gave a quarter inch, and he met her halfway.

His lips touched hers.

*God, they were cold!* she thought, stunned. Icy.

*God, she was warm,* he thought, stunned. Blazing.

Fascinated, Vengeance pressed his mouth more snugly to hers. He knew he was supposed to use his tongue somehow, but wasn't certain he understood the mechanics of it.

"Taste me," she breathed against his lips. "Taste me like you would lick juice from your lips."

*Ah,* he thought, understanding. Mesmerized by the softness of her lips, he touched the tip of his tongue to them, running it over the seam, and when her lips parted, he tasted her like he was trying to remove a bit of cream from the center of a pastry.

She was infinitely sweeter.

And then his body seemed to take over, to understand something he didn't, and with a hoarse groan, he plunged his tongue into her mouth and crushed her against him, locking his arms securely behind her back. But that wasn't good enough, he quickly decided, he needed her head just so, so he slipped his hands deep into her hair and clamped her face firmly, kissing her until they were both breathless.

*It was incredible,* he marveled, stopping to stare at her. He touched a finger to his own lips; they were warm.

And she got prettier when he kissed her! he thought, awestruck. Her lips got all swollen and cushy-looking, her eyes sparkled like jewels, and her skin grew rosy. *He'd* done that to her, he thought, with pride. He could make a lass prettier merely by pressing his lips to hers. 'Twas a gift his king had ne'er told him he possessed. He wondered how much prettier she'd get if he touched his lips to her in other places.

"You are lovely, lass," he said in a voice utterly unlike his own normal tone—indeed, it came out raspy and thick. "Nay, doona speak, I haven't finished."

He pressed his lips to hers again, swallowing her words. With butterfly light touches, his thumbs caressed smooth circles on the delicate skin of her neck, along the line of her jaw, and over her face. Then he drew back and ran his fingers lightly over her face, as if he were blind, absorbing the feel of every plane and angle from the downy soft brows to the pert nose and high bones of her cheeks, from the shape of her widow's peak to the point of her chin.

Her soft, lush lips.

When he rested a finger there too long, she gently sucked the tip of it, and heat lanced straight down to his groin. The vision of her lips closed full and sweetly around his finger near made him crazed . . . reminded him of something else, long forgotten, something a lass might do that was sweeter than heaven. His breath caught in his throat.

She stared at him, her amber eyes glowing, wide, trusting, her lips around his finger. It made him nearly mad with some kind of pain in his breast.

Taking her face between his hands, he kissed her as if he could suck the heat of her right into his body, and indeed, it seemed he did. "I want to touch you 'til your skin smells of me," he growled, not knowing why. "Every inch of it."

But Jane understood. It was a purely male way of marking his territory, loving his woman until she bore his unique scent from head to toe. She whimpered assent into his mouth, her hands curled into fists behind her back because it was killing her to not touch him.

Then he lifted her from the stool, crushing her against him completely, holding her weight as if she were light as a feather, and his hard, hot arousal pressed into the vee of her thighs.

*I'm dying*, Vengeance realized dimly. The feel of her body against that swollen part of him that seemed to have never recovered from whatever rash he'd caught from the coverlet burned and throbbed angrily. He must be dying, because no man could withstand such pain for long.

Mayhap, he thought, once he'd undressed her as she'd directed in her parchments, he could doff his tartan, too, and she might tell him what was wrong with him.

But nay—he would press his lips to hers a few more times, for she might see the thing betwixt his legs and be disgusted. Flee him. For now, he was warm . . . so warm. He slipped his hands from her hair and down over her breasts. He shuddered, once, twice, and three times, before losing complete control of himself.

He had no idea what he'd done, lost to a madness of sorts, until he stood looking at her as she perched atop the small stool naked, tatters of her dress scattered across the floor. He had no clear memory of ripping her gown away, so urgent and fierce had his need been to bare her completely to his touch.

"Did I hurt you?" he demanded.

Jane shook her head, her eyes wide. "Touch me," she encouraged softly. "Find my most private heat. You may look for it wherever you wish," she encouraged, eyes sparkling.

He circled her slowly. She didn't move a muscle, merely stood naked on the stool as he marveled over every inch of her. And when he returned to face her, he sucked in a breath. She'd done it again—grown more beautiful. Her eyes were filled with some lazy, dreamy knowing he could only guess at. Glittering and sleepy and desirous, her skin flushed from head to toe.

He reached out with both hands and gathered the firm, plump weight of her breasts in his palms. They felt sweet, so sweet. Their eyes met and she made a soft mewing sound that shivered through him.

"Kiss—"

"Aye," he said instantly, knowing what she wanted, and lowered his head to the soft pillows of her breasts. Unable to comprehend why he wanted it so badly, he closed his lips over first one nipple, then the next. Unknowing why he did it, his hand slipped between her soft thighs, sought the warmth and wetness. . . .

And images assaulted him—he was someone else—a man who knew much of soft thighs and heated loving. A man who'd lost everything, everyone:

*"Aedan, please dinna go!" the child sobbed. "At least wait 'til Ma and Da come home!"*

*"I must go now, little one." The man crushed her in his arms, brushing helplessly at her tears. " 'Tis only for five years. Why you'll be but a lass of ten and three when I return." The man closed his eyes. "I left a note for Ma and Da . . ."*

*"Nay! Aedan. Dinna leave me," the child said, weeping as if her heart would break. "I love you!"*

"Ahhh!" Vengeance roared, thrusting her away, clutching his head with both hands. He bellowed wordlessly, backing away until his spine hit the wall.

"Aedan! What is it?" Jane cried, jumping off the stool and scurrying toward him.

"Doona call me that!" he shouted, his palms clamped to his temples.

"But Aedan—"

*"Haud yer wheesht,* woman!"

"But I think you're remembering," she said frantically, trying to touch him, to soothe him.

Another wordless bellow was his only reply as he raced from the hall as if all the hounds of hell were nipping at his heels.

# Eleven

***Above all else, it would be unwise to seek the company of*** female humans or permit them to touch you.

It would be unwise.

How had he overlooked such nonspecific phrasing?

It would be unwise. Vengeance didn't feel particularly wise at the moment. Nor did he intend to eat bland food, nor did he intend to circumvent Kyleakin because "it might be best."

Just as he'd begun to suspect, his king had, in truth, not issued a single order at all.

*How and when did I meet him?* Vengeance wondered for the first time. Had he been born in Faery, pledged to the king from birth? Had he met him in later years? Why couldn't he *remember?*

Vengeance sat in silence beside the gently lapping ocean, slapping the blade of a dirk against his palm.

Fairies didn't bleed. They healed too quickly.

Vengeance made a fist around the blade.

Blood seeped from his clenched hand and dripped down the sides. He spread his fingers and studied the deep cuts.

They remained deep, oozing dark crimson blood.

A harsh, relieved breath escaped him.

How old was he? How long had he lived? Why could he not recall ever changing? Why did humans gray on their heads, yet Vengeance remained unchanged?

*Nothing changes in Faery.*

If he never went back, would his long black hair one day silver, too? Strangely, the thought appealed to him. Thoughts of a child rose unbidden in his mind. He imagined hugging one of the wee village lasses in his arms, wiping away her tears. Teaching her to climb trees, to make boats out of wood and sail them in the surf, bringing her a litter of mewing kittens whose mother had died birthing them.

"Who am I?" Vengeance cried, clutching his head.

It occurred to him that, in truth, mayhap the right question was—who had he once been?

*Jane watched him from the front steps of the castle. He* sat with his back to her in the deepening twilight, clutching his head, staring out to sea. Blood was smeared on one of his hands, dripping down his arm. Suddenly he stood up, and she caught a gleam of silver as he flung a blade, end over end, into the waves.

A salty breeze whipped at his hair, tangling the dark strands into a silken skein. His plaid flapped in the breeze, hugging the powerful lines of his body.

He seemed dark and desolate and strong and utterly untouchable.

Jane's eyes misted. "I love you, Aedan MacKinnon," she told the wind.

As if the wind eagerly whisked her words down the front lawn to the sea's edge, Aedan suddenly turned and looked straight at her. His cheeks gleamed wetly in the fading light.

He nodded once, then turned his back to her and walked off down the shore, head bowed.

Jane started after him, then stopped. There'd been such desolation in his gaze, such loneliness, yet a great deal of anger. He'd turned away, clearing demonstrating his wish to be alone. She didn't want to push him too hard. She couldn't even begin to understand what he was going through. She was elated that he was remembering and equally anguished by the pain it was causing him. She watched, torn by indecision, until he disappeared around a bend in the rocky shoreline.

# Twelve

***He didn't come back for three days. They were the most*** agonizing three days of Jane Sillee's life.

Daily, she cursed herself for pushing him too far too fast. Daily, she berated herself for not going after him when he'd begun walking down that rocky shore.

Daily, she lied to the villagers when they came to work, assuring them he'd only gone to see a man about a horse and would return anon.

And nightly, as she curled with Sexpot in the bed that was much too large for just one lonely girl, she prayed her words would prove true.

# Thirteen

***It was the middle of the night when Aedan returned.***

He awakened her abruptly, stripping the coverlets from her naked body, sending Sexpot flying from the bed with a disgruntled meow.

"Aedan!" Jane gasped, staring up at him. His expression was so fierce that her sleep-fogged brain cleared instantly.

He stood at the foot of the bed, his dark gaze sweeping every inch of her nude body. He'd braided his hair. His face was dark with the stubble of a black beard, shadowing his jaw. In the past few weeks, he'd lost weight, and although he was still powerfully muscular, there was a leanness to him, a dangerously hungry look, like a wolf too long alone and unfed in the wild.

He didn't say a word, just stripped off his shirt and kicked off his boots, then moved toward her.

She never would have believed it of herself, but he radiated such barely harnessed fury that she scuttled back against the headboard and crossed her arms over her breasts protectively.

"Och, nay, lass," he said with silky menace. "Not after all the times you've tried to get me to touch you. You willna naysay me now."

Jane's eyes grew huge. "I-I—"

"Touch me." He unknotted his plaid and let it fall to the floor.

Jane's jaw dropped. "I-I—" she tried again, and failed, again.

"Is something wrong with me?" he demanded.

"N-no," she managed. "Uh-uh. No way." She swallowed hard.

"And this?" He palmed his formidable erection. "This is as it should be?"

"Oh," Jane breathed reverently. "Absolutely."

He eyed her suspiciously. "You're not just saying that, are you?"

Jane shook her head, her eyes wide.

"Then give me those kisses of yours, lass, and be quick about it." He paused a moment, then added in a low, tense voice, "I'm cold, lass. I'm so cold."

Jane's breath hitched in her throat and her eyes misted. His vulnerability melted her fears. She rose to her knees on the bed and extended her hands to him.

Never breaking eye contact, staring into her eyes as if the invitation in them was all that was sustaining him, he placed his hands slowly in hers and let her pull him onto the bed, where he knelt facing her.

She glanced down at their entwined hands, and his gaze followed. Her hands were small and white, nearly swallowed by his work-roughened and tan fingers. She flexed her fingers against his, savoring the first *real* feel of holding Aedan's hand. Until that moment, she'd only touched him in her dreams. She closed her eyes, savoring every bit of it, drinking the experience dry.

She opened them to find him regarding her with expectancy and fascination.

"Sometimes I think I know you, lass."

"You do," she said, with a little catch in her voice. "I'm Jane." *Your* Jane, she longed to cry.

He hesitated a long moment. Then, "I'm Aedan. Aedan MacKinnon."

Jane stared at him wonderingly. "You've remembered?" she exclaimed. "Oh, Aedan—"

He cut her words off with a gentle finger against her lips. "Does it matter? The villagers think I am. You think I am. Why should I not be?"

Jane's heart sank again. He still didn't recall.

But . . . he was here, and he was willing to let her touch him. She would take what she could get.

"Jane," he said urgently, "am I truly as a man should be?"

"*Everything* a man should be," she assured him.

"Then teach me what a man does with a woman such as you."

*Aw,* her heart purred. The look in his eyes was so innocent and hopeful, nearly masking the ever-present despair in his gaze.

"First," she said softly, raising his hand to her lips, "he kisses her, like so." She planted a sweet kiss in his palm and closed his fingers over it. He did the same with both her hands, lingering over the sensitive skin of her palm.

"Then," she breathed, "he lets her touch him *all* over. Like this." She slid her hands up his muscular arms and into his hair. Removing his leather thong, she combed her fingers through the plait until it fell dark and silky around his face. She laid her palms against his face, staring into his eyes. He was still beneath her touch, his eyes unfocused.

"More," he urged, a stray tomcat, starved for touch.

"And she touches him here," she said, skimming his shoulders, the muscles of his back, down over his lean hips, and back up his magnificent abs and muscled chest. Unable to resist, she dropped her head forward against his chest and licked him, tasting the salt of his skin.

A rough groan escaped him, and the heat of his arousal throbbed insistently against her thigh.

Jane whimpered at the contact and pressed against him. She tasted his neck, his jaw, his lips and buried her hands in his hair. "Then, he brushes his lips—"

"I know this part," he said, sounding pleased with himself.

Fitting his mouth to hers, he kissed her; a deep, starving soul-kiss, and dragged her hard against his body.

The feel of her naked body against his bare skin made his head swim. Made him burn. Made him tremble with wonder. He'd never known . . . he'd never suspected what pleasure was to be found in touch. The feel of her wee hands on his body made him hotter than any fire could and brought him crashing to his knees inside himself.

She'd said that he was fashioned as a man should be, and she touched him as if she desperately craved his body. He liked that. It made him feel . . . och, just feel and feel and *feel*.

He nibbled and suckled at her lips, then plunged his tongue deeply, thrusting. His body moved to a rhythm, innate and primal. She went supple in his arms, dropping back onto the bed, and he followed, stretching his body atop her lush softness. "Christ, lass, I've ne'er felt aught such as you!" Intoxicated, he kissed her deeply, his silky hot tongue tangling with hers. When she shifted her legs beneath him, the swollen part of him was suddenly flush between her thighs, and he thrust against her instinctively. She raised her hips, pressing back, and he thought he would die from such sensation. He cupped her bottom and pulled her more firmly against him. Digging his fingers into the softness of her bare bottom filled him with a wild and fierce sensation—an urge to possess, to hold her beneath him until she wept with pleasure. Until he shuddered atop her. Images came to him then:

Of a man and a woman rolling naked across a bed. Of the firm pistoning motion of a man's hips, of slender ankles and calves raised near a woman's breasts, of the musky scent of skin and bodies, the sweat and rawness and heat of—

*"You have no clan. You have no home," the dark king said.*

*"Nay, I do! I have clan all o'er the Highlands.* My *Highlands.* My *home." 'Twas the thought of his clan that sustained him. Along with yet a more exquisite thought—but the king had tried to steal that other, most important thought from him, so he'd built a tower of ice around it to keep it safe.*

*"Everyone in your clan died a hundred years ago, you fool. Forget!"*

*"Nay! My people are not dead." But he knew they were. Naught but dust returned to the Highland soil.*

*"Everyone for whom you cared is dead. The world goes on without you. You are my Vengeance, the beast who serves my bidding."*

*And then the darker images, as the pain, the unending pain began . . . and went on and on until there was nothing left but a single frozen tear and ice where once had beat a heart that held the hallowed blood of Scottish kings.*

He pushed her away, roaring.

Stunned, Jane fell back on the bed. Bewildered by his abrupt leave-taking, she stammered, "Wh-what—" She shook her head, trying to clear it, to understand what was happening. One minute he'd been about to make wildly passionate love to her, the next he was five feet away, looking horrified. "Why did you stop?"

"I can't do this!" he shouted. "It hurts too much!"

"Aedan—it's just—"

"Nay! I canna, lass!" Eyes wild, trembling visibly, he turned and stormed from the bedchamber.

But not before she saw the remembering in his dark gaze.

Not before she saw the first faint hint of awareness of who and what he really was.

"Oh, you know," she breathed to the empty room. "You *know*." Chills shivered down her spine.

And he did. She'd seen it in his gaze. In the pain etched in his face, in the stiffness of his body. He'd left her, moving like a man who'd gone ten rounds in the ring, whose ribs were bruised, whose body was contused from head to toe.

She had the sudden terrifying feeling that he might leave her, that he might simply go back to his king so that he wouldn't have to face what he would now have to face.

"Aedan!" she cried, leaping up from the bed and chasing after him.

But the castle was empty. Aedan was gone.

# *Fourteen*

***Jane trod dispiritedly into the castle, shoulders slumped.*** It had been a week since Aedan had left, and she had only two more days before . . . before . . . whatever was going to happen would happen. She had no idea exactly what would come to pass, but she was pretty certain he would be gone from her, forever.

No longer in this castle. No longer even in her dreams.

Leaving her to a life of what? Only memories of dreams that *nothing* could ever compare to.

Reluctant to go in search of him, in case he returned only to find *her* gone, she'd been crying off and on for a week. She'd barely been able to converse with the villagers when they came to labor every day. The castle was progressing, but to what avail? Both the "laird and lady" would likely be gone in a matter of forty-eight hours, no more. How she would miss this place! The wild rugged land, the honest, hard-working people who knew how to find joy in the smallest of things.

Sniffing back tears, she mewed for Sexpot who, for a change, didn't come scampering across the stone floor, tail swishing flirtatiously.

Glancing around with tear-blurred eyes, she drew up short.

Aedan was sitting before the hearth, feet resting on a stool, with Sexpot curled on his lap.

As if him being there, petting the "wee useless beastie" wasn't astonishing enough, he'd propped the painting Elias had unearthed weeks ago against the table facing him and was staring at it.

She must have made some small sound, because without looking up, hand moving gently over the kitten's silvery fur, he said, "I walked about the Highlands a bit. One of the villagers was kind enough to ferry me to the mainland."

Jane opened her mouth, then closed it again. Such intense relief flooded her that she nearly crumpled to her knees. She still had two more days to try. *Thank you, God,* she whispered silently.

"Much has changed," he said slowly. "Little was familiar to me. I lost my bearings a time or two."

"Oh, Aedan," she said gently.

"I needed to know this place again. And . . . I suppose . . . I needed time."

"You don't have to explain," she hastened to assure him. The mere fact that he'd returned was enough. She'd nearly given up hope.

"But I do," he said, his staring fixedly at the portrait. "There is much I need to explain to you. You have a right to know. That is," he added carefully, "if you still wish to share these quarters with me."

"I still wish to share these quarters, Aedan," she said instantly. Some of the tension seemed to leave his body. How could she make him understand that she wished not only to share "quarters" but her body and her heart? She longed to share *everything* with him. But there was something she had to know, words she needed to hear him say. "Do you know who you are yet?" She held her breath, waiting.

He looked at her levelly, a bittersweet smile playing faintly upon his lips. "Och, aye, lass. I am Aedan MacKinnon. Son of Findanus and Mary MacKinnon, from Dun Haakon on the Isle of Skye. Born in eight hundred ninety-eight. Twice-removed grandson of Kenneth McAlpin. And I am the last of my people." He turned his gaze back to the portrait.

His words, delivered so regally, yet with such sorrow, sent a chill up her spine. "Beyond that, you need only tell me what you wish," she said softly.

"Then I bid you listen well, for I doona ken when I may have the will to speak it again." That said, he grew pensively silent and gazed into the fire, as if searching for the right words.

Finally, he stirred and said, "When I was a score and ten a . . . man of sorts . . . came to this castle. At first, I thought that he'd come to challenge me, for I was heralded the most powerful warrior in all the isles, descended from the mighty McAlpin himself. Mayhap I was a bit pleased with myself." He grimaced self-deprecatingly.

"But this man . . ." He trailed off shaking his head. "This man—he terrified even me. He looked like a man, but he was dead inside. Ice. Cold. Not human, but human. I know that doesn't make sense, but 'twas as if all the life had been sucked from him somehow, yet still he breathed. I feared he would harm my people and mock me while doing so. He was great and tall and wide, and he had powers beyond mortal."

When he paused, lost in his memories, Jane whispered, "Please go on."

He took a deep breath. "Ma and Da were away at sea with all my siblings but the youngest. I was here with my wee sister." He gestured to the portrait. "Rose." He closed his eyes and rubbed them. "Although I may have suffered my share of arrogance, lass, all I'd e'er wished for was a family, children of my own, to watch my sisters and brothers grow and raise their children. To live a simple life. To be a man of honor. A man that when he was laid into the earth, others said, 'He was a good man.' Yet on that day, I knew that such things would ne'er come to pass, for the man who'd come for me threatened to destroy my entire world. *And I knew he could do it.*"

Eyes misting, Jane hurried to him, sank onto the footstool, and placed a gentle, encouraging hand on his thigh.

He covered it with his own, staring at the portrait.

After a few moments, he turned his head and looked at her, and she gasped softly at the anguish in his eyes. She wanted to press kisses to his eyelids as if to somehow kiss all the pain away, to make sure nothing ever hurt him again.

"I made a deal with the creature that if he left my clan in peace I would go with him to his king. His king offered a bargain and I accepted, thinking five years would be a hellish price to pay, wondering how I could withstand five years in his icy, dark kingdom. But it was ne'er five years, lass—'twas five hundred. Five hundred years and I forgot. I *forgot.*" He slammed a fist down on the arm of the chair. Thrusting the kitten at her, he leaped to his feet and began pacing. Sexpot, alarmed by the sudden commotion, scampered off for the calm of the bedchamber.

"I became just like him—the one who'd come to claim me. I lost all honor. I became the vilest of vile, the—"

"Aedan, stop," Jane cried.

"I became that thing I despised, lass!"

"You were tortured," she defended. "Who could survive five centuries of . . . of . . ." She trailed off, not knowing what he'd withstood.

Aedan snorted angrily. "I let them go. To escape the things that the king did to me. I let memories of my clan, of my Rose, go. The more I forgot, the less he punished me. God, there are things in the dark king's realm, things so . . ." He snarled, shaking his head.

"You *had* to forget," Jane said intensely. "It's a miracle that you survived. And although you might think you became this Vengeance creature who came for you—you *didn't*. I saw the goodness in you when I came here. I saw the tenderness, the part of you that was aching to be a simple man again."

"But you doona know the things I've done," he said, his voice harsh and deep and unforgiving.

"I don't need to know. Unless you wish to tell me, I need never know. All I need to know is that you are never going back to him. You're never going back to him, are you?" Jane pressed.

He said nothing, just stood there, looking lost and full of self-loathing. His head bowed, his hair curtaining his face.

"Stay with me. I want you, Aedan," she said, her heart aching.

"How *could* you? How could anyone?" he asked bitterly.

Ah, she thought, understanding. He hungered to be part of the mortal world—that was why he'd come back to Dun Haakon, rather than turning to his king—but he felt he didn't deserve it. He feared no one would want him, that once she knew what he'd been, she would cast him out.

He glanced at her, then quickly glanced away, but not before she saw the hope warring with the despair in his gaze.

Rising to her feet, Jane held out her hand. "Take my hand, Aedan. That's all you need do."

"You doona know what these hands have done."

"Take my hand, Aedan."

"Begone, lass. A woman such as you is not for the likes of me."

"Take my hand," she repeated. "You can take it now.

Or ten years from now. Or twenty. Because I will still be standing here waiting for you to take my hand. I'm not leaving you. I'm *never* leaving you."

His anguished gaze shot to hers. "Why?"

"Because I love you," Jane said, her eyes filling with tears. "I love you, Aedan MacKinnon. I've loved you forever."

"Who are you? Why do you even *care* about me?" His voice rose and cracked hoarsely.

"You still don't remember me?" Jane asked plaintively.

Aedan thought hard, pushing into the deepest part of him, that part that still was iced over. A hard shining tower of ice still lay behind his breast, concealing something. Helplessly, he shook his head.

Jane swallowed hard. It didn't really matter, she told herself. He didn't have to remember their time together in the Dreaming. She could live with that, if it meant she could spend the rest of her life here on this island with him. "It's okay," she said finally with a brave smile. "You don't have to remember me, as long as you—" She broke off abruptly, feeling suddenly too vulnerable for words.

"As long as I what, lass?"

In a small voice, she finally said, "Do you think you could care for me? In the way a man cares for his woman?"

Aedan sucked in a harsh breath. If only she knew. For the week he'd wandered, he'd thought of little else. Knowing he should do her the favor of never returning, yet unable to stay away. Dreaming of her, waking to find his arms reaching for nothing. Until, unable to push her from his heart, he'd faced his memories. Until, scorning himself for a fool, he'd returned to Dun Haakon to force her to force him to leave. To see the disgust in her gaze. To be sent away so he could die inside.

But now she stood there, hands outstretched, asking him to stay. Asking him to make free with her body and heart.

Offering him a gift he hadn't deserved but vowed to earn.

"You wish that of me? I who was scarce human when you met me? You could have any man you wished, lass. Any of the villagers. Nay, even Scotia's king."

"I want only you. Or no one. Ever."

"You would trust me so? To be your . . . man?"

"I trust you already."

Aedan stared at her. He began to speak several times, then closed his mouth again.

"If you refuse me, I'll cast myself into the sea," she announced dramatically. "And *die*." Not really, because Jane Sillee wasn't a quitter, but he needn't know that.

"Nay—you will not go to the sea!" he roared. Eyes glittering, he moved toward her.

"I am so lonely without you, Aedan," Jane said simply.

"You truly want me?"

"More than anything. I'm only half without you."

"Then you are my woman." His words were finality, a bond he would not permit broken. She had given herself to his keeping. He would never let her go.

"And you'll never leave me?" she pressed.

"I'll stay with you for all of ever, lass."

Jane's eyes flared, and she looked at him strangely. "And then yet another day?" she asked breathlessly.

"Oh, aye."

"And we could have babies?"

"Half dozen if you wish."

"Could we start making them now?"

"Oh, aye." A grin touched his lips; the first full grin she'd ever seen on his gorgeous face. The effect was devastating: It was a dangerous, knowing grin that dripped sensual promise. "I should warn you," he said, his eyes glittering, "I recall what it is to be a man now, lass. *All* of it. And I was ever a man of greedy and demanding appetites."

"Oh, please," Jane breathed. "Be as greedy as you wish. Demand away."

"I will begin small," he said, his eyes sparkling. "We will begin with the pressing of the lips you so favor," he teased.

Jane flung herself at him, and when his arms closed around her, she went wild, touching and kissing and clinging to him.

"Woman, I need you," he growled, slanting his mouth across hers. "Ever since I remembered the things a man knows, all I could think of were the things I ached to do to you."

"Show me," she whimpered.

And he did, taking his sweet time, peeling away her gown until she was naked before him, kissing and suckling and tasting every inch of her.

He experienced no difficulty whatsoever finding her most private heat.

# *Fifteen*

***The Unseelie king sensed it the precise moment he lost his*** Vengeance. Though the mortal Highlander had not yet regained full memory, he loved and was loved in return.

The king's visage changed in a manner most rare for him; the corners of his lips turned up.

*Humans*, he thought mockingly, *so easily manipulated.* How infuriated they would be if they knew it had never been about them to begin with, and, indeed, rarely was. His Vengeance had performed precisely as he'd expected, twisting his three nebulous suggestions, and with obstinate human defiance, aiding the king in his aim.

Eons ago, a young Seelie queen for whom he suffered an unending hunger had escaped him before he'd been through with her.

She'd not risked entering his realm again.

His smile grew. If he must stoop to conquer, it was not beneath him.

He swallowed a laugh, tossed his head back, and let

loose an enraged roar that resonated throughout the fabric of the universe.

***The Seelie queen heard the dark king's cry and permitted*** herself a small, private smile.

So, she mused, feeling quite lovely, he had lost and she had won. It made her feel positively magnanimous. Sipping the nectar from a splendidly plump dalisonia, she rolled onto her back and stretched languidly.

Perhaps she should offer the dark king her condolences, she mused. After all, they were royalty, and royalty did that sort of thing.

After all, she had won.

She could simply duck in and back out, gloat a bit.

And if he tried to restrain her? Keep her captive in his realm? She laughed softly. She'd beaten him this time. She'd *proved* that she was stronger than she'd been millennia ago when he'd caged her for a time.

Feeling potent, inebriated on victory, she closed her eyes and envisioned his icy lair . . .

***The iciness of his realm stole her breath away. Then she*** saw him and inhaled sharply, sucking in great lungfuls of icy air. Her memory had not done him justice. He was even more exotic than she'd recalled. A palpable darkness surrounded him. He was deadly and powerful, and she knew from intimate experience just how inventively, exhaustively erotic he was. A true master of pain, he understood pleasure as no other could.

"My queen," he said, his eyes of night and ice glittering.

Even as powerful as the Seelie queen was, she found it impossible to gaze into his eyes for more than a moment. Some claimed they'd been emptied of matter and pure chaos spooned into the sockets.

She inclined her head, averting her gaze ever so slightly. "It would seem you have lost your Vengeance, dark one," she murmured.

"It would seem I have."

When he rose from his throne of ice, and rose and rose, she caught her breath. Not quite fairy, his blood mixed with the blood of a creature even the Fae hesitated to name. His shadow moved unnaturally as he rose, slithering around him, wont to move independently of its host.

"You seem unperturbed by your defeat, dark one," she probed, determined to savor every drop of her victory. "Care you not that you have lost him? Five centuries of work. Wasted."

"You presume you knew my aim."

The Seelie queen stiffened, staring into his eyes for a moment longer than was wise. "Pretend not that you intended to lose. That I have been manipulated." Her voice dripped ice worthy of his kingdom.

"Loss is a relative thing."

"I won. *Admit* it," she snapped.

"I doubt you even knew what game we played, young one." His voice deep, silky, and mesmerizing, he mocked, "Did you come to gloat because my defeat made you feel powerful? Did it make you feel safe in seeking me? Careful. A being such as I might be inclined to find you reason to condescend. To sink to my depths."

"I have sunk to nothing," she hissed, feeling suddenly foolish. She *was* young by his standards, for the king of darkness was ancient—sprung from the loins of an age she'd heard of only in legend.

He said nothing, merely regarded her, his stare a palpable weight. She repressed a shiver, remembering her last excursion to his land. She'd nearly failed to summon the power to leave. But, she conceded with a thrill of sexual anticipation so intense that it nearly brought her to her knees, she'd not quite been in a hurry to leave the dark king's dangerous bed. And therein lay double the danger . . .

"I came to offer my condolences," she said coolly.

His laughter alone could seduce. "So offer, my queen." He moved in a swirl of darkness. "But offer that for which we both know you hunger. Your willing surrender."

And when he was upon her, when he had gathered her up and his great wings began to flap, she let her head fall against his icy breast. Darkness so thick it had texture and taste surrounded her. "Never."

"Heed me well, light one, the only thing you are never with me—is safe."

Much later, when he possessed her completely, a full blood moon stained the sky above the Highlands of Scotland.

*Aedan made love to Jane like a man who understood that* this day, this moment, only this *now* was securely in the palm of his hand, taking her with the passionate urgency of a tenth-century Scotsman who knew not what tomorrow might bring: brutal war, drought, or crop-destroying tempest. He made love like a drowning man, desperate for the surety of her body—she was his shore, his raft, his harbor against what storms may come.

And then he made love to her again.

This time, with exquisite gentleness. Brushed his lips against the warm hollow of her neck in which her heartbeat pulsed. Kissed the slopes of her breasts, tasted the salt of her skin and the sweetness of her passion glistening between her thighs, and flexed himself deep within her innermost warmth.

He became part of her. Finally, he knew the kind of loving that made two one and understood Jane was his world. His ocean, his country, his sun, his rain, his very heart.

And that sleek, iced citadel behind his breastbone—

behind which he'd concealed from the dark king that which was most infinitely precious to him—cracked at the foundations and came crashing down.

And he finally remembered what he'd sealed away there . . . his Jane.

*"Jane, my own sweet Jane," he cried hoarsely.*

Jane's eyes flew wide. He was buried deep within her, loving her slowly and intensely, and although he'd called her name aloud many times during the loving, his voice sounded different this time.

Could it be he'd finally remembered all of it? All those years they'd spent together in dreams, playing and loving and dancing and loving?

"Aedan?" His name held the question she was afraid to ask.

Framing her head with his forearms, he stared down at her. "You came to me. I remember now. You came when I slept. In the Dreaming."

"Yes," Jane cried, joyous tears misting her eyes.

There were no words for a time, only the soft sounds of passion, of a woman being thoroughly loved by her man.

When finally she could catch her breath again, she said, "You were with me always. You watched me grow up, remember?" She laughed self-consciously. "When I was thirteen, I nearly dreaded seeing you because I was so gawky—"

"Nay, you were no such thing. You were a wee lovely lass, I watched your womanhood ripening and saw what you would become. I ached for the day you would be old enough that I could love you in every way."

"Well, you didn't have to wait *quite* so long," she voiced a long-harbored complaint. *"Mmm,"* she added, gasping, when he nipped her nipple lightly with his teeth. "Do that again."

He did. And again, until her breasts felt ripe and exquisitely sensitive. Then he rubbed his unshaven cheek lightly against her peaked nipples, creating delicious friction.

"I claimed you when you were ten and eight," he managed finally.

"Like I said—long. I was ready way before then. I was ready by sixteen . . . *ooh!*"

"You were a wee babe still," he said indignantly, stilling inside her.

"Don't stop," she gasped.

"Doona think for a minute 'twasn't difficult for me to naysay you. 'Twas that my mother insisted all her sons forgo impatience and give a lass time to be a child before having bairn of her own."

"Please," she whimpered.

Heeding her plea, he thrust without cease, and she cried out his name over and again, digging her fingers into his muscular hips, pulling him as deep as she could take him.

He kissed her, taking her cries with his lips until her shudders subsided.

"Have you had time enough, wee Jane?" he asked later, when she lay drowsy and sated in his arms. "We may have made one this very day, you ken."

Jane beamed. His shimmering eyes were again a warm tropical surf in his dark face, his lips curved with sensuality and tenderness. He'd finally remembered her! And she might have his baby growing inside her. "I want half a dozen at least," she assured him, smiling.

Then she sobered, touching his jaw lightly. "When I was twenty-two, the dreams seemed different. They became repeats of earlier dreams."

His jaw tensed beneath her hand.

"I lost you," she said. "Didn't I?"

"The king discovered I was gaining strength from my dreams. He prevented me from joining you there," Aedan said tersely.

She inhaled sharply. "How?" she asked, not certain she wanted to know.

"You doona wish to know, and I doona need to speak of it. 'Tis over and done," he said, his eyes darkening.

Jane didn't press, and let it go, for now, knowing the time would come when he would need to speak of it, and she would be there to listen. For now, she would wait while Aedan became fully Aedan again.

He smiled suddenly, dazzling her. "You were my light, wee Jane. My laughter, my hope, my love, and now you will be my wife."

*"Ahem,"* she said pertly, "if you think you're getting off with that lame proposal, you have another thought coming."

He laughed. "Your headstrong nature was one of the first things I favored in you, lass. So much fire, and as cold as I was, your tempers kept me warm. Saucy like my mother, demanding like my sisters, yet tender of heart and weak of will when it comes to passion."

"Who are you calling weak?" she said, with mock indignation.

Aedan gave her a provocative glance from beneath half-lowered lids. " 'Tis obvious you have a weakness for me. You spent the past fortnight trying to seduce me—"

"Only because you'd forgotten me! Otherwise *you* would have been chasing *me* around!"

Certain of it, she scrambled from beneath him and slipped from the bed, then dashed out into the great hall. Sure enough, he followed, stalking her like a great greedy dark beast.

And when he caught her . . .

*And when he caught her, he made wild, passionate love to her. Celestial music trumpeted from the heavens.* ~~*Celestial music trumpeted from the heavens.*~~ *(It did. I* swear.*) Rainbows gathered to shimmer* *above Dun Haakon. Heather bloomed, and even the sun's brilliance paled in comparison to the luminosity of true love.*

*And when he proposed again, it was on bended knee, with a band of gold embedded with tiny heart-shaped rubies, as he vowed to love her for all of ever. Then yet another day.*

Excerpted from the unpublished manuscript
*Highland Fire* by Jane ~~Sillee~~ MacKinnon

# *Epilogue*

*"Don't forget the latest chapter, Aedan," Jane reminded* as he slipped from their bed. "I missed last week, and Henna said they're going to storm the castle if I don't let them know what's going on with Beth and Duncan."

"I won't forget, lass." Donning shirt and plaid, Aedan picked up the parchments from the sidetable. He glanced at the top page.

> *She held her breath, waiting for him to kiss her, knowing that she would never be the same once she'd tasted the passion of his embrace. Her braw Highlander had fought valiantly for the Bruce and had come home to her wounded in body and heart. But she would heal him . . .*

"You know, the men say that since their wives have been reading your tales they're much more . . . er, amorous," Aedan told her. Downright bawdy, the men had actually said. Insatiable. Plotting ways to seduce their men at all hours. Her stories had the same effect on him. Reading one of her love scenes never failed to make him hard as a rock. He wondered if she suspected that before delivering her pages to the eager women, he stopped in the tavern where the husbands listened, with much jesting and guffawing, as he read the most recent installment. Although they made sport of the "mushy parts," not one of them failed to show each Tuesday when he made his weekly trip to the village. Last week, three of them had come looking for *him* when he'd failed to appear with that week's installment.

"Really?" Jane was delighted.

"Aye," he said, grinning. "They thank you for it."

Jane beamed. As he pulled on his boots, she reminded him, "Oh, and don't forget, I want peach ice, not blueberry."

"I willna forget," he promised. "You've got the entire village making your favored dish. I vow when the spring thaws come and they can't make your icy cream they may go mad."

Jane smiled. She'd been unable to resist teaching the villagers a few things that she deemed reasonably harmless. It wasn't like she was advancing technology before its time. Pushing the drapes aside, she glanced out the window behind the bed. "It snowed again last night. Look—isn't it beautiful, Aedan?" she exclaimed.

Aedan pulled the drapes back over the window and tucked the covers more securely around her. "Aye, 'tis lovely. And damned cold. Are you warm enough?" he worried. Without waiting for her reply, he stacked several more logs on the fire and banked it carefully. "I doona want you getting out of bed. You mustn't catch a chill."

Jane made a face. "I'm not *that* pregnant, Aedan. I still have two more months."

"I willna take any chances with you or our daughter."

"Son."

"Daughter."

Jane's laughter was cut off abruptly when he took her in his arms and kissed her long and hard before leaving.

At the doorway he paused. "If 'tis a lass," he asked softly, "do you think we might name her Rose?"

"Oh, yes, Aedan," Jane said softly. "I'd like that."

After he left, Jane lay back against the pillows, marveling. Seven months had passed since her arrival at Dun Haakon, and although there'd been some difficult moments, she wouldn't have traded it for anything in the world.

Aedan still had a great deal of darkness inside him, of times and things he rarely discussed. There had been somber months while he'd grieved the loss of his clan. Then finally, one morning she'd come down from their new bedchamber above-stairs and found him hanging the old portraits in the great hall. She'd watched him, praying he wouldn't have that stark expression in his eyes. When he'd raised his head and smiled at her, her heart had soared.

" 'Tis time to honor the past," he'd told her. "We have a rich history, lass. I want our children to know their grandparents."

Then he'd made love to her, there in the great hall. They'd rolled across the floor, paused for a heated interlude on the table, and ended up, she recalled, blushing, in a most interesting position over a chair.

All of her dreams had come true. The village women waited with bated breath for the latest "installment" of her serial novel. They lapped up every word, savoring the romance, and the magic of it spilled over into their hearth and home. And no one ever complained about purple prose or typos.

She was a storyteller with an eager audience, a mother-to-be, had a milking cow of her own, reasonably hot water, the scent of her man all over her skin, and she slept each night held tightly in the arms of the man she loved.

Dreamily, she sighed, resting her hand on her tummy. Sexpot gave a little pink-tongued yawn and snuggled closer beside her.

Life was *good.*

# Author's Note

My younger sister has long entertained me with Silly Jane Jokes. What is a Silly Jane Joke? Elizabeth is so glad you asked!

*A carpenter asked the very curvaceous Silly Jane to help him. He'd hurt his foot and needed someone to climb up the ladder and retrieve his bucket of paint from the top. But Silly Jane was no fool. She knew that he just wanted to look up her dress and see her panties when she climbed it. So she tricked him. She took her panties off first.*

This story is a work of fiction. Any resemblance between Silly Jane and Jane Sillee is purely coincidental. Really.